OAKLAND PUBLIC LIBR

CALIF. 94612

P9-ELT-069

OAKLAND PUBLIC LIBRARY, CALIF. 94612

WITHDRAWN
FROM THE
COLLECTION

Oakland Public Library
Oakland, CA
www.oaklandlibrary.org

Plenty Good Room

Plenty Good Room

Cheri Paris Edwards

West Bloomfield, Michigan

WARNER BOOKS

NEW YORK   BOSTON

This book is a work of fiction. Names, characters, places, and incidents are the product of the author's imagination or are used fictitiously. Any resemblance to actual events, locales, or persons, living or dead, is coincidental.

The Scripture quotations contained herein are from the New Revised Standard Version Bible, copyright ©1989 by the Division of Christian Education of the National Council of the Churches of Christ in the U.S.A. Used by permission. All rights reserved.

Copyright © 2005 by Cheri Paris Edwards

All rights reserved.

Published by Warner Books with Walk Worthy Press™

Warner Books

Time Warner Book Group
1271 Avenue of the Americas, New York, NY 10020

Walk Worthy Press
33290 West Fourteen Mile Road, #482, West Bloomfield, MI 48322

Visit our Web sites at www.twbookmark.com and www.walkworthypress.net.

Printed in the United States of America

First Printing: April 2005
10 9 8 7 6 5 4 3 2 1

Library of Congress Cataloging-in-Publication Data

Edwards, Cheri Paris.
    Plenty good room / Cheri Paris Edwards.
        p. cm.
    ISBN 0-446-57647-6
    1. Women social workers—Fiction. 2. Foster home care—Fiction. 3. Girls—Fiction.
I. Title
    PS3605.D878P57 2005
    813'.6—dc22

                                                                    2004017869

Book design by Charles Sutherland

Dedicated especially to my sons,

to my feisty girls,

and

to all those individuals who work with youth, to all the loving foster parents

who are committed to opening their homes to displaced children and teens,

and to all the young people I've met throughout the years!

In memory of Mrs. Verne Woodson, Mrs. Helen Heath, and for Laura.

Acknowledgments

A Prayer.

Lord, I ask You to help me maintain a balance in my life. The narrow road I endeavor to travel on through life is not too far to the left or right. Calm me when, like an out-of-control pendulum, I swing from one extreme behavior to another as I try to find my way. Comfort me with the inner peace You offer as You guide me back to that middle road I strive to travel on.

O God, help me to remember those things I would rather forget, and to forget those things I should but that instead I choose to remember. Create in me a clean heart as I strive to become transparent with people, unafraid of what they might think. Lord, help me to forgive others as I want them to forgive me.

Lord, I thank You for the grace You have covered me with throughout my life. I know that the good that others may see in me is because of Your greatness, the manifestation of Your spirit in me.

Lord, it is my prayer that this book honor You and affirm Your love for every kind of person in every kind of circumstance.

In Jesus Christ's name I pray,

Amen.

Acknowledgments

Thank you.

Thank you to my family.

From the bottom of my heart, I thank my mother, Jeannetta Justice, who taught me through her example to serve people. And, more important, I thank her for teaching us all to love God and to seek for Him to be a part of our lives. Thank you to my stepfather, Vernell, for providing us with a life that we could not have experienced had you not been there for us.

All my love and appreciation to my sister Vikki Paris Rhodes, who has always been the rock of our family, to my brother-in-law, Freddie Rhodes, who can "burn on that grill" like no other! Much love to my brother, Maxie, his wife, Leslie, and their sons, Jarod and Justin. Love to my sisters, sweet-spirited Joanna and baby sister Olivia, who always makes us all laugh. Love to my nephews, Theo and Matthew—Matt, we love you, and we know you will be home soon—and to my niece, Amanda. To my cousin Kevin, thank you for being so supportive. To my cousin Joycelyn, I love you like my own sister. Love to Marcus, Imani, Chris, and Aisha as well.

To my son Charles: you are so very bright, handsome, and creative, yet I know that you struggle inwardly as you look to find your place as a young man in this world. God will help you if you let Him! Sam, you, too, are my shiny boy, full of potential and intelligence; keep your eyes on the Lord and let Him lead you. I love both of you with my whole heart and soul, I am so blessed that God brought you into my life, and I know that He has a special purpose for each of you!

Thank you to all those I worked with at UMS for so many years. In particular I thank Mr. Clyde Wicks, Mr. Gradis Upshaw, and my former Outreach coworkers, Mr. Lyndell Clemons, Mr. Dayvon MacCarroll, Ms. Eula Hamilton, and Ms. Vernettia Flemons. Also, thank you to Ms. Tammy Crosby, Ms. Karla Shelby, Ms. Tonya

Acknowledgments

Kearns, Mr. Bob Boyden, Ms. Sheila Jenkins, Ms. Sandra Mozier, Ms. Teri Medwed, Mr. Chico Wilson, Mr. Lee Pruitt (dec.), and Mrs. Val Summerville.

A special thank-you to Ann Williams for reading the manuscript first for me and being kind in your review, even though it was poorly edited at that time! To all of you: we shared lots of laughter and tears together as we served the young people we worked with, and I love you all!

To the staff at Continuing Education at UIUC, thanks so much for your kindness. It's been a pleasure to work with all of you!

Thank you to Linda Gibbens, Christina Donaldson, Dr. Gene Amberg, Marian Krier, Blanton Bondurant, and Patrick Russell. A very special thanks to Dr. Preston Williams for taking a chance on me even though I didn't have my "papers." My love and thanks to Shirlene Jones for your positive nature and support, and know that I've remembered and leaned on your words and sweet demeanor long after your departure!

Thank you to my Truant's Alternative family: Mary Brooks, Alice McGee, Debbie Montegerard, Sandra Gonzalez, Donna Mackey, and Bertha Kent—love keeps you coming back to work with youth each year, and it's your love that makes the difference for so many young people! The very best of wishes to my ex-boss, Mr. John Muirhead, and your wife, during retirement—you always treat others with the greatest of respect, and that means so much!

Thank you, Rayco, for just being you—strong, beautiful, and regal—and giving so much to young people while expecting highly of them! We need more like you! Thank you for taking time to read the manuscript, and thank you for your positive comments! Thank you, Dayanna Shelby, for your soothing manner and comforting hands—you are a great mom, and I admire your business savvy!

Acknowledgments

To Donna Tanner Harold, Hattie Paulk, Kim Seward, and Gigi and Norm Lambert: I admire you so for all the years you spent working to make the lives of displaced youth better. To "my girls" Shemika, Laura, Kia, and Kim: if I didn't say it right or do it right, I'm sorry, but know that I love you and I will NEVER forget you, and God hasn't, either—He loves you! To my school girls, my two Briannas, Adrianna, Tasheba, and LaToya: I love you all, and I expect great things from you! To DeMario, Marlon, Justin, Gerald, Ricardo, and all my other young men: stay strong and look to God to be your Father!

Thank you, Joyce Jones, for telling me and showing me so many years ago that God loves me! Truly your words and actions were the catalyst for my walk with God. Thank you, Imani, for the sister-girl gift many years ago; what one does in anonymity I believe is truly from the heart! Thank you, Mrs. Elaine Harmon, for talking with me and encouraging me from the workplace during difficult times.

Thank you, Denise Stinson, for Walk Worthy Press! God certainly has blessed writers of Christian books by anointing you to be so successful in the publishing industry. I feel personally blessed that through your company I've been afforded this wonderful opportunity as a first-time writer to have these words I've written from my heart published. I am grateful that God filled you with the fortitude, experience, and intelligence to create Walk Worthy. I knew when I heard your voice that you were about business, and I immediately thought, "That's the person I want to work with!" Thank you for your supportive words, the new title, and your comments. God has been my main partner throughout this endeavor, and all other help meant so much to me!

A special thanks to Frances Jalet-Miller for excellent editing! I am so glad we got to work together; hopefully we will again soon.

Thank you, Reverend B. J. and Mrs. Tatum, for being kind to

me during rough times in my life; and thank you, Reverend Harold Davis, for your moving ministry. A special thank-you and lots of love to Bishop and Sister Gwin of the Church of the Living God, for being so loving all the time. I came to the church long before you even knew me; you helped me and were loving to me, and it was the love I felt that brought me back for more, years later. Thank you to the Love Corner family for allowing God's love to shine through you as well. It is love, love, love that changes us and can change the world!

I cannot say how much the ministries of T. D. Jakes, Bishop Eddie Long, and Joyce Meyer have impacted my life. Whenever I need worship and a word from the Lord, you bring it to me in my home. Those times have been many for me in the past years, and God has used you on many occasions to speak to my heart and circumstances. Thank you to TBN for being an outlet to bring the Word to so many.

To Daddy: I wish that I'd had a longer time with you, but I'm thankful for the moments we had. I looked into your face and saw my own, and I know you gave me what you could: your love for music, your laughter, and your lessons in "street-smarts." I love you and I miss you. Thank you, Beverly and Donna Jean, for accepting me with open arms. You didn't have to, but you did, and I will never forget your kindness. Grandmother, I wish I'd known to love you when you were here, but I know that your spirit watches over me and that we will one day be together again.

To Mrs. Heath, you encouraged me to write a book and now I have. I know that you are with the Lord now and you are proud. I'll miss you.

To anyone I've forgotten or not mentioned: I appreciate your presence in my life as well. Thank you for the good times and the laughter, and even more important, thank you for the difficulty; thank you for the tears. It is through the difficulties that I've learned to lean on God, and so they have truly been a blessing in disguise.

And finally, thank you to all the young people I have had the pleasure of meeting throughout the years. YOU are my heroes, and it is you who have filled me with the truest joy of my life. Your vigor, determination, and intelligence in spite of difficulties give me all hope for the future. *Always* remember that your life is no accident. God has a plan for you, and whatever hardships you may face today can develop character in you for tomorrow's challenges.

No matter what life hands you, *never, ever give up*! Keep on pushin', fight the good fight, pick yourself up, dust yourself off, and get back in the race, and whenever life hands you lemons, make a big ol' pitcher of lemonade! In other words, tell yourself whatever is necessary to keep you striving for your goals. Know that even in your hardships God loves you and that these tough situations will make you strong and give you the ability to be compassionate toward others. *Never, ever forget that ALL things work out for the good for those who love the Lord!*

Dream high, believe in yourself, be positive, strive to do the right thing, listen to the people God puts in your life to help guide you, and always, always, always keep your head to the sky! God loves you!

John 14:2

In my Father's house are many mansions:
if it were not so, I would have told you . . .

1.

Runaway

The girl looked worriedly up into the dark sky when she heard the first roar of rolling thunder. The thick humidity weighing down the night air foretold the coming storm, and with one hand she reached under the old baseball cap she wore, and wiped beads of moisture from her forehead. With a frown, she impatiently looked again at the traffic light, waiting for it to change so she could cross the busy street.

"Hey there, girl, what you know good?" a gravelly male voice said from behind her. The man seemed to have appeared from nowhere, and when the girl felt his feathery-light touch on her elbow, she turned to look at him. His shadowed features seemed ominous to her. Her surprise swiftly changed to fear once she saw the red-rimmed, faded brown eyes of the old white man. With a gasp, her mouth fell open, and she shuddered at his wide grin with its many dark gaps where his teeth should have been.

Truly scared now, the girl quickly pulled in her elbow, and in her haste to escape the gray-haired man, she began to step into the crosswalk, with no thought of the oncoming traffic. Right at that very moment, as if in answer to her need to cross the busy intersection, the red Walk light changed to green and she took off across the street. Without one glance backward, she began to run, darting in and out of the crowds of people walking down the avenue. She ran faster and faster.

Suddenly a huge fork of lightning split the dark sky directly in front of her, and the steamy night was lit brightly for a moment. Then, seconds later, an explosively loud clap of thunder shook the ground, followed by low rumblings in the distance, which only added to her alarm. The smell of the imminent spring rain wafted into her nostrils. Sensing that the downpour would begin at any moment, she instinctively began to look for shelter.

Ahead, the girl spied a small alleyway, and with a quick, furtive glance over her shoulder to assure herself that she wasn't being followed, she disappeared into the darkness of the alley. She gathered several pieces of heavy, stiff cardboard scattered around a large metal trash bin in the alleyway, along with some thick plastic and a large corrugated box. Quickly she built herself a makeshift shelter in an area behind the garbage container.

Moments later, in response to the howling wind, she huddled in the corner of the box and tucked her head between her knees. The rain started to pummel her shelter. Her small body was paralyzed with fear, at least until another loud thunderclap caused her to jump involuntarily. When the heavy rain finally began to drip into her cardboard coverings, she could be brave no longer. Tears began to fall one by one from her eyes, and she sobbed from fear and frustration.

The girl's thoughts wandered back to the home she'd left behind, and to what he had tried to do to her before she ran away tonight, and suddenly her tears flowed even more profusely— only now she cried from anger, too. Forgetting about the storm, the girl harshly wiped her wet eyes and her runny nose, and as she rubbed her damp hands on her pant legs, she vowed aloud, "I don't care what I have to go through—I will never go back there again! *Never!*"

2.

Night Visitor

Tamara Britton sat straight up in the bed. She tilted her head sideways and listened. Suddenly fully alert, she threw her legs over the side of the bed and slid her feet into her fuzzy slippers. She grabbed her robe from the end of the bed, wrapped it around herself, and tied it quickly as she walked down the long hallway toward the front door.

"Who could this be?" she whispered to herself. She glanced over at the wall clock when she walked past the living room, and noted that it was almost three o'clock in the morning.

At the front door she peered through the peephole and looked directly into the worried face of her coworker Lynnette Moore. The woman was accompanied by a fair-complexioned, scowling, skinny girl who looked to be in her early teens.

Lynnette Moore and Tamara had worked together for the past seven years at the Care for Kids Agency. Both women worked in the Child Protective Unit, which offered a wide variety of services for children and their parents. Counseling and other services were available for families struggling with domestic issues. The more structured Stabilization Services, whose goal was to keep families intact, helped parents at risk of losing their children to Child Protective Services. Tamara worked in Stabilization, while Lynnette was a field caseworker for the Foster Care Division.

Taking a deep breath, Tamara tightened the belt on her flowered terry robe, unlocked the deadbolt, and then opened the door wide.

"Hey, girl . . . what you doing?" said Lynnette saucily, as if she had just stopped in for a casual visit and it were not the wee hours of the morning, when most folks were sleeping.

"Hi, Lynnette," she replied, and following the woman's lead, she made no acknowledgment either of the lateness of the hour or the unexpectedness of her visit.

Then, in what seemed to Tamara to be a strange manner of self-introduction, the young girl accompanying Lynnette clicked her tongue loudly, put one hand on her hip, and looked at both women as she said derisively, "*Excuse me,* but do we have to stand in the hallway?" Her gaze locked on Tamara, and with disdain apparent on her small face, she added, "What's up with the *house*pitality?"

With a slight raising of her eyebrows, Tamara wordlessly slid to the side of the doorway while gesturing with one hand for them to come inside. "*House*pitality?" she mouthed to Lynnette as the young girl came forward.

"Go 'head, Miss Thang," said Lynnette to the girl, who then rolled her eyes at both of them, turned her head dramatically, and sauntered into the house. Once inside, she ignored them and immediately began to check out Tamara's house thoroughly. Turning, Lynnette stared at Tamara meaningfully, shook her head, and then breathed out heavily through flared nostrils.

Stepping close to Tamara, she said in a low voice, "She's my new case—just got dropped off tonight . . . *runaway.*"

She had already figured that the young girl was a new case of Lynnette's, since she knew that field agents sometimes had chil-

4

dren placed temporarily with them until a more permanent home with a foster family could be located. These kids had usually just been removed from their families' homes or were runaways and had been brought in by the police, which could explain the young girl's foul mood.

Tamara closed the door, and together she and Lynnette watched the girl as she slowly proceeded through the house, stopping at tables to pick up small knickknacks, examine them carefully, and then, with a twist of her lips, put them back down. Finally, when she seemed to have finished scrutinizing Tamara's home, she walked over to the couch and, with a loud plop, sat down hard.

It was only then that she noticed the two women looking at her. *"What y'all looking at? Y'all act like you ain't never seen a person befo!"* she said haughtily. Then she closed her eyes for a long moment and rolled her neck. Clearly angry, she propped her head up on one hand, and with a deep scowl on her young features, she avoided their gaze.

Lynnette looked at Tamara and rolled her eyes, made a face, and then said with feigned sweetness, "Sienna, honey, this is Tamara. Remember, I told you about her."

The girl turned her glare to Tamara and looked her slowly up and down from her head to her feet and back again. *"So?* I don't care *nothin'* 'bout no Tamara."

Lynnette made another face and, ignoring the girl's rude comment, continued cheerfully, "Tamara, this is Miss Sienna Larson."

Tamara said nothing as she really looked at the young girl closely for the first time. To have such a bad attitude, the girl was actually a pretty little thing, small-boned and petite, with reddish, naturally curly hair that was pulled into a tight, curly ponytail high on her head. A spattering of freckles covered her nose and cheekbones. Long black eyelashes framed her small, dark eyes that turned upward on the ends, and her small pink lips were bud-shaped but tightly drawn in anger.

Noticing Tamara's curious stare, the girl snapped, "Look, I don't know who you think you lookin' at, but *I* am not the *one!*"

Surprised by the girl's unexpected anger, Tamara turned away quickly and silently but gave Lynnette a long, questioning glance.

Seething now and unable to hold her temper any longer with the teen, Lynnette, who was not short on sassiness herself, held one hand up to Tamara as if to forestall her comment and said angrily, "Girl, I don't care where you been and who did what to you, but you do *not* talk to grown folks like this. I have had all I'm gonna take of your smart mouth tonight! Now, what you *do* is sit there and *shut your mouth* while I talk with Tamara in the kitchen."

The teen's face reddened, and she appeared ready to retaliate verbally, but then wisely she seemed to reckon within herself that Lynnette was in no mood to be trifled with. Through turned-up lips she made the loud clicking noise with her tongue again, and then mumbled under her breath as she set her head in her hand hard and turned her eyes away from the two of them.

"Come on, Tamara, let's go talk where we can have some *privacy,*" Lynnette said as she gently pulled her coworker by the arm toward the kitchen. It frustrated her that her coworker was not more assertive in standing her ground when people disrespected her or made her angry. Actually, sometimes Lynnette thought it was a little strange that Tamara was so reserved all the time. It wasn't as if Tamara was actually afraid, but instead it was almost as if she were powerless to respond when people pushed her around, as the girl was doing. *Not me,* Lynnette thought spiritedly. *I'm not taking any crap from anybody!*

After one more furtive glance over her shoulder at the young girl perched petulantly on her couch, Tamara sighed and followed her friend into the kitchen.

Lynnette was already seated at the table in Tamara's small kitchen area, with a bright smile plastered on her face. Helpfully pulling out the chair next to her and patting the seat with her hand, she said to Tamara in a voice laced with sweetness, "C'mon, girl, sit down. I know you tired, and I know that it's late and I woke you up. *I'm so sorry.*"

Tamara glanced at her coworker skeptically now. During the several years they had worked together, she'd grown to know Lynnette well, and she was aware that once that sugary tone was in her voice, she wanted something. By now she'd seen her use that tactic enough times on other people to recognize it for the manipulative strategy that it was. In fact, it was becoming clearer by the moment that tonight Lynnette wanted a favor from her. Thinking about the pouty-faced young girl sitting on her couch in her living room, she was quite certain Lynnette's request was going to be something that she did not want to do.

Lynnette raised one French-manicured finger to push her microbraided hair away from her face as she fixed her wide-eyed stare on Tamara. She batted her eyes dramatically several times before speaking, another clear indicator to Tamara that she was about to ask for something. She said breathlessly, "Now, Tam, girl, I know that you are wondering why I came here this late at night and stuff."

Tamara shook her head in mute agreement, with her eyes locked on her friend's. As she noticed Lynnette's attire, it began to dawn on her that her friend was quite overdressed for the errand of accompanying this young girl. In fact, it did appear to her that Lynnette had been out on the town, perhaps on a date or maybe even "shaking her booty" somewhere.

Now quite sure that Lynnette wanted something, Tamara was ready to dispense with this preliminary buttering-up tactic and get to the point. In a low, firm tone she asked, "Lynn, what is it? Is there something you need from me? Please, Lynn, tell me what you want!"

Lynnette seemed to realize then that Tamara was growing impatient with her delaying tactics, and breathed out heavily, saying in a rush, "Okay, Tamara, I'm gonna stop beating around the bush . . . here's the deal. You know how it is. As a field caseworker, I've got to find a placement when a child comes to me in an emergency, like Miss Sienna out there—or I have to keep her with me."

"Right . . ."

"Well, they dropped little Miss Thang off tonight, and I have plans that I'm in the middle of, and, girl, *these* plans might continue into tomorrow, if you know what I mean." Her large eyes seemed even wider than usual as she pleaded with her friend and coworker for understanding. "Tam, I just *can't* have her with me this weekend."

Tamara asked with a small smile, "You have a date, huh?"

Lynnette batted her eyes and shook her head energetically. "Yeah, girl. Actually I was in the middle of a date when I got beeped, and it's been a long time—well, maybe not that long, but a sistah got to have some male companionship now and again, if you know what I mean."

Tamara knew what she meant, and although she wasn't sure that it was true, she still tried to understand Lynnette's perspective.

Lynnette kept her wide-eyed stare steadily fixed on Tamara as she added quickly in a low tone, "So, I was wondering if she could stay with you, just till tomorrow, and then I promise I'll come get her and work on finding her a placement."

"Lynn, I don't know," said Tamara hesitantly as she thought once again about the young girl's foul demeanor. "She's a little wild, it seems, and she appears to *dislike* me."

Lynnette threw her hand out in a dismissive gesture and said, "Girl, that child don't like *nobody.*" She snickered as she continued, "She's a little hellcat, and her mouth should be declared a lethal weapon—that's why she can't keep a placement. She's snappin' and cussin' out folks and stuff. Believe me, Tam, what she said here is mild compared with some of the stuff she's said at other folks' houses. It's going to be a challenge to place her, I know. I'm sorry I can't tell you much else about her, 'cause I don't have all the paperwork; but I do know that she's not violent or anything like that."

Tamara sat and quietly looked down at her hands. "I didn't think she was violent or anything. It's just . . . oh, Lynn, I'm ashamed to say, I don't know if I can handle someone so 'outspoken,' even for a day or two."

Lynnette reached over and squeezed Tamara's hand gently. "C'mon, Tam, you really gotta stop letting everyone run over you. In fact, I think Sienna will be good for you, because eventually, girl, she'll make you so mad, you will have to say something back," she said with a chuckle.

Tamara's heart was beating really fast, and she did not want to do this favor for Lynnette, but instead of saying no as she wanted, she acquiesced, albeit reluctantly, responding hesitantly, "O-okay, Lynn, but you need to leave me a number where I can get in touch with you—j-just in case."

Lynnette rose from the table quickly, obviously preparing to make a hasty escape before her friend could change her mind. She smoothed down the jacket of the close-fitting deep turquoise knit pantsuit she wore, and her silver bracelets jangled jauntily as she waved her hand at her friend and said, "Girl, no problem. Just call my cell or beeper—you got the numbers—and if she acts up, girl, I promise you I'll drop whatever I'm doing and come get her."

Tamara rose slowly from the table and followed her friend

into the hallway. She was relieved to see that Sienna had laid her head on the arm of the couch and now slept deeply, her small chest rising and falling rhythmically.

"See, girl, she's tired, and she'll probably sleep late tomorrow, too. She's been running the streets for days now, so the child probably ain't had *no* rest. Shoot, I bet she'll sleep all day, and you won't have to deal with her very much at all," Lynnette added as she made her way toward the front door.

"We'll be okay, I'm sure," said Tamara, although she certainly did not feel the confidence that her comment suggested.

Lynnette's eyes were on Tamara's as she said, "C'mere, girl," and hugged her close. "Thank you, Tam, I can always count on you. You are the sweetest person I know, and I will pay you back for this one day soon."

Tamara said shyly, "That's okay; we've worked together a long time, haven't we?" and opened the door for Lynnette.

Lynnette tossed her hair over her shoulder and replied, "Yeah, girl, and you are really a friend, 'cause you've been there for me a million times."

Tamara opened her mouth to speak, but before she could, Lynnette's back was to her and the woman was off, leaving the night air fragrant with her Elizabeth Arden Splendor perfume.

Tamara watched her walk away, then sighed loudly, closed the door quietly, and locked it. For a moment she stood there, unmoving, her back stiff against the door, and then, with another small sigh, she padded quickly down the hallway. Moments later, she returned to the living room with some extra bedding, gently laid the young girl's head on a pillow, then covered her with a blanket.

She walked over to the recliner. Covering herself with another blanket, she lay listening to the young girl's quiet breathing until she fell asleep.

3.

Rude Awakening

"Dang! Don't you have nothin' in this house to eat?"

Tamara opened her eyes and sat up with a start, catching herself just before she fell out of the easy chair, where she'd spent the night. Sleepily she attempted to shake the grogginess away, and when she found herself gazing into the almond-eyed stare of her new temporary roommate, the events from the previous evening flooded back to her.

"I'm hungry and you don't have *nothin'* in your kitchen to eat," the girl repeated even more loudly, this time in a tone laced with rudeness.

Although not fully awake yet, Tamara got up from the chair and walked into the kitchen. She reached up into the cabinet over the refrigerator, took out three boxes of cold cereal, and put them on the counter. Next she opened the fridge, removed the gallon container of milk, and placed it on the table.

By rote she began to follow her morning routine: she scooped coffee into a new filter and, after pouring in enough water for her daily allotment of caffeine, turned on the pot to brew. Then, without looking at the young girl even once, she left the kitchen area, went into the bathroom, and closed the door behind her.

Tamara walked over to the shower, pulled the curtain closed, and started the water. She shed her clothes and entered the shower, where she stood very still for blissful seconds, letting the briskness of the welcoming, warm spray wash over her. Finally

11

feeling fully awakened by the steady stream, she washed, and then stepped out of the shower. After drying herself, she tied a large towel around her so that it covered her like a bright pink terry cloth sarong.

With a face towel she wiped off the steamy mirror and then stood thinking as she watched her reflection. She was surprised that although several minutes had passed, her heart was still beating fast from this morning's rude awakening by the girl. Just thinking of Sienna's unpleasant words again, her breathing became shallow and she felt much more uncomfortable than she had in a long, long time.

Calm down, Tamara, she told herself. She's only a little girl. Don't let her get to you.

There in front of the large bathroom mirror, she stared un-seeingly into her own upturned dark eyes as she attempted to relax herself. Her rich coffee-brown skin was smooth, and her face, though a bit wide, was offset with high cheekbones that provided it with balance. She had an almost pertly small nose, a full mouth with small white teeth, and deep dimples that appeared in her cheeks when she smiled. A gold, shiny silk scarf that she wore during the night covered her finely textured hair, which was cut stylishly short. With one hand she slipped the scarf from her head and, still watching her reflection, absent-mindedly began to use her slim fingertips to push her hair into its regular style.

Thankfully Tamara noticed that her heart was not beating quite as fast now. In her head she began to will herself calm, re-peating the mantra she used to compose herself whenever she was upset: *everything is going to be just fine, Tam . . . everything is going to be just fine.* Inhaling once more deeply, she felt relaxed again and continued her morning grooming, brushing her teeth next before washing her face and applying a thick, creamy mois-turizer to her skin.

Without warning, a loud knocking shook the bathroom door and too quickly interrupted her moments of silence.

The girl yelled into the closed door, "I hate to tell you, but that milk you took out ain't no good! Shoot! I guess you tryin' to poison me or somethin', huh?"

Tamara rolled her eyes but kept her irritation to herself as she said, her own voice oversweet now, "Could you *please* wait and talk to me when I get out of the bathroom? You know, it is not polite to bother people when they are using the bathroom."

There was a momentary silence, and then to her relief the girl replied, "Well, excu-u-use, me!" But just when Tamara thought she was gone, the girl added spitefully, "I'm leavin', but your stupid milk still is rotten!"

"I cannot believe her!" Tamara said aloud in a voice brittle with anger. "Who does she think she is, talking to people like that?" Her dark eyes were flashing with annoyance now, something else out of the norm for her. *In fact, this entire situation with this girl is making me feel totally off-balance,* she thought before flinching in pain and saying peevishly, "Ow!" Distractedly thinking about the girl, she'd wiped off the moisturizer a bit too briskly with the cotton pad, scraping the tender skin on her face.

Tamara was irritated that she was feeling reccurring discomfort following each unpleasant interaction with the girl. But still she was unable to stifle her frustration with the teen and continued her one-woman discourse, chattering to herself angrily in a low voice, "Why, I bet she's not even ninety pounds wet, and she's talking like she's a grown woman or something." Lifting her head, Tamara suddenly caught sight of her angry reflection in the mirror, and feeling ashamed at her obvious loss of control, she willed herself quiet. In an instant she was silent. During the next few minutes of stillness, her heightened emotions subsided, and once again feeling composed, she opened the bathroom door and stepped out.

"*Dang!* It's about time! What was you doing in there any-way?" the young girl said as she looked her up and down from where she stood leaning against the wall, with one tiny hand placed on her small hip.

Tamara glared at her without speaking, then walked past her into the kitchen. Picking up the container of milk, she twisted off the cap and wrinkled her nose when she smelled the foul odor that came from the plastic jug.

"Empty it into the sink, please," she said to the teen, who was now standing next to her.

The young girl looked at her incredulously. "Are you talkin' to *me*? I'm not throwin' nothin' away. I didn't come to your house to work. You the one supposed to be workin' here, takin' care of me!"

Tamara's jaw dropped, and her calm demeanor evaporated so quickly that without even thinking, she almost retorted, but something inside caused her to bite her tongue and say nothing. She clamped her jaw so tightly it hurt as she emptied the rancid milk down the drain, opened the refrigerator door, and peered inside, searching for food.

Seated at the table behind her now, the girl talked loudly. "Anyway, I was just minding my own business last night and somebody had to go call the police. I told them I was eighteen, but for some reason they didn't believe me."

Wonder why, thought Tamara as she glanced at the small girl. She looked twelve, although she was supposed to be fourteen, but eighteen? *No way.* Still silent, Tamara blocked out the angry rambling of the teenager. Placing a skillet on the stove, she cooked sausage and eggs, then toasted bread in the oven. With a spatula she slid the food onto two plates and placed one before the young girl at the table.

The girl stared at the plate of steaming food sullenly for a moment and then looked up at Tamara and smiled widely.

"Now, this here is what I'm talkin' 'bout! This *here* is breakfast," she said as she gestured down at the plate with one small finger.

Tamara watched unbelievingly as the small girl began to shovel in the food so quickly that she did not seem to breathe at all between bites. Totally immersed in the act of eating, she did not look up once. Now that Tamara could see how hungry the tough-talking teen was, her heart immediately softened.

"Can I have some more?" the girl asked without even looking up from the once-full plate. Tamara noticed that this was the first time since they had met that the girl did not have a rough edge to her voice.

"Sure," said Tamara. She retrieved the plate of food that she had prepared for herself, and set it in front of the girl.

The girl gave her a wary look then. "Is this yo' plate? What you gonna eat? Shoot, I don't need *nobody* givin' me *nothin'* 'cause they feel sorry for me or nothin' like that," she said as she eyed the plate of food with hunger still apparent on her face.

"I wasn't hungry anyway," Tamara lied, "so I would be throwing it away if you didn't eat it."

The girl looked at her for a moment and then said, "Well, ain't no use in lettin' no good food go to waste, is it?" She pulled the plate in front of her and attacked it with vigor, just as she had the first.

As she watched the petite girl, who still seemed famished, Tamara was astonished by the enormousness of her appetite. She had never seen someone so small put away such a massive amount of food in such a short time.

With the girl's attention diverted, she examined her more closely, noticing that her smooth skin, pale as vanilla cream, made scattered freckles stand out in her small heart-shaped face. In fact, Sienna Larson reminded her of a small wood sprite, or a fairy from a storybook, with her uptilted eyes, delicately placed features, and wildly curling reddish hair. Suddenly that thought seemed so funny to Tamara that she had turn away to hide the smile that had suddenly lifted the corners of her lips.

She walked over to the sink and began to scrape the dishes and wash the pots and pans while the girl continued to eat.

"Can I have something to drink?" Sienna asked loudly. "You know a sistah gets thirsty when she eatin' all this food."

"A *sistah* does, huh?" Tamara said with a small smile as she poured the girl a glass of cranberry juice. With her light complexion and unique hair texture, Sienna certainly looked biracial to her, yet it was clear from her comment that Sienna considered herself *all* African-American. With a slight sigh she cleared the girl's plate from the table. She had no intention of asking her to do anything right now, since she had no desire to experience the girl's fiery temperament yet again this morning.

The girl picked up her glass, loudly gulped down the juice, and then pursed her lips and frowned as the tartness of the cranberries affected her youthful palate. *"Dang!* What kinda juice is that? It gots a bit of a twang to it, whew!" she said as she wiped her mouth with the back of her hand and loudly placed the glass on the table.

Tamara frowned, tired of hearing the girl's coarse language, and replied, "Young ladies should not repeatedly say 'Dang.' It does not sound right, and I do not want you saying it while you are here."

The girl twisted her mouth, made another annoying loud click with her tongue, and rolled her neck as she turned her head from Tamara's gaze.

"Young lady, *did you hear me?*" Tamara said quietly, but insistently.

"My name is *Sienna,* not 'young lady,' first of all; and *I heard you!*" the girl said loudly, with the streetwise edge fully apparent in her tone again.

Then, before she knew what happened, Tamara heard herself retort loudly, *"Don't yell at me!"*

The girl gave her a surprised look but this time mumbled under her breath, "Shhhooot! I'll yell anytime I get good and ready."

Tamara turned away, more than a little surprised that she had actually raised her voice at the girl. She was thankful that Sienna had given in this time with no further argument, since she really needed a respite from all this heated back-and-forth talk. Exhausted and even feeling a little sick now, she realized she was unused to this type of drama. Her head was beginning to ache from it all, and her stomach was a little queasy, too.

By contrast, Sienna was gazing at her complacently, sucking her small teeth loudly while using one fingernail to remove a bit of food from between them. "Do you have TV in this spot, or what? I ain't seen none yet."

"In the living room, inside the cabinet. Open the doors, and the remote is in there as well," Tamara said without looking at her.

She was surprised at how relieved she was to hear the girl's fading footfalls on the carpet. *Finally,* she thought gratefully, *a few moments alone.*

As she finished cleaning the kitchen, Tamara glanced up at the wall clock and said aloud in a weary voice, "I can't believe it's only ten! This is going to be one long weekend." She heard the TV playing loudly now, and as she thought of her unexpected visitor sitting in her front room watching it, she shook her head ruefully and added, "Lynn, I think you will owe me for this one, *big-time!*"

4.

Anyway

Jayson put the cup of steaming coffee down in front of Tamara and, standing with one arm leaning on top of her cubicle, said sympathetically, "Tam, it sounds like you had one heck of a weekend." He rubbed his neatly trimmed goatee, as he did whenever he was anxious or pondering a thought, and then ran one hand over his bald, shiny head.

Jayson Johnson was six feet two, chocolate brown in complexion, and had worked for the Care agency for about five years now. Although thin, Jayson's taut body was naturally muscular, and his dark eyes were mischievous. He flashed his white, dimpled smile often, making it clear to those who knew him that he considered himself quite a ladies' man. Tamara and he worked closely together and often traveled together as a duo of Stabilization and Family Training caseworkers.

With a solemn shake of her head, Tamara replied to her coworker while wrapping her fingers around the hot coffee cup, "That's putting it mildly, Jayson. Thank you for the coffee—this *is* decaf, right? I've been overly hyped up since Sienna has been at my house, and I certainly don't need anything to add to my anxiousness."

"Did you get any sleep at all?" Jayson asked, concerned that Tamara looked a bit tired. Like Lynnette, he worried that Tamara's naturally reserved manner made her too much of a pushover, and while one saucy sister like Lynn was more than

18

enough for him at the workplace, he did wish that the young woman could be a little more assertive.

Actually, he was surprised that Tamara was being so forthcoming today, since this was the first time she'd ever revealed this much about her personal life to him. He had often wondered what she thought of him, because he found her very attractive, even though he'd never even tried to get next to her, as he did with most women. Jayson was pretty sure Tamara wouldn't give him no play anyway, but normally that didn't stop him from trying. Something was different about this girl, though, because without even trying, Tamara brought out a protective and caring side in him that he hardly recognized in himself.

Tamara wiped her eyes as she answered his question with a yawn. "I got very little sleep, Jay—very, very little. In fact, it seemed like each time I closed my eyes, Sienna was complaining or going on about something or other, and for some reason she had to do so in a rude or unpleasant fashion every time. One thing I can be thankful for, though: she tried to be sneaky or greedy or something and drank up about two gallons of cranberry juice . . . Jay, the coffee is decaf, right?"

Pushing his wandering thoughts about her from his head, Jayson glanced at the coffee she held, and replied, "The java juice . . . it's decaf, Tam—I know what you like by now." And then he questioned her, "Now, tell me about the cranberry juice. What's that about?"

Tamara smiled and took a swallow from the now lukewarm cup of coffee. "If you have ever drunk lots of cranberry juice, you'd understand, Jay."

"What do you mean?"

"Well, one cup can clean out your system, if you know what I mean, and when you drink too much . . . suffice it to say that Miss Sienna spent almost all of Saturday night and Sunday in the bathroom. She was so busy running in and out of there, she had no time or energy to terrorize me anymore. *Thank God!*"

Jayson blurted out a loud laugh and then looked behind him toward a larger office as he put his hand over his mouth to stifle his continuing chuckle. "I got you now, Tam. Little Miss Sienna was riding that bathroom seat, huh?"

"Shhh! Don't say that, Jayson!" Tamara's face reddened, and her dimples deepened as she pursed her lips disapprovingly. "Jay, it just doesn't sound right when you say it like that, and anyway we wouldn't want Joan to hear you—you know how she is," warned Tamara.

Joan Erickson had joined the agency several months ago as the new director. She was aggressive and ambitious, and at times it seemed to them that the white woman was more than a little bit racist as well.

Jayson made a face and added flippantly, "I'm not thinking about Joan, 'cause she shouldn't be watching us all the time like she's waiting for us to do something wrong!" Gesturing toward their supervisor's office, he added, "The girl is such a racist, and the sad part is, she doesn't even realize what she's doing, does she?"

"I don't think she does, Jay. She actually believes she is being fair to everybody, but in truth it seems like when white people who look like her do wrong, she doesn't even notice."

Shifting the subject, Jayson said, "Anyway, after that weekend, I bet you want to kill Lynnette, huh, Tam? And where is little Miss Sienna now, anyway?"

"I was kinda mad with Lynnette. In fact, I suppose I was actually pretty 'salty,' as you say, Jay. I called Lynn's pager number and her cell phone repeatedly, and she didn't call me back the entire weekend. She didn't even return my messages!"

He turned his lips up and rubbed his goatee. "That's a shame.

You know, I love that girl, but Lynnette can be pure-D triflin' sometimes. She must have been out on a hot date or something."

"She was—on a date, that is . . . Well, I don't know if it was hot or not," she added with a small giggle. "But she was out on a date."

"So, Tam, where's the child now?"

"I was desperate, Jay, and actually didn't know what to do, so I brought Sienna in with me this morning. It was pure luck that we ran into Lynn in the parking lot. By then I was already upset 'cause I thought—well, *knew*—that Lynnette was trying to dodge me. Then, to add insult to injury, before Sienna got her things from the car, do you know what that little girl said?"

"What?"

"First of all, she slammed the door really hard when she got out of the car; then she stuck her head in the window and said, 'I didn't want to stay at your dumb house another day anyway!' Then, in a huff, she got her belongings out of the backseat, slammed that door loudly, and flounced her little self over to Lynn's car, and before they drove off, she rolled her eyes at me."

Jayson's eyebrows rose in disbelief. "She didn't. She ain't that bad, now is she, Tam?"

Tamara nodded her head affirmatively. "Oh, Jayson, yes, she did do that, and believe me, she is that bad! In all fairness, I'm sure she must have a good side, but I certainly didn't get to see it. This weekend she cussed like a sailor and was nasty and unpleasant most of the time. I actually yelled, and that's not usually my way, you know?"

With a small smile, her coworker replied, "Well, you getting mad and yelling some might be a good thang. Tamara, everybody needs to let their anger out sometimes, even you! You are just *too* nice, Tamara, *too nice.*"

Tamara got tired of Jayson and Lynnette always riding her about the fact that she was reserved and slow to anger. She ignored Jayson's comment, but she reminded herself reassuringly that she was just not the "snapping" type; that type of aggressive interaction was just not her style.

Abruptly she changed the subject. "Jay-Jay, how was your weekend?"

Always ready to share nuggets about his love life, Jayson grinned and raised his bushy eyebrows dramatically. "Girl, let me tell you 'bout my weekend: it was *sweet,* Tam."

"Sweet?"

"Oooh, I had a date with a *sweet* honey, took her out to a *sweet* play, and then we went to dinner, and then we went to her place and 'thangs' got even *sweeter.*"

Her interest piqued, Tamara suppressed a giggle and asked, "Really, Jay? Is this someone I know?"

"You remember Desiree?"

Tamara frowned and asked, "Isn't she the one that I met at lunch that day when you, me, and Lynnette went to Simply Salads downtown? Didn't you say that you weren't going to ask her out anymore? In fact, wasn't she the one who flattened the tires on your car and then called you and told you about it?"

Jayson looked a bit sheepish for a moment as he said, "Yes, that's her—she's a bit feisty, I guess."

"*Feisty?* Are you sure about that? I mean, slashing someone's tires is behavior that is sort of criminal to me!" said Tamara in a concerned tone.

"Aw, come on, Tamara, she ain't no criminal, now."

"But, Jay, if you had called the police and pressed charges on her about your car, she would've been," the girl said seriously.

Jayson stroked his chin and said, "Well, you know what, Tamara? You right about that—I could've gotten her locked up. And getting those tires fixed wasn't cheap, either."

"So, why are you seeing her, then?"

He grinned widely and winked at her, "I guess the girl just gots some assets that I can't fully explain to you."

Tamara looked at Jayson quizzically and then reddened and turned away quickly once the assets that he was speaking of became clear to her.

"Uh-oh, somebody's comin'; look busy, now," said Jayson as he slid down into his chair and disappeared from her sight. She heard him sit hard with a loud thud.

Joan Erickson and her peculiarities were one thing Tamara did not feel like having to deal with today, not after the weekend she'd had. Quickly she spun around and began busily typing her contact notes into the computer terminal, documenting the family visits she had performed during the past week.

5.

Tricked and Bamboozled

"Good Morning, Joan," Tamara heard Jayson say, and she knew he was flashing his best dimpled smile at the woman when she passed his cubicle. His deep voice was dripping with feigned sincerity when he added, "That's a slammin' outfit that you are wearing today! But then, you always look good, and you know it!"

"Thank you, Jayson!" cooed Joan in a girlish tone.

Tamara made a face and stiffened in her cubicle while thinking how much she hated it when Jay did that phony flattery stuff with Joan. Silently she prayed, *Please just let her walk right by my desk. After the weekend I've had, I am in no state of mind to talk with Joan Erickson today.*

But instead, almost as if on cue, the smell of her boss's Clinique Happy perfume wafted into the air in front of her nose.

"Tamara, may I speak with you for a moment in my office?"

Tamara rolled her eyes and then tightened her lips before looking up. Quickly gathering her emotions, she turned to face Joan Erickson. As usual, the woman was dressed stylishly, today in a black crepe de chine pantsuit with a beige silk shirt. A matching peach, copper, and beige print silk scarf was casually tied around her neck.

The woman's hair was streaked with just the right touch of buttery blond highlights, and her makeup had been applied with a light, natural touch. Her thin lips were pressed into a closed-mouth smile, and Tamara quickly twisted her own, fuller mouth into the same expression as she rose to follow her boss to her office.

As the two women walked by Jayson's cubicle, Tamara hastily answered his quizzical expression by raising her eyebrows expressively while shrugging her shoulders slightly. Tamara truly had no idea why Joan wanted to speak with her, and she just hoped that it wasn't about some of the nitpicky borderline-racist stuff that Joan was becoming well known for among the African-American employees.

Once seated in Joan's office, Tamara looked into the white woman's green eyes and tried to cover her own curiosity about the purpose of their meeting.

"Before we get started, there's one small thing I want to talk with you about, Tam," said Joan with a quick, upturned twist of the corners of her lips. "Then I'll get to the thrust of why I called you in here."

Tamara cringed inside at the woman's shortening of her name. She really hated when Joan called her "Tam," since it was a pet name of sorts that Jayson and Lynnette had given her, and not to be used by everyone. She said nothing about it, though. Again reciprocating the closed-mouth smile the woman had given her, she said, "Sure, Joan."

"Not that I'm just singling you out or anything, but I couldn't help but notice that you seem to get back a few minutes late from your break on a regular basis," Joan commented while gazing at her intently. "You know, I really do like you, Tam," the woman said, and then quickly curved her lips upward again, "But, if I let you do it, soon everyone will think it's okay, and we can't have that, can we?"

"No, Joan, we can't," said Tamara in her usual professional tone, but even while she was saying the words, she was thinking of all the other employees who routinely arrived late or left early, and she began to understand that there *were* different standards for white employees. Joan probably did not even notice what they were doing, because she was far too busy watching the black folks all the time.

Joan's large diamond ring glittered in the office light as she opened the file folder that was lying on her desk. Then she looked up at Tamara, smiled quickly again, and said in an almost saccharine-sweet tone that she often affected when talking to the employees, "Now, Tamara, I just want you to know that I think you are one of our most valuable employees. You work so well with foster families, and your training and coordination of services have helped a number of them to keep their kids and not lose them to the system."

"Thank you, Joan," said Tamara, but the woman's uncharacteristic solicitousness made her more and more concerned about just what the real purpose of this impromptu meeting was.

"I do have a small favor to ask of you, though," said Joan. "As you know, as an agency we require all of our employees to take foster parent training so that if we are ever in an emergency situation, *we* can become the example for the community by helping kids who are without homes."

"Right," Tamara said. "I've finished my classes, and I'm licensed at all three levels: Regular, Specialized, and Intensive Services."

"I am aware of that, and I think it is great that you showed the initiative to take all three classes—that was not required." Joan smiled, actually showing her small, even teeth this time before adding, "That is truly going the extra mile, Tam, and you should pat yourself on the back for that."

Tamara's own smile was bright and earnest then, since compliments that seemed genuine, like that one, were few and far between from her boss.

"Thank you, Joan," she replied gratefully.

Joan's face became serious again. "Now, Tam, I am calling on you to use the skills that you have been trained in. We have an emergency situation. We have tried many options, but right now they have not worked, and I'm turning to you for help because I truly believe *you* possess what it takes to do the job."

Her confidence high from the earlier praise, Tamara nodded her head, smiled again, and said, "Okay, Joan. I will do what I can to help out."

"Thank you, Tam. I knew I could count on *you*."

"You can, Joan."

Joan's hazel eyes then locked on Tamara's. "Here's the rub, though. We have a child that we are unable to place right now. We know that because of the difficulties she has encountered in previous placements and because of her issues, we will have to select the next home for her in a very careful and measured way for it to be successful."

Tamara crossed her legs and smoothed her pant leg down with her hand. "That's understandable. While I have worked more closely with the parents than with the youth who are placed in foster care, I do realize that many of the kids have lots of baggage, and it's difficult for them to transition easily into homes."

"Exactly," said Joan. You are one of two employees here who are trained at the Intensive level, and that is exactly the type of services that she will need; and we would like to place her with you—*temporarily,* of course."

Tamara began to think quickly, asking herself, *What problems can one little girl present?* Then, in her typical manner, she began to reassure herself mentally, *I can do this. After all, it won't be for long.* Having made up her mind, she gave her boss a direct gaze and replied confidently, "Okay, Joan, I can accept a *temporary* placement, until you can find a permanent home for her."

"Oh, excellent, Tam! I knew we could count on you! You are well prepared to deal with her issues through your training. Tamara, you can have a tremendous impact on her with your professionalism and work ethic. Most importantly, you and the girl share cultural similarities. Like you, she is African-American—at least partly."

All of a sudden, Tamara got a strange feeling in her stomach. Could the placement be Sienna? "Partly?"

"Yes, she is biracial."

Attempting to stay composed, she asked, "Just how old is this 'little' girl?"

Joan opened the folder and put the glasses hanging around her neck on her nose before running one pink-manicured finger down the page and looking at Tamara over the reading spectacles. "I've seen her, and she is quite a petite little thing, but it says here she is fourteen."

Tamara's lips tightened. She was getting the strong impression that she had been hoodwinked, bamboozled, and tricked. Still carefully hiding her rising emotions, she replied, "Oh, really; fourteen, huh? That's not really a 'little' girl, now, is it?"

Forcing a smile, Joan said, "Well, that *is* a matter of opinion, right, Tam? She's such a tiny little thing, I actually thought that she was younger myself. But I tell you what, she is as cute as a button, too."

Now sure that her suspicion was correct, she asked, with more tension in her voice than she intended, "What's her name, Joan?"

"Sienna Larson."

Tamara had to use all her reserves at that moment to keep herself in check. "Sienna Larson?" *Oh, my God, she thought, it is the girl!* This had to be some sort of cruel joke. If Lynn was behind this, she would not forgive her this time for setting her up with the girl again. *It's simple,* she surmised, *I cannot do it, because I just cannot deal with her.* The weekend's events flickered through her mind rapidly.

"Tamara? Is something the matter?" asked Joan as she looked with concern at the girl's stricken expression.

The sound of Joan's voice cut through Tamara's musings and brought her abruptly back to the present. "I'm fine, Joan. Fine."

"So, it's all settled, right?" Joan asked as she dropped her glasses from her nose to let them land on her beige silk blouse.

Hesitantly Tamara cleared her throat and asked, "And just why is it she can't stay with a regular foster family, again?"

Joan flashed her another quick, closed-mouth smile and said, "Well, from what I hear, her oppositional disorder makes her a bit difficult to get along with." Dropping her voice to a whisper, she crinkled her nose as she added, "I think she can be a bit mouthy at times."

Before she could stop herself, Tamara replied in an incredulous tone, "A bit?"

"Did you say something?" her boss asked.

"Yes," said Tamara, and before she knew what she had done, she heard herself say, "I said, I'll do it."

"Good! Good!" said Joan. "I *knew* I could count on you!" She reached out her freckled hand to shake Tamara's deep brown one. "We've got her in a short-term placement right now, and we should be able to give you about a week to prepare for her to move in."

Dazed now, Tamara stood up from her seat, turned from Joan's bright, shiny smile that seemed to reveal all her teeth, and walked to the door. She turned the doorknob, stepped outside, and closed the door behind her. There she paused a moment, and as she began to walk to her cubicle, all she could do was say over and over, under her breath, "What did I do? What did I do?"

6.

Ridin' Duo

Jayson looked away from the road toward Tamara and, with the same incredulous tone in his voice, asked again, "Why, Tam? Why didn't you just say no?"

Tamara refused even to look at Jayson this time, though.

29

Asking the same question over and over was not going to change what she'd already agreed to do, and besides, his repetitive inquiries were really beginning to annoy her. So, ignoring him totally, Tamara stared out the window, contentedly watching the colorful trees as she enjoyed the passing fall scenery while thinking quietly.

The two of them had been asked, or rather required, by Joan to drop off some information to the State Agency. The implication by their boss had been that the fat manila envelope contained documents that she'd not known were to be included in an initial funding request she'd sent earlier in the week. They'd said nothing then, but later she and Jayson reasoned that the new director probably had forgotten some crucial part of the paperwork and just did not want to admit her mistake to them.

Nonetheless, today was the deadline for the package to be in Springfield, and for very different reasons she and Jayson were glad to be the couriers selected to drop it off.

"Tam . . . Tam?"

Shaken from her musings, Tamara whipped her head around. "What, Jayson? What?"

"I don't know why you are just trying to ignore me and what I'm saying to you. I'm only telling you what you already know. There's *no way* that you could've wanted that smart-alecky, foulmouthed little girl to stay with you!"

Tamara acquiesced reluctantly. "Okay, Jayson, you're right. No, I did not want her to stay with me. And the truth is, I really don't know if I'll be able to deal with her. She is very angry," Tamara added, recalling how the girl's pretty features were distorted throughout the weekend by her ire.

Jayson lifted his Kangol cap a bit, scratched the front of his head, and replied matter-of-factly, "You know, Tam, I'm oldschool. In other words, when I grew up, whether I was angry or not did not matter. My parents didn't care. See, my mama and daddy used to break me off a little piece, if you know what I mean, when I acted like a fool. The way you described how she was talking to y'all, it's obvious that this little girl ain't had no parenting. Ain't nobody broke her off a piece, not no time lately anyway. Sounds like to me, this little girl is used to doing what she wants, saying what she wants, whenever she wants, and, sistah-girl, that's gonna be rough for you!"

Tamara agreed quietly, "You're right, Jay. Sienna has been on her own quite a lot from what I've read in the information we do have on her. She's lived more on her own than in a home with anyone. So, you see, there's no way she could have gotten much 'home training,' as you say, because she's never had a home."

Jayson's concern shifted, and he asked, "But, Tam, what do you know about her really? Did they give you all of her information from her past placements? Did you get information about her early history?"

Tamara replied calmly, "Jay, all I know is that she is a transfer case from the Chicago area. Joan had only a small amount of information, and she gave that to me, but much of her background documentation hasn't come into the agency yet. Right now the agency's and my knowledge is limited about Sienna's past."

Jayson turned his gaze from the road just long enough to give her a quick but clearly worried glance. Whistling between his teeth, he asked, "Chicago? Whew! It can be rough in the Windy City, and if that girl has been on her own for any period of time, there's no tellin' *what* she's been through there. Tamara, she could be violent or something."

"Oh, Jay, stop it! I'm sure she's not a violent person."

His tone became even more serious, and he added, "For real, Tam, that girl could be an ax murderer or something. You don't know what you're getting into." He stroked his goatee thoughtfully. "And anyway, are you sure that Lynnette didn't have something to do with this? I love that girl, but you know how good she is at twisting folks around her little manicured pinky finger."

"I don't think so, Jayson, and anyway, I can't get out of it now—I've already said I'd do it." Then, in a small voice, she added, "Plus, she might just need a chance, huh?"

Jayson gave her a skeptical glance before drawling sarcastically, "Riiiight . . ."

Glancing out the window, Tamara saw the sign indicating their exit. With one leather-gloved finger, she pointed to it and said, "Jayson, don't miss the exit. It's this one."

He twisted his lips, demonstrating his frustration while quickly pulling his car over into the exit ramp. "Now, see, Tam, I'm thinking about you and Little Miss Sienna so much that I've lost focus on what *I'm* supposed to be doing."

Tam patted Jayson's arm awkwardly and said, "Don't worry, Jay—it'll be all right. Sienna will probably calm down once she's been with me a while. I'm sure I just saw her at her worst the other day."

Quiet ensued in the car as Tamara watched the road and Jayson concentrated on maneuvering in and out of the early afternoon traffic. While Springfield was not an extremely large city, especially in comparison to urban areas like Chicago or St. Louis, traffic was typically congested during the day as commuters made their way to work from smaller towns.

Tamara, no longer worried about her new housemate, was inwardly enmeshed in plotting a strategy that would allow her to use this unexpected trip to her advantage this afternoon. During the past year or so, Tamara had embarked on her own escapade of sorts, delving into the master state files and computer information data whenever she could manage on to these trips.

"Jay-Jay?" she said innocently.

"Huh, Tam?"

Tamara gave Jayson a sideways glance from under her eye-lashes. "You know, after we pick up the information packages and touch base with the area caseworker, I have a friend I need to do a favor for."

"A friend? I didn't know you were from Springfield. I thought you were from Ohio or somewhere—and not Spring-field, Ohio, either."

"Oh, I'm not from Springfield. I met this friend back when I was at college."

Jayson's attention was immediately piqued now, since in his mind any female could be a potential love match for him. A friend of Tamara's would be a good bet, too; since she was pretty, that made it a strong possibility that any acquaintance of hers would be fine, too.

Jayson glanced at his friend, raised his eyebrows, and asked, "So, what's your friend's name?" With a smile he asked flirta-tiously, "Does she know that you have a handsome, single, male coworker?"

"Her name is Yvette," Tamara replied, ignoring Jayson's at-tempts to gain more information.

He said the name aloud: "Yvette? Nice name . . . so what's sistah girl look like?"

Anxious about her afternoon plans, Tamara replied a bit snip-pily, "Must you always be concerned about how a girl looks, and whether you might get a date with her?"

Tamara's snappish reply was out of character for her, and Jayson gave his friend a quizzical glance before saying, "Okay, Tam. I apologize—it's all good. I'll keep myself busy for about an hour or two, 'cause I think that's what you're asking me to do, right?"

Glad to have discouraged any more questioning from him, Tamara did not notice his curious gaze as she exhaled gratefully and replied, "Thank you, Jayson."

Now, she thought to herself, *I've got at least an hour, maybe more, and if I work fast, I can make a lot of headway in that amount of time—I have to!*

7·

Mission Accomplished

It was ninety minutes later when Tamara finally settled in front of one of the data computers located in the back of the State Child Welfare building. Tamara glanced at her watch and, noting the time, thought disappointedly, *only forty-five minutes—that's all I have left.* It had not taken long to drop off the envelope for their boss, but it seemed to have taken forever for her to lose Jayson. Still certain Tamara was holding out on him about this friend of hers, he'd seemed determined to stay with her until she told him exactly who the girl was.

Out of desperation she finally said to him, "Jay, I need about an hour, remember?"

Finally realizing Tamara wasn't going to let him in on whatever secret he was certain she was hiding, Jayson dropped his shoulders dramatically and stuck his hands deep into his pockets before walking away, mumbling, "I guess I'll go get some lunch."

Tamara's adrenaline ran high now, for she had so much to accomplish in such a short time. With trembling hands she reached into her briefcase and pulled out the familiar manila folder, forcing herself to ignore her apprehensions and focus on the job at hand.

"Yvette Bailey" was handwritten on the worn tab of the folder, and opening it, she quickly scanned through the loose pages of information she had painstakingly researched and gathered over time.

"Sissie Bailey, today is the day that I'm gonna find you. I can just feel it," she said under her breath while entering her state password ID and waiting impatiently for the computer to allow her access to the files. "Bingo," she whispered when the large state logo appeared, indicating she was in the system. Tamara's fingers flew across the keys as she began to retrace the now familiar data pathway that she knew would lead to the cluster of files she was searching for.

Even though it seemed that only seconds had gone by since she'd sat down in front of the computer, glancing at her watch, Tamara was shocked to see that almost thirty minutes had passed already.

"C'mon, c'mon . . . where are you, Sissie?" she asked as her eyes scanned the small print on the page, searching for that one name in particular.

Finally spying the woman's name, Tamara pressed the key and brought the woman's background information file to the screen. "'Celestine Bailey, also known as Sissie,'" she read aloud.

Her eyes began to follow the words on the screen carefully as she read to herself:

Celestine Bailey (aka) Sissie Bailey, has a long criminal history precipitated by her addiction to drugs. She is the mother of four girls, now ages 12, 11, 10, and 8. Repeated attempts on the part of the state to reunite the mother (Sissie) with her children have not proved effective to date.

Silently, Tamara skimmed over several more pages of information documenting the various interventions, treatments, and services given to Sissie Bailey by the State of Illinois in an effort to keep her family intact.

> While not a drug user, Sissie has had a procession of men in and out of her home. Her pursuit of these relationships has resulted in the girls' suffering from neglect and physical abuse. She has left them alone for hours at a time or with neighbors and near strangers.

Unfortunately, the scenario she was reading about was not uncommon to her. In her role as a Stabilization worker, she had many clients who were parents who had neglected their children, leaving them alone in similar situations. Yet no matter how many times she came across this type of abuse, Tamara always asked herself the same questions, and she asked them again while reading about Sissie Bailey's obvious neglect of her kids: Why would they have children if they did not want to care for them? How could they leave *children* alone? Her eyes swept over the information again as she wondered, didn't Sissie realize that her children were not old enough to be left alone, or didn't she even care?

These irresponsible parents often seemed truly unaware of their shortcomings. Tamara knew in theory that they should ultimately be held responsible for these children they'd brought into the world. But the sad reality was, these parents were not unlike children themselves—selfishly absorbed by their own desires and often trying to fill an empty space inside themselves with little thought of the consequences of their actions. Far too many times when Tamara looked into their eyes, these parents were as confused and lost as the kids that they were supposed to be caring for.

Tamara took a deep breath and looked at her watch quickly. She had to get to work before time ran out. She needed to focus;

this was no time to ruminate over these difficult questions that she had no real answers for. Glancing at her watch again, she sighed, realizing Jayson would probably be back in just a few minutes, and that there was no way she would have time to read all the information in front of her before then.

Scouring the unfamiliar keyboard, Tamara located the Start button for the printer and pressed it once, twice, then three times. Holding her breath while swinging her crossed leg nervously, she watched the silent metal box furtively, willing the pages to quickly begin their transit through the machine. Tamara exhaled gratefully when she finally heard the whir of the motor, indicating that the first pages were being printed. Then her eyes were drawn back to the words in front of her on the computer screen, and again she read silently:

> Witnesses say that the girls were often running through the neighborhood asking for money from people they barely knew. They were disheveled and unkempt, and their behavior unruly and rude. Although, as mentioned before, the mother had many boyfriends, there is no knowledge as to whether there was any sexual abuse of the girls.

Tamara's eyes widened and her jaw dropped a bit when she read the next shocking statement. Even though Tamara had a good inkling by now that Sissie Bailey had led a wild life, this was even more than she expected:

> All of the girls were taken into final custody by the state in 1965, when Sissie Bailey was arrested for involuntary manslaughter.

Involuntary manslaughter? What was that about? Tamara knew that it meant Sissie had more than likely spent time in the correctional system. And so it may not have been her neglect of her girls that caused her to lose them in the end. Instead, her criminal behavior may have been what finally separated the family for good.

Quickly she scanned the rest of the text. *Where is she . . . where is she now?* she thought while nervously tapping her nails on the desk. Quickly checking her watch one more time, she used her finger as a guide on the computer screen while scanning the words. But there was nothing, not one more word about Sissie.

The distant thud of a closing door in the outer room brought her back into the present. Tamara knew it signaled the ending of the lunch hour, since people were filtering back into the outer office area, and that meant Jayson would be here very soon. Carefully she closed off the document window and gathered her papers from the printer area.

As Tamara was stuffing the last of the papers into the manila folder, the door was flung opened behind her, and she spun around, startled yet readying herself to invent a quick excuse for her presence in the area if necessary.

"Tam, do you know what time it is? I've been looking all over for you," Jayson said.

To her dismay, for an extraordinarily long moment Tamara was unable to utter a word. Instead, she stared mutely at Jayson with her eyes wide open, willing her brain to function again so that she could speak.

Jayson gazed at Tamara, waiting for her reply, when it dawned on him that something was a little off balance with her. "Tam? Are you all right?" He peered into her eyes closely. "You look funny . . . Did you eat lunch or sit in here and work? Where is that friend of yours, anyway? I wanted to meet her . . . I thought you was going to hook a brotha up!"

Of course, Tamara knew there was no friend for him to meet, and she *had* to think quickly to come up with something, *anything,* to distract him from that whole subject.

Finally finding her voice, she replied, "Okay, Jay-Jay. I'm on the way now," as she hurriedly stuffed the manila folder inside her briefcase.

Keeping her eyes averted, Tamara sensed him giving her another long, searching look. "So you okay, then, huh? But, where's baby girl?" he added, flashing his dimpled smile at her.

"Jay, I did *not* say my friend would be here. You misunderstood me. I said I needed to do a favor for a friend," she said as she smiled back at him. Then on impulse she added, "And besides, she wouldn't be interested in you, because she has a boyfriend, and they are in loooove."

Jayson said in a whining voice, "Awww, see, why are all the good girls already taken?" Then he turned his cap backward and held the door open for her as he added mournfully, "I bet she's fine, too."

"C'mon, Jayson, you can't win 'em all," Tamara replied with a nervous giggle, relieved that the tense moment had passed as she followed him out of the computer area.

8.

Running, Again

"Don't go to sleep; don't go to sleep . . . " the girl kept repeating to herself over and over in a whispered voice that only she could hear. Finally, after she had lain there for what seemed hours, she moved her head to the left slowly, careful not to make a sound as she turned toward her roommate.

She noticed with relief that Latisha Mayfield was sleeping

soundly in the next bed. The large girl's mouth was open a bit, and she could hear the air softly move in and out as she breathed.

Now that it was safe for her to get up, she yanked back the coverings with one hand and, with another swift, silent movement, planted her feet on the floor before stooping to reach under her bed for her green duffel bag. Sadly, she would have to leave many of her belongings behind because, as usual, she could only carry a small amount with her. Pulling the already packed bag from beneath the bed, she placed it over one shoulder and stepped lightly toward the window.

From the back pocket of her overalls she took out an old baseball cap and with both hands pulled it down low over her face. After pushing errant hairs under the old cap, the girl pulled her hood up until only the frayed bill of the cap could be seen.

Swiftly she moved over to the window and then gripped it with both hands, hoping hard that the old wood would not creak noisily when she opened it. Magically, the window slid upward smoothly. After hoisting the bag through the window first, she put one foot over the ledge, then the other, and, with a small leap, landed quietly on the soft ground. Once safely outside, she spun around quickly and, using an old hanger she'd thrown outside earlier, closed the window without a sound and crouched there in the bushes outside the window, with her heart beating a mile a minute.

While she was standing there, all sorts of thoughts were running through her mind. Flashbacks of the just past Fourth of July holiday made her smile when she thought about how they'd all sat around the table together and eaten barbecue, baked beans, and potato salad that the house mom and dad cooked for them. The girl emitted a small giggle remembering how she and Latisha had gobbled down the feast and then how they couldn't stop laughing whenever they looked at each other, lips shiny from the food that they had eaten so quickly.

Yes, she would miss them all. She'd even miss Rosemary with her odd mood swings and dark stare. Some of the others called Rosemary crazy, but not her, 'cause she wasn't even sure what that word meant anymore. Sometimes, living as she did, she felt a little crazy herself. Fondly she thought about her roommate, Latisha, once more, with her raucously loud laugh and bright smile. And then there were Mr. and Mrs. Cooley, who seemed almost like parents to them, even though they were in state care.

"I can't stay, though," she whispered to herself. "I just can't." And then, after a furtive glance left and then right, the girl did the one thing she knew how to do the very best.

The girl ran.

9.

Cold Feet

Tamara finished making up the full-size bed with the thick multicolored comforter that she'd bought yesterday after work, at the T.J. Maxx store out by the Riverton Mall. When she was done, Tamara crossed her arms and surveyed her work critically. The beautiful down-filled printed comforter looked warm, and it was a perfect match to the pale peach walls of the room.

In the far corner was a wooden rocker that Tamara had purchased years ago. She'd thrown an ethnic-patterned blanket on the rocker's back, painted in shades of corals, greens, and peaches similar to the comforter, and had placed a matching peach cushion on the seat. Woven baskets decorated the walls, as well as colorful framed posters of African-American children of various ages.

Nestled against the largest wall was a natural wicker mirrored dresser covered with colorful bottles of assorted lotions and shower gels that Tamara had begun picking up days ago, for Sienna's impending arrival at her home. A small color television sat on the matching wicker bookshelf, and the other shelves held magazines like *Vibe* and *Young Teen* that Tamara thought might appeal to the girl.

Sienna's gamine face suddenly flashed through Tamara's mind, pushing thoughts of the beautiful room into the background, and she stared with glazed eyes out the window in front of her. Adrift in her thoughts of the teen, Tamara didn't even notice that the swirling colors in the new curtains hanging from the window completed the colorful decor of the room and helped give the space a pleasant air.

During the past week, each time Tamara had thought of the uncomfortable weekend she'd spent with Sienna, she'd felt anxious and had pushed the discomfort away, mindlessly shopping and decorating while not allowing herself to think of the girl at all. Gazing at the completed room now, though, she could no longer deny the inevitable, and her heart suddenly beat wildly; she felt panicky at the immensity of what she'd agreed to do.

"I can't believe it . . . I've opened my home to a stranger . . . ," she said aloud. "Oh, God, what was I even thinking? I can't do this."

I really need to talk with somebody, she thought. Rushing into her bedroom and finding her purse, she reached into her wallet and retrieved her Black Day Planner from her nightstand. With a pale, pink-nailed finger she turned the pages quickly until she found the number that she was looking for. Gingerly she sat down on the edge of the bed, picked up the telephone, dialed the number, and listened hopefully for a familiar voice to answer.

"Hello," said a male voice at the other end of the line.

"Mr. Jackson?" she asked tentatively. "This is Tamara Britton. How are you?"

"Oh, Tamara . . . hello. I am just fine, baby. How 'bout you?"

Tamara's heart rate slowed a bit, just that easily lulled into relaxation by the rich, deep timbre of Leonard Jackson's warm tone. He was a tall, thin man with a thick crop of silver and black curly hair. As he spoke, she instantly pictured his face in her mind, his deep brown skin; and she remembered how his thin cheeks creased into long dimples whenever he showed his easy, white smile.

"I'm okay, Mr. Jackson. I was just wondering if I could speak with Mrs. Jackson for a minute or two—if she's not busy or anything," she said. Her shoulders fell, a sure sign that her confidence also was failing, as once again she thought of the impending arrival of her new roommate.

"Hold on, Tam, baby. You hold on, now. I'll get Denise for you."

"Thank you," said Tamara, and she held the phone under her ear with her shoulder while staring at her hands, lying tensely balled into two fists on her lap. Anxiously she waited to hear the voice of the foster parent she'd worked with so many times.

She was thankful at this moment to know Denise Jackson, the parent member of their foster parent training team. In the classes they taught together, the woman shared practical knowledge with potential foster parents based on years of experience, and Tamara was continually amazed at the generosity of these two special individuals who had opened their home to so many children. Suddenly, her own concern about one little girl moving in seemed quite selfish, especially in comparison to these two, who had parented hundreds of children over the years.

While waiting for the man's wife to pick up the telephone, she wondered incredulously, *How* do *they do it? How do they just open their homes and their hearts to strangers?* "I just hope you can help me, Mrs. Jackson," she whispered to herself.

"Tamara? . . . Tamara?" the woman repeated when she did not answer the first time.

Denise Jackson was a couple of years younger than her fifty-eight-year-old husband, and the two of them had been foster parents for almost twenty years now. Between their own two kids and the hordes of others that they had kept on a temporary or permanent basis, their home was full of life with the constant commotion and the daily drama that colored the lives of the young people living there. Well known in placement care, Denise and Leonard Jackson had been chosen foster parents of the year time after time because of their huge hearts and their constant commitment to kids.

The woman's demeanor was always upbeat. Her smooth skin was light brown, and her thick hair was long and most often worn pulled back into a bun or pinned up in a French roll. More than a little overweight, she was always on the verge of starting an exercise program that she never quite seemed to have the time to actually fit into her busy life.

"Mrs. Jackson . . . hello," Tamara replied. "I'm sorry . . . I was daydreaming a bit, I guess."

"Tamara! Baby girl, I was beginning to wonder if you was on the phone or what," said Denise Jackson with her trademark hearty laugh. "Are you okay?"

"Mrs. Jackson, I am fine," said Tamara, and her voice sounded calm and professional as usual. "Do you remember I told you that I would be having a houseguest for a while?"

"Houseguest? Baby, do you mean the little girl that's moving in with you—the one with the *real* bad mouth that you told me about the other week when you was by the house?"

Tamara smiled at the apt description she'd given her of the girl, and said, "Yes, Mrs. Jackson." Then, struggling to keep composed, she added, "She's moving in tonight."

Years of experience with emotionally damaged youth had taught Denise Jackson well, and Tamara's efforts to disguise her feelings did not go unnoticed. Waiting for a new placement produced some level of anxiety in even the most experienced foster parent, since any new persons moving in *were* still strangers even though they were children.

"Tamara," she said knowingly.

"Yes?"

"Now, baby, I know you're nervous 'cause the little girl's gettin' ready to move in over there, and it's natural that you'd feel that way, 'cause somebody new is coming into your house. Right now here's what I want you to do. I want you take a deep, deep breath, and then I want you to say aloud, 'everything is going to be just fine.'"

Dropping her facade completely, Tamara, rather than follow the woman's request, instead interrupted in a voice that was rushed and shaky: "But what if it's not? What if I've made a big mistake? What if she hates it here? Mrs. Jackson, the girl didn't even *like* me during that weekend she stayed with me. She was cursing and argumentative, and most of the time she even looked at me as if I was dirt."

"Tamara! Stop it, now!" said Mrs. Jackson, her voice strident. "Now, girl, don't you ever forget that the enemy Satan is the master of what-ifs. He loves to put just those type of doubts in our minds, and he hopes that when we are focusing on our fears, he will keep us from doing God's work."

Tamara nodded as if the woman could see her, but said nothing. Was this God's work that she was doing? What did she know about God, really? To be honest, much of the time Tamara wondered if God even knew she existed.

The woman continued, "This *is* a good thing you are doing, baby. You are opening your home to a young person who doesn't have one. Only a person with a heart would do that. You've worked at Care Agency for a long time now and you've stood on the outside watching others open their homes to these children, and now God has put something inside you that's made you become a joiner and not just a watcher."

As Tamara listened, she silently wiped away teardrops that were threatening to spill from her eyes. Retrieving a tissue from her nightstand, she wiped her nose, careful not to sniffle, because she didn't want Mrs. Jackson to know that she was crying. Not only anxious about Sienna's arrival, now Tamara was also filled with guilt that Mrs. Jackson was crediting her with a much more noble motivation than she deserved regarding her decision to allow the girl to live with her.

She doesn't know that I'm a coward, Tamara thought morosely. *She doesn't know that the only reason I said yes is really because I was tricked into it, or maybe I just was too scared to say no.*

Unaware of the younger woman's inner notions, Denise Jackson continued, "Never, ever doubt that you can do this, baby girl. God would not put it into your heart to do something that you cannot do."

"Mrs. Jackson . . . do y-y-you think I can?"

"I know you can," said Denise Jackson firmly. "You have *everything* it takes to do this and do it well. You have the training and the skills, and most importantly, you have the heart to do it—that's why you agreed to it!"

"I can do this," said Tamara, more to herself than aloud.

Denise Jackson heard her, though, and said, "Say it again, girl!"

"I can do this," said Tamara more firmly.

"One more time, baby girl—say it like you mean it!" said Denise Jackson as fervently as a pep rally leader to a lifeless crowd.

"*I can do this!*" Tamara said quite loudly.

"That's what I want to hear! You *can* do this and you will! Now, Tamara, be prepared; this girl *is* gonna act up. You know this, or if you didn't, you know it now! These kids are displaced into a whole new environment, and actin' up is often how they let off steam, so expect it, okay?"

"Okay."

Mrs. Jackson continued, "Baby, teenagers can be moody and difficult to handle anyway, just cause their hormones are raging. Lots of these kids are strong-willed, too; because they've lived through such craziness in their early lives, they have to be full of spirit to survive the hardships."

Her voice tentative again, Tamara asked, "Mrs. Jackson, do your kids act up at your house?"

"*Oh, baby* . . . Yes, they do! But when they get to clownin' 'round here, I just get on 'em and love 'em anyway," she finished with a hearty laugh.

Immediately Tamara tensed when she heard the word "love." *Love?* Love was something she wasn't even ready to think about, let alone give to anyone. She might grow to like the girl, but she wasn't really planning on loving anyone. In fact, as far as she was concerned, love had nothing to do with any of this!

"You have to be firm. Set your rules and boundaries about what is acceptable behavior and what is not, and stand tough on those expectations. She may try you at first, but the girl *will* come around, take my word for it. Now, Tamara . . ."

"Huh?" she said.

"I gotta go, 'cause Leonard and I are heading out to Bible study in a minute. Remember, baby girl. Don't forget what I told you—stand firm with your expectations, and she will come around. Remember, God loves you and so do I!"

"Okay . . . Thank you, Mrs. Jackson; I really needed someone to talk to," said Tamara gratefully.

"Baby girl, once that little girl moves in, you might need to talk to someone even more. 'Specially if she's sassy as you say she is! Anyway, you call on me anytime you need me, now—*anytime,* Tamara," replied Mrs. Jackson encouragingly.

Softly she put down the receiver as she thought to herself, *I am so thankful for Mrs. Jackson's help. I feel so much better now . . . She really knows what she is talking about, I can tell.* Tamara pursed her lips, and her brows furrowed as she thought how Mrs. Jackson was wrong about one thing: love had nothing to do with this at all!

10.

Sharing Space

"Sienna!" Tamara said as she let herself through her front door and wrinkled her nose at the odors of burnt food. Worriedly she hurried into the kitchen area and was greeted by scattered dirty dishes on the counter. Crumbs covered the area around the open loaf of bread, and a spoon filled with peanut butter and jelly lay next to it, while a once-cold gallon of milk with no cap was warming on the counter by the refrigerator.

"Look at this mess!" Tamara said aloud. While she in no way considered herself a neatnik who insisted that everything be "just so" in her home at all times, she found this chaotic scene in the kitchen definitely unacceptable!

"Sienna!" Tamara shouted, and stood waiting for the young girl to appear around the corner . . . but she did not.

Irritated and still mumbling under her breath about the disarray she'd just seen, Tamara turned her back disgustedly on the messy kitchen. She made a quick stop in the living room to drop off her briefcase and, once there, heard the thumping low notes of the compact CD player she had bought for the teen, which only added to her aggravation.

Single-mindedly Tamara stalked down the hallway and threw open Sienna's bedroom door, and there was Sienna in the middle of the floor, dancing suggestively to the booming bass of the rap song. The tiny girl was moving in a seductive manner, looking like one of the writhing girls on some of the latest music videos that Tamara had happened upon on TV late at night. Taken aback at the explicitness of the young women's provocative moves, Tamara would stare at them openmouthed before hurriedly switching channels, quickly surfing to a station less shocking to her.

In a similar state of surprise, Tamara just stood there several moments with her eyes glued on the teen, who did not even know she was there. Sienna's almond eyes were closed tightly as she rapped along loudly with the male voice on the CD, ". . . girl, yo' butt is so fine; that's why every day I can't help but wish that you was mine!"

"Sienna!" she said again, but the girl kept right on undulating to the music as if she had not heard her. *"Sienna!"* she called, loudly enough this time that her voice could be heard over the music.

Sienna's eyes flew wide open, and she immediately stopped her X-rated dance moves, obviously shocked to see Tamara standing there. In only moments, though, Sienna's look of shock disappeared, replaced by the tough, streetwise persona she affected most of the time.

Sienna rolled her eyes and said dramatically in a voice filled with attitude, "Cain't you knock? Last time I looked, this *was* my room, right?"

Tamara purposely ignored the girl's disrespectful tone and replied, "If I had knocked, you would not have been able to hear me anyway," and the coolness in her tone belied the simmering heat she was feeling inside.

"What?" said Sienna.

"Sienna, turn the music off."

"Uh?"

"Sienna, turn the music off!" Tamara shouted. *"Now!"*

To her surprise, the girl flinched noticeably, evidently frightened at the sound of her raised voice. Almost running, she quickly cut the stereo down. Determined not to appear weak, though, Sienna replied with feigned bravado, *"Okay, okay,* you don't have to *holla* like that!"

"Sorry, but you could not hear me for that music."

With a plop the teenager sat down hard on her bed, pretending to ignore Tamara as she began to thumb through one of the teen magazines lying there. Sullen now, she asked, "What you want anyway?"

Expectantly Tamara looked at Sienna and waited for the girl to meet her gaze, but the teen, obstinately defiant now, stared steadily at the magazine, refusing to make eye contact with her.

"What kind of music is that you are listening to, Sienna? Those lyrics that I heard when I came in this room did not sound appropriate for a young lady."

The girl looked at her now and popped her small lips loudly. "I don't know what no *appropriate* means, but I know that music sounds good to me." She smiled dreamily. "I love Lil' BigDog; *he the bomb*!"

"Well, I don't care if he *is* 'the bomb.' I simply cannot allow that type of music to be listened to in this house. From what I heard just now, it has cursing in it, and that is not acceptable."

Sienna gave Tamara a quick angry glance; then without comment she began to turn the flimsy pages of the magazine loudly. "Oh, so I don't have no choice about what I even *listens* to in your house, huh?"

"You may *listen* to whatever you like, just as long as it does not contain language that is lewd or vulgar," she replied.

"Oh, I guess just 'cause *you* don't listen to no music or nothin', you don't want nobody else to have no fun," she mumbled.

"Excuse me, what did you say?" asked Tamara.

Sienna clicked her tongue again, even more loudly this time. *"You is excused."* Then she continued, "I *said,* just cause you don't like music or nothin', that doesn't mean other people don't like it."

"And just what makes you think that I don't like music? Is it because I don't like that vulgar stuff you were listening to?"

The girl looked up at her. "You don't even have *no* music! You got a big ol' nice stereo CD player with no CDs in there."

Tamara was silenced for a moment. It had been her intention when she purchased the CD player to buy some CDs. She was especially partial to the contemporary jazz music she heard on the radio sometimes, and she would hum along with many of the melodies since she knew them by heart, although she didn't really know any of the artists by name.

Confidently she replied to the girl, "I've just not gotten around to purchasing the music yet. I am going to buy some soon, though."

With a skeptical grunt, the girl said in a voice laden with sarcasm and doubt, "Right. And just how long have you had that stereo anyway?"

Tamara's lips tightened. Sienna had no right to question her this way. In fact, it was none of her business when she'd bought the stereo.

Pushing her irritation away, Tamara replied nonchalantly, "I've had it for a few years."

"Years? Years? See what I mean? You've just got it sitting in there going to waste, but when I use mine to listen to some slammin' sounds, you wants to get mad at me, like I'm wrong."

Tamara grew reflective for a moment, thinking how quickly time had passed since she'd moved into this place, and suddenly wondering why so many of her plans, especially those having to do with her personal relaxation, never came to fruition. Suddenly she caught herself, and became irritated again. *I don't know why I'm even thinking about this—it is not like me,* she thought as she turned her focus back to the girl.

Noisily Tamara cleared her throat. "Sienna, whether or not I use my CD player is not your concern. Your choice of music does concern me, though. It is not acceptable, and I will not allow it in this house."

"B-b-but—"

"No buts," she said crisply.

Sienna gave her a lengthy stare and then turned away and, with a voice that was sullen and hard, asked, "Anything else?"

Tamara thought about the disorder in the kitchen that had brought her into Sienna's room in the first place. Mrs. Jackson had advised her to set the rules early. The girl had made the mess, and it was her responsibility to clean it, but then Tamara recalled Sienna's overreaction when she raised her voice a few minutes ago.

She slowly surveyed Sienna's room, noticing how everything was carefully in its place and that the room looked much like it had on the day she moved in. Then she glanced again at Sienna, who now sat upright on the bed, turning the magazine pages with one small freckled hand. The teen's posture was stiffly erect, and she was sitting so still that it almost seemed to Tamara that she was holding her breath while waiting for Tamara's next response.

With a sigh, Tamara said in a soft, quiet voice, "Good night, Sienna."

Out of the corner of her eye, Tamara saw the teen exhale through her nostrils as her stiffened stance immediately relaxed. Then, with another small sigh, Tamara closed the door to Sienna's bedroom and headed into the kitchen to clean up the mess that the girl had made.

11.

Making Connections

Tamara closed the car door before glancing furtively around the barren neighborhood. Her work in child welfare brought her into public housing many times, so she was well aware that these "project" areas were often dismal and depressing, and this one was certainly no different.

In fact, with only one look around, anyone would know that life was rough here. *Shoot,* Tamara thought, looking down at the hard, bare, cracked soil, *even the dirt here is too dry and stony to let any blades of grass squeeze through.* The graying brick buildings were small and squat, and the unpleasant combination of bug spray, cigarettes, marijuana, and urine permeated the late fall air.

It was a cold afternoon for early October, and Tamara could see her breath as she made her way toward the sidewalk. She scanned the numbers on the row houses, searching for Sissie Bailey's address. While Tamara had been elated to find the woman's address in the pages she'd hurriedly printed that day in Springfield, at the same time, after searching so long for Sissie Bailey, she was finding this moment strangely anticlimactic.

Tamara had read so much about the woman that she felt as though she already knew her in a way, and now she was only minutes from meeting Sissie Bailey face-to-face. Despite the coldness of the day, anticipatory warmth was spreading quickly throughout her inner core, and this interior heat was a familiar, telltale sign of nervousness for her. Tamara breathed deeply, forcing her anxiety aside, well aware that after all this time these uneasy feelings were to be expected.

"Hey, pretty lady, watch yourself, now!" a man said in a husky voice that broke into her thoughts.

Startled, Tamara glanced into the dark eyes of a deep-brown, muscular young man who seemed to appear from nowhere and now was standing in front of her. The dark hood of his sweatshirt was pulled up tightly over his head so that she could not see his face clearly, and he wore his pants loose and low-hanging, as many young men did these days.

"Hello," Tamara replied in a voice tight with tension. His unexpected appearance frightened her, and with another darting glance into his dancing eyes, she pulled the belt on her soft lambskin black leather coat tighter and stepped around him. The heels of Tamara's short boots clicked dully on the concrete sidewalk as she walked even faster. Finally spying the woman's address, she headed toward her destination with her head down, bracing herself against the frigid wind.

"Nice to meet you, too," said the young man, in a voice dripping with sarcasm, as she rushed by him.

With one last glance back toward the young man who was disappearing into the dusky darkness, she walked up to the door and knocked loudly.

Seconds later, Tamara was looking down into the small, round face of a butternut-brown little boy. The boy gave her a long, curious look with his large hazel eyes, as he rubbed his runny nose with the back of his hand. Wiping his wet hand on his pant leg without speaking to her once, he turned and yelled loudly in a voice that seemed strangely deep for one so small, *"Granny Sissie, somebody at the door!"*

The boy then turned his unwavering wide-eyed stare back to Tamara. She searched his small face for a long moment, then nervously began to pull at her belt as she looked away from him.

An old woman appeared, barely visible in the dimness behind the boy. "Who is it?" she said gruffly as she moved the boy out of the way with a heavy hand and gave Tamara the once-over.

Despite the fluttering in her stomach, Tamara reached out her hand in a professional gesture and said loudly, "I'm Tamara Britton from Children's Protective Services, and I'd like to speak with you a moment if I could."

The woman turned up her nose, ignoring Tamara's outstretched hand, and complained loudly, "CPS? *Oh, shoot!, what now?* Them doggone kids of mine gonna drive me crazy. I ain't *even* heard from three of them girls in years. Now what? I am just one old lady, and there ain't nothin' I can do if they messin' up again!"

Tamara dropped her hand and replied contritely, "I'm sorry to have disturbed you, but I just have a question or two. I won't take but a few minutes of your time."

The older woman studied Tamara closely for a moment or two through her faded brown eyes and then, opening the door wide, said resignedly, "C'mon in, gal." She furtively glanced around outside and then shut the metal door loudly, obviously annoyed, and added, "I cain't have folks like you standin' 'round on my porch—folks'll get to talkin'. They nosy 'round here."

Tamara stood uneasily in the square front room and with one glance quickly took in all of her surroundings. Oversize black and chrome furniture crowded the modest living room area, and one whole wall was covered by the large TV that sat on a huge, shiny black entertainment center in front of the couch and love seat.

Gesturing toward the couch with one hand, the woman said harshly, "Well, sit down, gal; you in here now! Don't just stand in the floor looking crazy."

"Sorry," said Tamara as she perched uncomfortably on the edge of the soft-cushioned couch. Pushing herself back awkwardly on the overly cushy sofa, she cleared her suddenly dry throat and said, "Well, Mrs. Bailey, I suppose you're wondering why I'm here."

Sissie Bailey gave Tamara a hard-eyed stare. "That's a stupid question. Of course I wanna know why you here, gal—even though I know it can't be nothin' good."

Tamara swallowed hard again. For some reason, the woman's toughness was not what she'd expected, and this brusqueness made her uncomfortable, but she continued, although haltingly at first, "The th-thing is, for years I've been sorta m-moonlighting on a c-case. You see, I met a girl a long time ago—actually, we went to school together—she was in state care and she never knew her mother and father."

"Hmph!" said Sissie Bailey flatly as she continued to stare at her, hard-eyed.

"Well, anyway she—my friend, that is—was always so sad

because she did not know where she came from." Tamara went on, glancing surreptitiously at Sissie Bailey, trying to gauge the woman's reaction to her friend's situation.

The woman's lined face was unreadable, though, and Tamara forged ahead hopefully. "Well, one day my friend abruptly disappeared. I found out later that she'd been removed from her foster home and sent away to another city. I never saw her again, and I really want to find her, and I also would like to surprise her with information about her parents."

"And just what does that have to do with me, gal?" said Sissie as she slapped at the little boy's hands. Lying sideways in the woman's ample lap, the boy was chuckling while using his dirty hands to play with errant gray strands of the woman's hair.

"*Boy, stop!* Dontay, you see I'm tryin' to talk. Get yourself up, boy, and get out of here," Sissie said roughly before slapping him hard on his small behind.

Tamara stared silently at the two of them for a moment before turning her head to gaze at the television set.

The woman gave her a defiant glare. "I suppose you gonna report me for that, uh? Well, you go 'head if you want to, and you just see who'll be there to take his bad tail. Just me, that's all who wants 'im . . . just me."

Tamara watched the boy run from the room and answered, "I would not report you for that, Ms. Bailey. That is not considered child abuse." Even though Tamara thought the woman hard and mean-spirited, and knew all about her rough past, she was witnessing no abusiveness now. Yet she did wonder how Sissie had gotten custody of the boy, with her criminal background and all.

As if she'd read her mind, the woman said defensively, "And in case you wonderin', I don't get nothin' for keepin' him. The daddy had him and didn't want him no more and dropped him off one day and never looked back." As if challenging Tamara to do something about it, she continued, "He been here a whole year now, and we lives on my SSI—that's how *we* lives."

Tamara sighed imperceptibly. *This is not my purpose for being here,* she thought. Telling herself that the boy was with family— Sissie *was* his grandmother—Tamara reassured herself that the woman must care for him, because if what she'd just said was true, he'd already been with her longer than her own daughters had. None of them had ever lived with her for a solid year. In fact, according to the records, Sissie Bailey's life with her daughters had been interrupted by the state every few months, until the state finally took the girls for good.

"Mrs. Bailey, I'm not here to discuss Dontay," she replied. The woman was going to be even more defensive now and might even change her mind about talking with her. Tamara quickly got to the point for her visit. "Now, to answer your question about what this has to do with you, to tell the truth, I'm really not quite sure yet. I was just hoping that you wouldn't mind taking a moment or two to answer some questions for me."

Glancing at Sissie again, Tamara was dismayed that the woman's flowered housedress had fallen open and she was either oblivious or didn't care that her undergarments were fully exposed.

The woman calmly stretched out one plump leg before pushing back a piece of the graying hair from her eye as she looked at Tamara suspiciously. "You mean I don't have to answer any of yo' questions if I don't want to?"

Tamara was silently praying the woman would talk with her, but she knew that there was no way she could make the woman cooperate against her will. Uncomfortably she forced herself to maintain steady eye contact with the nearly nude woman and replied, "This is not an official visit."

Sissie Bailey looked down then and, without saying a word, pulled her robe closed tightly and gave her a brittle smile. "Oh, it's not, huh? You sho' you not tryin' to gather some stuff on one of them kids of mine on the sly? Somethin' you gone come back to me with later, are you?"

Unwaveringly Tamara continued to look the woman in the eye and replied, "I give you my word, that is not why I am here."

Sissie Bailey sat with her eyes locked searchingly on Tamara's for a long moment and then laughed harshly and said, "Okay, gal, it probably cain't hurt nothin' to talk to you. What the heck, you in here now. Go 'head then; ask me what you want to know."

Less than an hour later, Tamara was back in her car, thinking that she had not been mistaken about one thing: Sissie Bailey *was* an unpleasant woman. Clearly life had been rough on the woman, because she seemed steely-hard and determined not to let anything or anyone come near any soft part of her again.

Sissie really hadn't said too much about her own kids, either. In fact, she only knew the whereabouts of one daughter: the one whose son Sissie had living in her home. Tamara had disliked the harshness in Sissie's voice when she'd spoken with the boy, and more than once Sissie had swatted him on the arm or behind, but the boy continued to play and laugh as if used to that type of treatment from the woman. A couple of times he'd hugged her hard around the neck and nuzzled his small head there as he giggled joyfully.

For just that moment anyway, it looked to Tamara as though the woman's face softened. The moment was fast and fleeting, though, and when Tamara blinked again, the hard lines and stony demeanor were back on Sissie's face.

Tamara started her car, and as she backed out into the street, she forced the woman's hard countenance and raspy voice from her mind. At least she'd gotten information on one daughter—that was a start.

"Central State County Correctional Center for Women, uh?

59

Well, I guess I'll be meeting Samyra Bailey soon, and I sure hope she's nicer than you, Sissie," she said as she pulled her Toyota onto the main street and began the long drive home.

12.

Troubled Waters

Disgruntled, Tamara stared down disbelievingly at the stack of work that had accumulated on her desk. *I don't know how I can have so much to do already,* she wondered. "It's almost as if these stupid forms multiply," she muttered to herself in frustration.

Joan's clipped tone, coming from behind, stunned her, "Talking to someone, Tamara?"

Sitting straight up in her chair, she spun around quickly and found herself staring directly into her boss's hazel eyes. It was aggravating to Tamara that the woman seemed to sneak up on Jayson and her, almost as if she was *trying* to catch them doing something that they should not.

"No, Joan . . . I'm only talking to myself. Just going over what I need to do," she added with a forced laugh.

Without another word, Joan walked around Tamara's cubicle and then, leaning over her shoulder, peered closely at the paperwork on her desk. "Well, it does seem like you have quite a stack of work there. How *did* you get so far behind, Tam?"

I can't believe her, thought Tamara while quickly stacking the papers into a neat pile on her desk to prevent Joan from reading them. "I'm really not too far behind," she added through tightened lips, working hard to hide her agitation at her boss's interference.

Joan straightened up abruptly and patted her shoulder patronizingly. "Well, I know that you are quite competent, and you will meet any designated deadlines, I'm sure, Tam."

Tamara turned to glance at the woman and replied in a quiet but confident voice, "Yes, I will."

As soon as she heard the woman's footfalls softly and steadily moving away from her cubicle, muffled by the indoor carpeting that covered the floor of their office, she murmured under her breath caustically, "And you can stop calling me Tam, too . . . like you really like me or something."

"I heard that," said Jayson. He rolled his chair back, as he often did, and stuck his head around the partition dividing them, so that he was looking into her cubicle.

Tamara jumped and then spun around quickly and said, "Stop doing that, Jay-Jay! You're going to give me a stroke one day, easing around that corner like that!"

Jayson stroked his goatee and asked, "Tam, doesn't it make you sick when she tries to act all friendly and everything?" He pointed his finger toward their boss's door in a dramatic gesture. "That woman don't care about nothin' but getting the work done and riding us black folks to do it."

"Oh, c'mon, Jayson, we don't know that." Tamara was trying hard to be fair to the woman—after all, she was in a new position, and they did not know her all that well yet. "Maybe it's us; maybe we're being too hard on her. Maybe *we're* being racist or something. In a way it seems like she's trying real hard to let us know she does care about us."

In a shocked tone, Jayson replied chidingly, "Tamara, girl, you know better than that! Racism is a tool of those in power!

And that is white folks! We don't have the power to be racist, and we're not even being prejudiced—we did not judge her before we knew her. She is the one that treats *us* like we still on the plantation. She acts like she don't know those days are long gone!"

Tamara looked up at Jayson and said quietly, "I don't know—well, maybe you *are* right, Jayson."

"Maybe? Maybe? Girl, you know I'm right!" Jayson looked at Tamara with concern written on his handsome face. "Tam, I know you be gettin' mad sometimes, and you really need to start letting your anger out, or one day you are going to explode! It's not healthy to hold in everything like you do. C'mon, you know that you are sick of Joan, too!"

"W-w-well, kinda," Tamara added falteringly.

Shifting gears a little, Jayson asked, "And what about that wild girl you let come live with you when you didn't even want to do it? *She* browbeat you into it!"

Skeptically Tamara answered, "Well, it wasn't actually like that, Jay; I could've said no. For some reason, I just didn't."

There was no stopping Jay, though; clearly he'd been waiting for this chance to voice his opinion about Sienna again, and he added, "Tam, let's face it. You didn't say no, because she is the boss and you were simply afraid to say no. Plus, Joan knows that you are sorta meek, and that's why she asked you in the first place. She knew that you would not say no."

"I am *not* meek!" Tamara said more loudly than she intended.

Jayson put one finger to his full lips "Shhh! We don't want her back over here checkin' up on us again, now!"

"Sorry, but I'm *not* meek! I'm just a *little* reserved sometimes," added Tamara firmly, with what she hoped was a stern look on her face.

Jayson replied sarcastically, "Right, Tam, and I'm not a ladies' man."

"You're not," said Tamara. "You only *think* you are!"

Playfully Jayson pushed Tamara's slender shoulder and said, "Well, I guess you ain't meek, girl; in fact, you might be a little *too bold,* when you start questioning Jay-Jay's prowess with the women."

Tamara emitted a sputtering giggle before she could stop herself.

Jayson's gaze turned serious then. "For real, Tamara, how is that child of yours? Is she still clownin' and cussin' you out and stuff?"

"First of all, Sienna is not my child; she is a young teen staying with me *temporarily,* and actually she is *not* acting up," said Tamara. She added a bit smugly, "Surprisingly, things are going rather well; Sienna has been minding her business, and I've been taking care of mine. She is usually in her room doing homework when I get home—I think her grades will be quite good."

Jayson was not satisfied, though. Clearly feeling that Tamara's rosy representation of the situation was suspicious, he asked, "Does she help you around the house? Does she clean up behind herself or do dishes or anything? Have you given her chores to do every day, or are you just working your own pretty little fingers to the bone after putting in long days here?"

Tamara ran her fingers through her hair before replying offhandedly, "She takes care of her room, and that's all I ask."

Jayson sucked his lips loudly, and asked sardonically, "That's all you ask, or that's *all she'll do,* Tamara?"

Frowning now, Tamara chided the man. "Be quiet, Jayson! Besides, you don't have to worry about the two of us. I think everything is going to be all right."

Jayson gave up then. Clearly, Tamara was intent on painting everything with a rosy brush today. "You go, girl, then; I guess you got it all together now!" He began to push his chair back around into his cubicle as he whispered, "I guess we better get to work, before *she* comes back. You know this time she'll be flashin' that ring, tryin' to bling-bling, and if I have to see that thing *one more time today,* I think *I* might snap out and tell Ms. Joan a thing or two."

Before Tamara could reply, the intercom on her desk buzzed loudly. She swiveled around in her seat, picked up the receiver, and listened silently before hanging up moments later.

Worriedly she told Jay, "I've gotta go now. That was the school, and Sienna evidently is really misbehaving today, and they want me over there right away."

Tamara's concerned expression told Jayson to stifle himself; now was not the time to criticize her decision to allow the girl to move into her home in the first place. Instead he replied encouragingly, "Everything will be okay, Tam. Don't worry—kids her age act up all the time."

The tension in Tamara's face relaxed a little as she asked him, "Really? You think so, Jay-Jay?"

Standing up, Jayson retrieved Tamara's leather jacket from the coatrack and, while helping her put it on, assured her, "It'll be just fine, Tamara; you'll see. I'll tell Joan where you've gone. You can take comfort in the fact that there's not much she can say about you leaving early, since it was her idea that Miss Sienna-girl move with you in the first place, huh?"

"That is right, isn't it?" Tamara took a deep breath as she pulled her leather gloves over her slim hands. She opened her bottom drawer, got her purse out, and then turned to Jayson and said, "I'll see you later today, hopefully."

"Now, don't worry, Tam—everything will be just fine," Jayson said again with a reassuring smile on his face. He watched her walking down the hallway toward the door, and as soon as Tamara was out of earshot, he shook his head while saying to himself, "Lord, have mercy on her! That poor girl *don't have a clue* about what she's in for. I've got a feeling that little

Miss Sienna-girl is gonna take Tamara on the ride of her life—and it's only just beginning!"

13.

Fast Getaway

The girl stood uneasily in the dinner line, trying her best to look older than her young years. Though paranoid that someone might notice her youthfulness and call to report her as a runaway, she stayed put, realizing that in only moments the servers would begin to ladle food onto her Styrofoam tray. Tonight the girl's usual caution took a backseat because her thoughts were consumed by her hunger; she'd not eaten since she ran away last night. In fact, it had been her overwhelming desire for food that had driven her to venture into this shelter for a meal in the first place, even though she knew that by doing so she was taking a big chance.

Tentatively she looked up from under the bill of her cap to find herself staring right into the blue eyes of a friendly-faced, light-haired woman who was spooning out stew and hashed browns. The woman stopped what she was doing and, gazing at her curiously for a moment, said, "Well, aren't you a pretty little thing?"

The girl smiled quickly before instinctively becoming wary of the strange woman's friendliness. Tucking her chin tightly into her chest, she kept it that way even though she could sense that the woman was still watching her, evidently waiting to look into her face again. With her hands out in front of her, the girl held the tray with stiff arms, praying that the woman would not bring unwanted attention to her that might cause her to have to run away without eating. She needed to eat tonight; she was so hungry.

Impossibly long moments passed, and then finally, out of the corner of her eye she saw the feet of the person next to her move, so she sidestepped as well, without ever raising her head. *Just keep moving,* she thought, desperately hungry now, especially since the aroma of the food was wafting into her small nostrils, and her stomach was reacting to the smell by clenching and un-clenching in anticipation of being fed.

Ignoring her inner rumblings, the girl moved down the line, keeping her eyes straight ahead, too afraid now to look up at all. Finally, at the end of the line, she grabbed a juice from the open box sitting there, muttered a quick thank-you, and headed toward a vacant corner. Sitting on the floor, she crossed her legs and then slid on the dusty floor until her back was supported by the wall behind her.

The curious stare of the serving lady was forgotten as the girl attacked her food; her eyes were glued on her platter while she ate ravenously. Starved, she savored each bite; the food tasted so very good to her. She contemplated her next move. First she had to recover her things—right now they were hidden in a place where she hoped that they would be safe. Her eyes darted quickly around the room. She thought, *I sure couldn't bring them here.* After all, street people found out quickly that shelters had a well-deserved reputation for being places where people stole from one another—nothing was really yours for long when you were in a shelter.

With her bread she soaked up the brown gravy of the stew. Then she took a long, quenching drink of the orange juice, and while it normally was not her favorite drink, today it tasted wonderful. She wiped at her mouth with the back of one hand and then rubbed it on the side of her already dirty coat.

Much too soon the tray was clean and the girl sat staring at it, wishing that she felt brave enough to go back for seconds. Within moments her eyes grew heavy, and soon her long lashes rested on her cheeks, and she was nodding ever so slowly toward the tray in her lap.

The tired girl had no idea she was being watched with curiosity. The rotund lady sitting on the cot closest to her nudged the rasta-haired friend sitting by her and said, "Hey, look at little miss over there. She gonna fall right in her food." She chewed a bit more as she continued to observe the girl, adding, "Poor thing is probably a runaway or something. She don't look too old, do she?"

Her friend looked up then and gazed around the room until she spotted the sleepy girl over in the corner. "Oh, you talkin' 'bout that little girl over there?" she said while sucking loudly at her fingers, which were brown with gravy from the stew. Then she said knowingly, "Yep, that girl there done ran away. She probably just bad and don't want to be at home. You know how these kids is nowadays."

The first woman nodded her head in agreement, adding, "Don't I know? My kids is what got me in this situation I'm in. Tryin' to do for them and stuff and they clownin' and one went to jail and I puts my house up to try and help 'em and he skips off and they take MY house. Now here I am with nothin'— nothin'!"

The rasta-haired friend, listening to show support, was thinking to herself that she'd heard this same story about a million times, it seemed. Yet she understood the woman's need to talk. They were in a shelter after all, and it was a hard life, and everybody had a story, and sometimes they needed to tell it, just so it would seem as if somebody cared.

Suddenly, the small girl's head drooped even closer to her plate, and the first woman yelled, "Hey . . . hey, girl!" The woman got up from the cot, put her tray down, and walked over toward the girl, who seemed deeply asleep on the floor. Gently she touched the tired girl's shoulder, but before she could say a word, the girl's eyes flew open.

Startled to see a strange face, the girl froze. For a moment she couldn't recall where she was, but once she remembered, she jumped up so quickly that her Styrofoam tray tumbled right over on the woman's legs.

"Hey, girl! Look at my pants!" yelled the woman. "Ain't no cause to act like that—I was just trying to wake you up before you tumbled over into your food."

The girl didn't hear one word the woman said, though. After one look at the mess the brown stew gravy had made on the woman's pants, she took off for the door, barely missing a man.

With two hands she shoved the double doors of the big Community Center doorway hard, and with one furtive look to the left and one to the right, she headed in the direction of where her belongings were.

Running again.

14.

Stormy Weather

"Well, aren't you gonna say something?" asked Sienna haughtily while looking at Tamara out of the corner of her eye. The two of them were on the way home from the meeting with the dean at her school, and the deep silence in the car was becoming too much for Sienna to bear.

Tamara was preoccupied, though, still thinking about the meeting that she'd just attended about the girl's behavior. Dean James was neither mean nor unfair, as Sienna had described her more than once. Instead, the dean, a short, attractive brown-skinned woman, had an extremely pleasant demeanor and took the time to carefully explain that Sienna had been extremely disrespectful to a teacher, and that was why Tamara had been called.

Sienna had been asked to stop talking a number of times, because her persistent chatter was disrupting the classroom, and instead of complying, the girl had laughed raucously and began to talk about the teacher in a rude manner. Other students had joined in the laughter, with the escalating situation threatening to get totally out of control. Finally, when she called the teacher a "trick" and a "ho," Sienna was sent from the room with a referral to see the dean.

Well aware that she'd been out of line, Sienna knew there was little Tamara could say to defend her behavior, and was not surprised when Tamara just listened quietly as the dean talked.

Once Dean James finished speaking, Tamara turned and asked, "So, Sienna, do you have anything you'd like to say?"

Though not usually at a loss for words, Sienna felt so flustered as she gazed back into Tamara's calm brown face that she didn't want to speak at all. So she just mumbled, in an intentionally bored tone, "Whatever she said." She shrugged her small shoulders in a nonchalant way. The dimples showed in Tamara's brown face as she pursed her lips, clearly upset, turning away from Sienna without further comment.

The two women had sent her into the hallway, and there she'd sat in a chair watching Tamara through the open doorway, attempting to read the young woman's reaction to the dean's news as she studied her erect posture. She'd soon given up, though, because Tamara was perched on the edge of the seat, with her back straight as an arrow, unmoving and revealing nothing to Sienna that would help her figure out what the woman was thinking.

Sadly, Sienna thought, *This is it . . . I bet she's probably gonna make me move now, and no tellin' where I'll be tomorrow.* Continuing her morose self-talk, she began to make plans, telling herself that she didn't care if they moved her or not. *In fact,* she decided, *if they move me and I don't like it, I'll just run away again!*

Moments later Tamara had emerged from the dean's office and, without glancing at her once, said quietly, "Get your things together. Let's go, Sienna." Scared to say a word, Sienna swallowed hard, grabbed her book bag, and walked behind her out the brown double doors of the school.

Even now as they were riding home together, each time she dared to steal a glance at Tamara, Tamara still refused to look her way but instead kept her eyes on the road ahead.

Again Sienna asked Tamara, "Ain't you gonna say somethin'?"

After what seemed an eternity to the girl, Tamara spoke in a faraway tone. Instead of sounding angry, as the young girl had expected, Tamara's voice was calmly professional and even quieter than usual. "What, exactly, do you expect me to say, Sienna?"

"I don't know. Just somethin', I guess," the girl said, sullen with frustration at Tamara's nonresponsiveness.

"Sienna, I will ask you again, exactly what happened today? I cannot really comment on the situation if I have not heard your side of the story."

Suddenly, Sienna replied loudly in a voice that was hard and rough, "That teacher don't like me! She asked me a question and I answered it. *That's all!*"

Through tightened lips Tamara responded, "From what I understand, it is the *way* you answered the question that caused a problem with the teacher. After asking you several times already, your teacher again asked you to please be quiet, and somewhere in your response to her you called her a derogatory name or two. . . . Did you or did you not call her a 'trick'?"

"*No!* I was saying something to my friend Rick! She just thought I said that, and she don't like me no way! You could go and ask anybody in the class and they will tell you that teacher don't like me! Really, Tamara, she don't like *nobody,* and nobody likes her, either!"

They sat at the red light silently. Tamara knew that the girl was lying, and this was intolerable to her. Rick? What kind of dummy did she think she was to believe such a see-through excuse?

Without warning, booming bass sounds emanated from her car's speakers, shattering her thoughts. Startled, she glanced at Sienna, who was now nodding her head to the loud rap beat blasting through the car, while smiling at a group of teenage boys who were stopped next to them at the red light. Sienna had taken advantage of Tamara's distractedness and, in an instant, slid some vile CD into her car stereo. Now it was blaring loudly for the world to hear, from *her* car.

"Give it to me, baby," Sienna sang suggestively, clearly unconcerned with Tamara while she busily flirted with the boys in the car next to them.

"Sienna, you stop that!" said Tamara forcefully. But the teen, ignoring her, sang even louder. Aware that she had a captive male audience in the neighboring automobile, Sienna grew even more boldly suggestive in her facial expressions and began to dance even more wildly.

A honking horn from behind alerted a distracted Tamara that the light had changed to green. Reflexively she pressed the accelerator much harder than she intended. The car responded with a screeching of the wheels as it lurched forward jerkily, and they took off down the road fast.

"What the heck are you doing?" shouted the girl at the top of her lungs as she looked at Tamara. Then she rolled her eyes and asked loudly, "Don't you know how to drive this stupid car? If you don't, then pull over and let a pro get behind the wheel!"

Shaken now, Tamara seemed to be unraveling fast. Unused to losing her cool this way, she ignored Sienna's rude comment and struggled to focus on driving. The loud, jarring music, coupled with the girl's provocative moves toward the boys in the nearby car, had her rattled, and now she needed a quiet moment or two to relax. "Calm down, Tamara," she said aloud to herself while ejecting the vile CD. "Just don't say anything."

Sienna gave her a sideways glance. "Who you talkin' to? Please, don't tell me they got me livin' with a crazy lady who talks to herself."

"Sienna, you need to stop talking," replied Tamara in as calm a voice as she could muster.

"Sienna, you need to stop talking," the girl repeated mockingly as she laughed to herself.

The tires of the automobile screeched even more loudly this time as Tamara suddenly turned the vehicle into a parkway area. She pulled the Toyota Corolla adjacent to the curb. She could feel Sienna's questioning gaze on her. Breathing in deeply through her nostrils, she turned to face her. Though Tamara's dark eyes were flashing with anger, she spoke in an even tone.

"Don't ever, *ever* mock me," she said to Sienna as she pointed one perfectly polished pale pink nail at her. "Your behavior in this car has confirmed what Dean James told me about your attitude today. You have a nasty, nasty mouth, little girl, and you need to start behaving much more respectfully to adults."

Clearly, her sudden move with the car had taken Sienna by surprise. The teen's eyes were open very wide, and her freckles stood out in the paleness of her heart-shaped face. Sienna was clearly shaken. Though she tried to appear nonchalant, her apprehension was apparent to Tamara. Meanwhile, Tamara was overcome by her own distress. "Now, you are kicked out of school for three days, and I have to find something for you to do over that period of time, or someone to care for you. I clearly cannot leave you on your own while I am at work. Not after what I just saw with those boys back there."

Sienna, seeming to toss her previous anxiety aside just as quickly as it had come over her, murmured under her breath through turned-up lips, "You just trippin' 'cause you old. This is the two thousands, and *all kids* act like this."

Tamara, though taken aback at the teen's quick recovery, maintained her equilibrium and replied in the same carefully controlled tone, "You are a little girl, and you need to start acting like one. That type of behavior could get you in a lot of trouble."

"Ain't no trouble I ain't already seen," said the girl before making the impudent clicking noise with her tongue that Tamara found so irritating. Sienna's quick reversion to her insolent

habits informed Tamara that now the girl was fully back in her attitudinal saddle once again and ready to petulantly ride that argumentative pony to a gallop once more.

Tamara was tired now, and she had no desire to spar further with Sienna. With a sigh, she turned from the girl and started the car. As they pulled away from the curb, she heard the girl add saucily, "And I don't need no babysitter, either."

Moments later, when she dared to glance at Sienna again, the teen was calmly looking out the window as if nothing at all had happened. Sienna might be right about one thing, Tamara thought. *I must be one real crazy lady, because it seems I've really got myself a big load of trouble here wrapped up in a deceptively cute, small package.* Then, with one last long, silent sigh, she turned her attention back to the matter at hand and forced herself to focus on the short drive home.

15.

Building Bridges

That night, after tiptoeing lightly into Sienna's room and hearing the girl's soft, rhythmic breathing, Tamara went into her own room and shut the door behind her. From the nightstand she retrieved the now-worn manila folder containing Yvette's information and sat on her bed, and after kicking off her slippers one by one, she pulled her legs under her. With all of Sienna's drama at school and in the car, it had been an exceptionally long day, and Tamara was grateful to be able to relax at last.

Leaning back on the gold satin pillows, she stared into space before abruptly sitting up and opening the folder in front of her.

The ring of the telephone interrupted, and after a quick glance at her watch, Tamara picked up the telephone and answered hesitantly, "H-hello?"

"Tamara? Is that you?"

Tamara immediately relaxed once she recognized her friend Denise Jackson's voice at the other end of the line. In fact, after the day that she'd had with Sienna, she was actually happy to hear from the woman tonight.

"Hello, Mrs. Jackson, I'm so glad you called," Tamara responded.

Denise chuckled deep in her throat before saying, "Uh-oh, that little girl must've been clownin' on you today. You not too much of a talker, Tamara, and normally when I'm callin' you, it's somethin' wrong on a case, and I know you don't want to have that problem this late at night."

"You're certainly right about that, Mrs. Jackson, *please, please* don't tell me it's a caseload problem. You are also right that Sienna had a hard day."

Denise Jackson added knowingly, "See, I know what I'm talkin' 'bout, baby girl; in fact, I know you better than you think! If you happy I'm callin' this time of night, God must've sent me yo' way 'cause he knew you needed somebody to talk to!" Then, chuckling again, she asked, "Now, you said *she* had a hard day? From what my little daughter Sabrina, who is the same class as your Sienna, told me, Sienna was clownin' today, so I'm sure *you* had a bit of a hard day yourself, girl."

Next time I'll unplug my telephone after Sienna gets in trouble, since she's gotta tell everyone about it, Tamara thought peevishly. But aloud she agreed somewhat grudgingly, "Okay, you're right, Mrs. Jackson; I guess I had a rough day, too."

"Tamara, baby girl, why is it so hard for you to ever admit you have a problem? Ever since I known you, you always actin' like everything is just fine. Nobody's life is as easy as you make yours out to be, and once you brought that child into your house, I told you to expect that yo' whole life is gonna be turned upside down."

"What do you mean exactly when you say 'upside down'?" Tamara asked worriedly. Even though now it seemed a little unrealistic, she'd been hoping that today was the worst and that from this day forward it would be smooth as silk between her and Sienna.

Sensing Tamara's seriousness, Denise Jackson answered in a gentle but firm tone, "Tamara, baby, don't think that today was the worst. You will be fooling yourself if you do. These kids are in the *system,* baby, and they have been through a lot, and some of them truly don't know how to act."

"Mrs. Jackson, I guess I just find it hard to believe that Sienna doesn't know any better. Are you telling me that she doesn't know that she's being thoughtless and rude when she speaks to people like she does?" asked Tamara with much more emotion than she'd intended to let slip.

"I'm telling you that she *may* not know what she is doing. And then, it could be that she is doing it on purpose and her behavior may be her way of preventing people from getting close to her—she may try to attack them before they attack her. Or it could just be them hormones. She is a teenager, and from what I understand from you all, she's naturally feisty."

Tamara ran her hand through her hair while thinking about the events that had occurred during the trip home today.

She replied resolutely, "Oh, Sienna is feisty, all right, Mrs. Jackson. In fact, now that I think about it, 'feisty' is a bit understated, actually. It's a little too low-key to describe her accurately."

Try as she might, Denise Jackson couldn't keep from laughing loudly at Tamara then. It was more than a little ironic that the young woman was one of the instructors of the classes designed to train foster parents; and yet obviously she had not really listened to her own instructions. Denise could picture the serious look on Tamara's pretty brown face now as she sat pondering Sienna's bad behavior while still struggling to be professional and remain calm about it all.

In between gasping laughs, the woman said, "Tamara Britton, only you would say it like that: 'feisty is a bit understated, actually.' Baby girl, what you really tryin' to say is, that girl is *baaad*!" Mrs. Jackson continued to laugh heartily at the other end of the line.

Tamara's dimples deepened in her cheeks, and she could not help but smile as she pictured Mrs. Jackson holding her hand over her generous mouth, trying to stifle her laughter. Then she remembered how Sienna was talking to her earlier in the car, all the while moving her neck back and forth while she pointed her little finger with emphasis. One small giggle erupted from Tamara, and then another and another, and in a minute she was laughing right along with Denise Jackson.

"M-M-Mrs. Jackson, you-you-you should've seen how she was looking at those boys! And better yet, you should have seen how they were looking at her—it was like they were in shock to see such a small girl behaving so wildly—and I honestly believe she thought they were looking at her because they thought she was attractive or something."

Between gulping laughs, Denise Jackson said, "And I know they was looking at you like, 'Can't you control your daughter or sister or whoever she is to you?' I know 'bout that, baby girl, 'cause I been there, done that—seen that look many a time myself, you know?"

"Exactly!" said Tamara, holding the telephone tightly under her ear with her shoulder while rubbing her favorite cotton pajamas back and forth with a brown, slim-fingered hand as she talked. "I was pretty embarrassed. In fact, the truth is, I was embarrassed all day, even at the school."

Denise Jackson exhaled loudly before saying, "Now, in all seriousness, Tamara, let me give you a good piece of advice. Baby, now that you are in this foster care thang, you might as well put your embarrassment away. *You* are *helpin'* this girl, but it will take time before everything smoothes out. It don't matter none what other folks think, long as you know what's going on."

In her heart Tamara knew what Denise Jackson said was true, but Tamara had lived alone so long now that she was set in her ways, and she abhorred standing out in a crowd, preferring to mesh into the background. That was going to be hard to do with Ms. Sienna around, since behaving in a low-key manner was hardly her style!

"Are you there, Tamara?"

"I'm here, Mrs. Jackson. I'm just thinking, that's all."

"Well, Tamara, I'm gonna tell you what I think. I think you are some great young lady to take this little girl in like you have. You are a pretty young woman, and you could be busy dating and partying and doing all that stuff that young folk do nowadays. She's blessed to have you in her life."

The woman's comments caught her off guard, and she replied shyly, "Thank you. I hope that I made a good decision."

"Be assured that you did. God put it in your heart to do, and that's why you did it. I just called to check on you, and I can see you are just fine. You get yourself a good night's rest, Tamara. Tomorrow's another day."

"I'll do that, and thank you for calling me, Mrs. Jackson. You've really made me feel better."

"You're quite welcome, Tamara. Remember, call me anytime, and you both have an open invitation to come visit my church. That little girl needs to learn about the Lord, and you might find that you like it, too."

While not opposed to religion or God, Tamara tensed at the idea of attending church. She knew there would be many people there that might try to talk with her, and get to know her, and she just wasn't that type of sociable person. But thinking of Denise Jackson's kindness and supportiveness toward her, she answered genuinely, "Okay, Mrs. Jackson, maybe sometime soon we'll take you up on that offer."

"I hope so; God would love to see you in his house. Bye, now, Tamara."

"Good-bye," she said, and as she hung up the telephone, she thought, *God? Would God really want* me *in his house?*

Leaning back on her pillow, Tamara drifted tiredly in and out of her own thoughts until her hand touched the folder that had been forgotten when the telephone rang. Sitting up straight, she picked up the folder, holding the familiar information that she'd read time and again. She opened it very slowly, her expression placid as she thumbed through the papers. Only a very perceptive eye could have noticed the slight trembling in her slim fingers as she held the pages and began to read.

16.

Food Fight

"These people *do* need to hurry up," said Lynnette petulantly. Clicking her tongue loudly through her perfectly lined red lips, silver bracelets dangling noisily from her upraised arm, she snapped her slim fingers, tipped in long manicured nails carefully lacquered in graduating tones of red.

Simultaneously, Jayson and Tamara looked at each other, and he rolled his eyes upward meaningfully. The two of them had planned this luncheon weeks ago, since they rarely saw Lynnette in the office anymore. And though she assured them she was out because she was working in the field a lot lately, they both hoped she wasn't just skipping work, since they knew how carefully Joan watched them, and they were certain she would inevitably catch her.

"Just chill, Lynn," said Jayson with a touch of irritation in his voice. "We have time, and anyway me and Tam are probably the only two going back to the office, right?"

Lynnette gave him an annoyed glance and then replied dismissively, "I know what you tryin' to say, Jay, but I do my time at work, just like y'all, so you can quit acting like I don't. I just have other things to do sometimes—you know, places to go, people to see, and all that. Fieldwork *is* part of my job, remember?"

Jayson really did love Lynnette, but her high-and-mighty attitude infuriated him sometimes, and that comment was a perfect example of the arrogant stance that he detested from her. He hated it when she talked down to anyone, let alone him! Her words had been clearly more than a little condescending, and he responded in an annoyed tone, "Why is it that every time we go out together you gotta act like the diva from hell? You are *not* Whitney Houston or Celine Dion, you know."

Tamara raised her eyebrows in a silent response to Jayson's remark and inwardly winced, preparing herself for Lynnette's scathing comeback. She knew Lynnette well, and there was no way that girl was going to let Jay get by with that statement without sending a biting, snappy retort his way.

Sure enough, once Lynnette fully digested her male coworker's words, she dropped her arm and whipped her head around to face Jayson. With her silver-ringed index finger she slowly moved the hair back from her face. As usual, her hair was impeccably styled, microbraided into a bobbed cut that flowed saucily over one eye, thanks to her new, shorter extensions.

Then, in a slow exaggerated move, she dropped her hand from her hair while giving Jayson a long, withering stare. Her large eyes gazed at his as she spoke slowly, her perfectly enunciated words cutting through the warm air of the restaurant like verbal ice. "Well, *I* don't have to be Whitney Houston to expect and demand good service. After all, *I* am paying my hard-earned money to eat here, and *I* have the right to expect that *I'm* waited on promptly and with courtesy."

Jayson raised his own eyebrows then before giving Tamara a quick glance out of the side of his eyes. He wiped his hand over his mustache and goatee and breathed in deeply. He could see that Lynnette was really angry, and twenty-twenty hindsight told him that he had started something that he might not be able to finish.

Lynnette continued to stare unblinkingly at Jayson. Her round eyes were unwavering, and her full lips were pursed tightly. Replying then with feigned sweetness dripping with sarcasm, she asked, "What? No comment, Jay-Jay? I mean, is it okay with *you* that *I* expect good service? I realize that I'm not Celine Dion, because I am a *sistah*—you know, an African-American woman! You tell me, is a little good service too much for a sistah to ask for?"

Jayson, unsure of what to say now that would not escalate the situation any further, silently returned her gaze. For several moments the two continued to stare at each other, clearly at an impasse, since neither of them was saying anything.

Though Tamara had grown used to her friends' social squabbles, this whole situation seemed to be getting pretty serious. Gazing from one to the other smilingly, Tamara said cheerfully, "Okay, you guys, that's enough. We all came out here to have a bite to eat and enjoy one another's company. Let's just make up and be friends." When there was no change in her friends' angry demeanors, her cheerful composure began to slip a bit, and she added hopefully, "Okay?"

Almost simultaneously, the two of them turned their solemn stares on her, and she gave them a small, awkward smile, which began to fade when they did not reciprocate right away.

Abruptly Lynnette broke the tense moment. "Girl, you look so pitiful, I'll stop fussing just so I don't have to look at that little sad face of yours."

Jayson smiled, glad for a reprieve from the woman's ire, and added, "You right about that, Lynn. Tam know she can make you feel bad for her. She's talkin' to us like she's the teacher and we are actin' up in school or somethin'. It's that look on that cute little face of hers that makes you feel so bad you just can't stand it."

"Stop, you guys," said Tamara shyly. "I'm not that bad, and I wasn't talking to you like I was a teacher, was I?"

Lynnette and Jayson looked at each other and then turned to her and said in unison, "You were," and they all laughed.

The heaviness of the moment seemed to lighten. Flirtatiously Jayson winked at the waitress now standing at their table. He gave her his order, then said to Tamara conversationally, "You know, little Miss Sienna really could use some manners. That's who you need to be trying to teach something, Tam, not us."

"What do you mean?" asked Tamara.

"Tamara, give the girl your order," said Lynnette with a diva-like wave toward the waitress.

After placing her order, Tamara again asked Jayson, "What do you mean—you know about Sienna and the manners, that is?"

Lynnette glanced at Jayson and then said conspiratorially, "Girl, when that child calls the office for you, she is *awful* on the telephone. Even *I* know this, and according to y'all, I'm *never* in the office. Instead of 'hello' or anything halfway courteous, Miss Sienna just asks me in a smart-alecky little tone, "'Where's Tamara?'"

"Ummm-huh," agreed Jayson as he leaned back in the booth and nodded his head. "She did the same thing to me when I answered the telephone the other day."

"She did?" said Tamara, trying to ignore the immediate quickening of her heart rate. She remembered Mrs. Jackson's advice about not taking the teen's poor conduct so personally.

Lynnette added, "Girl, the day when I happened to answer the phone, I just asked the girl how she was—tryin' to be friendly with her, you know?—and she was just rude and nasty. 'Just put Tamara on the phone,' she repeated, and when I told her you weren't in, that little heifer hung up the phone—*hard*!"

Wincing when Lynnette said the word "hard," Tamara was both disappointed and surprised to hear that Sienna was still behaving so rudely. "I had no idea she was acting that way. I wish you all had told me before. I will talk to her about it."

"Talk to her?" said Lynnette in the strident tone that invariably led to her talking too much, and usually saying the wrong thing in the process. Jayson sensed this was about to happen, and frantically kicked her shin under the table, but she ignored him.

Still attempting to shut her up, he glanced at Lynnette warningly. "Just talk to her, Tamara, okay?" he said soothingly.

Lynnette wasn't about to let the subject rest, though. She pointed her finger at Tamara and added saucily, "You *need* to do more than just talk to her. Shoot, it seems to me, in your house she's the one doing all the talkin', and that's part of the problem. Tam, sooner or later you are gonna have to snap at somebody—and it might as well be Sienna's bad behind! It is not healthy to *never* get mad." She turned to Jayson, seated beside her in the booth. Rubbing her ankle, she said, "And stop kicking me! Those big size twelves you wearin' ain't no joke."

Jayson gritted his teeth then to keep from tearing into Lynnette about her insensitivity. Mortified, he watched as Tamara sat quietly staring down at her folded hands, her brown face red-tinged with embarrassment, her expression sad. He whispered, raspy-voiced, out of the side of his mouth as he elbowed Lynnette and gestured toward their coworker with his head, "Shut up!"

After she looked at Tamara's distraught countenance, finally it dawned on Lynnette what Jayson had been trying to tell her. Tamara was clearly taking her criticism personally, and Lynnette had obviously hurt the girl by making her feel as if her efforts with Sienna were inept.

Immediately repentant, Lynnette apologized, her words coming out in a rush. "Oh, Tam, I am so sorry. I suppose I need to learn to be less rude myself sometimes. I know I can talk too much, and then I say things that I have no business saying. I am so sorry, girl; after all, if it weren't for me, you wouldn't even have little Miss Sienna in your house."

She stopped talking then, and her red lips formed an O as she realized that she shouldn't have let those words out. It was too late to take them back, though—they had gone from her big mouth directly to Tamara's ears, and now she was going to have some explaining to do!

Tamara slowly raised her head and looked into Lynnette's large eyes with her almond-shaped ones and asked, "What do you mean, Lynn? Sienna wouldn't be at my house if it weren't for you? I've been under the impression that it was all Joan's idea that she move in with me."

Jayson glanced from woman to woman as he listened with quiet interest now, certain he was about to be privy to some juicy information. Maybe, just maybe, he thought, this might be the moment he'd get to see Tamara really "snap out" on somebody, and he would love that somebody to be Lynnette!

"I'm waiting, Lynnette," said Tamara in a calm voice as she continued to stare unblinkingly at the other woman.

With a frown Lynnette realized she had trapped herself this time, and finally gave in, saying, "Okay, okay! I admit it—I sorta gave her the idea to ask you. Joan wanted me to do it, and I just have too busy a schedule to have a little girl living with me. And I figured you wouldn't mind, since you *are* always at home anyway."

Tamara looked at her friend, still not wanting to believe that she could be so insensitive and selfish. In a deep, strong tone, she said, "Your schedule or mine is not really the point, Lynn. You could've—you *should've*—asked me first, before you volunteered me to do it. Maybe, just maybe I might've had some other plans for *my* life, too. You were wrong to volunteer me for this behind my back without bothering to ask me, Lynnette. You were very, very unfair to me."

Lynnette was taken aback by the unmistakable anger evident in Tamara's calm voice. She had never heard her friend speak so forcefully. Realizing that this meant the normally placid woman was very upset, Lynnette began to apologize profusely for the second time that afternoon.

"I *am* sorry, Tamara." Leaning across the table, she touched the upset girl's arm with her hand. "Really, I am. You are absolutely right, Tam. I do know how pushy Joan can be when she wants you to do something, and I know that it was even more difficult to make a clear-headed decision, because you were taken by surprise when she asked, and that was unfair."

Jayson could stand it no longer; he was champing at the bit to add his two cents into the conversation between the two women. He pointed his finger at Lynnette and said, "You should be ashamed of yourself, 'cause that is exactly why she said yes, 'cause she was taken by surprise."

Lynnette turned around, gave Jayson an incensed glare, and said shrilly, "*You* don't have anything to do with this! You need to shut up and mind your own business, Jay!"

Jayson wasn't about to back out this time, though, and he retorted, "I beg your pardon, Lynn; I do have something to do with this, too, because I was the one there when she was traumatized about saying yes when she wanted to say no. As usual, you were 'working in the field' that day!"

Tamara sighed heavily. She was certainly in no mood now to hear the two of them snipe at each other again. She said quietly, "There's no point in arguing about it . . . It doesn't even matter how it happened. Sienna is here, and she lives with me. She's my problem now, so the two of you don't need to worry about it."

Glancing up, she noticed that the young waitress was standing at the side of their table, looking a little overwhelmed and obviously waiting for a quiet moment to inform them of her presence. The girl's nervous smile could not disguise her look of embarrassment. She'd stood there long enough to have heard quite a bit of their heated conversation.

"Excuse me . . . I have your orders," said the waitress bashfully, turning quickly to the metal cart holding their covered lunch platters.

Jayson and Lynnette glanced at Tamara's despondent face and suddenly quieted, finally seeming finished with the constant bickering they had done all afternoon.

Everyone's nerves were frayed and sensitive, and the carefully planned lunch that was to serve as a social outing for the three of them seemed to be now officially a bust. Instead of laughing and talking together as they'd expected, the three of them began to eat quietly, each enmeshed in recollections about the events leading up to Sienna's arrival at Tamara's home.

17.

Jailhouse Blues

White-lipped from pressing her mouth closed tightly, Tamara held one leather-gloved hand unconsciously to her stomach, which was churning anxiously in anticipation of today's meeting. She'd postponed this day for a while, not exactly eager to visit the inside of this particular place and unsure of what sort of response to expect from Sissie Bailey's daughter, Samyra.

The deep breath she took to clear her head didn't help much, since the pungent odor of Pine-Sol permeated the jailhouse air, and inhaling the overwhelming smell into her nostrils only made her feel queasier.

"Tamara Britton," said the guard from the check-in window.

The man's baritone voice interrupted her meandering thoughts, and she stood so quickly that she dropped her briefcase. Hastily Tamara bent over and picked up the leather satchel before replying in a voice that sounded much too loud to her in the empty room, "I'm right here."

The guard's keys jingled as he unlocked the outer door for her from the inside. The heels of her leather boots clicked loudly on the linoleum floor and echoed down the corridor as she followed him through the long passageway leading to the cell-block areas.

In a small room located at the end of the hall, the tall, bald African-American man turned, looked down at her, and gave her a sad smile. "Miss, I'll have to search you now. Sorry. It's just part of the job. You'll have to set your bag on the table there, 'cause I'll have to look through it, too."

With a small, nervous smile, Tamara put the bag on the table that faced the holding cell, raising her arms as indicated, and looked up while he patted her body lightly.

"That wasn't so bad, was it?" he asked once he was finished, but before she could reply or even glance his way, he'd begun to check her bag as swiftly as he had examined her.

"Follow me, miss," he said, striding toward a door made of finely meshed steel wire.

Tamara grabbed her bag from the table and then quickly caught up with the long-legged man, who was using his key now to open the heavy door in front of them.

He turned his head and looked down at Tamara, and though his large eyes met her own, she felt as though he were looking right through her. Apparently attempting to calm her obvious nervousness, he explained, "We'll just have to walk through this short hallway. Normally we hold only a few ladies here, but we've had a lot of business lately," he added with a wry laugh.

Tamara's eyes were on his face as he spoke, and when he finished, she inhaled deeply and shook her head up and down. Her throat was suddenly so very tight that she dared not try to speak right then.

The man touched her arm briefly. "Don't be scared, Miss. Just ignore them when they yell stuff at you. They're just sad and lonely women for the most part—remember that. But you can't let 'em see you scared."

"I'm fine," Tamara replied, her voice still crackling hoarsely despite attempts to clear her throat. Somehow she managed to keep her gaze steady, though, and even turned her stiff lips up into a slight smile.

With his large fingers he gave the key a turn before tossing over his shoulder to her, "Okay, miss, here we go."

Once the door opened, Tamara squinted, trying to see down the dimly lit hallway, noticing that the pungent, piney odor was mixed now with a slightly musky one. As Tamara's eyes adjusted to the lighting, she saw some women sitting on their cots, and others standing at the bars of their cells; most were looking at her curiously. Though not brave enough to look any of them in the face, Tamara could feel their gazes on her, and she saw their shadowy profiles out of the corners of her eyes while walking by.

A couple of times women shouted words toward Tamara as if they were flirtatious men and she was their prey, "Hey, sweet baby! Who you comin' to see, Miss Sunshine? I sho' hope it's me!"

Tamara knew what the women were talking about, and couldn't help but wonder if the women were really "that way" or if it was only the desperateness of their situations that led

89

them to pursue love in one another's arms. Continuing forward, Tamara stared straight ahead, the words of the guard ringing in her ears. "These are only sad and lonely women," he'd said. He need not have told her this, since Tamara innately understood these women. Not naive, she knew that they had been found guilty of crimes, yet their incarceration in this dark and shadowy place still saddened her deeply.

The guard made a sharp turn to the left, and she followed closely behind.

"You can have a seat, miss," he said, gesturing for her to sit at an old, round wooden table in the corner of the small room.

Tamara sat stiffly upright in the well-worn wooden-backed chair, still clutching her bag tightly. Then she set her briefcase on the floor, and, taking a deep breath, stared at the door and waited expectantly.

She flinched when the door opened and the guard moved sideways to allow a short, heavyset, caramel-brown-complexioned woman to enter the room. The tall man towered over the shorter woman for a moment or two before turning to lock the door again.

"This is Samyra Bailey," he said to her.

With a glance at both women, he added, "Now, ladies, I'll just be here in the back. Y'all go 'head and talk now." He laughed and gave them a flirty wink. "Don't you ladies worry about me—I won't listen to a word."

Tamara watched as his long legs took him up the short flight of stairs two at a time to a glass-partitioned area overlooking the room. He took a seat in a chair and, after glancing down at them once, picked up a newspaper and began to read it.

When she turned her attention back to Samyra Bailey, the short woman was staring at her curiously. Noticing Tamara's attention focused on her, she pulled with pudgy fingers at the red and white bandanna wrapped and tied around her head, Aunt Jemima–style.

She rolled her eyes then and said conspiratorially to Tamara, "Guess we s'posed to be stupid or some kinda fools, uh? That is, if we believe he ain't listenin' to us. Dag, it's his friggin' job *to* listen to us," she finished with a hard laugh.

Roughly she wiped one hand over her light-brown face, then carefully folded back the sleeves on her blue denim work shirt as she walked over to the table. Tamara couldn't help but notice that the woman's mannerisms and walk were overtly masculine. With one small hand she pulled out the other rickety wooden chair, turned it backward, and straddled it. Her face was close to Tamara's now, and her red-rimmed eyes stared unblinkingly at her. She asked in a rough, raspy voice, "Now, just why *is* you here, anyway? What do you want from me?"

Tamara's own eyes widened then. Face-to-face with this streetwise and life-hardened woman, she was speechless for a few moments.

The woman sucked at her teeth and said, "C'mon girl, what you want? I know you didn't come here 'cause you think I look good, did you?"

Jolting into life, Tamara sputtered, "N-n-no!" Quickly regaining her composure, she launched into the discourse about her intentions just as she'd told it to Sissie Bailey. Once again she explained about Yvette's problem and, though nervous, tried to convey to Samyra her empathy for the girl, which had sparked her deep interest in finding the young woman again, as well as her birth family.

When Tamara finished explaining, the woman looked at her closely for a moment before asking, "You mean you come all the way out here to help somebody else? Shoot, that girl could be dead or somethin'—you don't know, 'cause you ain't talked to her in years, you say.

"Oh, no," said Tamara. "Yvette is not dead; I am quite certain of that."

Again the woman gave Tamara a long, lingering stare while she slowly stroked at her chin as though running her fingers through a well-groomed beard. For a moment Tamara thought the woman would question her more. Instead she said, "I'ma do it just because I hate the daggone system so much and what it can do to a person—because of that, I guess I can try to help you best I can."

Tamara had been holding her breath hopefully as the woman pondered her request, and exhaled now imperceptibly with a grateful "Thank you."

Shooting a quick glance toward where the guard sat, still apparently immersed in his paper, Samyra smiled widely, her mouth full of dark gaps where teeth used to be.

She emitted a harsh croak of a laugh and added, "And anyway, talkin' to you will at least get me out of that cell for a minute, and maybe you'll even put a coupla dollars on my books, huh?" She looked up at Tamara as she picked at some dirt from under her long and uneven fingernails. "Thataway at least I can get a pack of smokes out of this little visit, you know?"

Tamara gave her a weak smile as she nodded her head in agreement.

"I will be happy to leave you some money for cigarettes— even though they are bad for you."

The woman snickered again. "I got worse things to worry 'bout in here than smokin', gal."

Wanting to waste no more time, Tamara reached in her bag, grabbed her small tape recorder, set it on the table, and turned it on.

"Why you got that tape player? How'd you get it in here anyway? You not gonna use this against me in some kinda way, are you?" asked the woman suspiciously.

With a nod toward the guard, Tamara replied, "He checked my bags and let me have it—and anyway, how would I use it against you? This is just a way for me to make sure that I don't miss any important information."

Samyra squinted at her suspiciously now. "How'd you know I was here anyway?"

"Sissie Bailey told me—she *is* your mother, right?"

The woman sucked her teeth and then turned up her pink lips to one side of her face and flicked some dirt from under her nail.

"I guess you could say that, although that woman ain't never did a friggin' thang for me. She birthed me and my sisters, and that was about it . . . Seemed like we wasn't nothin' but a bother to her, and the truth is, she wanted to get laid more of the time than she wanted to be bothered with us."

Thinly veiled beneath her tough exterior was a sadness in Samyra's eyes when she spoke of her mother. Tamara was almost overwhelmed with an unexpected wave of compassion for the woman, who obviously had experienced much instability as a child.

Samyra stared into space then, and her hazel eyes glazed over as she continued to reminisce. "Shoot, we was in and out of the house, in some dang foster home or back with her, until she went to jail for killing me and my sister's daddy," she said with a grunting laugh. "Then the state took us out for good . . . I wasn't but six then."

"What happened to your sisters?"

"Didn't my so-called mama tell you?" she asked sardonically.

Falteringly Tamara replied, "S-s-she didn't seem to know much about them. Really, I think she only knew where you were because she has your son living with her—you know that, though."

The woman sat up straight in the chair and said, "Yeah, I

93

know it, and I hate it, too! I wish every day that Dontay could be anywhere than with her . . . well, almost anywhere, that is. I don't want my son in the system. Gal, you can get lost in there and nobody could even find you."

"I guess I've never thought of it that way," Tamara said quietly.

The woman glared at her. "Why would you think of it? You work for the system—you don't know nothin' about how it is to be moved from home to home. Every now and then you get one who really cares, but most of them don't care nothin' 'bout you—and anyway it just don't seem the same as blood family, you know?"

For a long moment, Tamara said nothing; then she asked again, quietly, "Your sisters? Do you know where they are, or did they get lost in the system?"

Samyra took a deep breath and replied, "We all got separated; only me and Lanisha grew up in the same town, but I think I know where they are." She glued her eyes onto Tamara's. "Last I heard, Lanisha locked up just like me in Lake County Correctional Center, and Kaytriona live in Dayton, Ohio. She married, got a coupla kids, and probably want to forget she was ever a member of the Bailey family." She looked at Tamara, turned her lips down, and snickered, "Cain't blame her for that, now, can we?"

Tamara gave her a sympathetic smile before asking, "What about Jannice—where is she?"

The woman eyed her as she said, "You know all about my family, huh? Know everybody's name and everything. You is a *real* good friend to this girl that you *used* to know. Gal, ain't nobody in my whole life never helped me like you helpin' her—shoot, I *needs* a friend like you!"

"I really miss her," said Tamara earnestly, missing the sarcasm dripping from the woman's statement. "I hope that when I find her again, she will be happy to get this information . . . She was always so unhappy about not knowing her family."

Sensing Tamara's straightforwardness, Samrya gave up her derisive stance and asked, "What does Jannice have to do with all of this, anyway?"

"I think Jannice is my friend's mother."

"Oh, yeah?"

"Yes."

The woman stared into space and began to muse over long-ago recollections of her sister. "One thing I gotta say: that Jannice sho' was pretty. Dark skin so black it was shiny almost. She got that from our daddy—he come from Mississippi and was just as black as he could be. She was slim with long, pretty hair that was thick and shiny, and she had sparkly, dark eyes that was a little turned up on the ends."

Hopefully Tamara asked, "Where is she?"

Turning lifeless eyes toward her, in a flat voice the woman replied, "She dead."

"Dead?" That was an answer Tamara was totally unprepared for.

"'Bout five years ago now. She was a pretty girl, real smart and funny, too, but my sister took a lot after ol' Sissie even though she didn't live with her long. State moved her up to the Chicago area, and the city can be rough, 'specially when you in the system. She growed up way too fast, had kids young; she was a bad mother, lots of men always around, and the worst habit she got up there in the city was wantin' that horse."

Tamara's expression was curious. "Horse?"

"*Her-on,*" the woman said. "Smack . . . She left her kids alone, sold herself—shoot, she'd even leave a man for that her-on. She told me one day that when she hit it the first time and the warm calm spread over her body like a fuzzy, safe blanket, it was the feelin' she longed for her whole life. I really think it only took a couple of times, and from then on when she was high was the *only* time she felt good."

Tamara pushed aside the sick feeling that came over her when she thought about the young woman addicted to the powerful drug. "What happened to her kids?"

She said disgustedly, "Shoot!, the state got 'em all. That girl had seven kids, and I bet she didn't spend more than a month with any one of them. I swear, she was just *straight-up triflin'* in that way . . . a couple of them babies she just dropped and walked out on. It got so bad toward the end that whenever the state found out she was pregnant, they just waited for her to have the baby, so they could take it from her. I don't think she spent a day with the last three."

Tamara exhaled heavily and then asked, "Where is the father of the kids?"

"*Daddies,* you mean." The woman rolled her large eyes toward the ceiling and stroked her round chin again, "Let's see, Danny Stewart is the papa to the middle three, and he's dead, too . . . least that's what I heard through the grapevine, and Victor Davis was papa of the two at the end, and he's incarc'ated, as they say, just like me."

"What about the oldest two? Do you know where their father is?"

The woman twisted one side of her lips up into smile. "Ol' Three, that's what we called him, but Maurice Lewis the Third was his name. His name even sound like he was some kinda prince or somethin'! Whoo-wee . . . he was one fine man, too! Big and tall and dark-eyed with long, pretty eyelashes. His skin was smooth and dark, and he had thick, naturally wavy hair." She patted her leg hard and looked at Tamara in the face and said, "Girl, if he hadn't been my sister's man, I'da went for him—back then, anyway. I mean he *looked-ed* dat good!"

Still overwhelmed by the unexpected news about Jannice's

death, Tamara nodded numbly before asking, "Do you know where this 'Three' is?"

The woman twisted her full lips downward and said, "Sho' don't, baby gal. I haven't heard nothin' 'bout that brotha in years. He mighta went back to the city—he was a local boy, but he'd ran away to Chicago when he was 'bout seventeen, you know. Used-ta run numbers on Fifty-fifth Street. Jannice met him up there when she was only sixteen; he was ten years older. It weren't till later on she found out that he was born downstate, too."

Tamara sighed deeply and turned off the tape recorder—she couldn't get Jannice's death off her mind. "How did she die?"

Samyra turned up her lips disgustedly and replied, "Do you really have to ask, Miss Lady? My sister died the way most drug addicts do—she OD'd."

"Where?"

Samyra was quiet for a moment, and Tamara could see that the woman's eyes were shiny with unshed tears when she turned to look at her. "She died all alone up there in an old warehouse on the streets of Chi-town. My sister died all alone, just like she'd left them kids all them times, you know?" Her raspy voice was hard when she added, "I guess what goes around really does come around, huh?"

Tamara was silent, and her own heart felt heavy in her chest as she thought of the woman's cold, lifeless body lying alone in some abandoned building in that large city.

The woman repeated softly, "What goes around comes around . . . well, at least it was thataway for Jannice."

Tamara cleared her throat and said, "I'm sorry."

The woman wiped her eyes hard with the back of her hand and said, "Well . . . I guess it be's like that sometimes, huh?" With a half smile, she asked, "Any more questions, baby gal? I'm kinda tired now."

"No. Thank you, Samyra, for speaking with me."

The woman blinked her eyes a couple of times, wiped them with a finger, and then got up and said, "Guard, I'm ready to go."

Deep in thought, Tamara's eyes watched Samyra as she walked toward the door, where the guard met her. Once there, the woman turned to her and said, "Hey, sweet sista, don't forget to put some money on my books for the smokes, huh?"

"I'll do that," said Tamara, but her lagging reply was too late—the door was already closed, and Samyra Bailey was gone.

18.

Stopped Cold

After pulling her frayed cap down lower on her head, the girl moved as fast as her short legs would allow, turning the corner onto the darkened street. After a quick glance behind her, she hurried down the side of the old, dark underpass. The girl hurried past the small cardboard lean-tos scattered here and there in the grassy area serving as home for those with no other place to lay their head at night. Inadvertently she kicked an empty bottle with the side of her foot, and she stopped in her tracks, holding her breath as she watched it slowly travel down the grassless incline until it came to rest with a quiet thud by a pile of paper and an old pizza box at the bottom of the hill.

Certain that the noise had brought no undesirables from

their hiding places, she began her descent again. At the bottom of the hill, she slid through a large, leafless bush with prickly branches into the small space behind. Then, without hesitation she slid her agile body down into a huge concrete drainage pipe obscured by the leafy growth in front of it. After the new expressway was built, this dead-end street was traveled only by a rare lost automobile, whose driver hurriedly U-turned to get back on the main road once he found himself in this obvious camping ground for the homeless.

The large duct must have been long forgotten by some construction worker and was now almost an ingrown part of the hill. This nature-made back wall insulated the tube from the wind and weather, and she'd wedged an old plaid blanket between the outer edge of the pipe and the grassy dirt, creating a colorful, wooly partition. Then she'd pushed her meager belongings back into that far corner hidden away from the probing eyes of any chance passerby.

Once safe inside, the girl reached outside the opening to pull over some loose brush she kept there to conceal the entrance from passersby. Then, with her head hunched between her small shoulders, she walked down the length of the pipe and gave the old duffel bag that held her few belongings a swift, hard kick. She was taking no chances today! Just yesterday she had her hand poised to open the bag, and without warning a huge rat reared its ugly head out of the top of the bag and bared its yellow fangs at her. Newly frightened by that sobering memory, she gave the old green duffel bag another kick, even harder than the first.

Finally satisfied that there were no unwanted visitors inside the bag, the girl removed an old towel and then sat down in the tight space. Next she got the old sleeping bag that she'd lucked upon walking by a Dumpster one night, then pulled out another faded blue towel, folding it over carefully twice before she rolled it tightly into a coil.

Reaching inside her pocket, she pulled out a chocolate candy bar. Her mouth watered as she removed the wrapper from the Hershey bar she'd hoarded all day. Carefully she broke it into tiny pieces. Placing it piece by piece into her mouth, she slowly chewed each small morsel, savoring the taste of the chocolate until there was nothing of its sweetness left on her tongue. Finished much too soon with her dinner for that night, the frustrated girl crumpled the paper, angrily stuffing it back into her pocket, unwilling to throw the wrapper outside and have it land next to her "home."

I'll find someplace to throw it away tomorrow, she thought as she yawned sleepily.

The girl hated nighttime. Though tired, she was constantly aware of her vulnerable position, alone and out in the wide open, mindful that a bad dog or a rodent, or even a crazed street person, could attack her while she slumbered. But much of the day she walked, constantly moving, too afraid of being caught to sit still very long anywhere. The continual movement exhausted her, and she was bone tired at the end of each day.

With a sigh she retrieved a heavy old blanket from the worn bag, pulled her cap down hard over her eyes, and lay her head on the towel that she had rolled so carefully into a tight coil earlier. Covering herself with the blanket, she let her weariness overcome her anxieties and quickly drifted off.

"Hey . . . hey . . . you!" the girl heard a voice say loudly, and for a long moment she thought it was part of her dream and continued to lie there unmoving.

When she heard the voice again, she knew this time it was no dream. "Hey, you in there!" the man said, even more loudly this time.

The girl forgot where she was when she first sat up. It seemed as if it was daylight, and she thought she was in a real home for just a moment, because everything was so bright. But then her grogginess subsided, and remembering now that she was inside her old damp pipe home, she knew immediately that something was wrong. She held up one small hand to shield her face from the light in front of her and squinted to see who was there at the end of the pipe.

"You in there . . . come on out, *right now!*" said the voice demandingly. It was definitely a man speaking, and it was not a voice that she recognized from any time before. "Come on out, now! You don't want me to come in there after you!"

Resignedly she moved the old blanket to the side and, without attempting to stand, shimmied her way down the old pipe. At the opening the man moved back enough to allow her to get all the way out and stand up.

A look of interest creased the older man's face, and he said wonderingly, "Well, I be darned, boy, what are you doing there in that old dirty pipe?" Then, studying her more closely through squinted eyes, he added, "Heck, you ain't nothin' but a kid. Where's your folks, anyway? I bet you're a runaway, and somewhere, somebody is worried sick about you."

No one is worried about me, she thought sadly, *and I can't be a runaway really, 'cause I don't have a home to run from . . . not really.* She said nothing, though, and just stood there mutely with her head held down, hoping that if she kept quiet, he might just go away and leave her alone. But deep inside, she knew that was not going to happen.

"Hey, boy!" the man said again, louder, and he reached out his hand in an effort to touch her shoulder and get her full attention. As his hand got close to her head, she moved back instinctively to avoid his touch. The man sensed her movement backward. Overcompensating in his attempt to tap her shoulder, he instead accidentally caught the frayed bill of her hat, flipping the old baseball cap right off her head.

The man shielded his eyes with his hand and squinted again at her for a long moment before saying in an astonished voice, "Well, my, my, this is no boy here; this is a little girl."

Weary from walking all day, she just stood there staring right through him. Her small shoulders slumped gently as she just gave up. She didn't have any energy or strength to run this time.

Sadly she realized, she was caught!

19.

Popcorn and Pepsi

"C'mon, Tamara, hurry up! Get yourself a pop! You takin' too long!" yelled Sienna over her shoulder as she headed toward the living room to get the movies ready that they were going to watch. It had been Sienna's idea to stop at the video store tonight, but Tamara agreed wholeheartedly that a movie night would be great way for the two of them to spend some casual time together.

She had yet to speak with the girl about the telephone behavior that Lynnette and Jayson had brought to her attention weeks ago, and Tamara's plan was to have that talk tonight. While Tamara was aware that she should have addressed Sienna's uncalled-for rudeness much sooner than today, she'd been so grateful for the temporary lull after the school incident and their stormy blow up that she'd kept quiet.

"You takin' too long, Tamara. Can you get the popcorn or *something?*" asked Sienna in an annoyed tone as she grabbed bowls and napkins to carry into the front room.

Thinking about Sienna's rude behavior, Tamara removed the popcorn from the microwave oven and distractedly pulled the hot paper bag open before it had time to cool off, almost causing the hot steam from the buttery kernels to burn her face.

"Ow!" she said as she sucked air in between her teeth. "Okay, Tamara," she said aloud to herself, "this is getting serious now . . . You are constantly worrying about that girl! You *must* address her behavior tonight, before you seriously hurt yourself!"

Preoccupied, she'd not heard the girl enter the kitchen again until Sienna interrupted her thoughts. "There you go again, talking to yourself." Then with a sarcastic laugh she added, "Shoot, I *still* think they got me living with a crazy lady half the time."

Tamara glanced at Sienna without speaking, and though she maintained a calm exterior, inside she was quite distressed. She noted with a sigh that her purposefully chosen method of ignoring the girl's behavior was not working, since the teen continued to speak to her as if she were an adult—and a rude one at that. In fact, each time Tamara ignored her disrespect, the girl seemed to grow more boldly insolent in her interactions with her. At this rate, Sienna soon would step over the boundary line that Tamara had yet to define to her clearly, and when that happened, the two of them were bound to collide hard—and it would be all Tamara's fault.

Abruptly breaking into her thoughts again, Sienna looked at her impatiently and said impertinently, "Tamara, can you come on?"

This time Tamara was so aggravated by Sienna's tone that her stomach churned at the blatant disrespect the teen was showing toward her. Highly agitated now, Tamara poured the popcorn into a plastic bowl, grabbed a hunter-green-striped kitchen towel, and threw it over her shoulder before leaving the kitchen.

"Tonight," she said with conviction. "I must talk to her tonight."

When she entered the living room, Sienna's back was to her as she busily worked to figure out how to program the DVD player with the remote. "I bet you don't even know how to use this thing," Sienna commented flippantly as she pressed buttons on the control. She added derisively, "Folks like you always got a bunch of sh—stuff, and they don't even know how to use half of it."

Tamara laid out the towel on the cocktail table with one hand and set the popcorn on it. Then she sat on the couch and looked at the girl before replying dryly, "For your information, Sienna, I do know how to program the DVD player."

"Well, Excu-u-use me—my bad," retorted Sienna with a cynical laugh. "Maybe you smarter than I thought you was."

Tamara opened her Pepsi and poured it into her glass. She watched the fizzing soda for a moment before taking a couple of kernels of popcorn. Tamara put them in her mouth one at time, chewing them slowly as she watched Sienna, who, unlike her, was hungrily gobbling popcorn with one hand while looking over the movies for the umpteenth time with the other.

Sometimes Tamara was convinced that the teenager had no understanding of just how rude she really was. She reasoned that Sienna may have been disrespectful for such a long time now that she actually thought that her way of speaking to adults was quite normal. Nevertheless, Tamara wiped her hands on the towel she had thrown over her shoulder and, after taking a deep breath, jumped headfirst into a talk that was long overdue.

"Sienna . . . I don't know if you realize it or not, but there are a lot of times when you could be perceived to be quite rude when you are interacting with adults."

Still chewing loudly, Sienna stared hard at Tamara and cocked her head to one side. "Huh?"

Tamara rolled her eyes upward and inhaled again. "Sienna, the fact is, you *are* rude many times to adults when you talk to them. Young ladies should not behave in that way—it's disrespectful, and frankly, it's not very nice."

The girl twisted her lips after smacking them loudly. "I ain't *tryin'* to be nice," she said as she wiped her salty hands on the sides of her jeans.

"Well, we certainly know that to be true. You are *not* trying to be nice, and you are *not* being nice at all. Moreover, you are not even being respectful."

"So?"

"So, you should try to do better. You represent yourself when you speak with people, and when you are rude, people think badly of you. This is especially true since you are still really a little girl."

"I'm not a little girl!"

"Well, I'm sorry, a young teen, then. I want you to know that people at my job have said that you are quite rude when you call there for me."

"They just lyin' on me!"

"Sienna, now you stop that! First of all, stop yelling. I can hear you perfectly fine. Now, every time you get in trouble, you say that the person is lying on you, and that just cannot be true. You must learn to take responsibility for your behavior sometimes."

"You listenin' to them 'cause you don't like me no way."

Tamara blew out a small breath. This whole thing was taking a turn for the worse now. Reaching over, she picked up her glass and took a long drink of the soda in front of her. Her dry throat was unused to the sweet soda, though, and it caught right there in her windpipe.

Unable to speak or catch her breath, all Tamara could do was grab the side of the couch and gasp for air. Sienna took one look at her widened eyes and sprang into action, quickly jumping from the floor and rushing behind her. Gently the girl began to rub Tamara's mid back with a firm hand, and just like a milk-filled newborn, Tamara loudly released the pocket of gas caught there, allowing the liquid to flow freely down her throat again.

The girl gazed at her, repeating worriedly, "Are you all right Tamara? Are you all right?"

With a grateful look Tamara replied softly, "Thank you."

Sienna shrugged her small shoulders and smiled almost sheepishly before affecting her usual streetwise demeanor. "It wasn't nothin'. I saw somebody do it on a TV show once, that's all. I'm gonna start a movie now, okay?"

Without waiting for an answer, Sienna turned out the lights and, after starting the DVD player, sat on the floor, crossed her legs, and leaned her back comfortably on the couch.

Tamara turned sideways and curled her legs under her. Even though this was the first time Sienna had shown any kindness toward her, for some strange reason the teen's caring gesture did not make Tamara feel happy.

In fact, the entire evening had not turned out the way she had planned. She was supposed to be in control tonight, letting Sienna know her boundaries and outlining her expectations to her. But, her close call with the soda changed the agenda, and to Tamara now it seemed that Sienna was in charge of tonight's situation and *she* was the one who was out of control.

Troubled by this unexpected turn of events, Tamara laid her head back on the arm of her floral print sofa. But instead of watching the movie, Tamara's gaze rested on the shadowy silhouette of the girl in front of her, and there it remained until her eyelids grew heavy and she fell asleep.

20.

Round Table

Seated at the huge table in Central High's conference room, Tamara stared mindlessly at the papers in front of her while trying to ignore her growing uneasiness. From the time that she had received the telephone call asking her to appear today, Tamara instinctively knew this would be no easy meeting, and while no one had been outwardly impolite since her arrival, she was certain the coolness in their greetings was an indicator of what was to come.

"Ms. Britton, is it? I can see you're looking over Sienna's progress reports, and once you're done, we can have a brief chat with you before she joins us," said the teacher who'd done most of the talking so far.

Tamara glanced up silently at the blonde geography teacher who obviously had been designated the spokesperson for the entire group. Counting quickly as she glanced around the table, again Tamara was dismayed to realize there were ten other adults sitting there. How was it possible that one little girl could need so many people to educate her? she wondered.

Compounding her discomfort, all the teachers assembled were white, with the exception of Dean James, whom she'd met when Sienna got suspended. The dean had given her a quick but unreadable smile when she first arrived, and now all Tamara could see was the top of her salt-and-pepper hair as she studiously looked down at her own set of papers. No, there was no friendly face in this group to make her feel more at ease; instead, Tamara felt as though she was facing covert hostility all on her own.

With a quick upward twist of her pink-painted lips, the blonde teacher glanced quickly at her watch before informing her, "Ms. Britton, we are waiting for one more person. Mr. Perry is Sienna's history teacher, and he should be here momentarily. He was teaching, but the bell should be ringing in a moment."

Tamara returned the woman's half smile and then looked down at the papers, willing herself to concentrate on the information. Her eyes came to rest on the Quarterly Grade Report. Where had the time gone? Tamara had not realized that the quarter was already over, and she stifled her shock once she realized that the document said Sienna was failing every class!

That couldn't be correct, she thought. Each time Tamara checked on Sienna in her room, the girl was busily writing or reading something. No, there had to be some sort of error, Tamara told herself, and as soon as they got started, she would make sure it all was cleared up.

When the bell buzzed loudly announcing the end of classes, Tamara glanced up again and purposefully looked around the table at each of the individual teachers. One or two gave her a quick smile when she caught their eye, but the others simply dropped their gaze.

Embarrassed, Tamara lowered her head again. *What must these people think of me? I'm her guardian, and what if she is failing? I didn't even know!*

Inhaling through her nostrils, Tamara sat back against the chair and, holding her back very straight, crossed her legs under the table while running her fingers through her hair. She was prepared now, calm and collected and ready for whatever this group of teachers was going to tell her about Sienna.

Just then a stocky brown-skinned man came rushing through the door. Within moments he'd pulled out a chair, sat in it, and said in a husky voice, "I'm sorry, everybody; I'm late—got held up by a student."

Tamara stared at him, her almond eyes wide with surprise. Sienna had one African-American teacher, all right, and *he* was a good-looking one at that!

Mr. Perry turned his wide smile toward her and, reaching over the table with his hand extended, asked, "So, you are the parent of our Miss Sienna?"

"Y-y-yes, that's me," Tamara managed to say falteringly, before looking down again quickly. Her previous composure was now shattered, leaving Tamara feeling overwhelmed and ill at ease.

The blonde teacher interrupted. "I think we should get started—some of the teachers in here have classes to teach next period. I've arranged for Sienna to join us during the latter half of the meeting, and there are a few things we should discuss before she does. Let's begin by introducing ourselves to Ms. Britton."

All the teachers introduced themselves quickly, along with the school psychologist, social worker, and counselor.

Mustering the courage to speak, Tamara let her eyes sweep around the table, and she commented more timidly than she would have liked, "I've been glancing through this information, and I'm not sure that this paperwork is correct. This report says that Sienna is failing every class. That just can't be so. Each day when I go into her room, she's working feverishly, and I know Sienna is an avid reader as well."

Brusquely the older English teacher, who had introduced

herself moments ago as Mrs. Madison, broke in. "Well, I must say that Sienna has not read one book in my class. In fact, Sienna *refuses* to participate at all. She does no homework, and all that she really does is socialize and disrupt the classroom. I've had to send her out numerous times this quarter."

Evidently, the woman's comment broke the ice, because one by one, each teacher began to recount the same sort of negative information about the girl's behavior and academic progress. By the time it was Mr. Perry's turn to talk, Tamara's shoulders were drooping low, heavy with the weight of all the negative, depressing information.

"Well, Ms. Britton, I have a few problems with Sienna's behavior in class. But she actually participates well and does in-class assignments," said Mr. Perry.

Tamara shoulders relaxed a bit—she was relieved to hear *something* good about the girl—and she looked into his eyes hopefully.

Mr. Perry held her dark eyes with his own and continued gently, "However, Ms. Britton, I'm sorry to have to agree with the others and tell you Sienna has done *absolutely no* homework this quarter, and no matter how well she participates in the class activities and quizzes, Sienna *must* complete the homework assignments to pass this class. Ms. Britton, we are well into the second quarter, and the fact is that Sienna will fail the semester if she does not begin to complete her assignments."

"I know . . . I—I—I just assumed that she was . . . doing her homework, that is. I asked her, every day . . . and she assured me she was working," said Tamara falteringly. Then feeling self-conscious, with no idea of what else to say, she looked down and began to study the papers again silently.

The door slammed hard then, and Tamara glanced up right into the face of Sienna, who was smiling widely as her eyes swept over the gathering around the table.

"Dang . . . *everybody* up in here! Why *all* my teachers got to be here?" the teen asked, but her large grin clearly showed that she was basking in all the attention of the moment.

Mr. Perry gave her a stern stare said firmly, "Sienna! Don't you question these adults, young lady! Come over here and sit next to Ms. Britton."

Tamara glanced at him, grateful for his help since she was unable to speak. She felt then as though a vise were squeezing her body. The air in the room seemed stifling, and the mostly white faces around the table seemed to be pressing in closer and closer. Swallowing her discomfort, Tamara turned and awkwardly pulled out the chair next to her for Sienna.

Sienna took one look at Tamara's somber face and asked loudly, "Dang, Tamara! What's wrong with you? You look like somebody died or something!"

Unspeaking, Tamara gazed at Sienna with one question whirling around in her brain: *What kind of foster mom am I?* All of her efforts to help the teen seemed useless now. In her powerlessness, her voice was caught down deep somewhere in her throat, and all Tamara could manage to do was look at her foster daughter and smile weakly.

"Tamara?" said the girl again, a little quieter this time, as she looked at her with curiosity written on her face.

"Yes, Sienna," she finally managed while glancing around the table at the blur of faces one more time. Tamara felt as though she, not the teen, was in the hot seat there at the table, and she was painfully aware of the watchful presence of the girl's teachers. Their negative comments seemed to reflect their opinion that she was unable to guide the girl in the right direction. Then, thankfully, she gazed into the dark eyes of Isaiah Perry, and he smiled at her warmly.

Then, as if it were his responsibility to do so, Isaiah looked Sienna squarely in the eyes and said sternly, "Okay, young lady, you have some explaining to do!"

21.

Stand-Up Girl

"So, Tam, please tell me that you *at least* put Miss Sienna on punishment for those grades," said Jayson in a half whisper from the back of the cubicle.

"I did, Jay," said Tamara firmly. "Sienna cannot watch TV at all, and I took her CD player from her, too."

"Well, at least you are trying. I know you wanted to *kill* her for making you go up there and be embarrassed in front of all those white folks like that," added Jayson through tightened lips. "I know I would've choked that little girl once we got outside."

Tamara emitted a small giggle before replying chidingly, "You would not, Jay! I *was* humiliated, though. To tell the truth, no matter how hard I tried not to, I was taking their criticisms of Sienna very personally. It really seemed as though they were blaming all of her bad behavior and failures on me."

Jay shook his head understandingly. "Shoot, I would've felt the same way, Tam. She lives with you, and so folks gotta think you got something to do with it if she's not doing well."

"I know, but . . . you know Mrs. Jackson, right?"

"You mean our Denise Jackson, whose husband is Leonard? The same ones with all the foster kids?"

"Exactly. They really do amaze me. I honestly don't know how they do it. Mrs. Jackson and I talk now and then since I've had Sienna. I really don't know how I would manage without her, Jay. She's been so supportive to me whenever I needed it. Anyway, we talked only a few days before the meeting, and she advised me then to stop taking Sienna's behavior personally. She reminded me that I'm not responsible for her choices."

Jayson gave her a skeptical look. "Good advice, Tam, but easier said than done, I would think."

Tamara reluctantly agreed. "Jay, it is difficult to remain objective, and although I was trying hard, I just couldn't do it that day. I'll tell you, I felt just awful and so incompetent." She turned her chair around to face his, "Jay-Jay, she'd hidden the first progress report, and the truth is, I was so out of touch with what was going on at school that I was not even aware that it had come out. To top it all off, Sienna had evidently intercepted dozens of calls to my home from teachers and even the dean—told them that I could not be disturbed at work and so they did not call me here, either."

Jayson stopped for a moment and then held his finger to his lips and said, "Hold on, hold on—I hear something."

Tamara spun around quickly and began to type on her keyboard until Jayson, confident that it was not Joan heading their way, added, "Tam, you know what? That girl is just good at being bad, but then, most kids who decide to act up at her age usually are! You are really a good one, though, 'cause I know I could not handle Sienna as calmly as you. Shoot, I'd probably have to send her back to wherever she came from just to keep from *killing* her little behind!"

Once again facing Jayson, Tamara crossed one leg over the other while smoothing the navy blue pin-striped pant leg with one hand in a deliberate fashion. She looked up at Jayson and said in a slightly baffled tone, "What was strange, Jay, is that Sienna was not embarrassed at all. Instead, she was *enjoying* having all the attention focused on her, even if it was in a negative manner." With a deep sigh, she added, "Jayson, I must admit I am a bit overwhelmed by it all, you know?"

As Jayson looked at his friend with empathy in his eyes, he noticed how beautiful the young woman was. He could detect no makeup on her high-cheekboned face, yet Tamara's smooth brown skin was even and clear, and her almond-shaped eyes slanted just enough at the corners to make her face look a bit exotic. Her slim hands lay on her knees, and the tips of her nails were painted pale pink. When she spoke, Jay saw deep dimples in her cheeks. But what Jay had always found most attractive about Tamara was her unassuming nature and her complete lack of pretentiousness.

For just a fleeting moment Jayson actually thought about asking her out, to see if their friendship could move to another level. But just as quickly he nixed that idea, deciding that he valued Tamara's friendship too much to risk losing it. Besides, he still enjoyed the ladies a bit too much to think about settling down with one woman.

"Jayson? Did you hear me?" Tamara asked.

"Tam, I'm sorry. I lost myself in a thought for a moment," he said with a flash of a grin accompanied by a mischievous look in his eye. "I know you are overwhelmed by all this. In my opinion, Sienna is just a lot for you to handle, and I know you're not going to like what I'm getting ready to say, but the truth is, anytime you can't deal with it anymore, just tell Joan."

"Tell Joan what?" Joan Erickson asked from behind the two of them.

Dumbstruck, neither Jayson nor Tam could disguise their surprise that their boss was standing there behind them. Engrossed in their conversation about Sienna, neither of them had seen or heard the woman walk over to their area.

The woman gave them her brightest smile and repeated, "Tell Joan what? I'm here right now."

Jayson looked at Tam and raised his eyebrows before he answered smoothly, "Oh, nothing really, Joan—only that we were hoping that we will have our next reports in on time."

Both of them noticed that the woman was still showing off her ring, dramatically using the hand with the glittery diamond on it to slowly move her coiffed hair away from her face. As she gave the two of them a quick upturn of her lips, she said, "I hope so. It is our expectation that we receive our reports on time."

Without further comment, Jayson moved his chair over to his cubicle, and Tamara turned her chair back around. Beginning to type her report, Tamara sensed the woman's presence behind her still, and hoped she would just leave.

"Tamara?"

Reluctantly Tamara spun her chair around so that she was half-facing Joan. "Yes?"

"I couldn't help but notice that it seems that you are out of the office quite a bit more than normal. In fact, you have been gone for at least two entire mornings and one afternoon. I happened to be going through my schedules and noticed that those times you were out of the office were not designated field days, either."

Tamara now spun her chair all the way around to face the woman, frowning as she tried to remember the times that Joan spoke of. Two of the days she was at Sienna's school, once for the conference and once when Sienna was suspended. The other was when she took Sienna to the doctor for her physical. She'd always indicated on her time sheet the purpose for her absences, but evidently Joan had not checked that part.

Slightly irritated now, she responded, "Joan, those times I was out were connected to Sienna."

The woman gave Tamara the closed-lip, condescending smile she hated. "Oh. Hmmm, I do realize that kids take time, but we don't want to miss too much of our valuable work time, now, do we, Tam? Perhaps, we could work harder to schedule these things on our off time or later in the day to minimize their impact."

Tamara looked at the woman incredulously. How dare Joan question her as if she lacked integrity in taking time off to care for the girl, when it had been Joan's idea for Sienna to move into her home in the first place!

Annoyed, Tamara retorted in an uncharacteristically clipped tone, "Joan, I do take offense at what you are saying. *You* asked me to take this young girl in as a personal favor to you, and I did. I work for this agency, and the way I handle her as guardian certainly reflects back on us—and this would include you as my supervisor. So if I neglect to pick her up when she misbehaves, or if I miss a conference or doctor's appointment, it would be a bad reflection on us all."

Joan looked shocked to hear Tamara address her in this fashion. Never had she heard the woman use this curt tone; in fact, now that she thought about it, she'd not heard Tamara speak much at all, really.

Tamara's nostrils flared angrily now, and she ignored her rapidly beating heart, continuing to speak while keeping her brown eyes locked on the white woman's hazel ones. "Furthermore, I am doing the very best I can to work with this young lady, and be assured, it is not always easy. Sienna has been left on her own a lot; she's had almost no home training, is often rude and disrespectful to adults, and is a chronic liar. Additionally, she is failing all of her classes in school, and from what her teachers have told me, she has consistent behavior problems."

Joan's eyes widened as she listened. She realized that Tamara *was* actually upset with her, and for good reasons. "Tam, maybe this is a misunderstanding. I didn't realize that you were going through so much with our Miss Sienna," she said, her tone sweet and low now.

"Well, now you know that I am," Tamara assured her tersely. Her almond eyes were still locked on Joan's as she said, "And one more thing, Joan. Don't take this the wrong way, but I really don't like it when you call me Tam—that's a nickname reserved for *friends*."

After a moment's silence, Joan answered contritely, "I'm very sorry if I offended you, Tamara." With one last glance at the young woman's grave expression, Joan added quickly, "Well, I guess I'll let you go on with your work."

Tamara turned her chair around quickly to face her desk again. She felt dizzy and struggled to type her report because her hands were shaking so badly that they kept inadvertently hitting the wrong keys.

"You go, girl! I'm so proud of you! It's about time you stood up for yourself!" said Jayson with enthusiasm.

Tamara jumped, startled by his presence behind her. Then, taking a deep breath, she faced him and smiled brightly, all the while holding her hands tightly together in her lap so that Jayson would not notice just how badly they were shaking.

22.

Solitary Moments

The girl's eyes moved so quickly over the text that she seemed to absorb the words rather than read them. She loved to read, and the written words provided her with a ticket to visit places far away and were her only escape from a here and now she often wanted no part of. Immersed in the novel, she did not hear the guard's footsteps approaching her room, and jumped when he rapped on the small window of the white door.

Looking up then, she saw the white-clothed middle of the man's body through the opening in the door. "Your dinner is served," he said, and his disembodied voice was emotionless as he pushed a tray through the small slot.

Without replying, the girl rose from the bed and retrieved the tray from the opening. Expressionless, she carefully examined the food on the tray. A Styrofoam bowl was half-filled with watery noodle soup, and the entrée was a creamy-looking chicken casserole, served with green peas and a big white roll.

It doesn't really matter what they give me, she thought to herself with a small shrug, but she was glad that today there was no meat. There was no point in giving it to her anyway, since she had no way to cut it. They would only allow her to have a spoon, because for some dumb reason they thought that she might try to do something to herself with a plastic fork or knife.

Then, without warning, her memory flashed back to the night they brought her here for the first time. The girl was looking down on the chaotic scene as if she were floating outside her body, and hovering there above it all, she could see herself as she was when they brought her in that night, screaming and flailing wildly at the nurses and guards.

"Stop it. Stop it—don't touch me!" she heard herself say over and over while she lay there writhing on the linoleum floor.

The visual image continued to play in her brain. She saw four of them then—no, wait a minute, five of them—surrounding her body there on the floor, and they were all dressed in white. One nurse managed to grab her arms, tightly pinning them close to her small body, and then two others held her legs, and swiftly they lifted her up high onto a small table. All the while

118

she was yelling as loud as she could, screaming at the top of her lungs.

"I can't take any more!" she was yelling. "I can't take any more!"

"Little girl, you need to calm down!" said the nurse, who looked alarmed at the sight of her writhing there so out of control.

There on the table she squeezed her eyes shut tightly now and flopped her head from side to side, harder and faster, and then suddenly she began to shake all over.

"I think she's convulsing," she heard the nurse say.

When the girl opened her eyes, she was no longer floating above the scene but was inside her body. Everything she saw looked distorted. The girl felt as though she were trapped in a long, dark tunnel, and no matter how hard she tried, she could not see anything to the left or to the right. Her head simply would not move on her now stiffened neck . . . She could not turn in either direction. Instead, she could only stare upward into the faces hovering eerily above her as she felt her body jerk hard time after time.

Somebody asked, "What's causing it? There is no history of epilepsy in her records . . . Do you think she's taken some sort of drugs?"

Another voice replied, "I don't know, but we'd better get her a shot of something—now!"

Even then, though she could not speak, the words played in her head repeatedly: *I can't take it anymore . . . I just can't take it anymore.* She thought she was crying then, but she couldn't stop shaking long enough to move her arms so that she could touch her own face. Instinctively the girl knew she was lost in another place, far away from the real world, and she wasn't really sure she would be able to make it back.

"This is going to burn a little bit," said a voice again.

There was the prick of a needle in her behind, followed by an intense burning in her left buttock. She had only a moment or two of total lucidity after that; her body was finally still, and she gazed up into each of the concerned faces looking down at her. White faces, black faces, green eyes, blue ones, and brown ones . . . and then she was asleep.

Back in the present, the girl blinked her eyes one time as if turning off a movie that made her uncomfortable. And then, with no further thought about that night, she sat on the side of the bed, rested the tray on her small knees, and picked up her book again. Quickly she was engrossed in the story as she distractedly spooned the now lukewarm food into her mouth with no regard to its taste.

Then she put the book down by her side, chewing silently while thinking about the girl in the story. That girl lived in a house, with a mother and a father and her real brothers and sisters. But she was unaware of her fortunate situation and often angry at them for some reason or other—this was difficult to comprehend.

Thinking about that lucky girl in the book, she felt small and alone here in the locked room, silently eating from her Styrofoam tray. She'd never known her mother or father. She'd lived in many foster homes, and years passed before she learned, through counselors and caseworkers reluctant to tell her the story, that her own mother had been totally uncaring about leaving her alone when she was a small baby.

Supposedly, one of the neighbors had heard her mewling cries that night and called the police, and she'd never lived with her mother again but had been in the "system" in some form or fashion ever since. She knew nothing at all about her father— who he was, where he was, or whether he was even aware of her existence.

With her small fingers she tore off a piece of the hard roll, put it in her mouth, and chewed distractedly. *Shoot,* she thought, *I would be just happy to have a mom or a dad, or an aunt or uncle even . . . just somebody who is family to me.* With a sigh she thought dejectedly of how there was no family that she knew of, and with no knowledge of her biological parents' whereabouts, there was no way to find anyone. Long ago she'd realized that not one blood relative cared enough about her to try to find her, either. She was all alone, and she knew it.

It was still hard for her to believe that she'd lived in so many different foster homes. *Twenty-five different places I've lived,* she thought with amazement, and though they called them foster "homes," none of them had really felt like home to her. Her eyes grew wet then, and she stopped chewing for a moment. Bad things had happened to her in a couple of those homes, and she just couldn't stay in any of them after that. No matter how much the girl liked it, in a few weeks or months, she had to go, to leave . . . to run.

When they caught her this time, something inside her snapped, and when the girl woke up from whatever place she'd gone to inside herself, she was strapped down on this bed in this room. They said she had gone crazy. And judging from what she had recalled moments ago, just maybe she had, for a while.

But she was herself again now, and when she glanced around the square room again, her eyes rested on the locked door. *I might be stuck in here right now,* she thought. *I can't go anywhere, but sooner or later they're going to open that door, and whenever they do,* I'm outta here.

Then the girl got up and replaced the empty tray in the slot in the door. She padded back to her bed, lay on her side, picked up her book, and began to read again.

23.

Hairy Situation

"Here," said Sienna, handing Tamara the blue plastic-bristled brush. "I need help brushing out the back of my hair."

Tamara was surprised by her request but had little time to comment before the girl had sat on the floor in front of her, scooting her body into the narrow space between the couch and the cocktail table. Tamara's body stiffened involuntarily as Sienna took one arm and placed it on each of her legs, then shimmied her small body backward until she seemed quite comfortable.

Well, this was quite an icebreaker, Tamara thought, astounded by the teen's overtly friendly behavior. Since the school conference the other week, and her clumsy attempt to talk it out with the girl during their movie night, there had been a chill between them, and their conversation had been limited, to say the least. To address the problems at school, Tamara had set strict consequences for any misconduct from Sienna, and surprisingly, Sienna had accepted them without argument.

"What you waiting for?" the girl asked impatiently. "Don't you know how to brush hair? C'mon, Tamara, all you do is take some hair from the bottom and then, starting at the top, brush out the naps slowly. Don't worry, I ain't tender-headed or nothin'."

Tamara took a good look at the girl's reddish-brown hair,

noticing how it sprang up in wavy tendrils all over her head. She had not seen it loose and free like this for weeks, since usually Sienna's hair was in stylish braids, which she tightly bound by herself or with the help of a friend.

"C'mon, Tamara," the girl repeated. "Just brush okay?"

Gingerly she parted the girl's hair, her brown fingers in stark contrast to the paleness of the girl's light pink scalp. Then, even more tentatively, she gathered a small amount of the soft hair into her hand and slowly began to pull the brush through the curly strands ever so lightly.

Sienna was obviously still not pleased with her hair-grooming method and commented loudly, "Tamara! I said I *ain't* tender-headed! You can brush harder than that!"

Pulling the brush a bit harder through the hair then, bit by bit she continued to take small pieces of the coiled locks and repeat the process, brushing each section carefully until it lay smooth and soft on the girl's small back.

"Dang, Tamara, you never brushed a girl's hair before? You sho' act like you ain't."

"No, I have not ever brushed anyone's hair before."

Growing up, Tamara had never spent time clustered with other girls, laughing and sharing secrets with one another. Sometimes she'd watch them curiously from the corner of her eye from where she sat alone, noticing how they combed and brushed one another's hair while giggling and talking conspiratorially.

"Why not?" asked Sienna. "Don't you know no other girls? Shoot, I got a lotta friends: Janetha, Marilyn, Sabrina, Tory, and Terry . . . We fix each other's hair all the time, 'cept Terry don't fix no hair though, 'cause he is a boy. Do you think Sabrina could spend the night one day, or can I stay at her house?"

"Sabrina?"

"*Sabrina!* Tamara, you know her foster mom is Mrs. Jackson, yo' friend. C'mon, Tamara, don't tell me you didn't know that. *She yo' friend.* You should know her kids' names. Terry is her son; he my age, too . . . He been living with her forever."

"Terry? I didn't know about him, either." *She's right, I should know Mrs. Jackson's children's names,* Tamara thought. But, unwilling to admit her ineptness to the girl, she instead replied, "I guess I've never had a lot of friends, so maybe I'm still learning about it. I suppose I'm sort of a loner."

"What you mean, a loner?"

"A loner is a person who does not have lots of friends. That's because loners enjoy spending time alone."

Sienna clicked her tongue almost imperceptibly and said, "Hmmph, ain't no 'sorta' to it! If that's what it means, than believe me, you *are* a loner."

"Why do you say it like that?" she asked with a quaver in her voice, while pulling the brush a little too hard through the girl's hair this time.

Sienna flinched, "Tamara, I ain't tender-headed, but you ain't gotta try to kill me, now. I say that 'cause it ain't like you the most popular person in town. Your phone don't ring that much, and you don't never go out on a date or nothin'."

"Sienna, please don't use 'ain't.' It's improper English . . . No, I guess I don't get a lot of phone calls, and I really don't date."

The girl wiggled her little body noticeably and said, "Shoot, if I was pretty like you and had all them nice clothes and stuff, I'd be goin' out all the time. I'd have so many boyfriends, payin' my bills and buyin' me cars and all that!"

Tamara smiled, flattered by Sienna's almost concealed compliment, and replied, "Oh, you would, huh? Do you actually think there are men who buy women cars routinely?"

"Shoot, I know so! Anyway, that's what Destiny Child say— you know, the song. 'Can you pay my bills, bills . . . ?'"

"Well," Tamara laughed, "I suppose, to date a man, I would need to have something in common with him, and I definitely do not have the expectation that he would pay my bills, bills, bills," she said with a small laugh.

The girl continued to sing the song to herself as she popped her fingers and danced to her own beat.

Hmmph! Her singing voice is not half bad, Tamara thought, brushing the last section of Sienna's hair flat. Then, gathering the entire mane of hair, she gently brushed it upward and then down her back again. The reddish-sandy hair was shiny and full of waves when she finished.

Not bad for my first time, she thought, and satisfied with her work, she handed Sienna the brush and said, "All done."

The girl turned around then and looked her squarely in the eye. "Tell the truth: why don't you have a boyfriend? Is it because of me?"

Tamara was taken aback by the unexpected question and quickly shifted her eyes away from the young girl's probing view. "I—I—I don't know why I don't have a boyfriend, Sienna; it isn't because of you, though. I suppose I don't want a boyfriend. And even if I did, I guess I don't know that many guys, and I really don't know where to meet any."

"You could go out to a club or something. That's what one of my foster mamas and her friends used to do." She closed her eyes and swayed from side to side as she mimicked their adult voices and said, "Par-ty—that's what they liked to do." For a moment she looked sad when she said, "It was okay there, but sometimes they came home drunk, or high or something, and sometimes she didn't come home at all, and I'd be scared."

"Oh, I'm so sorry," said Tamara.

This time the girl avoided Tamara's gaze. She shrugged her small shoulders, "It's no big thang, you know. Really, she was an okay foster mama and everything. I liked her and stuff; I just don't want to live with her."

"I understand," said Tamara quietly, thinking of the young girl, scared and home alone, waiting expectantly for the adults to arrive from their late-night partying.

Then, from out of the blue, while slyly glancing at Tamara from the corner of her eyes, Sienna said, "Mr. Perry, he think you look good."

Tamara stiffened at this undesired shift in the conversation and asked, "What are you talking about?"

"You know, Mr. Perry—my teacher at school. He's not married, either, and like I said before, I know he think *you* look good."

She had not forgotten who Isaiah Perry was. His generous smile and calm, positive demeanor had been the only thing that had helped her survive Sienna's school conference the other week.

Hoping to sound nonchalant, she asked, "And how would you know that, Sienna?"

"'Cause he keep asking me questions 'bout you."

"Well, my goodness! Just what kind of questions would he ask you about me?" she asked. Her cheeks were growing warm as she repeated, "What could he possibly want to know about me?"

She could tell that Sienna seemed to think her obvious discomfort with this conversation was amusing, since the girl was smiling widely now. "He want to know stuff like if you married, or if you dating somebody, and how old you are. You know, that kind of stuff."

Tamara felt her cheeks burning now, and she averted her face, hoping that Sienna would not notice.

Sienna gave no indication that she was aware of this new escalation of Tamara's uneasiness, and instead asked, "How old are you anyway? I don't think you too old, are you?"

With a smile, Tamara quipped, "That depends on what you think 'too old' is. I am thirty-two years old."

"Whew," said the girl. "That *is* kinda old! But Mr. Perry, he older than you! He's thirty-four—I know 'cause I asked him."

Tamara was surprised to hear herself emit an involuntary giggle, and she replied good-humoredly, "Okay, okay, Sienna, no more questions!"

"All right . . . But you really ought to start thinkin' 'bout havin' a boyfriend. You not gettin' no younger, you know," said the girl earnestly as she jumped up from the floor with the brush still in her hand.

Tamara had little time to reply to the girl's sardonic warning before she was gently pushed to the floor and Sienna was now seated behind her, brush in hand.

With firm strokes she began to run the stiff bristles through her short, dark hair. "I'll do you now," she said without giving Tamara time to protest.

Tamara tensed, unused to the strange sensation of having Sienna's small hands in her hair. But within moments, the gentle, rhythmic brushing unexpectedly induced a calming effect on her. Slowly Tamara's stiff shoulders began to loosen, and then her entire body began to slacken, leaving her more relaxed at that moment than she remembered feeling in quite a long time.

24.

Singing Praises

Tamara glanced over at Sienna, who was gazing around the Temple of Hope Church openly with interest. To her surprise, the teen had not objected at all to attending early service this Sunday morning. Instead, last night Sienna eagerly prepared herself, spending over an hour styling her hair in a new way just for today.

On the other hand, Tamara was trying hard to quell her own nervousness, which had begun in earnest yesterday morning, well before she'd informed Sienna of her decision. Once she'd told Sienna, the two of them made a trip to the mall in the afternoon, where the teen chose several dressy outfits suitable to wear to church. Back at home, Tamara's free-floating anxiety continued to build even while she shook her head in numb approval of each outfit the excited teenager modeled for her.

Sienna really did look beautiful in all of them, but she finally decided on a long black and fuchsia print skirt and a matching pink stretch button-front cotton shirt with three-quarter-length sleeves. The chunky, black Mary-Jane platforms added enough inches to Sienna's height to put her at eye level with Tamara.

Staring straight ahead, Tamara tried hard to ignore the knot in her stomach and not allow her discomfort to make her second-guess her decision to bring Sienna today. Right now, though, she felt edgy and uncomfortable and found herself wishing to make a hasty escape from the small, crowded room.

Tamara began to read and reread the announcement booklet the usher handed her when she came in, and even though she was anxious, she still listened curiously to the chattering voices around her. Every now and then she glanced around, surreptitiously watching the people in the congregation as they chatted or hugged one another in greeting.

Just then Denise Jackson's voice broke into her thoughts. "Tamara, is that you?"

As soon as Tamara heard the familiar voice, she stood up, wearing a smile of relief and happiness.

"Hi, Mrs. Jackson . . . w-w-we made it . . . ," Tamara said shyly.

The woman was smiling widely. "Yes, you did! And, little girl, I'm *so glad* to see you at church! And you know what? God's glad, too, 'cause He loves it when we praise Him," she said in Tamara's ear as she hugged her hard.

Tamara was actually overjoyed to see Mrs. Jackson's face today and, as usual, enjoyed the warm feeling the woman's encouraging comments gave her. Strangely, Tamara felt almost childlike when Mrs. Jackson called her "little girl," as she just had, and even weirder was that she deeply enjoyed that momentary sensation of youthfulness.

"Oh, Lord!" exclaimed the woman after a quick glance at her watch. "I'm running late as usual, and I still got to go get my robe on. But I thought I saw you when I came in, and I just couldn't believe it was you, and I had to come see for myself!" she added with her throaty chuckle.

Sienna had stopped looking around the church and was now watching the two of them curiously, so Tamara introduced her. "Mrs. Jackson, this is Sienna Larson."

Denise Jackson gave the girl a long, approving look while asking, "Is this the Ms. Sienna that I've heard so much about?

Not just from Tamara but from my Terry and Sabrina, too. C'mon, girl, you come give me a hug, too."

Tamara suppressed a smile when she saw Sienna's small body almost disappear in the woman's substantial bulk as Mrs. Jackson hugged her tightly, but it didn't seem to bother the teen at all. When she sat back down, smelling now like Denise Jackson's Elizabeth Arden Red Door perfume, she was wearing a wide, satisfied grin that she made no attempt to hide.

When Denise stood back, she stared at Sienna smilingly for another moment and then added, "Stand back up now, baby; let me look at you! Now, don't you look as cute as a little bug in a rug in that outfit?" Then, with another quick glance at her watch, Denise Jackson said, "Oooh, I gotta go before I really am late!" and then hurried off.

Tamara smiled, happy that Mrs. Jackson's exuberant greeting had calmed her jumpy stomach. Her calm was short-lived, however, because when she glanced over toward the sanctuary entranceway, to her astonishment she saw Sienna's teacher, Mr. Perry, step inside—dressed in a choir robe! Totally thrown off guard at the unexpected sight of the handsome man, Tamara quickly turned away from the door with her heart pounding hard and fast.

Sienna began to call her name excitedly then, using her small, bony elbow to poke her as she clamored to gain her attention. "Tamara, Tamara!"

Tamara was irritated now. Before, it had been Isaiah Perry's name that turned up at an unlikely time, and now he was here in the flesh! *"What?"* she asked in a tight voice.

Sienna was breathless with excitement by now and grinning from ear to ear. "I just saw Mr. Perry, and I think he goes to *this* church! He had a choir robe on!"

Without letting on to Sienna that she had spied him first,

Tamara again pretended to read her announcement booklet. Trying to sound nonchalant, she said, "Oh, he does . . . how nice."

Tamara's outer calm was a facade, though, because in her head she was now chiding herself animatedly. *This was* not *a good idea, she thought angrily. Now I'm here . . . trapped; I can't leave, and I can only hope that Isaiah Perry did not see me over here!*

Not even one full minute had passed, though, before Tamara immediately recognized the man's husky tone beside her. "Hello, Ms. Britton . . . nice to see you here."

Nervously smiling, Tamara spun around quickly to face him, hastily nodded at him without even speaking, and then hurriedly averted her gaze. She sensed his silent presence there for a few long moments and then, from the corner of her eye, saw him turn and walk away.

Sienna glared at her disappointedly. "Tamara, why didn't you say something? *I told you he likes you!*"

Frowning, she glared back at the girl. Ignoring her comment, she placed a finger to her lips and whispered, "Shhhhh!"

Sienna shot her a disgusted look while mumbling under her breath, "Shoot, I can see why *you* ain't got no boyfriend . . . and you always talkin' 'bout *me* being rude and stuff."

Tamara silently listened to the girl's ramblings, and in her heart she knew, this time Sienna was right. She had no legitimate excuse for her reluctance to talk with Isaiah Perry. There was just something about his quick, wide smile and dancing dark eyes that made it difficult for her to think clearly, and that was just not a feeling she enjoyed at all!

In fact, with only one glance from him, Tamara's tongue seemed to thicken, and it was as though her brain stopped functioning. With a long, quiet sigh, she reasoned, *I am obviously incapable of having a decent conversation with the man; therefore, it's in my best interest to avoid any conversation at all!*

Tamara's meandering thoughts were interrupted by music

from the front of the sanctuary, and her attention was immediately drawn to the large choir now assembled there, wearing colorful blue and white robes. The soloist stepped to the front and, in a clear voice, sang the opening lyrics to the song. Then, at the chorus, the choir joined in, thunderously loud and harmoniously pleasing to hear. Shyly Tamara began to sway slowly to the song with the rest of the congregation.

Sienna was singing next to her in a voice loud enough for her to hear clearly:

"When I think of what the Lord has done for me . . .
I can only praise Him joyfully!
My God has loved me like no other . . .
Stayed closer to me than a sister or brother!"

Tamara stopped to listen then and was stunned at the quality of the child's voice; she turned and stared openmouthed at Sienna, whose own eyes were closed as she sang.

"And I want to thank You, Jesus!
I just want to praise Your name!
Because of Your loving kindness,
My life won't ever be the same!"

While she'd heard Sienna sing at home, this was the first time she realized that the girl might be truly talented. For one so small in stature, the teen's voice was surprisingly full. Rising and falling in all the right places, her tone was impeccable. And to Tamara's amazement, Sienna knew all the words to the song!

Well, will wonders never cease! Tamara mused, continuing to watch Sienna from the corner of her eye. *Not only does she seem to know gospel music very well,* Tamara thought, *but also she can sing, I mean* really *sing!*

Like Sienna earlier, Tamara was now observing the entire service with curiosity. Once the large ensemble choir finished, the young people in the junior choir sang, and then she and Sienna contributed their offerings as the men's choir sang. Then the large church choir assembled again to sing its selection for the day.

This time Tamara clapped her hands while she rocked in her seat with the upbeat melody. Then, still flushed with exhilaration from the praise offerings of music, Tamara stood with the rest of the congregation when the selection was over. She watched Minister Walker stand, smiling broadly at them from the pulpit.

Cringing inside when he asked the visitors to come to the front to be recognized, Tamara hoped no one would point her out as a newcomer. It was a long walk to the front of the church. Lowering her head when she noticed a quick glance or two shoot her way, Tamara was thankful no one said a word, and even more grateful when the minister moved on to the morning prayer.

With her head bowed, Tamara closed her eyes and listened intently to the minister's baritone voice as it filled the room: "Lord, let us learn to love one another, just as Jesus Christ loved us. Let us strive to follow God's word, to live righteously. It is truly just as the choir sang so well a minute ago: 'I never seen it, Lord . . . never seen a righteous man or woman forsaken.' O Lord, we just want to live good lives, Lord God, to thank You for all You've done for us . . . Lord, every day we want to represent You in a manner that will make You proud."

"Amen," said the deacons.

He continued, "We know that we just can't do enough to thank You, Lord . . . There's nothing that we could do that would be enough to thank You for giving us Your son, Jesus! Jesus, who *loved us* so much that He willingly shed His blood for our sins. *Jesus,* who was still able to love those who had treated Him so cruelly . . . O Father, we remember His words: 'Forgive them, for they know not what they do.' Father, today we pray, Lord, that You will open our hearts and let us see past our own hurt and the things that people have done to us that were unfair, and let us begin to forgive them as You forgive us."

As the minister spoke, Tamara began to feel a strange stirring inside, and she knew that it was not her nerves this time. Then, without warning, her eyes began to prickle wetly. Surprised by this uncommon public display of emotion, she was unwilling to give in further to the unfamiliar sensation.

The minister continued to pray, his voice quieter now: "And, God, teach us to be loving *with ourselves,* because once we truly learn to walk in love for ourselves, it is always much easier for us to love others. Once we can accept our own failings, because, yes, while we wish we did not, we *do* sin. In fact, God, sin is our ever-humbling error; it is what makes us human; sometimes sin is what brings us back to our knees and to You when we get too haughty.

"But the wonderful thing about You, God, is that You continue to love us despite our sins. And so, Lord help us to learn to love ourselves as well. Lord, we just thank You today for all of our blessings, and we magnify Your name O Lord, and we love You and praise Your name." The minister raised his head then and said loudly, "C'mon, church, say amen!"

"Amen," said the congregation in unison.

With another wide smile he added then, "Thank you so much for coming out today to praise the Lord and to hear His word! You all may be seated." Clearing his throat, he said, "Church, today we are going to begin a new teaching, that will last for quite a long while, I'm sure. This is a powerful teaching that every Christian needs to understand: learning how to open our hearts to love like our Lord, Jesus. I really believe you gonna enjoy these lessons, church, 'cause after all, it's His love for us that first set us free!"

Love? Immediately perturbed, Tamara squirmed uncomfortably in her seat, thinking, there was that word again! *Love?* Un-

consciously she held herself stiffly erect now, and then purposefully smoothed her navy Ultrasuede skirt over her legs with one
hand several times. Then, with a deep exhale, Tamara stopped
resisting the moment, relaxed her shoulders, leaned back in the
cushioned blue velvet pew, and, with her head and heart now in
a dither, listened intently to the minister's words.

25.

Street Walker

Whew! I sure wish I'd worn my comfortable flats today . . .
It feels like I've been walking for hours, thought Tamara
as she again looked pensively at her raw heel. She eased back into
the plastic-covered booth of the small diner at Fifty-fifth and Ab-
erdeen, where she was finishing a cup of decaffeinated coffee.

"Ow!" she said, squirming uncomfortably and then sliding
away from a large, jagged tear in the vinyl seat that had just
pierced painfully into the small of her back. Tamara sighed then,
determined not to give in to frustration, even though it had
been a long day already, and she had not yet accomplished what
she'd come to the city of Chicago to do.

Massaging the sore place in her lower back absentmindedly,
Tamara stared out of the big plate glass window. Chicago was
huge. Never in her life had she seen so many African-Americans
all in one place. As soon as she pulled onto the expressway leading to the city, that's all she'd seen: all sorts of black people,

everywhere! Even more amazing, the few whites that she did see seemed quite comfortable living among all these diverse-looking people of color.

The trip up had been mostly uneventful, thanks to Jayson's great directions along with his warning about the busy Dan Ryan Expressway. Just as he said, the fast-moving highway proved to be hectic and challenging for her. The traffic moved incredibly quickly. Overwhelmed at first, she'd gotten caught in the wrong lane and missed her exit. Carefully moving from lane to lane then, she managed to get off on the next exit ramp and, through pure luck, found her way here by maneuvering through the city.

Tamara could tell that Jay really wanted to accompany her on the trip when she had told him yesterday of her plans to visit the city. Clearly worried that such a big city would be too daunting for someone as timid as he believed her to be, he'd even intimated that the journey might be dangerous, in an effort to convince her to change her plans.

Earlier this morning he'd even stopped by, and his handsome face was somber and full of concern as he'd repeated over and over, "Tamara, you don't need to go up there by yourself."

Proudly Tamara thought, *Well, Jayson I'm here now, all in one piece and no worse for the ride. I just wish I didn't have to walk right now, though,* she thought with a wry smile, tentatively attempting to slide her foot back into her shoe and wincing when her almost-raw heel touched the hard leather. Her throbbing foot would not weaken her resolve, though. While it would have been nice to have Jayson along, she really needed to do this alone. There was no way Tamara would explain to him her motivation for being here, and even if she did, chances were that he still wouldn't really understand anyway.

The pain in Tamara's foot faded into the background of her thoughts as soon as she reached into her bag and tugged out the manila folder containing her research information. She opened it and searched quickly through the papers inside once again. Today's trip to Chicago was certainly a fishing trip, since all her research efforts before today had netted her only a small amount of information on Maurice Lewis III.

Though Tamara knew that the man had lived in the central part of the state for a while, so far she'd been unable to link him to anyone locally. Maurice was not mentioned at all in the state computer data, unlike the Bailey family, whose involvement in the system helped her get information about them. She just would not accept that she'd reached a dead end, though; she continued slyly to ask questions whenever she could, and amazingly had actually run into a couple of people who claimed to have known Maurice.

These contacts told her that Maurice had moved to Chicago on his own as a teenager. At eighteen, he was too old to be considered a runaway exactly, but he had still been young enough to make lousy choices and end up getting involved at that early age in some unsavory street activity. There was, in fact, little possibility of finding him through career information, either, since Maurice Lewis III had an aversion to working a regular job, instead choosing to use various sorts of hustles throughout the years to make his living.

She checked her notes once more and then closed the folder. This street was his old hangout, where he allegedly ran numbers, which to her understanding meant he ran some sort of gambling game. Though the idea of finding the man with such a small amount of information seemed far-fetched, Tamara fought the feeling that she was on a wild-goose chase.

Nonetheless, she took one long swallow of her coffee before tearing a piece of the stiff white napkin and placing it gingerly in the back of her tender heel, which had resumed its throbbing again as if anticipating the painful walking to come. With a quick, sure touch she turned on her cell phone and then pushed it back down into her shoulder bag, laid a five on the speckled Formica table for the coffee, and squirmed out of the booth.

The icy wind took Tamara's breath away when she stepped out of the door. Much too cold to stop and pull on her leather gloves, she stuck her free hand into her shallow pocket and proceeded hurriedly toward Fifty-Second Street.

A brick building occupied the corner, with its two dingy windows looking out on both streets. An old red-and-white-striped pole by the door hung adjacent to the cracked black letters spelling, "The Corner Shop."

This was the place Tamara was looking for. Anxious to escape the frosty day, she quickly squeezed the cold metal handle of the door hard, causing it to fly wide open. "Whew!" she said under her breath, relieved to feel the rush of heat greeting her just inside the shop. Behind her the bitter wind blew the heavy door, pushing it closed with such a loud bang that she jumped.

Glancing around the room, Tamara hoped her mask of composure hid the inner anxiety she was feeling right then. The oddly shaped space was almost triangular. Three barber chairs, all occupied, lined each wall. A few men waited in chairs, aligned in two closely-spaced rows in the narrower portion of the room where she now stood.

Tamara realized she might be grasping at straws when she decided to pursue the lead she'd gotten from the skinny, round-eyed waitress in the diner about this old barber shop. However, the business had been located in this same spot in this neighborhood for years, and hair shops were known to be one of the hubs of the African-American community simply because so many came and went during the day. That would seem to be especially true of those like Maurice Lewis III, who were always looking for a captive audience because they had something to sell.

Unsure exactly how to begin her investigation of sorts, Tamara turned to a dark-skinned, scowling man sitting in the chair closest to where she stood, and asked rather timidly, "Excuse me . . . do you know Maurice Lewis the Third?"

The man's frown deepened. "Maurice Lewis the Third, you say?" He rubbed his salt-and-pepper beard and said the name once more, "Maurice Lewis—let me see . . . Wait a minute . . . is you talkin' 'bout *Three?*"

The barber nearest to them was a robust man busy with a client, but he stopped cutting hair abruptly and, turning an intense stare her way, growled, "Three, huh? Who are *you,* asking 'bout Maurice?"

Tamara lost her voice for a minute, feeling more than a little intimidated by the huge man with his rumbling voice and intent, glaring look, but she knew there was no turning back now. And so, gathering her wilting courage, she cleared her dry throat and replied in a small but firm voice, "He's my cousin."

The man's eyes looked huge to her as he roared, "What did you say, girl? You gotta speak up, now! It's noisy in here!"

Ignoring his distracting appearance, Tamara gazed at him steadily, forcing her eyes away from the slicked-back hair and his large gold-ringed fingers he held clasped over his substantial midsection. Again she cleared her throat and repeated, louder this time, "I said, he is my cousin."

Resolutely she tightened her lips then, offering no more information. Intuitively she knew that this was not the place to try to offer her full explanation for wanting to locate the man. She sensed that others in the shop were now staring at the two of them, and now the steamy warmth inside the shop, combined with her anxiety, caused beads of sweat to moisten her forehead. In fact, Tamara's discomfort was mounting quickly, and all she wanted to do now was to get some information about Maurice Lewis III and get out of this place.

The man chuckled ruefully as he gave her the once-over from head to toe with his large-eyed gaze. *"He's yo' cousin, huh?* Girl, I sho' didn't know ole Three had any 'cousins' look as good as you do, gal. Yeah, I remember him. *Three,* that's what we called him. In fact, we used to always tease him, 'cause whenever you said his name, the brotha had to add on 'the Third,' like he was some sort of prince or king or somethin'!"

He focused his round eyes on the barber working next to him and asked in his booming voice, "Now, tell me, Malcolm, how can you be the *Third* when you don't know who yo' daddy is, number one, and so you don't know who the heck is Maurice the first and the second?"

Everybody in the shop began to laugh raucously at his comment.

The barber turned and looked back at Tamara and asked without a trace of a smile on his face, "And how can you be his cousin, little girl, when you come here callin' him Maurice and everybody knows his name was Three? That's what he expected folks to call him."

Tamara's cheeks grew hot and she wanted to turn and run on her throbbing heel from the dusty room. But remembering how far she'd traveled to gain this information, somehow she managed to stand her ground, replying somewhat primly, "Well, just because *you* don't know about me does not mean that *I* do not exist. I *am* his cousin, and for your information, I always called him Maurice, and he liked it just fine. Now, do you or do you not know where he is?"

The barber picked up his clippers again and, gazing at her with raised eyebrows, replied, "Well, okay, then, Ms. Lady! Maybe you 'is' his cousin, and maybe you 'is' not."

"Do you or do you not know his whereabouts?" she asked again firmly.

"I do not," answered the man mockingly. "But I'ma try to

help you, little sister girl. You can walk down two blocks to Fifty-ninth Street, and on the corner there is a package store. Right inside the door is where that old brotha Benzo Taylor usually hangs out." He grunted out a hard laugh. "He's a salesman of sorts, just like ol' Three used to be; he just might be able to help you. I think they used to run around together, if you know what I mean."

She did not know what he meant, really, but smiled anyway, replying, "Thank you for your help." Immediately her attention was focused on her new destination, and Tamara never noticed the approving looks of the men silently applauding her determined stance, before she went out the door.

Though it should have been impossible, the cold wind blew even harder now, and she lifted the collar of her wool coat up around her neck, thankful that the pain in her heel was numbed by the low temperatures. Water ran from her icy-wind-assaulted eyes as she struggled to keep them on the buildings so she would not miss the package store described by the barber.

Tamara didn't have to look long; in fact, as soon as she neared the next corner, she spotted a man huddled inside the entranceway of the small package store. The small-boned, dark-skinned man was wearing a long, blue trench coat and holding the short end of a lit cigarette between his wind-whitened fingers.

"Benzo Taylor?" she asked squinting her eyes tightly against the cold.

Without making eye contact, the man flicked the rest of the cigarette to the ground and opened his coat with one quick motion. Tamara's eyes widened once she looked inside the flimsy coat, which was lined with dangling watches, rings, and bracelets.

"Something you want? I got it all right here, baby: gold chains, watches, the finest of fourteen-karat—whatever you want, miss, I got it right here," he said barking out an obviously well-used litany reminiscent of carnies working the small fairs that seemed to spring up overnight in small towns every summer.

"I—I—I didn't come here to buy anything," she said.

He closed the coat and buttoned it with fingers that were stiff and slow-moving from the bitterly frigid air.

"What *do* you want, then?" he asked suspiciously.

Tamara looked at Benzo hopefully. "I'm trying to find my cousin, and the barber in the shop down the street thought you might know his whereabouts."

"*Yo' cousin's whereabouts?* That doggone Dwayne, he shouldn't be sending nobody to me for no dumb stuff like that. Shoot, I'm trying to make some ends—I ain't got no time for the bull."

"Sorry," she said. Then, ignoring Benzo's obvious irritation, she decided to forge ahead, saying, "Maurice Lewis the Third—that's his name. My cousin . . ."

The man spun around quickly and stared at the girl with a distrustful look on his face. "Maurice, huh? You mean Three?"

"Yes . . . Three," she replied expectantly. She couldn't miss the look of recognition in his eye when he heard Maurice's street name, never mind how foreign it sounded coming from her mouth.

Benzo Taylor searched the girl's face for a few moments, and then his own seemed to soften. "Come on, girl, let's go cop a squat somewhere, and I'll tell you about my man Maurice. Can you buy a broke man a cup of coffee at least?"

Two hours later Tamara left the small coffee shop for the second time that day. Jittery, she also had a small headache now and could only step gingerly because the heel of her foot was pulsating far too painfully for her to place all her weight on it. To top it off, it was early-winter dark, and the dimly lit street was silent and empty as she rushed, half-limping, to the corner of Sixtieth Street, to hand the parking attendant her ticket.

"That'll be fifty dollars," he said.

"Fifty dollars? I've only been here for a few hours!" she said with a look of disbelief on her face.

"Ma'am, that's how much it costs to park here—read the sign," the red-nosed white man replied flatly.

That coffee had to be caffeinated, Tamara thought while looking at the man miserably. Her head was throbbing in earnest now, and suddenly she wanted badly to be out of this neighborhood and out of the city itself. With no energy left to barter, Tamara sighed, reached into her purse, and handed three twenties to the waiting attendant.

"Thanks, miss!" he said in voice that was a little less flat, before shooting her a quick facial gesture that resembled a smile.

Tamara didn't have the heart to tell the man she hadn't intended to give him a tip, and so, chalking the other ten up as a loss, without speaking, she hobbled slowly and painfully to her car. Once inside the automobile, gratefully Tamara removed her shoe, careful not to touch her irritated heel again. Cell phone in hand, she dialed Denise Jackson's number.

Mrs. Jackson, as usual, was completely supportive, cheerfully agreeing to pick up Sienna at school so the teen could spend that night with her while Tamara was out of town. Thankfully, Sienna liked the woman, too, and was excited about staying, since she and Sabrina were growing to be closer friends day by day.

The phone rang several times before Sienna's voice at the other end of the line caught her off guard.

"Hello," the girl said.

"Sienna, is that you?" asked Tamara, even though by then she'd recognized her voice.

"Yeah . . . it's me."

Then the girl seemed to catch Tamara's voice, too. "Tamara, is this you? Are you okay?"

To her surprise, Tamara could clearly hear anxiety in the teen's voice. "I am just fine. I was checking on *you.*"

The girl's tone became insolent then. "Ain't *nothin'* wrong with me! You was the one who took off and went up there to Chicago all by yo'self. I'm *from* Chicago, but you must not know *anything* can happen to you there, or maybe you just don't care! Anyway, here's Mrs. J," she said, and without allowing Tamara time to comment, she was gone.

"Tamara?" asked Denise Jackson.

"Yes, Mrs. Jackson, it is me. Thanks again for picking up Sienna for me today. She's behaving a little strangely, though . . . I know Sienna wanted to spend the night with you and Sabrina, but just now she sounded upset with me for some reason." Without waiting for Mrs. Jackson to respond, Tamara added, "I just wanted to give you a quick call, to check on her, and let you know I'm running a little late. I'm still here in Chicago, but I will just be leaving the city in a moment."

"Okay, Tamara." The woman lowered her voice to a whisper. "Baby, Sienna's just upset because she is worried. Let me tell you something, Tamara Britton, this little girl of yours is just crazy 'bout you. Don't you let her fool you if she act like she ain't. She ain't done nothin' but ask me 'bout you ever since she got here."

Mrs. Jackson's statement caught her completely by surprise, and she replied, "Are we sure we're talking about Sienna? *Crazy about me?*" She laughed dryly, "Mrs. Jackson, you must be mistaken."

Denise Jackson laughed throatily to herself then and said, "Oh, I'm not mistaken, baby girl; don't let her fool you. Sienna really does love you. I know about these things now!" Then, abruptly, the woman changed the subject. "Tamara, baby, let me get offa here. I gotta get back in here and finish up dinner, and we will see you when you pick Sienna up tomorrow. Don't forget to give me a quick call tonight, though, to let me know you made it okay, when you get home. I worry about you—you becoming like one of my own, too." She laughed again, "And anyway, that girl of yours ain't gone let anybody get a wink of sleep if you don't!"

"Okay, I'll do that," said Tamara softly.

Denise added, "You be careful on that expressway, too—them city folks drive like fools up there."

Tamara mustered a small laugh even though her head was beginning to thump harder now. "You are right about that, Mrs. Jackson, but I'll be just fine."

Tamara attacked the Dan Ryan Expressway much more confidently on her exit from the city, actually managing to maneuver her way out of Chicago quickly. While driving, she thought peevishly that the long trip certainly had not proved as fruitful as she would have liked. Though she knew Maurice Lewis III better now, Benzo Taylor's information had sent her right back where she started: home to her own neck of the woods to search for him.

Out of the city, on the straightaway toward home, Tamara let her mind wander, and it drifted back to Denise Jackson's words about Sienna. *Crazy about me? That is not possible, is it?* Tamara had just not counted on the girl's growing close to her when she agreed to allow her to live in her home. In fact, the last thing she wanted was emotional ties with anyone, and this whole situation with Sienna was just supposed to be a *temporary* living arrangement.

Tamara knew by now that too much emotion in any form made her uncomfortable, and so she worked hard to keep her own feelings in check, choosing to focus instead on the tangible and practical things that she could control in her life. In fact, just thinking about all these feelings now was causing her to feel dangerously unsettled. Rubbing her aching forehead with one hand, she sighed and forced herself to focus on the highway.

Feeling a cramp threatening in her overtaxed leg, Tamara stretched her sore left foot out before arching the toe downward to stretch it after all the walking she'd done earlier. Distractedly, she pulled the foot back too quickly, though, hitting the leather seat squarely with her raw heel. "Ouch!" she yelled, and the un-expected burning pain caused tears to spring into her eyes.

Jerkily she pulled the Toyota over to the shoulder of the highway and sat there crying like a baby while carefully holding her foot in her lap, until the stinging subsided a bit. While an overreaction to some extent, the burning pain provided Tamara with an ample excuse to release all the pent-up emotions she'd been holding inside. Almost ten minutes later her sobs finally slowed, and though still hiccupping and sniffling, Tamara was finally able to maneuver her midsize car back onto the highway.

What is wrong with me? she thought miserably as she peered down the highway through swollen eyes. Tamara knew the an-swer to that question, though; she knew exactly what was both-ering her. Her life had changed in more ways than she'd bargained for since Sienna moved in with her. And part of her was quite certain that she did not like it at all!

26.

Hostile Takeover

Weeks later, Tamara tiredly turned her car into the circular road leading to her parking lot and sighed with relief that the long day was finally winding down. Right away she noticed lights glowing brightly yellow from each window of her apartment. *That's strange,* she thought, *usually when I come home, Sienna only has the small light on in the front room.* She was used to that familiar, welcoming glow reflecting through the pale yellow front-room curtains.

Her heart caught tightly in her chest, and she tried to quell the panic she felt suddenly as she thought, *What if something's happened to Sienna?* Alarmed now, she hurriedly parked in her assigned space, grabbed her briefcase quickly, opened the door, and stepped out of the car. As soon as she shut the car door and turned to lock it, she could hear the loud thumping of music, much like the unpleasant bass line emanating far too often from teenagers' low-riding cars.

"That can't be music!" she said aloud. The apartment complex was usually very quiet, and the peaceful atmosphere was one of the reasons she had lived here so long.

Quickly she walked toward her apartment, and as she got closer, she realized with shock that the loud thumping sound in the air was coming from her own apartment! In fact, the music sounded like a CD she'd heard Sienna play before. *Oh, no,* she thought before glancing both ways as she hastily twisted the key in the lock, *what can my neighbors be thinking about this?* More anxious than ever to get inside now, she pushed the door, but it did not open. The top deadbolt had been locked from the inside.

Now certain that this was Sienna's handiwork, she fumbled for her deadbolt key with her one free hand as she said under her breath incredulously, "She's locked me out of my apartment!"

Finally, she found the key and, with a trembling hand, put it in the top lock and opened the door.

The same type of loud, lewd rap lyrics that she'd chided the girl about before pumped loudly from the CD player. Tamara rushed into the living room and tossed her briefcase toward the couch. In her haste to get to the stereo, she almost tripped on an unfamiliar platform shoe lying in the middle of the floor, before managing to turn the volume on the pulsating, rhythmic rap all the way down.

"Sienna, where are you?" she said aloud. Gazing around the room now, she noticed an unfamiliar small scattering of shoes and book bags in the front room area.

"I'm gonna see what happened to the music," Tamara heard someone say from the hallway. Oblivious to her presence, the teenager continued, "Probably just this cheap old stereo of yours, Sienna."

As soon as she rounded the corner into the living room, the cute brown-skinned teen's eyes widened once she saw Tamara standing there.

For a moment Tamara glared at the teen steadily before stating crisply, "Sienna does not own this stereo equipment. This is *my* stereo equipment, and for your information, it is *not* cheap. In fact, it is top of the line and was quite costly."

Tamara's clipped words were unplanned, and while it was unlike her to speak out in such a manner, she was not sorry. In fact, she realized that it had actually been quite liberating to do so.

The girl stood there, obviously too shocked to speak; then her lips formed an O, and she half walked, half ran from the room without saying a word. In a few seconds Tamara heard the familiar footfalls of Sienna in the hallway.

Throwing a nonchalant look her way, Sienna tossed out, "Oh, Tam, girl, I didn't know you was home." Then, totally ignoring Tamara's nonplussed expression, she continued, "Why you turn the music down, anyway? We was getting our jam on."

"Girl?" replied Tamara incredulously. "Do not address me like that again, and for your information I turned the music off because it was way, way too loud. I do have neighbors, you know."

The girl postured in a streetwise manner, "Aw, girl—Tamara, I mean—the neighbors prob'ly like this kinda music, too. They know that Ja Rule is the sh—stuff."

Tamara glared at her unbelievingly for several moments and then sighed deeply when she abruptly remembered they were not alone. Where was the girl who fled the room so quickly moments before?

Turning her attention back to Sienna, she admonished her, "Sienna, you know that you are not to have anyone over while I'm at work."

With an insolent tilt of her small head, Sienna shrugged her shoulders and tightened her lips but said nothing.

Tamara crossed her arms meaningfully in front of her and said firmly, "Please tell your friends to leave."

When the girl did not move for a few seconds, she added, "Now!"

Seconds passed, and Sienna turned around, surprisingly mum, and stalked out of the living room. After Sienna stomped loudly through the hallway, Tamara heard her say, "Y'all just get yo' stuff and go on home now. As you can see, *somebody* is home and she don't want *nobody* in *her* house."

She's got her nerve acting as if I'm the one wrong, Tamara thought while busily picking up small odds and ends scattered around the living room. Agitated anew, she ignored them when they came in to pick up their books and backpacks. The teen she'd spoken to earlier stopped in front of her hesitantly and said, "E-e-excuse me, I n-need to get my shoe." Clearly embarrassed, the girl picked up the errant shoe quickly, grabbed her backpack, and turned hurriedly into the hallway.

"I told you we shouldn't have turned it up so loud," she heard the girl say to Sienna.

A young man's voice added, "And at least we could've been listening to some Hezekiah or some other gospel, and she wouldn't have gotten mad about the words."

"Shut up, Terry!" said Sienna loudly. "Bye, Sabrina!"

After hearing the slam of the front door, Tamara glanced up just in time to see Sienna return from escorting her friends out.

Purposely refusing to offer the girl eye contact, Tamara busily wiped invisible debris from under the sofa pillows before fluffing them and then began to stack and arrange the magazines and books that were haphazardly lying around.

"Sienna, you did not answer my question earlier. Why did you have people over here when I was not home? We have spoken about this before, and you are well aware that you are disobeying a household rule when you do so."

The girl scowled back at her and crossed her arms defiantly. "Well, some nights seems like you ain't never comin' home. I get tired of stayin' in this ol' apartment by myself."

Tamara continued to arrange the magazines, moving them to the glass-top table now, as she pointed out calmly, "Sienna, you know that I have to work late sometimes. Don't I always leave you money so that you can order you a pizza or have Chinese delivered?"

"Ain't nobody said you didn't feed me."

Tamara stopped her busy movement for a moment and glanced over at Sienna, still standing by the doorway.

Unexpectedly, she felt a pang of guilt at the thought of the girl spending so many hours alone, and quietly commented, "I'm just not sure what else you would have me do, then, Sienna. I do have a job. I am sorry you're home alone, but you are not to have parties in my home when I am not here."

The girl looked down at her white-socked feet. "Wasn't nobody havin' no party or nothin'. It wasn't nobody but Sabrina and Terry, and we was studying, anyway."

"That was Denise Jackson's Sabrina and Terry? Nonetheless, what I heard when I came in here was not studying. I heard lewd rap music playing, and you disrespected the neighbors and me by having that vulgar music playing loudly."

"I did not have no lewd music playing." The girl paused a minute then and asked, "What's 'lewd' mean anyway?"

Tamara stifled an unexpected smile as she replied, "'Disgusting'—it means 'disgusting,' Sienna."

To Tamara's grateful astonishment, Sienna said nothing. Instead, during the short silence that followed, she seemed to contemplate the situation while leaning in the entranceway, watching one small foot that she was twisting into an indentation she'd made with her toe in the plush carpet.

Deep in their own thoughts, they both jumped at the extraordinarily loud and off-key sound of the telephone's ring disrupting the silence.

Clearly happy for a reprieve from the admonishment she was receiving, Sienna almost ran over to the telephone and hurriedly picked up the receiver.

"Hello," she said, and then widened her eyes expressively at Tamara, who was staring at her with curiosity, wondering just who it was at the other end of the line.

Without saying another word, the girl handed the receiver to her.

"Hello?" Tamara said tentatively, as she leaned back on the couch.

Sienna grabbed the remote before plopping down loudly next to her and clicking on the television.

"Ms. Britton? This is Mr. Perry."

"Mr. Perry?" she repeated, now gazing at Sienna, who was staring back at her mirthfully, wearing a mischievous smile on her gamine face.

"Oh, maybe you don't remember me," the man said in his husky voice. "I am Sienna's African-American History teacher."

"I—I—I remember you," she said haltingly.

In fact, just that quickly his deep-brown, handsome face had appeared quite plainly in her mind. Then, just as effortlessly, she envisioned his wide, white smile, and she was even surprised to recall clearly that his two front teeth were separated by a small gap.

Isaiah's voice shook her back into reality. "Ms. Britton, I'm calling to tell you about Sienna's progress in my class."

"Please don't tell me she's doing anything wrong," she replied, immediately concerned as she stared at the girl. Sienna petulantly folded her arms in front of her and pushed out her lips at Tamara's comment before turning again toward the television, using the remote to turn quickly from channel to channel.

"Oh, no, just the opposite. Actually, since our meeting, Sienna's been doing a great job, and I just wanted you to know!"

"Really?"

"She's completing her homework assignments now, and as I said before, she was always quite active in class participation. In fact, as of now she's pulling a solid B in my class."

"Really?" she asked again, chiding herself instantly for so

foolishly repeating the same word as if that were the extent of her vocabulary. Unbelievably, the same odd thing was happening to Tamara again! Each time she spoke to Isaiah Perry, her brain went blank and her tongue seemed to freeze. Why, the man probably thought she was an imbecile or, at the least, someone with a very small vocabulary!

"Yes, Ms. Britton, really." He paused a moment and then added, "I really don't think you are that shocked. In fact, I'm sure you know Sienna is quite intelligent. Like a lot of young people, she just needs to apply herself."

Tamara looked over at Sienna; the girl's posture was rigid. Tamara seriously doubted that she was as immersed in the television as she appeared to be. Though Sienna was doing her best to act uninterested in the conversation, Tamara was certain that the girl was probably listening to every word.

Isaiah Perry's positive comments about the teen proved so uplifting to Tamara that she finally regained her poise enough to respond wholeheartedly, "I do agree, Mr. Perry. Sienna is a very intelligent young lady. She has the ability to go very far in her life if she chooses to do so."

Out of the corner of her eye, she saw the girl relax, and then, with her eyes on the television set, Sienna pushed herself back on the sofa until she was sitting right next to Tamara.

"Well, Ms. Britton, that's all I wanted. I thought that you had gotten so much bad news on the day that we'd asked you in that I just wanted to call you and give you a positive update."

"Thank you," said Tamara sincerely. She added shyly, "Mr. Perry, I never thanked you for your kindness that day at the conference. I was overwhelmed, and you really helped me. And I really do appreciate you calling me to let me know that she's doing better."

After a moment of silence he replied, "You know, you don't

have to call me Mr. Perry. You're not one of my students. My name is Isaiah."

"Isaiah?"

"Yes, it's Isaiah, just like in the Bible. My mama, God bless her, just loves the Lord *and* His word, and so, quite naturally, she named me after a prophet," he finished with a laugh.

She laughed, too, even though her Bible knowledge was so limited that she was not sure who Isaiah was or exactly what he had accomplished to make him worthy of being written about in such an important book.

"Well, Ms. Britton, I'll let you go. I'm sure you have lots of other things to do."

"Okay, Mr. Pe—Isaiah. Thank you again for calling," she said.

"Oh, anytime, Ms. Britton. Anytime," he said, and Tamara held the receiver to her ear until she heard him hang up.

Until now she had not noticed just how close Sienna's small body was to her own, or how the girl's slightly fuzzy head rested gently on her arm. Tamara felt awkward, but she did not move away even when the girl pulled her arm up and placed herself under it so that she could snuggle her sandy mop even closer.

"You should've told him to call you Tamara," Sienna said in a sleepy, muffled voice.

"Hmmh?"

"When he said call him Isaiah, you should've told him to call you Tamara."

"Oh," she replied. Tamara's emotions were askew now, stirred up by the girl sitting so close to her and by the husky-voiced Isaiah Perry's telephone call.

Unseeingly she stared, expressionless, at the television screen for a few moments while her thoughts drifted into space. By the time she glanced down at Sienna again, the girl had fallen asleep there cuddled close to her, with her small legs tucked tightly under her compact body.

Reflecting once more on Isaiah Perry's unexpected telephone call, Tamara sighed, again considering all the changes that seemed to be taking place in her life so quickly. Wearily she glanced over at Sienna, sleeping comfortably in the crook of her arm, and she thought ruefully, *The truth is, my whole world is changing, turning upside down day by day, and I don't think there's any way to stop it now.*

27.

Lonely Night

After taking only a taste or two of the watery red punch, the girl set the small paper cup on the table next to her and then picked absentmindedly at a brightly colored, confetti-sprinkled Christmas cookie she held in her hand.

The holidays were the most difficult time of the year for her. All around were reminders of the family that she did not have. Though they meant well, this small party organized by hospital personnel, given to help kids locked up in this barren facility to have some semblance of a celebration, only made her feel more forlorn and sad.

Cynthia, the tall, thin African-American woman who worked on her unit, had clearly taken the small, lonely girl under her wing. Often when the nurse came on shift, she stopped by the girl's room to offer her homemade snacks to eat, or books to read, or sometimes just to say a special hello to the girl. Today she handed her a brightly wrapped present, saying, "This is for you, sweetie."

"Thank you," the girl said shyly as she took the small present.

Placing her cookie on the plywood table beside her, the girl carefully opened the package. Inside she found a book titled, *Hind's Feet on High Places,* by Hannah Hurnard.

Cynthia rubbed the girl's shoulder gently. "I know you've had hard times, but this book will help you, honey. It will give you comfort. One day everything is gonna be all right for you. I just know it." Before the girl could see the tears that sprang to her eyes, the nurse quickly turned away.

Her head averted now, Cynthia did not see the long, curious stare that the girl gave her before sliding the book into her pocket to read later.

The girl looked around the room and saw that several of the night nurses and other staff were in the lounge area, keeping the party lively for the small group of patients still here on this special day. Many had gotten to go home for the holidays, but even if she'd earned the right, she had no home to go to. She did feel fortunate to be out of her room, though, since she'd been on lockdown for almost three months now—ever since she'd had the "breakdown" that landed her in this hospital in the first place.

Just then the small, blonde nurse who always told her, "Just call me Evelyn, hon, not Ms. Stevenson, just Evelyn—the other makes me feel too old," turned on the CD player. Cheerfully she said, "Come on, everybody, it's Christmas now—sing!"

"Silent night, Holy night,
All is calm, All is bright . . ."

Cynthia mouthed the words to the Christmas hymn, but her

mind was still on the withdrawn, sad-faced girl. If her schedule had allowed it, Cynthia would have taken her home today and showered her with love and attention. Misty-eyed again, Cynthia glanced over at the small figure sitting alone. The girl was not singing with the rest of them; instead, she pulled the book Cynthia had just given her from her pocket and, ignoring the celebration going on around her, quite deliberately opened it and began to read.

28.

Unexpected Joy

Startled, Tamara sat up quickly, immediately glancing at the clock on her nightstand. Then she realized that it was Christmas morning and she had no reason to be up early, and stretching contentedly, she lay back down in the bed, gratefully closing her eyes again. Between work and Sienna, her schedule was always busy, and this year, before she'd known it, the holiday season had crept in.

With Thanksgiving's arrival, the two of them had been invited to Mrs. Jackson's, where they had feasted with her family. Tamara felt stuffed again now just thinking about all the food that she and Sienna had put away that day.

To her surprise, Isaiah Perry had greeted them at the door when they arrived. Denise Jackson had met the young man at the church when he first moved into town, and had taken him "under her wing," too, since all his relatives lived far away in the South. Isaiah was a frequent visitor to the Jackson home now, often having Sunday dinner with the family and spending holidays with them as well when he was in town.

But on that day, even Tamara's nervousness around Isaiah did not keep her from tasting as much as she could of the scrumptious dishes. In fact, watching with amazement as the two of them ate, he grinned widely and commented, "For two little bitty women, y'all can sure eat a lot!"

Tamara laughed and replied between bites of sweet-potato pie and warm peach cobbler smothered with Cool Whip, "I know I'm stuffing myself, Isaiah. I've just never seen so much food in one place, that's all. I'm gonna have to work out extra hard tomorrow, but I just have to try a little of everything today!"

Sienna had filled her plate again and again, feasting on hickory-smoked turkey and savory dressing, candied sweet potatoes, and buttery, cheesy macaroni. Even after the girl's stomach was clearly stretched to the limit, she tried to eat more, stating exuberantly, "Miss Jackson, this food is goo-ood!"

That was *a good day,* she thought; *Sienna and I had fun together.*

As if the girl knew she was thinking of her, Sienna's voice woke her out of her dream state. "Tamara, it's Christmas; c'mon, wake up!" said the girl excitedly.

"Okay, okay, I'm coming," she said, realizing her short-lived sleep-in time was over. Wiping the sleep from her eyes and pulling on her robe, she followed Sienna down the hallway.

"Sienna, put something on your feet!" she croaked froggily, and the girl obligingly stopped in her room, grabbed some thick white socks, and was back without missing a beat.

"Go on into the living room, Tamara; I'll get your coffee," the girl said, and before Tamara could object, she ran into the kitchen area. Tamara heard the swinging door close behind her with a small thud.

That's strange . . . Something smells wonderful right here, like fresh-cooked breakfast almost. It must be my imagination—I guess I'm hungry, Tamara thought, with a small laugh. She went into the living room and sat down on the sofa. Tucking her legs under her, she stared at the tree while waiting for the girl.

This was Tamara's first time decorating the house for Christmas, and in fact, it was the first time she'd celebrated the holidays in any real way. Each time she bought more festive ornaments, Tamara had told herself it was for the girl, but the truth was, she was enjoying all of it a lot more than she had thought she would. Tamara stared at the tree that they'd trimmed together in lavenders, blues, and beiges, and it was beautiful, glowing with twinkling lights and sparkly ornaments.

"Here's your coffee, Tamara."

"Thank you, Sienna," she replied as she took a sip of the steamy, fragrant coffee. "This is excellent—it tastes different from my regular coffee."

With a happy smile Sienna said, "It's French vanilla; I bought it with my allowance just for today. I knew you'd like it."

"Well, thank you again. Now, you open your gifts."

"Can I?" asked the girl, and her eyes sparkled with excitement.

"Yes, you can. They are for you."

One by one the girl opened each of the presents that Tamara had carefully picked for her over the past several months.

Inside the brightly wrapped boxes were color-washed and sparkly bell-bottoms with matching tops, as well as skirts with sweaters and blouses to match that were suitable for church. After she'd finished with most of the boxes, elatedly the girl opened up a large plastic container that Tamara had filled with inexpensive glittery and colorful makeups and perfumes.

"Oh, Tamara," Sienna said time and time again, alternately gazing at each newly opened package and then back at her again. "Thank you! Thank you!"

Tamara, meanwhile, sipped her French vanilla coffee, watching her tear open each brightly wrapped gift. She was surprised to find that she felt a strange contentment each time the girl showed obvious happiness with her choice.

Finally, only one gift remained, and Sienna struggled to retrieve the huge box that Tamara had placed almost in back of the Christmas tree.

"What is this?" she asked with a curious look.

"Well, you'll have to open it to find out," Tamara replied with a mischievous smile. "It goes along with that present right on top, so open it first."

Sienna grabbed the smaller, square present and pulled the paper off excitedly. Inside was a carefully chosen selection of contemporary gospel CDs, including the girl's favorites that she liked to sing.

"You bought me music!" said the teen exuberantly.

"Yes, Sienna, I bought you music. Now, open the other box."

The girl turned and began to rip away the bright wrapping paper that hid the mysterious package's contents. "Oh, Tamara, it's a karaoke machine!"

"Yes, it is." She put her coffee on the table, and her expression grew serious. "Sienna, you are gifted. You have a magnificent voice, and I think that this machine will enable you to practice singing some of your favorite songs at home."

"Do you really think I can sing?"

"Oh, my, Sienna, yes—I *know* that you can sing." Then, surprising herself, she added, "Perhaps if things continue to go well, we can look into procuring you some voice lessons in the future."

The girl's look became quizzical. "'Procuring'? What does 'procuring' mean?"

Tamara laughed and said, "I'm sorry, hiring you a voice teacher, Sienna—that's what I mean."

Though it hardly seemed possible, the teen's small eyes opened even wider. "Really? You'd hire a teacher to show me how to sing better?"

"I would, because you are just that talented."

"I have something for you, too," said the girl, pulling out a small box from the pocket of her robe.

Tamara looked at her questioningly. "I wasn't expecting anything."

"But it's Christmas, Tamara; everybody s'posed to get something. Open the box, Tamara! C'mon," she urged.

Tamara unwrapped the small gift slowly and then carefully removed the lid of the enclosed box. Inside was a pair of delicate gold earrings with a small diamond sparkling on the wire of each. "Oh, Sienna! These are just beautiful!"

Sienna's lips turned up into a satisfied smile, and she said, "Well, you know that's not a real diamond—it's a ZC or CZ or somethin' like that, the woman said at the store."

"Oh, don't you worry about that! They are quite beautiful, and I'm going to wear them as soon as I get dressed today!" she said.

Almost shyly Sienna added, "I'm glad you like them—you *are* kinda picky, Tamara; you always look so nice and everything, I didn't know what to get you."

"Well, you did good, and see? You know me better, *much* better, than you thought!" Tamara replied with a small smile as she glanced at the delicate earrings once more.

"Don't move, okay? I'll be right back," said Sienna with a mysterious smile on her own small face.

Tamara had little time to wonder just what the girl was up to before she rounded the corner into the living room, carrying a large tray.

"What's this?"

"I got up early and fixed you breakfast this morning. I made you some bacon and some eggs and French toast with syrup, and I poured you orange juice, 'cause that's all we have."

Inexplicably, Tamara's eyes grew instantly misty as she gazed incredulously into the girl's face, which was bright with happiness, "I don't know what to say, Sienna. Thank you."

Sienna made a face and said, "C'mon, Tamara, now, don't get all teary-eyed and stuff, it's just some microwave food, 'cept for the eggs, 'cause that's all I really know how to cook."

Not trusting herself to reply, she nodded dumbly and placed the tray on her lap. Though the food was lukewarm by now, for some reason it was the best breakfast Tamara ever remembered having. When she glanced up at Sienna again, the teen was dancing around the room happily, holding the karaoke microphone in her hand while singing to herself. Despite Tamara's efforts to restrain her feelings, the young girl's joyous expression caused her emotions to overflow. Quickly Tamara wiped away tears and, with a strange happiness filling her heart, finished eating her Christmas breakfast.

29.

Kickin' It

 "I don't know if I should be here," said Tamara, warily glancing around the crowded nightclub.

She had been happy at first that they were finally inside after waiting in line for such a long time, but now she was frustrated to find that they would have to stand again in these cramped, smoky surroundings. The murky darkness of the second-floor room made her a little claustrophobic, and all kinds of people she could not see well were rubbing close to her, which made her even more uncomfortable.

Even in her discomfort, though, Tamara was enjoying the smooth jazz sounds emanating from the superb music system. The loudspeakers accentuated the smooth instrumentals, and the rhythmic tinkling of the keyboards made her feel as if bubbles of music were exploding melodically inside her body.

"Tam, you needed this. That's why we *made* you come tonight. It's the perfect time, with the holidays and all, to get you out of the house, girl!" said Lynnette before turning to smile flirtatiously at a tall, well-dressed man who was squeezing by her.

Tamara looked at her friend uncertainly. "I don't know, Lynn . . . I've never been to a place like this before. Are you *sure* that I'm dressed okay?"

Lynnette turned to her friend and said, "Girl, you looking

good! Shoot! You was *hurtin'* Jay-Jay when you walked out of the house, 'cause I don't think he's never seen you in a dress before!"

"What do you mean, hurting him?" Tamara asked quizzically.

"Girl, in other words, I had to help that brotha put his eyes back in his head," Lynnette answered with a laugh. "He turned to me with his eyes all big and said, 'Tam's been hiding legs like those under pants all this time?'"

Tamara ducked her head, hiding a small, nervous smile as she felt her cheeks begin to burn. She wasn't really hiding her legs; she just rarely wore skirts, because pants seemed more comfortable to her, and then again, perhaps it was because she wasn't certain whether she *wanted* men to look at her legs at all.

"Whew! There's lots of folks here!" said Lynnette as she glanced around the crowded room. "I sure hope Jayson is scouting us a spot to sit down at while he's out getting our drinks, 'cause, girl, as they say, 'the joint is jumping tonight,' but these shoes were not meant for standing up long," she whispered to Tamara as she pointed to her feet.

Tamara looked at her friend's pointy-toed, ankle-strapped black spiked heels and nodded in agreement. Lynnette always dressed well, and tonight she wore a tight, short black leather mini with a black leopard print silk shirt. Casually she held a three-quarter-length matching jacket of the same soft lamb leather over her shoulder with a silver-jeweled hand. Her chunky silver necklace with earrings to match completed the outfit.

Tamara's own style was much less flashy and more understated. A deep burgundy suede stretch skirt skimmed her lower body closely, barely hinting at her curves and stopping right above her knee. The skirt was topped with a silky black stretch shirt that showed off her small waist and defined stomach, and she wore classic-styled black sling-backed alligator pumps. Although Tamara worked her treadmill more for the health benefits than anything else, her daily workouts were apparent tonight in the tautness of her toned body.

Leaning over the balcony railing, she observed with interest the people on the lower level as they interacted animatedly with one another. Most held drinks in their hands, and many seemed to know each other, while others stood in corners or sat at tables alone or with partners. A few sat stiffly erect, and their rigid posture made them appear to be as uncomfortable in this environment as she.

"Our drinks are here," said Lynnette from behind her.

Jayson had returned from the bar, balancing three drinks in both hands while maneuvering his tall, lithe frame through the crowd.

"Follow me," he said once they each had their own drink in hand.

Undeniably anxious now, Tamara breathed shallowly, trying not to lose sight of Lynnette and Jayson as they made their way through the throng of people. A couple of times she managed to toss a nervous smile toward a man in response to his appreciative comment to her as she passed by. Finally, Jay stopped at a table where a smiling young woman was already sitting.

"Thank you, baby," said Jayson, giving the girl a lingering gaze before winking flirtatiously and smiling her way with a flash of his dimples. Demonstratively he blew a small kiss at the girl and said, "I'll come get you for a dance in a minute, sweetheart."

"Okay, don't you forget me, now," said the girl, flirting herself now, tossing her long microbraids back and flashing her own large white smile in response.

Jayson turned to watch her walk away, sucked in a breath of air, and said, "Oooh, did you see that onion?"

Lynnette gave Jayson an annoyed glance and said, "Boy, sit

down. We don't care nothin' about that girl's 'onion', and you shouldn't either, with as many of them girls be tryin' to bring you drama."

"Okay, Lynnette, but, uh, don't you worry 'bout my drama," said Jayson flippantly as he motioned for Tamara to slide into the maroon leather booth before him.

Lynnette shook her head disgustedly as she watched him give an unsuspecting Tamara a thorough once-over as she sat down in the booth.

"See, that's just what I'm talking about!"

"What?" he asked, wearing an innocent look.

"Boy, you just a dog, that's all," she said through tightened lips.

"Well, if I'm a dog, then what does that make you, *a doggette*?" he asked with a sly smile. "You gotta lot of drama in your own life, don't you, girl?"

Unable to deny that her own relationships could get a bit complicated at times, Lynnette laughed, then added sheepishly, "Okay, you got me. I guess, I'll just shut up for now, anyway."

By now Tamara was used to the two of them sniping at each other, and she joined Lynnette's laughter, too, happy to be sitting down, and glad that the two of them had called at least a short-lived truce.

Sipping their drinks, the three of them listened appreciatively to the mellow sounds of keyboardist Kevin Toney. Wearing a look of intent curiosity, Tamara bobbed her head a little to the music while noting the fancy, smooth steps of some of the couples who were moving together on the floor. These dancers seemed to be totally in tune with each nuance of the music. Their feet would slide smoothly; then the man would allow the woman to turn and spin until they came back together in time with the music.

She elbowed Jayson and asked inquisitively, "What is that they're doing out there?"

"You mean the dancing?"

"Yes, I've never seen anything like that."

He widened his eyes emphatically and stroked his goatee as he looked at her disbelievingly. "Girl, you really haven't been anywhere. We gots to get you out more often. Back in the day they called that 'fast dancin'—we call it steppin' now. Now that I think about it, I suppose it's really a traditional dance of sorts in the African-American community."

She turned and smiled at him brightly, noticing now that the alcoholic drink was making her feel quite relaxed. "I like that, the way that they are moving together right with the music, and it's neat how everybody does it a bit differently, I see."

"You want to try it?"

"Oh, I don't know, Jay," she said skeptically.

Lynnette overheard the conversation and encouragingly prodded, "Girl, go 'head. This night is for you, Tamara. Girl, you been under some serious stress with little Miss Sienna and all, and it's the holidays, too! You really could stand to loosen up, Tam."

Jayson smiled again and said, "C'mon, Tam, ain't nothin' but a party."

"But, what about you Lynnette? I don't want to leave you sitting here all alone," replied Tamara, sipping the sweet-flavored drink again.

Lynnette, waving her hand nonchalantly at Tamara, glanced around the crowded club, batting her large eyes. "Don't you worry 'bout me, girl. I'm gonna have me another sip or two of this drink, and then I'll find someone to save our table and I'm gonna get on the floor and shake my booty, too . . . Shoot, y'all know I'm lookin' too fine to sit down all night."

"Lynn, you are lookin' good—that is, except for that extremely big head you got," Jayson commented facetiously with a huge smile before taking a deep drink from his own glass.

With a toss of her hair, Lynnette replied saucily, "I bet you one thang: my head ain't too big for *somebody* in this club, and this four-hundred-dollar leather suit right here ain't going to waste tonight."

Just then a new tune came over the speakers, and Jayson reached over, grabbing Tamara's hand. Pulling her up from the table, he left her no room to refuse.

"Girl, c'mon, this is my man, Paul Taylor, on the horn now; we gotta get up here and move."

At first she felt awkward as she moved self-consciously on the dance floor, unable to follow Jayson as he tried to show her the steps.

Jayson bent over then and whispered into her ear, "Tam . . . just relax. Listen to the music and let it flow through your body."

Tamara focused on the music, and suddenly the melodious sounds of the saxophone seemed to envelop her body, and she allowed herself to glide with the beat of the song. Soon the two of them were stepping in synch, until Jayson would spin her in concert with the music, back and forth, and then they would come back together in unison again.

After several minutes of their smooth movements, Tamara could see other couples watching them appreciatively from the edge of her vision, and their silent approval assured her that she must be doing it right. Time seemed to stop moving as they swirled and danced, and when the music finally ended, Tamara looked up at Jayson with bright, shining eyes.

"You like?" he asked with a smile on his face.

Her own deep dimples matched his as she smiled widely and said, "Yes, I liked it, Jay! Thank you! It was so much fun!"

At that moment, Tamara's heart was beating fast inside her

chest, leaving her wildly exhilarated. Though she'd said it was "fun," that word could not come close to adequately describing the wonderfully free feeling she'd experienced when the two of them were whirling and gliding in harmony to the wailing saxophone moments ago.

30.

Love Lessons

 "I'll meet you here in the front when your rehearsal is over, Sienna," Tamara told the girl.

"Guess what, Tamara? Tonight I get to practice for my first solo!" the girl tossed over her shoulder as she half walked, half skipped down the corridor toward the church auditorium.

As Tamara watched her walk away so obviously delighted, she quietly wished that she had shared the girl's eagerness to be part of the church. Entirely on her own, Sienna had walked in front of the entire congregation and joined the church the second time they came together, and soon after, she became a member of the mass choir. The teen never missed rehearsals or Sunday service, riding there with Mrs. Jackson on the days that Tamara did not go herself. Sienna had obviously been waiting impatiently for her to arrive home from work that evening, because as soon as Tamara turned the car into the driveway, she came running out of the house and hopped into the car.

Tamara, however; was still much less enthusiastic and only

169

agreed grudgingly to attend Bible study class this evening at Denise Jackson's prodding, once Denise discovered that Tamara was bringing Sienna to choir rehearsal anyway.

Oh, well, I'm here now, she thought with a huge sigh, *and Mrs. Jackson is right that attending church together is a great way for Sienna and me to spend some quality time together . . . well, sorta together anyway. At least I won't have to worry about having to talk to Isaiah Perry tonight, since he should be rehearsing with the choir, too,* she thought gratefully, comforted in the knowledge that they were practicing in the back auditorium. Entering the sanctuary, she was surprised to see Denise Jackson there. Tamara patted her shoulder as she slid into the pew next to her.

"Oh, I'm so glad you came, baby girl," said the woman as she hugged her enthusiastically.

Tamara smiled back at the woman, glad to feel some of her tenseness fade away at the sight of her friend. She wondered why Mrs. Jackson was not at choir rehearsal with Sienna, but before she got the chance to question the woman about her unexpected presence at Bible study class, Tamara heard a familiar voice beside her.

"Why, Ms. Britton, it's so nice to see you here tonight."

It can't be, she thought. *He's not supposed to be out here with us right now.* But sure enough, when she turned, she was gazing directly into the smiling eyes of Isaiah Perry.

Tamara attempted to sound calm and collected but instead revealed her anxiety when she stammered, "Uh, oh, hello, Isaiah. I—I brought Sienna to sing in the choir tonight, and Mrs. Jackson invited me to stay for B-Bible study."

"And I'm glad she did," he responded smoothly in the husky voice she'd grown to recognize.

Sienna is right, she thought incredulously. This time there was no denying the interest apparent in the long, lingering glance he'd given her, and she turned from him quickly to hide her reddening face.

Denise Jackson bumped her with her shoulder gently, and when Tamara quickly glanced at her, the woman giggled conspiratorially.

Showing no indication that he'd noticed her embarrassment, Isaiah Perry continued, "You know what? Now I'm really glad our choir practice isn't until Thursday night. Tonight only the soloists are rehearsing; the rest of us get a chance to hear Pastor's Bible study. So I guess this is my lucky night!"

Disheartened, Tamara discovered that once again she was unable to comment. Her tongue had grown thick and heavy, her brain was full of fuzz, and right now she could come up with nothing better to say than a lame "Uh-huh."

Relieved for the reprieve from Isaiah, she looked up at Pastor Walker gratefully when he cleared his throat into the microphone, announcing the beginning of the night's study session. The minister wore his usual wide smile as he looked at those assembled and said in his baritone voice, "Let's get started. We all know that when I get going, I can go on for a while, and I wouldn't want to keep you too late tonight."

There was an "amen" or two in response to his self-deprecating comment, followed by a peppering of laughter from the congregation.

"On your feet, please. Now, let us pray."

At the conclusion of the prayer, they were all seated, and Minister Walker said robustly, "Church, tonight we are going to continue our study about love. We're going to delve deeper into how we can learn to walk in love. After all, church, love *is* why we are all here today. It is the love that God had for us that caused Him to give His son in sacrifice for all of our sins, and it was love that gave Jesus the heart and will to do it."

He took off his glasses, rubbed his eyes, and held them in his hand for a moment before replacing them on his face. The pastor's deep voice grew softer as he said, "I am aware that many, many clergy focus on teaching about the wrath of God and why we should fear Him, and I agree—we should have a reverent fear of the Lord. But I want my members to know about His love, because in my book, and even more importantly, in *His* book, it is *only* love that can change anything or anybody."

"Yes," said Denise Jackson as she nodded her head fervently in agreement.

Tamara's attention was riveted on the pastor. Even though again the subject of his text was love, and though she did not really want to hear it, still she could not seem to turn away.

The Reverend Walker continued, "Many times we listen to songs about love. I think you'll agree with me that it is *love* that the songwriters *love* to write about, isn't it? 'Love to Love You,' 'Can't Get Enough of Your Love,' 'Your Sweet Love,' and I could go on and on."

Again he took off his glasses and held them in his hand as he gestured, "They all talk about love affairs, spending time with the one you love, and y'all know all that ooh, baby, baby stuff; but they all miss one important fact about love. There is *only one* love affair that really can change our lives and our hearts, and that is the one that we have with our Lord Jesus!"

"Amen," said several people.

Minister Walker slipped his glasses back on and wiped his face with his handkerchief while saying in a voice vibrant with emotion, "Oh, my people, let us not forget that *it was Jesus* who stood in the gap for *each* of us; *it was sweet Jesus* who gave His own life, because it was the will of His Father . . . *It was Jesus* who was humiliated and scorned by His own people so that *we* could live and live more abundantly."

Opening his Bible then, he said, "Let's turn to First Corinthians, chapter thirteen. It is here that we will find our guide on how to love."

Tamara fumbled through her brand-new Bible that she had

bought just yesterday, especially for tonight's class. Isaiah Perry's rugged brown hand appeared then, and he gently turned the pages to the left until she was at the correct chapter. He pointed to the correct passage, and she put her finger there so that she could follow along with Minister Walker:

> If I speak in the tongues of mortals and of angels, but do not have love, I am but a noisy gong or a clanging cymbal. And if I have prophetic powers, and understand all mysteries and all knowledge, and if I have all faith, so as to move mountains, but do not have love, I am nothing. If I give away all my possessions, and if I hand over my body so that I may boast, but do not have love, I gain nothing.

Pastor Walker closed the book, took out his white handkerchief, and wiped his brow, which was beaded with sweat now. He looked at them all for a long moment.

"Do you know, church, how poignant that is? How *profound*?"

The pastor enunciated each word. "If I speak in tongues, I am *nothing* without love, if I can prophesy, I am *nothing* without love, and if I have all faith—enough to move mountains—I am still *nothing without love*. Even if I give away all that I have and sacrifice my own body, I am *nothing* without love."

"Amen," said many members of the congregation.

"Church, I am *nothing* without *love. Nothing*."

He opened the Bible again and said, "And, now that we know we are nothing without love, let's see what it takes to love, *to really love*."

"Let's read together . . . Begin with verse four."

Tamara read silently as she followed along with her slim finger:

> Love is patient; love is kind; love is not envious or boastful or arrogant or rude. It does not insist on its own way; it is not irritable or resentful; it does not rejoice in wrongdoing, but rejoices in the truth. It bears all things, believes all things, hopes all things, endures all things.

In a quiet voice, the minister said, "Oh, church, think about that. My, my, my, have *we* ever really *loved like that*? Paul wrote about the kind of love that Jesus showed us. Jesus didn't try to have His way, now, did He? If He had, He would not have been crucified, He did not necessarily *want* to die, but He sacrificed *Himself* for us, anyway. Follow with me for a moment, church. Hold your place there, but turn for a moment to Matthew twenty-six: thirty-nine."

Again, with the assistance of Isaiah, she found the place and read to herself with the pastor:

Going a little further, he fell with his face to the ground and prayed, "My Father, if it is possible, may this cup be taken from me. Yet not as I will, but as you will."

"In other words, church, Jesus asked His Father God to 'take the cup' of His sacrifice from Him, but then He said, 'Father, if it is *Your will* I will do it,' and why, church? Because He loved His Father, He submitted His will and His flesh . . . because He loved His Father and He loved us enough to give up His own life for us."

Tamara looked at Minister Walker; she was feeling a bit dazed by the magnitude of the sacrifice that Jesus made, giving up His *life* for people just like her.

"Now, let's go back to our description of love, church. Remember what we just read? Could *you* love like that? Could you sacrifice anything that you really cared about? Could you give up your *life*? The truth is, most of us don't even want to give up watching our favorite television show for any period of time, or let go of eating our favorite food for a while, but Jesus *gave His life* for us."

Tamara couldn't help but think of how often she was resentful about Sienna's intrusion into her life. It wasn't as if she even loved the girl or anything like that, yet she felt ashamed of being so selfish at this moment.

"Okay, church, let's continue to read together. Back to First Corinthians, chapter thirteen, verse eight now."

This time Tamara whispered the words to herself as she read along with the Pastor:

> Love never ends. But as for prophesies, they will come to an end; as for tongues, they will cease; as for knowledge, it will come to an end. For we know now only in part, and we prophesy only in part; but when the complete comes, the partial will come to an end.

Minister Walker's voice thundered through the walls of the sanctuary now: "Everything that we know will come to an end, *except for love. Love is Jesus, Love is God,* and *all* else that we understand in this world *will cease to be.*"

She watched him closely, and his voice fell again. "People talk about heaven, but the truth is, we don't know what it will be like then, because we only know in part now, but we know that God will be there, and *His love* for us will be there, too. And, church, that's all that matters."

"Preach, Pastor!" said one of the elder deacons.

"Verse eleven:"

> When I was a child, I spoke like a child, I thought like a child, I reasoned like a child; when I became an adult, I put an end to childish ways. For now we see in a mirror dimly, but then we will see face to face. Now I know only in part; then I will know fully, even as I have been fully known. And now faith, hope and love abide, these three; and the greatest of these is love.

Minister Walker closed his Bible, and his eyes swept over the small congregation. "Church, I'm telling you tonight, *now* is the time for us to grow up. Many of us have been Christians for a long time, yet we still have not put our youthful, immature ways behind us. Now is the time to give up these childish, selfish ways and begin to *Love in earnest. Love, for real!* Church, is it too much to ask of us, to love like Jesus loved us? I don't think so; after all, every day *we* benefit from Jesus' sacrifice for us."

Tamara gazed at the minister questioningly while he explained.

"Whether we know it or not, every, every day, each one of us can choose to walk in the light and experience God's love, and that is *only* because Jesus died so that we might live. Why? Because it was only after *He* sacrificed *His* life for us that God gave each of us His Holy Spirit inside, and whenever *we* choose, now, *we* can call on that Spirit and It will awaken within us."

The minister began to preach now, "Church, once that Spirit truly awakens, then God becomes the master of our lives, and just like Jesus, no longer will we *be able* to live how we want to and do what *we* want to do; instead we will find ourselves doing things, good things, without even understanding why."

"Preach, Pastor," said the elder again, now on his feet, listening to the minister.

"Oh, church, hear me now. It is time for us to begin to *walk in love,* every day, just like Jesus did for us. I like to call it *love walkin'* . . . whew! *Love walkin'!* It makes you feel *good* when you *walk in love,* and it makes you walk tall when you *walk in love,* and though some people think you're weak when you're in love, it really makes you strong when you can *walk in love . . . love walkin'! Love walkin'!*"

"All right, now . . . I'm walkin' with you, Pastor," said Denise Jackson as she stood up and began to rock from side to side with her Bible under her arm.

The Reverend Walker was preaching in earnest now. "Church, your fears can't stop you when you *walkin' in love,* and your sadness can't keep you cryin' when you *walkin' in love,* and your problems can't make you lose your joy when you *walkin' in love* . . . When you leave here tonight, let's do some *love walkin',* church, just like Jesus . . . *love walkin'!*"

Tamara stood up then along with the rest of the congregation. Pastor Walker's voice lowered as he looked at them all.

"Know that God's love for us is ever-flowing, never-ceasing, all encompassing, church. In First Timothy chapter one, verse fourteen, Paul writes 'And the grace of our Lord was exceeding abundant with faith and love which is in Jesus Christ.'" Pastor Walker added, "And in John, fourteen-one Jesus himself says to his disciples as the hour of his death drew near: 'In my Father's house are many mansions, or rooms; if it were not so, I would have told you. I go to prepare a place for you.'

"The Lord's love is unconditional, and so, church, we never have to worry about being left on the outside when it comes to our Father. Unlike Mary and Joseph when she was getting ready to birth Jesus Christ and could not find a place to lay her head, there's *always* a room in the inn for us! And what's more, God has promised us that we never have to sit in the back or settle for a place in the 'cheap seats'! There's *good* room always available with Our Father God!

"His heart is open to us, and there is always plenty room for us there—*plenty good room*—and whether we know it or not, just like our Father, once we learn to trust Him and to walk in His love, we discover that we, too, have plenty good room in our own hearts—plenty good room to love others, just as we are loved by Him!"

All of a sudden, Minister Walker opened his mouth and, in his rich, deep baritone, began to sing:

"There's plenty good room,
plenty good room in ma Father's Kingdom,
plenty good room, plenty good room
—just choose your seat and sit down."

"C'mon, church," he said, "You know the words to this old song. This is what our ancestors used to sing back when we were still in bondage. They knew that God's love made them free, even in slavery, to love and be loved in return."

Tamara closed her eyes and held her Bible close as she found her feelings again going awry in the sanctuary. The lyrics to the old Negro spiritual touched her heart, and her throat was so tight she could not swallow. Her eyes were wet with unshed tears. Isaiah Perry's close proximity was forgotten as Tamara listened to them singing and wrapped her arms around her body, wiping the reappearing tears away with one finger.

Tamara's feelings were intensifying each time she attended a church service, and this escalating emotion represented a loss of control that was almost overwhelming to her. Tonight it was proving especially difficult for her to maintain control. Standing there, struggling to regain her equilibrium, all Tamara could do was hug herself as she gently rocked back and forth, listening to the voices' singing that seemed to fill her insides.

31.

Night Flight

The girl slept fitfully, tossing and turning to and fro as she moaned and shook her head violently—obviously frightened of an unknown presence that only she was aware of.

Suddenly, her eyes popped open wide. Sitting upright quickly, she began to look from side to side and all around the room, as if she truly expected to see, hiding in the shadow, some unknown person or entity that would jump from under the bed or spring malevolently out of a closet.

"It was only a dream," she said aloud. "The same old dream."

It had been so long ago, yet it seemed like only yesterday that it happened, and still she couldn't get it out of her head. Now, as she sat fully awake, that day again came to her mind. She'd been playing in her new bedroom. Though not exactly like the ones she read about in her storybooks, she loved the room because it was bright and colorful, and most important, it was all hers, and that made it perfect.

The first night the girl moved into her new home, she was very frightened. But then, that was mostly because all of it had happened so quickly. One minute she was living with Wilma, and the next she was not.

Wilma's house was the fifth place she lived, and what she remembered most about Wilma was that she had a big, soft chest and she smelled powdery whenever she hugged her close. She liked how Wilma called her "baby," and the woman was mostly nice to her. The only bad part about living with Wilma, though, was that she was home by herself lots of the time.

Wilma's boy, Victor, was sixteen, and he didn't come home till late at night lots of the time. She didn't like him that much anyway, so it was okay with her that he wasn't there. But Wilma was gone a lot of the time, too, and when she'd come home from school that early-winter day, the woman was gone again, and for some reason it was dark in the house.

For a long time she sat there quietly in the dark, waiting for Wilma to come back, but after a while she grew tired of just sitting there waiting, and so she made a plan. Using all her strength, she pulled the big kitchen chair over to the wall. Carefully she stood on it, struggling to balance herself so that the wobbly metal legs would not bend or twist, sending her plummeting hard to the floor. With some maneuvering she was finally able to turn on the light switch, but nothing happened. Uncomprehending, she flipped the switch over and over, on and off, and still nothing happened. The lights in the house just weren't working for some reason.

Cautiously she got down from the chair and, after pulling it back to its place, ran and jumped into Wilma's bed and pulled the covers over her head. It was cold in the house now, and she felt lots warmer lying there under the blankets in the spot that Wilma slept in. She'd fallen asleep just like that, too, curled up in a tight ball lying on Wilma's side of the bed.

Her memory grew fuzzy then; she was drifting in and out of sleep after that and was unsure how much of her memory was real and how much was just a dream. She did remember clearly that a tall man picked her right up out of the bed, and even through the blurriness that she felt in her head, she heard him say, "Her little legs are freezing . . . There's no telling how long this child has been here alone."

The next time she awakened, she was here at this house, and a pretty brown-skinned woman was looking at her with concern in her eyes. In this house she was the only child they had, and they'd given her a brand-new doll, bought her new clothes, and given her a nice room to live in.

"Where's Wilma?" she'd asked over and over, but no one had told her one thing. One night when they thought she was long asleep, the girl overheard the woman and her husband talking in the front room, and she knew now that Wilma was gone to jail.

"She ain't nothin' but a crack addict, no way—they'll sell their mama for a hit," she heard the husband say then. The girl wasn't exactly sure what "crack" was, but she did understand that she would not be seeing Wilma anytime soon.

Soon afterward the lady told her, "I'm your new mama," with a big smile on her face. And even though she smiled mutely and ducked her head low, inside she wondered, how could that be so, since she already had a "real" mama somewhere, and she couldn't really have two, could she?

For a while everything was going really well for her in her new home. The house was always clean, and there was lots of food to eat. Her new mama took her shopping, and she even got her hair done at a beauty shop and everything. They went to church on Sunday, and she liked the music, and the people there acted happy, and that made her feel good, too.

The lady's husband was William, and he was a deacon at the church. Whenever the minister was preaching his sermon, she noticed it was almost always William who was the first one to say, "Amen," or "Preach it, Reverend." "He just loves the Lord," his wife said all the time, and the girl believed it, too, 'cause he went to church even when they didn't go, and that was almost every day, it seemed.

Nonetheless, there was still something about him that made her uncomfortable. For one thing, even though he always seemed extra happy when he talked to her, especially when her new mama was around, too, his smile looked scary to her. Sometimes she'd catch him staring at her, and when he noticed her looking at him, too, he grinned even more widely than usual. Quickly she'd turn her head with that feeling in the pit of her stomach that she used to get whenever she'd come home from school and discover that Wilma was gone again and she was alone.

Still, she liked it there, and she just tried her best to avoid William and his evil smile. One night she was sitting in the tub, slippery and wet with warm, fragrant bubbles, and he just walked right into the bathroom without knocking. He stood there at the door, watching her for a long moment, wearing that smile she hated, and then he turned around without saying a word and left, closing the door behind him.

With her heart thumping almost painfully in her small chest, the girl jumped out of the tub without even washing herself; she dressed, hurried to her room, and curled into a tight ball underneath her own covers. As days and weeks passed, finally the bathtub incident seemed to fade so far away into her memory that she no longer knew if it had really happened or whether it was something she just imagined.

Slowly she began to relax again, and she even let herself begin to think of them as her real family. The woman seemed truly happy to be her mother, and she was glad to be the daughter of someone who wanted to be a mother—at least until that last day.

She'd been playing with her doll, just like always, with her back turned to the doorway.

"You like that doll," William said from behind her, and now, since she was quite comfortable with him, she didn't even turn to look at him when she answered, "Yes."

Then she heard her twin-size bed creak under his weight as he sat down behind her. From under her eyelashes she glanced apprehensively to the side and saw his brown wing-tip shoes pointing forward from where he now sat on her bed.

"Come here and sit with me," he said as he patted the bed by him.

Pushing away her rising discomfort with his presence, slowly the girl had gotten up and leaned on the bed by him, but before she knew what was happening he'd swooped her up into his lap. Although she was eight years old, she was still scared. Physically she was very small, and she sat suspended in his large lap with her small legs swinging high up off the floor.

Within seconds William moved his hand into her underpants, and she felt his finger touch her private parts. It happened so very quickly that the girl did not have time to comprehend exactly what he was doing until he'd already done it.

"You like that, don't you?" he whispered, with a strange look on his face.

Without waiting for an answer, he laid her on the bed, and

she instantly closed her eyes, too scared now to see what was going to happen next. Suddenly she felt something burning hot inside her, but before she could scream in pain, he'd placed his large hand tightly over her mouth.

"Shhh! We don't want nobody to hear us, gal," he grunted, breathing heavily.

The girl felt the burning, jabbing pain a few more times, and then, after a last loud grunt, he got up.

"You might want to go to the bathroom," he said to her over his shoulder.

Then he walked from the room as if nothing had happened and left her lying there alone on the bed. Limping into the bathroom, the girl cleaned herself off as she cried, wincing from the searing pain that came alive anew with each touch.

Back in the room she'd loved only moments earlier, she lay across the bed, numb and frightened. Resignedly, she understood clearly now that this was not her home, and they were not her mother and father. Later, when the woman came home from work, she'd feigned sleep when she heard the woman call her name softly again and again.

She knew there was nothing she could say to her about what had happened earlier that night. After all, he was her husband, and she was not her daughter.

The girl waited until the house was quiet, and although still hurting, she clothed herself. Then, gathering a few things and putting them into a small plastic grocery bag, she tiptoed through the living room and right out the front door.

Once outside, she closed the door behind her and, forgetting all about the pain, with the wind in her face, ran just as fast as her small legs would carry her.

32.

Alone, Interrupted

Careful not to dampen the carpet, Tamara slid her wet shoes off one by one before she stepped through the door. Then she shook off her drenched trench coat and, with her wet things in one hand, tipped on uncomfortably moist toes through the hallway till she reached her bedroom. Once in her room, she put the soaked coat on a hanger and carried it along with the shoes back into the small storage area to let them dry.

Then she retrieved a fluffy white towel from the closet and began to dry her wet hair. *Of course it is just my luck it would rain today, and my umbrella is in my office, sitting in the corner of my cubby by my desk,* she thought irritably. Tamara went back into her room and pulled on a soft old pair of jogging pants and a cotton T-shirt, along with some thick white socks that felt wonderfully warm on her damp feet.

She sighed appreciatively, thinking, *At least I'm home . . . maybe I can warm up now.* Tamara had been out of the office doing fieldwork most of this gray and damp day, and now she was absolutely chilled to the bone.

Even though she'd been used to solitude, the town house seemed eerily empty now without Sienna. In fact, each time the girl was gone, Tamara realized how accustomed she'd gotten to Sienna's presence in her home, and without her the house was just too quiet and almost bereft of life and movement.

"I really should enjoy this little time I have to myself," she

184

said aloud with a slight smile, but even as she spoke, she could not help but notice the solitary echo of her voice in the quiet house. With a loud sigh, Tamara wrapped the towel around her head, turban-style, and went into the kitchen to make a salad for dinner.

Sienna was at choir rehearsal, and actually, Tamara could have met her there and attended Bible study herself. But, she had opted out tonight. The minister's lessons were trying enough for her when she was at her best, and as tired and vulnerable as she felt, Tamara was just not certain she could handle more talk about love from Pastor Walker tonight. Each time she attended the church, she became certain that one day she would not be able to hold down the strange quickening she felt in the pit of her stomach, and the thought of losing control like that made her nervous and uncomfortable.

Anyway, her own day had been really busy. She'd been booked back-to-back with home visits and appointments, and then she facilitated an evening training session for a new group of foster parents. While Sienna would miss her being there, the teen truly enjoyed being a part of the choir, and the members were happy to have her involved in the ensemble, especially since it quickly became quite clear to them that Sienna could actually sing. Each time Tamara heard the girl sing, she was newly impressed. Sienna's talent was genuine and quite extraordinary; with no training at all, she possessed a powerful voice with a full range of tone and depth.

Bushed from the day, Tamara decided to skip the salad and instead made herself a quick peanut butter and jelly sandwich, grabbed a napkin and a bottle of water from the refrigerator, and flopped down lazily on the couch in the living room. Catlike, she curled her legs up under her and, with remote in hand, snuggled back cozily in the corner of the sofa to watch the news while she waited for Sienna. Denise Jackson had agreed to bring the girl home when the rehearsal was over, and she was free to relax until then.

She turned up the television, took a big bite of her peanut butter and jelly sandwich, and was chewing contentedly when she heard a noise behind her. Instantly alarmed, Tamara laid the sandwich on the cocktail table and spun around toward the doorway just in time to see Sienna round the corner into the living room, followed closely by Isaiah Perry!

"I'm back!" said Sienna loudly.

"I see," managed Tamara, even though her mouth was still full of food. She looked at the girl quizzically.

"Mr. Perry gave me a ride home," said the girl, wearing the sly smile that Tamara was really beginning to dislike. She added, "Mrs. Jackson said that it would be all right because he don't live far from us at all, Tamara."

Tamara was struggling to swallow the peanut butter, which now seemed very dry, and her suddenly tight throat was protesting. With a strained look, she forced the lump down and then said hoarsely, "That was nice of Mr. Perry."

Tamara was so mortified, she literally wanted to disappear at that moment, and adding to her distress, Isaiah Perry stood behind Sienna now, smiling as if he was finding great humor in her suffering.

Tamara was mistaken in her estimation of him, though, because Isaiah was simply enjoying looking at Tamara right then. The woman's face was glowing, and she looked especially attractive to him sitting there on the sofa, obviously embarrassed, with a smidgen of jelly smeared on her top lip. Stepping out of the entranceway, he said to Tamara teasingly, "Why, thank you, Ms. Britton. We missed you tonight at Bible study."

Tamara swallowed a quick drink of water before attempting to clear her raspy throat once more. "Y-y-you did?"

"We did. Only our soloists were rehearsing again this

186

evening, and so many of us got to attend the lesson again tonight. I was disappointed when Sister Jackson told me that you would not be coming tonight. You missed an excellent study. Pastor Walker really took us deeper into the concept of God's Love."

"He did?" she asked. Inwardly she winced with frustration at her continuing inability to communicate with Isaiah. It was as though her vocabulary consisted of only one- or two-word sentences. Just as before, Tamara's brain seemed suddenly vacuous; there were no words of expression available, no well thought-out concepts in her memory for her to discuss, no funny witticisms for her to draw on—nothing for her to make any conversation of merit at all.

The ensuing silence lasted only a moment, though, because when Sienna looked from one adult to the other and sensed their obvious discomfort, she began to chatter in a clear attempt to keep the conversation flowing.

She smiled at them both and said brightly, "Well, I know I was likin' choir practice tonight. Guess what, Tamara?"

"What, Sienna?" she managed to croak weakly.

The girl pushed out her small chest and smiled widely. "I'm singing a solo on Sunday."

Tamara gave the girl a genuine smile. "You are? Well, I'm not surprised, because you really are a gifted singer."

Sienna grinned even more widely then and said, "I know."

With a husky laugh, Isaiah asked, "You're not too humble, are you, Sienna?"

"Humble? What's 'humble' mean?"

He looked at Tamara, and simultaneously they smiled at each other, both seeming to get the irony. It was quite fitting that Sienna would not know what the word "humble" meant, since she clearly was not displaying any humble tendencies.

"Are y'all laughing at me? What y'all smilin' about?"

"We're not laughing at you," Isaiah said. "We are just agreeing silently that humility is just not a trait that you have a lot of right now, Sienna."

"I got humbility," she said sincerely. "I do . . ."

The two adults looked at each other and once more began to laugh in earnest. "It's '*humility*,' Sienna," said Tamara.

"Oh, humbility, humility, whatever—y'all know what I'm talkin' 'bout," the girl said, now wearing a put-upon pout. "I'm going to hang my coat up."

After throwing Tamara a mischievous glance, she added, "Mr. Perry, you might as well give me your coat. Go 'head, just sit on the couch right there for a minute and talk to Tamara. She needs some company . . . '*cause she never has any.*"

For the second time that night, Tamara's mouth fell open, and again she found herself struggling to regain her composure while watching the petite girl take the man's coat and scurry from the room, leaving the two of them together.

"Well, I suppose you can sit down if you want," she said, even more self-conscious than before.

Ignoring the lack of enthusiasm in her invitation, Isaiah replied cheerfully, "I think I will for a few minutes, if you don't mind."

Tamara stiffly faced the television and tensed inwardly when she felt the weight of his body on the couch beside her. That Sienna was up to no good, she thought agitatedly. In fact, she seriously suspected that Sienna had orchestrated the entire event with Isaiah this evening. After all, Sienna had made it no secret that she believed that Tamara should be dating, and it was becoming clearer by the day that the girl favored Isaiah Perry as the perfect man for her to start with.

"Well . . . ," said Isaiah, his husky voice cheerful as ever.

"Well," answered Tamara, silently chiding herself again for

her recurring inability to do anything other than parrot his words.

"I wish that you could've made it to Bible study," he said.

"I do, too." Almost miraculously then, Tamara began to think with clarity about the last Bible session she attended. The minister's message had left her unsettled and full of questions.

Momentarily forgetting about her discomfort, she said, "To tell the truth, Isaiah, I'm having problems truly understanding parts of what Pastor Walker is talking about."

Isaiah looked concerned. "Really? Maybe I could help, if you'd like to talk about it . . ."

Tamara paused a minute and then said, "Well, I understand about love, I think. It's when two people fall for each other and then they get together. I'm just not sure what Jesus' love for us has to do with it all, and mostly I'm not sure why He loves *us* anyway."

Isaiah laughed and said, "Ms. Britton, are you sure that's *all* love is—when two people fall for each other?"

"Isn't it?" she asked.

"Well, yes, it is. But then, what about the love between a sister and a brother, or from one friend to another, or how about between a parent and a child?"

She laughed to herself a little. "You're right; I suppose that is love, too."

"You *suppose?*"

"Well, I know it is. I am guessing a big part of love is when you do things for others and they do things for you as well."

"So it's all about what you do, huh?"

Tentatively she replied, "Well, yes . . . I think it is, anyway."

Isaiah turned and looked at Tamara. "You are *exactly right*, really, Ms. Britton—Do you mind if I call you Tamara?"

She looked shyly into his eyes and said, "Oh, of course not . . . You may call me Tamara . . . *I'm right?*"

"Yes, you are right. Love is about what you *do,* and that is why the greatest love that we will ever know is the love of Jesus, just for that very reason."

"Could you explain that, please?"

"God loves us like a father, just like our parents love us and just like you are growing to love Sienna. Love often gives them the heart to do for us whether or not they feel like it or, more importantly, whether or not we have earned their gifts and support. That tendency of a parent to give time, attention, love, whether or not their child deserves it, is called *grace,* and it is *grace* that God gives us as well."

Tamara sat silently, listening intently to his words.

"Just like children, we continue to do wrong. Sometimes we do it out of ignorance, and sometimes we do wrong even when we know what's right; that seems to be just the nature of our humanity. But the wonderful blessing is that God loves us anyway and, through His *grace,* continues to bless us through His Word, and many times He even walks with us when we don't know Him yet."

"He does? But I still don't understand why Jesus died and what His death has to do with saving us."

The man gave her a long look and then asked, "I hope that you don't take this the wrong way, but you are not a Christian, are you?"

Tamara dropped her head. "Not really. I've been to church before, but I don't really know much about the Bible, nor do I understand much about the whole God and Jesus thing."

"Okay, I will do my best to explain it to you in my own words, but every person needs to study the Word of God, 'eat of the word,' as the Scripture says, for themselves. Each person's walk with God is a personal one, since only He knows what a person has been through in his life and what lies in his heart. Understand?"

190

"Yes, I do," she said sincerely.

"Okay, listen, now. God sent His son to die so that we may live. Before Jesus died, we had to go through another to get to God. In the Old Testament it tells of how men had to give sacrifices or ask certain anointed people to pray to God for them, but when Jesus gave up His life on the cross for us, died, and rose again in three days, God sent his Holy Spirit down to live in each of us."

"You mean His spirit is in me, too?"

"Yes, Tamara, His spirit is in you, too. Each of us has the Holy Spirit dwelling inside, and God is only waiting for us to ask so that we can feel the fullness of His quickening power within. We all have the power to love immensely, to give of ourselves unselfishly—to let God's light shine through us. In this world, we are His body, and He works His miracles of love through us. And so, Tamara, we all have the ability to love unconditionally, just like God loved us enough to give us his son, and Jesus loved us enough to die for us."

"That's very powerful," Tamara said, and she smiled brightly, feeling happy with this newfound knowledge about God's spirit residing in her.

"Yes, it is, Tamara, and when you really understand and feel it in your heart and in your gut, it's life-changing. God our Father loves us just as we are loved by our very own parents, and just as Jesus, who is our spiritual brother, loves us and gave His life just so that we could be in the family—Alleluia!"

Isaiah's face was animated, and his deep-brown skin glowed in the low lights of the living room. Tamara couldn't help but notice that he was quite a handsome man, and tonight she found it very comforting that he was so open about his obvious love for God.

"What up, y'all?" said Sienna, entering the room again,

oblivious of the deep conversation that the two of them were having.

"What up, Sienna?" said Isaiah, smiling broadly at the young girl.

Even though Tamara smiled, too, the enchanted moment was broken, and she was suddenly acutely aware of her grungy appearance: her now dry and unstyled hair, her bare, rained-on-and-dried face, and her old gray sweats and white-socked feet. Her confidence had waned just that quickly, to almost nothing, and now all she wanted was for Isaiah to get up off her sofa, get his coat, and go home.

The lighthearted mood of moments before had slipped away elusively, and Tamara felt intruded upon now by Isaiah, Sienna, God, love, and everything else new in her life. In fact, an unfamiliar pang of resentment prickled at her as she watched Isaiah and Sienna interacting so easily together, leaving her feeling more isolated than ever in her concerns. Turning her gaze away from them, she felt vague insecurities plague her once again as she wondered if all the changes were more than she could handle at one time.

33.

Heartbreak Hotel

Tamara stretched and yawned loudly. Trying to keep her eyes open was proving difficult this morning. Overly tired today, she regretted staying up later than usual last night to finish watching a television program with Sienna. Yet lately Tamara had been feeling guilty about all the time she spent away from home, so she took extra pains to find time for the two of them to be together. She knew that Sienna had already experienced some sort of neglect in her life, and there was no way she would purposely make her feel uncared for again.

Riding with Jay toward the north side of town, she drowsily sipped from the cup of cappuccino she had purchased at the Quick Stop. Although she and Jay normally did not do emergency field work, this morning they had volunteered their response to a hotline call on one of the families they'd worked with the past few months. The two of them had put quite a bit of time and effort into keeping this family together, and it was their hope that whatever situation they might find once they arrived at the home would be fixable, allowing them to salvage the family unit if at all possible.

"Tamara, you must really be tired!" said Jayson playfully. "Two cups of coffee in one day? That's wa-a-ay out of your comfort zone!" he added teasingly with a short chuckle.

Tamara smiled tiredly and yawned again. "You're right about that, Jay . . . I am tired."

With a sudden look of disdain marring his handsome face now, Jayson asked disapprovingly, "What did she do now? I know that little Miss Thang got something to do with this!"

"Her name is Sienna, Jay, and actually she doesn't have anything to do with it. I stayed up late of my own accord, watching television."

For a minute he looked at her skeptically, then relenting, replied, "Okay, then . . . my bad. It's just that ever since she's lived with you, she's either up to something or smarting off, and the person who seems to suffer the most for her bad behavior is you, Tam."

Tamara sighed, took a sip of the still-hot coffee, and then replied, "You know that's not really true, Jay; it's an exaggeration of what's happened, and things are getting better between the two of us. Last night we watched a movie, just spending time doing something together, since I'm not around much."

Jayson spun around and looked at Tamara with raised eyebrows. "But, Tamara, the only reason you are not around much is because you are working."

"I know that, Jay, but Sienna is just a young girl, and she does not necessarily understand that. A few weeks ago she actually told me that she got tired of staying home by herself, and after thinking about it more, I realized she may be lonely, and that may be why she misbehaves so often—she may be trying to get attention, you know?"

Dryly he asked, "And that's why you were up late, huh? Trying to make sure she got some attention."

"Well, I guess you could say that," Tamara admitted grudgingly.

With a knowing shake of his head, Jayson mumbled under his breath, "See, I knew she had something to do with it."

Tamara ignored Jayson's muttered comment. His constant negativity about Sienna was really beginning to bother her. "Look, Jayson, I appreciate your concern. I know you're worried about me, but I'll be just fine. Remember, Sienna's just a kid, and she's the one who's gone through a hard time, not me."

"Tam, I keep trying to remind myself of that, but all I can think of is what a hard time she's putting you through, and that seems unfair."

Glad to be able to change the subject, Tamara saw that they were quickly approaching the Smith family's neighborhood, and said, "Jayson, here it is . . . turn left here. Then we need to find Congress Avenue, right?"

Jayson turned the Chevy Malibu in at the trailer park. He was familiar with this neighborhood and quickly found the street they were looking for.

Totally alert now, Tamara sat up straight in the car, carefully watching the house numbers as they were driving by. "This is it; I remember now . . ."

Jayson pulled the blue Chevy into the short driveway by the small white trailer. A couple of old bikes and broken pieces of toys were scattered along the side of the house, and the windowless screen door flapped open wide, hitting the back of the railing with a rhythmic bang each time the wind blew.

Glancing quickly at Tamara, Jayson turned his black leather cap to the back and grabbed his clipboard from between the seats. He took a deep breath and said, "Okay, sister girl, let's go."

Inexplicably tense now, Tamara squeezed her shoulders high up around her neck and then relaxed them. The extra caffeine she just drank was probably why she felt a little wobbly, too. Inhaling deeply to shake off her jitters, she jumped out of the car and followed Jayson to the door.

Jayson rapped hard on the door. When there was no reply, he

knocked again even harder, and this time the flimsy door swung open wide. He raised his eyebrows, shot her a quizzical look, and then, with a shrug of his shoulders, stepped into the house.

Once inside the small trailer, Tamara's mouth fell open in disbelief at the disarray that greeted them. Following closely behind Jayson in the shadowy dimness, she could see garbage and debris littering the floor and the furnishings. The home felt cold. And it was dark.

"Try the lights, Tamara," said Jayson.

With a leather-gloved hand she flipped the switch, and her stomach clenched when nothing happened.

Jayson's face was barely visible in the dim room as he gave her a sobering glance. "This ain't lookin' good at all, Tam."

"Oh, God, Jayson," said Tamara with a confused expression on her face. "I don't understand . . . How can it even look like this in here? We just were out here a month ago and it was spotless!"

For almost six months now, they had been working with twenty-five-year-old Belinda Smith, the head of this single-family household, who had struggled with a drug problem on and off for years. Her two children; a girl named Santez, who was seven, and the little boy Jamez, who was five, had been removed from the home on several occasions already. The children were still receiving counseling to help them cope with the neglect they'd already experienced too much of in their young lives.

The final attempt by the state to keep the family together was their contracted Care Agency Stabilization Services, which had begun a few days after the young mother had completed the mandatory drug rehabilitation program. Then Tamara and Jayson set up monthly wellness home visits by nurses from the community health center, enrolled Belinda in job training services, and helped the young mother find affordable day care for her children.

From the moment they'd met her, Belinda had begged them

to help her get her children back again, and the young woman had complied with all the state's difficult stipulations in order to reclaim them. Stabilization resources had been used to assist her in renting this small trailer and had provided funding to furnish it as well, and when they came out for their regular visit just a few weeks ago, nothing was amiss. Stunned now at this fast deterioration around them, Tamara couldn't fathom what had happened to the neat home they'd last visited.

"What happened, Jayson? Just this quickly . . ." she asked, but Tamara knew that the most probable answer to her question would be heartrending. Her voice faltered as she continued to stare unbelievingly at the disorder in the small home.

Jayson's face was eerily shadowed in the dim room, but there was no mistaking the gravity of his expression when he turned to face her. "Tamara, I'm getting a *real bad* feeling about all of this."

His uncharacteristically somber look alarmed her, and she gazed at him through wide-open eyes now, her heart fluttery and beating so fast, she almost could not catch her breath. Tearing her eyes from his, Tamara again surveyed the filthy front room and said haltingly, "J-J-Jayson, *please* d-d-don't tell me you think that the children are in here somewhere . . . they c-can't be in here." With a slow, sinking feeling in her stomach, she asked pleadingly, "Please, Jay, don't tell me that you think they are in here somewhere . . ."

Jayson knew by her expression that Tamara's emotions were edging toward panic, and purposefully he kept his own voice evenly calm, "Tam, you know we're gonna have to look around the house, just in case. If you can't do it, go back to the car now, and I'll do it alone. But we *can't* leave this house until we are certain those children aren't in here."

His efforts to remain controlled paid off, for she drew a deep breath as if struggling to compose herself and then replied in a low voice, "No, Jay, I'm not going to leave you in here all alone . . . I'll look with you."

Carefully watching his step, Jayson walked to the window, maneuvering uneasily through the maze of old newspapers, food wrappings, and dirty clothes that lay on the floor. With a quick swoop of his hand, he pulled back the dark drapes, and a cloud of smoky-smelling dust particles filled the air as a burst of sun brightly illuminated the extent of the chaos around them.

Tamara blinked from the sudden brightness filling the room, and Jayson sneezed twice and then noisily began to slap his hands together to remove some of the soot from them. Then, with his clipboard tucked under his arm, he tried to wipe his hands clean, but they were still so damp, they left a brown trail on his khaki pant legs, and his hands' obvious clamminess revealed his own nervousness to Tamara.

They both avoided prolonged eye contact now, and Jayson was all business when he gave her a swift glance and said, "Okay, Tamara, let's go. I'll take the rooms down this hallway, and you look in the kitchen area first, okay?"

"Okay," said Tamara.

Tentatively she entered the small kitchen area and peered around. In the dim room she made out the shadowy outlines of garbage strewn around the floor and on the table. Following Jay's lead from moments ago, she made her way to the small back door window, where she pulled up the miniblind to shed some light into the room. No longer surprised by the extent of the decay in the home, she looked without emotion at the roaches sent scurrying by the light into the small cracks and crevices between the counter and wall.

Reluctantly Tamara opened the refrigerator door, recoiling from the stench of spoiled food that had been in the warm environment long enough to disintegrate into shapeless lumps of indistinguishable matter. Now, totally disgusted at the depth of the negligence she was witnessing, Tamara spun around and walked out of the kitchen area to find Jayson.

"Jayson," she whispered as she entered the narrow hallway where the bedrooms were located.

His voice seemed impossibly distant in the small space when he answered, "I'm here, Tamara."

The hallway was narrow, and Tamara turned into the nearest small bedroom. She stood watching silently as Jayson looked under the bed and in the closet. Her body was tense, and she felt as though she were paralyzed, unable to move—yet mentally she attempted to prepare herself for what they might discover at any moment.

"There's no one in here," he said, and she let out a small sigh of relief.

Tamara looked at him before saying hopefully, "They're probably not here, Jayson . . . Maybe they're at a relative's home or something."

Jayson's tone was still somber though. "Tamara, it *was* a relative who called the hotline. She was worried because she hasn't seen Belinda or the kids in a couple of days. But someone came by her house and told her that they saw Belinda out on the streets, and she was lookin' high."

Morosely she replied, "You're right . . . Oh, Jay, I really thought she was through with the drugs. I honestly thought she was through with them."

In a low tone, he replied matter-of-factly, "I was hoping she was, Tamara. But, for some folks, drugs are a powerful thing. They want to quit, but they just don't seem to be able to let go of them—or rather, the drugs won't let them go."

Tamara grew reflective for a minute as Samyra Bailey's face flashed in her mind, and she remembered her poignant statement about her sister Jannice's death. *"She died like most drug addicts do, alone."* Then she thought about how Jannice had neglected her children so many times, how the woman had left them alone because she, too, was addicted to drugs.

Resignedly she said in a determined voice, "Jayson, we *have* to keep looking."

"Yes, we do, Tamara," he agreed.

Silent now, they continued down the narrow hallway, turning into the second small bedroom, which was obviously the children's, since old plastic toys lay on top of the scattered debris. A blond-haired doll lying on the floor, nude, arms and legs akimbo, stared up at them unblinkingly with one round blue eye and an empty hole where the other used to be. There were no sheets on the two dirty bunk beds, and they were both covered with so much junk that there was little room for anyone to sleep on either. She stood behind Jayson, waiting tensely again for him to throw open the small metal closet door.

"Nope," he said once he'd opened it to find it filled only with more debris. She could tell this time that he was relieved as well.

"One more room," she said quietly, still silently hopeful they would find nothing there, either.

Together they walked over to the biggest of the three rooms. Softly they kicked papers and garbage out of their path, both still amazed that anyone could live in such disorder for any period of time.

Just like the others, the room was littered with clothes, papers, and other types of garbage. Cigarette butts had been squashed out indiscriminately, and there were ashes on plates and in bowls, intermingling with rotten food. The smell of the decomposing food and old smoke was rancid in the air.

The shades were open a bit in this room, admitting enough light to create a dull, hazy glow. In a hurry now to get the unpleasant task over with, Jayson went directly to the bed, lifted up the dirty white bedspread, and looked under the bed.

"Nothing," he said, and again they both looked at each other gratefully, since they both knew there was more than enough room under the full-size bed for two frightened children to hide.

She shadowed him even closer now as he made his way over to the closet. Holding her breath, she stared unblinkingly while he opened the door.

He threw back the closet door. They were not so lucky this time.

"Oh God . . ." was all she could say as she stared into the cluttered closet area.

Jayson spun around and locked his eyes on hers. "Tamara, dial nine one one. *Now!*"

Still staring at the closet floor, she reached into her pocket, grabbed her cell phone, and dialed the emergency number. She sighed deeply and wiped at the tears that suddenly sprang up in the corners of her eyes.

They had found the children. The girl, Santez, was seated in the back of the closet, staring wide-eyed right through them. She was unclean and obviously underfed, and yet her small hand was still caressing her baby brother, who lay cuddled next to her with his small, wooly head on her lap.

Jayson turned to Tamara with frustration, disgust, and anger written clearly on his face. His eyes were filled with unshed tears, and she knew he was so upset that he was just unable to articulate the enormity of his feelings. Instead, he just stared at her, struggling valiantly to maintain his composure while he repeated, his voice low and emotional, "Aw, man, Tamara, this don't make no sense at all. *Aw, man!*"

34.

Hunger Pains

The girl walked more and more slowly as the evening progressed. Each step was laborious and taxing. It seemed extra cold to her tonight, and she'd been walking for a long, long time. Overall, times had gotten tougher for her as she tried to make her way out on the streets these days, and she could only guess that one reason why things were so much more difficult now was her growing up. Though she was still small in stature, she finally looked closer to her age. Her more mature appearance too often attracted unwanted attention from strange-looking men, while making it lots harder for her to elicit the quick empathy reserved for young children.

Not that long ago, folks had given her money or food simply because she looked cute to them. Thanks to her well-practiced smile, flashed at them sweetly, they did not even think about reporting her as a runaway.

The girl sighed deeply, realizing that no one gave her much of anything these days without wanting something in return. In fact, most people nowadays were either trying to get something from her or sell something to her. No one called her in as a runaway, simply because no one cared. The truth was, she was invisible to most people, because street folks like her just didn't matter at all.

On difficult days like today, her only solace was that in a year she would no longer be a minor, and freedom would be hers. In a year, if she were picked up as a runaway, a judge could grant her freedom. No more running, no more fear of being placed in another foster home. Then she could get a legitimate job and support herself with her own pay.

Unable to walk one more step, she paused in front of an old brick building. Inexplicably, she felt warm in this spot, and looking down, she noticed that welcome heat was drifting up through the grating under her feet. It began to thaw her small, frozen legs. Basking in the momentary comfort, she sat on her old duffel bag and leaned her back against the dirty brick wall of the building just to take a load off her feet for a minute or two.

It had been days since she'd had a genuine meal, other than snacks of candy and crackers and other items she could pilfer here and there. For a while she'd used the well-known street trick of slipping into a vacant diner seat and buying one cup of coffee so she could surreptitiously pinch free crackers and other leftover foods from the counter. But she'd become such a frequent visitor that the small eateries were wary of her presence and sometimes sent her packing.

Embarrassment warmed her cold cheeks as she thought about the heavy blonde waitress today who had worn a look of disgust when she said, "Look, honey, I don't know what kinda problems you got, and I really don't want to know, but you can't just hang around here and eat up all our food for free. We got to make money, and you just takin' up a seat."

With her eyes down, she'd gathered up her bags and hurried from the diner as quickly as she could. The woman's scathing statement and disdainful look suddenly made her acutely aware that she had not bathed in weeks and that her worn clothes were dirty. Pushing the diner door open, she had run, hoping to find a place away from the probing stares of strangers, where she might safely shed her tears of frustration and shame. Finally, she had stopped in the doorway of an old building, where she turned her small body sideways to face the cold concrete wall. She wiped away the tears that were streaming down her face.

It was unlike her to feel sorry for herself, but unable to contain herself today, she gave in to her sorrowful feelings. "What did I do to deserve this?" she asked, and for several moments she sobbed softly, saying quietly between sniffles, "It's not fair . . . it's just not fair."

The thumping bass of a passing low-rider car reverberated through her small body, and wiping her eyes a final time, she turned to watch the loud automobile's progress down the street. Still sniffing, she reached into the pocket of her faded brown coat and wiped her face with a wadded-up piece of a napkin she'd grabbed before fleeing the dingy diner.

I don't care about that mean waitress, she thought, visualizing the woman's mocking face again. One day I'm gonna have a job and my own home and everything, and I'm gonna go back to that crummy old diner just so that she can remember me! I'm gonna order all the food I want, and then I'm gonna leave it there without touching it, with the money to pay for it on the table!

The girl's expression became resolute, and straightening her small shoulders and holding her head high, she began to walk down the street again, soon merging anonymously into the crowd on the busy avenue.

That had been hours ago. Now her head was aching, and still she'd had no food. Thankful for the heat still rising through the grating, she could feel herself becoming weak with hunger. Just then a door opened in the wall of the old brick building where she leaned, and a man walked out carrying a garbage bag. He looked at her, smiled widely, tipped his head in her direction, and said, "Good evening, little sister . . . you all right now?"

She wanted to yell loudly, "No, I'm not okay! I need something to eat! I need someone to help me right now!" but instead replied in a small voice, "I'm fine, thank you."

When he walked by, she caught the enticing odor of food in his clothes and in the bag that he carried. For the first time the girl looked up at the sign affixed to the building, and read, "The Temple of Hope Church," in blue letters.

The clang of a metal garbage can alerted her to his return; she stared straight ahead, trying hard to affect nonchalance. She sensed his attempt to make eye contact with her, but she would not oblige. From the corner of her eye, she finally saw him reenter the church.

After a few minutes, she could bear the hunger no longer. The girl knew that if she did not eat soon, something bad would happen. As good as the heated grating felt, she couldn't stay rooted in this warm spot all night long, yet she simply could not walk any farther without food.

Moments passed; then she stood and slowly made her way around the corner. She took a deep breath and set her bag on the ground by the dirty gray garbage can. In all the time she had been in the streets, she'd never had to resort to this, but tonight she had no choice. If she wanted to live, she had to eat something, and she had to eat it now.

Just as she grasped the lid of the garbage can, she heard a sound behind her. She spun around quickly and looked into the face of the same man from the church. She grabbed her bag and was preparing to break into a run, but the man held her back.

"You don't have to do that," he said in a low tone.

"Do what?" she asked, acting as if she did not know what he meant.

"Little sister, you always have a meal here. Please, come with me," he said, gently leading her back to the church.

Street experience had made her cautious. She knew he could

be a thief or worse, yet she was too tired to protest and far too hungry to run. Slowly she followed the man.

Inside the church, the bright lights overwhelmed her for a moment. He led her through the warm sanctuary, into a large back room filled with tables and chairs. She felt almost as if she were dreaming. On one table was a plate loaded with food. There was crispy fried chicken, potato salad, baked beans, and rolls.

Her eyes widened, and her mouth watered as she looked from the food to him and back again.

"Sit, little sister; eat," he said with a smile, and then he turned away.

Uncomprehendingly, the girl looked again at the man, but his back was to her. She dropped her dirty bag on the floor and sat down in the chair. Without even taking off her coat, she began to attack the food, eating ravenously.

She never noticed the man watching her compassionately now. He wondered just what, or *who,* this little girl was running from.

35.

Shut In

Tamara tossed and turned in her bed. One minute she was hot and could not stand the rough feel of the bedding on her flesh, and the next she was freezing and holding the blankets close, unable to control the trembling all over her body. Her head was pounding, and her throat felt rough and scratchy. Sneezing loudly, she pulled another tissue from the box that she clutched, and tenderly blew her sore nose. Then she laid her aching head back on the pillow and began to cough spasmodically.

"Tam, are you okay?" asked Sienna, standing beside the bed with a worried look on her face. "You sound really bad," she added anxiously.

"I'm okay; it sounds worse than it actually is," Tamara said reassuringly. She could see the concern in Sienna's face, and there was no way she was going to reveal just how awful she really felt.

"I'm gonna get you some more juice," said the girl. Sienna was really getting scared because Tamara looked really bad. She wanted to help, but didn't know what to do. She rushed to the kitchen for juice.

Tamara wanted to rest, but each time she closed her eyes, she saw the Smith kids all over again. They were there in the closet—Santez, with her eyes open, unblinking unseeing, and Jamez, dehydrated, his little stomach bloated, lying on his sister and unable to open his eyes at all.

"How could any mother do that to her children?" she said aloud. Tears again formed in the corners of her eyes, and she wiped at them despondently with a wadded-up tissue.

Even though it had been weeks since they found the two kids in the closet, Tamara was still unable to get that day out of her mind. She knew that after a short time in the hospital both children had recovered and were now safely in a new foster home. Their young mother, Belinda Smith, had not been found yet, but she would be charged with neglect and child abuse whenever she surfaced.

A familiar voice penetrated her thoughts. "Baby girl, are you all right?"

She turned her red-rimmed eyes toward the sound of the voice and was happily surprised to see Denise Jackson standing there by her bed. In her feverish state, her blurry vision caused the light to flow around the large woman in such a way that she looked just like an angel, complete with a bright, fuzzy halo around the top of her head.

Tamara could see the concern written clearly on Mrs. Jackson's face as the woman bent over, laid a cool hand on her hot forehead, and said, "Baby, you're burning up." She turned toward the door and glanced at Sienna, whose face was a mask of worry.

"Little Sienna baby, now, you go get me a cool washrag . . . and where's the Tylenol? We've got to get Tamara's temperature down."

Sienna rushed from the room, glad finally to have some instructions. Denise Jackson took off her coat and laid it across the chair.

Looking down at the young woman now, Denise chided her gently. "Tamara, you cannot let yourself get sick like this. Whenever you get a cold or the flu, you must take Tylenol for the fever, baby girl."

The girl looked at the woman and smiled weakly. "I thought I was taking it . . ."

"Here's the washcloth and the Tylenol," said Sienna.

Denise Jackson turned to the young girl and said, "Until she feels better, you must make sure that she takes the Tylenol every four hours for her temperature, okay, Sienna?"

The girl asked worriedly, "Is she gonna be all right? She looks so sick, Mrs. Jackson."

The older woman patted her shoulder reassuringly. "Don't you worry, baby; she will be just fine, especially with your help! Now, you go into the kitchen Sienna, and get you some of that fried chicken and macaroni and cheese that I brought over. I know you haven't had anything to eat, either."

"B-b-but what about Tamara?"

"You've done a great job, Sienna, sweetie, but I'll watch baby girl for a while, and you take a little break, okay?"

After one long, last look at Tamara, Sienna agreed reluctantly. "Okay, Mrs. Jackson . . . just call me if you need somethin'."

"Thank you, Sienna, baby," said the woman.

Once the teen was gone, Mrs. Jackson gazed down at Tamara worriedly. She did not look good. Her complexion was ashen, her breathing was labored, and she was staring ahead wide-eyed as if her eyes refused to shut.

Smoothing back the young woman's hair, she said, "Baby girl, you have to get some sleep."

In a cracked voice Tamara answered, "I can't go to sleep, Mrs. Jackson."

"You can't go to sleep?"

Tamara replied woodenly, "I keep thinking about them . . . I can't seem to stop it."

The woman looked puzzled. "Them? Tamara, you gotta help me out, now—just who is them?"

In the same flat voice, she answered, "The Smith kids."

"Is that one of your cases?"

Tamara nodded her head up and down. "We found them . . . Jay and I found them."

"Found them where, baby girl?"

Tears began to trickle from her eyes again. "All alone, Mrs. Jackson—that's how we found them. In a closet together, dirty, hungry, and all alone."

Finally it dawned on her what Tamara was talking about. This Smith case had actually made the evening news a few weeks ago, and she'd watched it sadly, with her own heart heavy for both the children and their mother. When she prayed that night, she included them in her time with God. My, my, if she had known that Tamara Britton was involved, she would have included her in the prayers, too—the sight of those two kids almost starved to death must have been devastating for her.

Tamara opened her swollen eyes as much as she could and said in a whisper, "Why does God allow this to happen, Mrs. Jackson? Those kids didn't do anything to anyone, did they?"

"No, they didn't, Tamara."

"Then, why? Tell me why?" the younger woman asked insistently, her voice crackly with the flu yet still demanding a reply.

Denise Jackson sighed as she sat on the edge of the girl's queen-size bed. "I don't know, baby girl . . . There is much about life I don't understand, either, and only the Lord knows why these things happen."

Tamara wiped her eyes and said, "But, I don't get it. If God is so loving and kind, then why would he make children suffer like they did?" The girl croaked out the last words before beginning to cough again, hard.

Denise Jackson pulled the sheet up around Tamara and said, "Shhhh! Now, calm down, baby girl. Things happen that we cannot understand . . . its like the Bible says in First Corinthians, remember? 'now we see through a glass darkly, but then face to face . . . now I know in part, but then shall I know even as also I am known.'"

The girl looked at her quizzically. "I do remember, Minister Walker had us read that in Bible study, too, but what does that mean?"

"Baby, what the Scripture tells us is that there are some questions we have that just won't be answered for us on this earth, but still we believe in God because of our faith. 'Faith is the substance of things unseen and the evidence of things to come.' We believe in God even though we don't understand it all. But, baby, we believe because we feel His presence inside."

She took Tamara's clammy hands in her own.

"His spirit lives in us, inside of you and me, and it is when we are still that we can most often feel the stirring of His presence within." Uncharacteristically sad, she added, "Baby girl, I don't have all the answers. I don't even wish that I did, because that would be just too much for ol' Denise Jackson to know. But what I do know is that God exists, and I know that He loves me, you, and that girl out there, and I know that He loved those kids, too, Tamara. God even loves their mother."

"I still don't understand," Tamara managed to add hoarsely.

"Because it's not for you to understand; it's for you to *believe,* baby girl; just have faith, Tamara, faith. Paul wrote in Romans five: four, 'We also boast in our sufferings knowing that suffering produces endurance, and endurance produces character, and character produces *hope,* and *hope* does not disappoint us, because God's love has been poured into our hearts through the Holy Spirit that has been given to us.'"

"Hope?"

"Hope, baby girl. Think about it, Tamara, just a tiny bit of *hope* makes you believe, makes you have *faith in something that you can't see,* because it only takes a little bit of hope to help you keep on keepin' on, even when the odds are stacked against you. That's why Pastor Walker's daddy named the church The Temple of Hope—to remind people to always keep the faith and be *hopeful,* because *hope* will never fail us."

"I guess . . . ," Tamara said, but her voice faltered uncertainly.

Denise Jackson turned the young woman's face gently toward her own, so that she was looking into her eyes, and continued, "Tamara, sometimes, hope is the only thing that keeps you going long enough for a miracle to happen and then that miracle, no matter how large or small, helps you make it even a little while longer."

Turning her eyes away, the young woman stared into space

and said, "Yes, I could see that happening—a miracle, that is. I guess I just wish one happened for those kids."

Denise shook her head in silent agreement while patting the younger woman's still-warm forehead with the cool cloth.

"Baby girl, I know that it's hard to understand all of the evil, unfairness, and injustice that sometimes seems to be everywhere in this world we live in. Believe me, even Christians have problems sometimes with those same questions and issues."

"Do you?"

"I do, but as I said before, *have faith,* baby girl. Keep your hopes alive and have faith. I remind myself during difficult times that God is real and His son Jesus is real, and He died for us because He loved us so. I know from my own experiences that love is real, and you can believe that no matter what those kids have been through, if they *just learn to love again,* they will be just fine."

Tamara continued to stare into space as she said, "That will be difficult for them, though, after all that they have endured."

"Yes, it will be hard, but they can start with loving God, because God's love and His Word is true and it *won't fail them.* He is the father to the fatherless, and His love will give hope to the hopeless. God is always available to us, and His heart overflows with love for us, and once we really understand that, then that knowledge of his unconditional love for us gives us the courage, no matter what we've been through, to love him in return. *Love* is the miracle we all can make happen in our own lives, since no matter how much we've been hurt, we can still choose to love again."

The woman began to sing then in her low melodic voice:

"The love I feel for Jesus,
I can hardly contain within;
He's loved me without condition
Before I even knew Him . . ."

With a shake of her head, Denise Jackson looked at her with eyes shiny with exuberance. "It's just so amazing to me that my God loved me even when I didn't love myself."

The Tylenol finally seemed to be taking effect, because Tamara was becoming more alert than she'd been all day. She responded, "Mrs. Jackson, love is difficult to give or accept sometimes, especially when you've been hurt by someone."

"I know, baby; that's because love requires you to *trust,* and trust is hard to give again when you have been let down by people time and again. So you can begin to trust by trusting God, because *He won't let you down.* His word is always true, and He will never fail you."

"Never?"

She finished by saying with her trademark chuckle, "*Never*—he can't fail us ever, 'cause 'He's all good,' as the kids say."

For a moment the two of them sat silently while she stroked Tamara's hair from her now cool forehead. Then Denise Jackson asked the question she'd wanted to ask for quite a while. "Baby girl, where are your parents? It would be nice if your mama was here for you at a time like this."

"She's dead," said Tamara flatly.

"What about your dad, then?"

"He's dead, too," she added, her tone still emotionless.

Denise Jackson covered her surprise. She'd always assumed that Tamara's family was absent either because of some temporary estrangement or merely because they lived in another city. It had never occurred to her that the poised young woman might be alone in the world.

"Oh, baby, I'm so very sorry to hear that. Are there any aunts, uncles, anyone else I can call?"

"No, there's no one I want you to call . . . but thank you so much for all of your help, though. Where's Sienna?" Tamara asked in a small voice as her eyes began to close.

Thankful that Tamara's fever had broken and that she finally seemed to be able to rest, Denise Jackson said soothingly, "You go to sleep now, baby girl. Don't you worry, Sienna will be just fine. I'll take care of her for you."

For a few more minutes Denise Jackson continued stroking Tamara's hair until she noticed her breathing becoming deep and even. Careful not to wake her, she rose from the bed quietly and stood watching her lie there in the large bed. Tamara looked small and helpless lying there alone, and her illness made her look vulnerable and even more fragile and innocent than usual.

It was hard for Denise to believe that Tamara had no one who could come and care for her now. Sighing, she pulled the covers up on the sleeping young woman and closed the door quietly. After a quick call to her husband to let him know she'd be here awhile longer, she'd check on little Miss Sienna—hopefully, she was getting some much-needed sleep, too.

36.

Friday Fun

Ruefully Tamara glanced at her watch once more. *I don't know why I agreed to chaperone tonight,* she thought miserably as she looked out into the rowdy crowd of kids. The music was loud, and talkative teenagers filled the room. This was her first real outing since her bout with the flu, and because she felt a little weak, all this noise and commotion only added to her discomfort.

These Hope Temple–sponsored Friday Teen Night gatherings tried for a "club" atmosphere, complete with a deejay playing loud music that was mostly upbeat contemporary gospel. Throngs of youth participated weekly and enjoyed punch and other refreshments as they chatted with friends, played in the Uno card showdown, or played video or board games. Even though Tamara was less than enthusiastic about being there tonight, she had to agree that these events were a great way for these teens to engage in some positive activities that were also fun for them.

Tamara had dropped Sienna off here at the church on previous Friday nights, but the teen made no secret of the fact that she loved the idea of Tamara's chaperoning. Having missed several days of work during her illness, Tamara's work schedule was even more demanding than usual as she struggled to catch up with overdue assignments. As a result, she and Sienna seemed to have less time than usual to spend together. So when Denise Jackson called and asked her to serve as a chaperone tonight, before she knew it, her guilt had caused her once again to place herself into an uncomfortable situation that she really did not want to be part of.

Thinking about it now, Tamara became annoyed at herself; she was just too wimpy to refuse a request from anyone, it seemed. Glancing at her watch yet again, she muttered under her breath, "Well, at least it's only for a couple of hours. I'm here now, and I'll just have to tough it out, I suppose."

"Why, Tamara, hello," said a now familiar voice.

It can't be him, she thought . . . *I must be mistaken.* But sure enough, when she turned to the left, there at her side was Isaiah Perry, looking as handsome as ever in a pair of well-fitting jeans and a soft blue pullover. With a quick spin of her head, she stared ahead again, thinking it strange how often this man kept turning up when she least expected it.

"Hello, Isaiah," she said without looking at him, in a voice loud enough for him to hear over the music. "I didn't know that you were going to be here."

He moved closer, perhaps so that she could hear him over the pulsating rhythm of the music, and she felt his breath in her ear when he asked, "You didn't?"

"No, Mrs. Jackson did not mention it to me."

"That's strange, because she called me and asked me to do it. You know, she told me that she was going to ask you, too."

Tamara gave him an incredulous look. "She did? Really?"

Isaiah smiled and laughed before saying, "You know, Tamara, I'm beginning to think someone is trying to put the two of us in the same room together at the same time—if you know what I mean."

"You think so?"

"I think so. And actually, there may be two culprits in this little game," he said as he scanned the youthful crowd until his gaze rested on Sienna.

She followed his glance curiously, but when she spied the girl watching the two of them and smiling broadly, her own face began to redden. "Sienna, too? I'm so sorry," Tamara sputtered as she felt her face burn with embarrassment.

He immediately noticed her red-tinged complexion and added, "Please, don't be embarrassed, Tamara—it's not a bad thing. Sienna and Mrs. Jackson just love you and want you to be happy, and I'm flattered that they think I might be a good person for you to get to know."

With her head still lowered, Tamara replied, "It is embarrassing, though. It's like I can't get a date or something."

He gave her a light bump with his elbow and said teasingly, "Oh, c'mon, Tamara, I know that no such thing could be true.

You are *far* too pretty to be unable to get a date. If you are flying solo, it is certainly by choice and not because you have to be."

Despite her embarrassment, she was surprised that her heart jumped a little when he said those words, and she smiled up at him and said shyly, "Thank you, Isaiah . . . I don't know that I'm all that pretty, but you are nice to say so."

His gaze was straightforward and intense as he added, "I don't know why you wouldn't know how attractive you are, Ms. Tamara Britton, but if no one's told you before now, then they've surely slighted you."

This time she leaned close to him so that he could hear her softening voice above the music, "I've never had anyone to tell me those sorts of things. M-my parents were not very demonstrative or talkative in that way."

He gave her a curious look. "What about a boyfriend? I know you've dated before, Tamara."

As Tamara gazed into the lively crowd, she noticed the easy way the teens were interacting with one another. Everyone seemed to be socializing: laughing, talking comfortably, and clearly enjoying one another's company. There was no way she could imagine herself in such a group when she was a teen. If she'd ever even had a circle of friends, more than likely she would have placed herself somewhere on the outskirts of the group, hoping to remain unnoticed there.

"Can I tell you something, Isaiah?"

He still wore a wide smile on his handsome brown face. "Of course, you can tell me anything, Tamara."

Without warning, there was a lull in the music as the deejay announced he was taking a short break, and the room became quiet. Tamara lowered her voice to almost a whisper and asked, "You won't laugh, will you?"

Serious now, he answered huskily, "No, Tamara, I won't laugh."

"I've never been on a date, Isaiah. Not really."

"Never?"

"No . . . never."

He let out a low whistle before, adding, "That's hard to imagine, Tamara."

"I know, that's why I don't tell anyone," she said as she looked down at her hands holding the Styrofoam cup of punch. "I know that people will think I'm strange."

"Is there a reason why?"

She shrugged her shoulders and, with a small smile, said, "Not one in particular . . . probably many in the beginning, that only I would understand. I suppose, then, that after not having dated for so long, I just never got around to it. After all, I spend lots of time at work, and then I busy myself at home when I'm off, and time just slipped away from me, I guess."

Isaiah expelled a breath of air and said, "Whew! That's really something. Then if that's the case, you really don't have much experience with men."

"No, I don't." She couldn't help but let go with a small laugh, adding, "I'm sure that you could tell that, since every time you talk to me, I couldn't really even speak back to you . . . I clammed up."

He laughed, too. "I did notice that. And actually, I'm glad to know this, because I thought I made you uncomfortable 'cause there was something you just didn't like about me."

"No, I like you just fine," she said quite clearly. Almost immediately, she raised her eyebrows, and her full lips formed an O as she realized what she'd said. "I—I didn't mean it like that," she said, embarrassed once again.

There was no way Isaiah was going to allow her to back out

of that statement now, though. He asked jokingly, "Oh, you like me, huh? That's good, 'cause I like you, too, Tamara Britton."

Laughing and then sipping from their cups, they chatted until Sienna and Denise Jackson's daughter Sabrina broke into their conversation. "What y'all doing?" asked Sienna, with curiosity clearly written on her face.

Isaiah looked at Tamara and, answering for the both of them, replied, "We're talking and watching you all—what we are supposed to be doing. What y'all doing, Miss Sienna and Miss Sabrina?"

The girls giggled again and said together in a singsongy tone, "Nothin'."

"Are you having fun?"

"Yes," they answered in unison, and then broke out in giggles at that.

"Praise the Lord, then!" Isaiah replied. "That's what we want you young folks to do, right? Have fun!"

Tamara took one look at Sienna's glowing face and could tell that the girl was having a great time. She looked cute tonight. Her distressed-denim bell-bottoms were topped by a red peasant-style matching shirt, and she wore matching Skechers striped in shades of red and blue.

She envied Isaiah his ability to banter easily with the girls, and she could see that his casual yet clear manner of communication made them feel comfortable talking to him. Tamara was certain that these same qualities were what made him an excellent teacher as well.

Sienna looked at Tamara inquisitively and asked, "How 'bout you, Tamara? Are you having fun?"

Tamara's answer was drowned out by a thumping beat right before the teen deejay announced to the crowd, "I'm back at y'all, okay? Now, c'mon, y'all, let's make some noise for the Lord, now . . . this is Donald Lawrence and the Tri-City Singers on the box." Warming the crowd up with his words, the young deejay introduced the music, adding, "Never, *never* let Satan have his way with you; and remember, no matter what you are going through, God's got the victory. Life is good, y'all; every day there's a new beginning, another chance for you to receive your miracle, and today is the first day of the rest of your life!"

"Girl, I like this song," said Sienna excitedly. "C'mon, Sabrina."

They quickly joined the crowd, who were clapping and waving their hands to the upbeat sounds. As they swayed to the music, many of the young people began to sing loudly along with the lyrics.

All her discomfort was forgotten as Tamara watched the joyful crowd while listening closely to the inspiring words of the tune. It was also dawning on her that the horror of the two Smith children, which had been weighing her down for weeks, seemed to lighten, and she realized happily that she had not experienced one unhappy memory during the entire evening.

Glancing over at Isaiah, she saw that he was nodding his head to the beat, watching the teens with a big smile on his face, and singing along with them.

His smile proved to be contagious, as were the song's catchy beat and optimistic lyrics. The music fully lifted her spirit, and by the time the song reached the chorus, she, too, smiled, clapped, and swayed along with the crowd, singing in a voice that no one but she could hear.

37.

Misjudged

Tamara slammed the car door and sighed to herself as she hurried along the sidewalk to Sissie Bailey's again. She really did not want to revisit the unpleasant woman again, but she had run out of options. All her avenues of inquiry had turned into dead ends, since no one around town seemed to know the whereabouts of Maurice Lewis III, or "Three," as he was known on the streets. Sissie Bailey was a long shot; the woman had not even known much about her own daughters, but Tamara still hoped she might know something that would lead her to Maurice Lewis.

After taking a moment to prepare herself mentally to face the tough woman, she knocked hard on the metal door. A moment later Tamara was gazing into the worn face of Celestine Bailey, better known as Sissie. The woman scrutinized her, trying to place her face. Once recognition dawned, Sissie asked coarsely in her raspy voice, "*You* again? What you want now? Didn't I answer all your questions the first doggone time you was here?"

Not really surprised by Sissie's coldness, Tamara cleared her throat and stammered, "Y-yes, M-Ms. Bailey, you did, but unfortunately all that information led me to was a d-dead end." She started to tell her what Samyra Bailey had shared with her about her daughters, but instead asked, "Can I come inside . . . just for a few moments?"

The woman placed her hands on her ample hips and said, "I

don't know . . . I really am busy right now, and I don't want no company."

In a low, insistent voice, Tamara added, "But, Ms. Bailey, I have some information about your daughters . . ."

Sissie gave her an incredulous look from the side of her eye. "My daughters—hmph! I might as well not have no daggone daughters. They don't do nothin' for me," she said in a hard, flat tone. But after only a few seconds, the woman moved back and opened the door wide enough for Tamara to step inside. "Sit on down. Don't come up in here standing up like you too important to sit down or somethin'."

Compliantly Tamara sat on the edge of the too-soft couch and said immediately, "Ms. Bailey, I saw Samyra."

"Umph!" said the woman through her turned-up lips. "Not that I care. I know where she is anyway, and she ain't even talkin' to me!"

Ignoring the woman's negative comments, Tamara added in a rush, "She told me where her sisters—your daughters—are, too. She said that Kaytriona is married with a couple of kids, and . . . I hate to be the one to tell you this . . . Jannice is dead."

The woman looked shocked for a moment. *"Dead?"*

Tamara said softly, "Yes, she OD'd."

The woman looked at her with flat eyes and said angrily, "They could've told me. Somebody could've told me. I know that I've been a bad mother. I know that, but they still my kids, and *somebody* should've told me."

Tamara looked at the woman sadly. "I agree, Ms. Bailey, somebody should've told you."

"I did love 'em, you know." It seemed to Tamara then that the wear and tear in Sissie's deeply lined face softened a bit, and she added with a tiny laugh, "I remember when each one of 'em was born, they was the prettiest little ole girls you ever wanted to see. All of 'em was fair-skinned and stayed that way, 'cept for

Jannice, and that girl just browned up after we was home 'bout a week."

"Jannice had seven girls herself . . . Did you know that?"

Sissie glanced at Tam then with a frown on her face. "I knew about the first three girls—Lord, when did she have four more, and what happened to them all?"

Tamara looked into the woman's eyes for only a moment and then shifted her glance away. "Unfortunately, all of them were eventually taken by the state . . . She lost them all. The older girls were together for a short time, but the others never lived together at all."

"The state got 'em all, huh?" Her sadness was evident as she shook her head and said mournfully, "Poor babies . . . poor, poor babies."

The unexpected tenderness of the woman's response caught Tamara off guard, but she pushed away her own sympathetic feelings and gazed at the woman intently. "Ms. Bailey, do you remember when I told you about my friend? Well, I think my friend is one of those girls taken into state care. She was the second daughter, and her name is Yvette."

Sissie got up from the couch then and wandered to the front window. Pulling open the side curtain so that her face was hidden behind it, she stood quietly at first. Then Tamara was stunned to hear the woman sniffling loudly, till finally she spoke in a muffled voice. "I don't know how this all happened. I was only fifteen when I had my first . . . One day I just had kids, and I guess I wasn't thinkin' 'bout them enough or somethin'. I was still young, and I just wanted to have a little fun, you know?"

"I can understand that."

The woman turned to her, and Tamara saw tears glittering in her eyes. Then Sissie quickly turned away again, gazing out of the window. "My own mama wasn't around, either . . . and when she was, she never acted like she loved me. I s'pose every now and then I wanted to feel somebody's arms around me and lovin' me, you know? Is that so wrong?"

For some reason Tamara remembered the words of the Reverend Walker, Isaiah Perry, Denise Jackson, and all that she'd been hearing about love. Understandingly she replied, "I suppose we all want to feel loved sometimes, Mrs. Bailey."

"But, the truth of it is, the love didn't last, and none of it turned out to be as much fun as I thought it would be, 'cause for a few moment of happiness, I lost everything, everybody . . . most of all I lost my kids. No matter what *nobody* think about me, life weren't never the same after that . . . always empty for me . . . No matter what nobody think, I never wanted to lose my kids."

Tamara felt her own eyes begin to prickle. Fighting to retain control of her emotions, quickly she changed the subject. She cleared her throat and asked, "Ms. Bailey, do you remember any of Jannice's boyfriends?"

Her voice gentler, the woman answered, "I really wasn't around her that much, 'tween me actin' a fool and them being in the system and then me finally getting locked up, you know? Bet you didn't know that it was Jannice and Sammy's daddy I killed." She looked at Tamara with her faded, dark eyes. "I hate I had to do the time, but I'm not sorry—ain't nobody ever gonna beat up on me like that and get by." She then sighed, "Anyhow, mostly what I know about her is from what I heard, you know?"

Again Sissie had thrown her a curveball, with her unexpected admission of killing Jannice's father and by telling her of the man's abuse. With much effort, Tamara resumed her questions. "I know, but I was just hoping that you might have heard something about the first boyfriend, or recognize the name Yvette."

Sissie wiped her eyes with a napkin before saying, "I do remember *hearing* 'bout Yvette . . . never did see her, but I remember Samyra telling me 'bout her when she visited me in jail.

That was a long, long time ago. Shoot, Sammy was only 'bout sixteen then, and she told me Yvette was the prettiest little ol' baby she'd ever seen . . . Said Jannice didn't have her a month. Tiny, brown, and looked just like her mama . . . Yes, I do remember hearing 'bout Yvette."

Tamara's voice lowered almost to a whisper. "Yvette's father was Maurice Lewis the Third—they called him 'Three.'"

"Three? Yes, I remember him . . . big guy. I used see him around before I went into the joint. He was tall and good-looking and quite a bit older than Jannice. Well known on the streets— really wasn't much more than a hustler, but you could tell he was real smart when you talked to him."

"Do you know where he is?"

"Naw, I don't know that."

Tamara's heart sank. The truth was that if Sissie didn't know where Maurice Lewis was now, Tamara had no idea where to turn. Still, she could not believe that after all these months of searching, everything was coming to a standstill here. She asked one more time, "Are you sure?"

"I'm sure," the woman said, and her tone became cross.

"Oh . . . ," said Tamara softly.

Then Sissie added, "He gots a sister, though . . . She lives somewhere in town."

Tamara snapped to attention and looked at Sissie hopefully. "A sister?"

"Yeah, a sister. She's quite a bit older than he is, about my age, I think, 'cause like I said, he wasn't no spring chicken hisself. Let's see . . . her name is Lillian. Lillian Lewis."

"Do you know where she lives?"

Sissie walked away from the window and sat back down next to her. "I don't know all that, now."

Tamara smiled at the woman. "Ms. Bailey, thank you so much . . . You have helped me. You've helped me a lot."

Sissie gave Tamara a piercing look. "So, I guess you trying to tell me that friend of yours might be my granddaughter, huh?"

Surprised at the question, Tamara answered after a moment's hesitation, "Yes, I suppose that's what I'm telling you."

"Like she'd want to be related to somebody like me," the woman said with a catch in her voice.

Tamara looked for words of comfort. "I'm sure she would like to meet you, Sissie. I'm sure she would," she said.

The woman looked at her with a little light now in her faded eyes and said, "You think? Do you really think after all I done, that she could forgive me?"

Tamara replied quietly, "It might take her some time, but eventually she may be able to forgive you." This unexpected glimpse of Sissie's soft side was profoundly moving for Tamara, yet also disarming, and she was ready to retreat from this emotional situation. She hastily brought the conversation to an end. "Thank you so much for your help, Ms. Bailey."

"Least I can do, huh? Other than that boy in there, I ain't got nobody who cares about me—maybe I'd like to change that."

"I'm sorry I had to bring you bad news today."

"It ain't yo' fault," said the woman grudgingly. "Stuff happens, don't it? Sometimes it just seems like all the bad stuff happens to folks just like me," she added sadly.

Once outside the house, Tamara walked quickly to her car. She was still shaken by the woman's show of emotion. Clearly Sissie was not as hard as she'd pretended to be; in fact, it seemed she actually had a heart. Tamara felt guilty at having judged the woman so quickly. Feeling emotionally wound up now, it was only when Tamara was back in the safe haven of her car that she was able to breathe deeply.

Though at first it seemed she'd gone full circle right back to where she started with Sissie Bailey, ironically, the woman *had* given her invaluable information almost accidentally . . . Maurice Lewis had a sister, and she lived somewhere in town. The truth of it was that she may actually have gotten quite lucky tonight, and she said aloud in the empty car, "I just might actually find Three . . . I might actually find him."

She allowed herself a small smile before sitting there several moments with her heart pounding hard in her chest.

38.

Locked up

The girl ignored the stares of the other kids outside in the common area. By now she'd grown accustomed to adjusting to life in different places, and though she still didn't like it, she considered herself a pro at facing these types of uncomfortable new situations. She could block out others' existence whenever she wanted, and today their faces were a mere blur to her as she searched intently for a place with a little privacy to settle in.

"Girl, you hear me talkin' to you," said the boy. "I guess you think you too good to talk to somebody, huh?" He'd been walking behind her ever since she'd come outside into the playground area, and though she knew he was there, she'd been purposely ignoring him, too.

"No," she said quietly, finally acknowledging that he was there.

"Did you say something?" the boy asked. He'd grown so used

to her lack of response that now he seemed shocked that she might actually have replied to him.

"I said no," she repeated in the same quiet tone.

"No, what?" he asked, so surprised now that she was talking to him at all, he forgot his original question.

"No, I don't think I'm better than anyone. I just don't feel like talkin', that's all," she replied unenthusiastically.

She sure was a pretty little thing, he thought as he gazed sidelong at her . . . small, just like he liked 'em, too. Nobody had said anything about her to him, so he must be the first one to have seen her. He could tell she was kinda shy, though, just by the way she held her head down, so maybe he'd cut her a little break, back off for a minute or two.

Careful to keep his tone neutral, he swiftly changed tactics and said, "Okay, then. You don't have to talk to me."

The girl glanced up at him for a moment, obviously suspicious at the sudden change in his demeanor.

"I tell you what . . . I can tell you don't want to be bothered, and I know a special place right out here where you can have a few minutes to yourself, too. Just follow me."

Just then she felt the stares of some kids who were now quietly watching the two of them curiously. One thing was certain, she thought: she was in no mood to answer lots of questions, nor did she have the energy necessary to continue to tune them out right now. All she really wanted was just to be left alone.

Warily she followed the boy as he led her around the fence to the side of the building, where there was a small doorway that was deep and wide enough for a person to sit in alone. Sizing up the small spot, she quickly surmised that if she turned sideways and pulled her feet up, the others could not even see her sitting there.

"Go 'head, sit on down . . . I'm not going to bother you," said the boy with a wide, toothy grin on his face.

His wide smile was unsettling to her . . . It reminded her of William. Shaking the memory of that evil man from her mind, she gave him a tiny smile and sat down on the cold stoop. She pulled her legs up close and rested her head back on the concrete doorway.

The girl finally relaxed when she heard the soft patter of his fading footfalls indicating that he was walking away. Then, pushing the sounds of the others' chattering into the background, she began to think about the events that had led her here in the first place.

"The Safe Haven Shelter Home," she'd read on the huge green and white sign outside the red brick buildings as they drove up last night. Even though it was not the place she wanted to be, she had to admit that it looked real pretty from the outside. The spacious buildings rested on acres of green grass, and tall, leafy trees surrounded the entire facility. A huge playground area covered one section, complete with a large swimming pool with a big blue plastic slide that twisted and turned to the right and left before its curved tip plunged close to the water's edge.

Feeling trapped and miserable, she had wedged her small body even deeper into the corner of the backseat of the big blue Chevrolet as they pulled into the long, curving driveway. The white caseworker kept trying to lighten the grave mood by talking about the weather and other inconsequential details before interjecting perkily her reassurance that the girl would "just love" this new place. The girl knew that the young blonde woman meant well but simply did not understand that she would never like it anywhere they *made* her live. It was far too dangerous when you lived with others, and she would never trust any people enough to live with them again.

Anyway, during most of the trip there, instead of listening to the woman's ramblings, her own mind was wandering back over the events that had led up to her being in this situation in the first place. Before that night, for the first time in a long time, everything had been going quite well for her. The Reverend Davis offered her a small room in the back of the sanctuary of the church after she'd eaten at Hope Temple Church that night, and she'd actually stayed there for several weeks.

He'd told her sadly that his wife died just last year, and she could tell he was grateful for her unexpected company. Each morning he would fix them both breakfast, and then she would leave as though she were going to school, but instead she wandered the streets until late in the afternoon. Part of her wanted to tell him the truth about what she did all day, but she just didn't have the heart to do it.

It didn't matter how late it was when she returned; there was always a plate left for her on the stove: deliciously cooked foods like fried pork steaks, rice, and gravy, or meat loaf smothered in tomato sauce with mashed potatoes and green peas. The kind minister was well loved by his church members, who often brought him wonderful desserts like fresh apple pie and luscious strawberry-covered cheesecake and rich, chocolaty frosted cakes.

The girl really liked it, living there with him in the church sanctuary, and that was part of the problem: she liked it too much, and she liked him too much, and she knew that she couldn't stay, because sooner or later someone would wonder who she was and where she came from. Then some well-intending church member would call CPS, and she'd be caught, and it was possible that the Reverend Davis might even get in some kind of trouble for letting her stay there.

There was absolutely no way she would let him get in trouble because of her. He had been too goodhearted for her to let that happen. The most that the minister ever asked from her was to go to church, and even though she never could bring herself to attend, he still did not get mad with her.

Her eyes filled up with tears then, and she reached down in her old duffel bag and touched the worn black Bible that he had given to her. Inside the cover he had written, "God loves you, never forget that." Though she didn't really know much about God, she would keep the Bible forever just because he had given it to her, and she knew that what she felt for him was probably the closest thing to love that she'd ever experienced in her young life.

That night before she left for good, he'd cooked a big dinner, almost like a going-away feast, except that he didn't know she was leaving. He baked fresh chicken stuffed with savory mushroom dressing and made freshly whipped potatoes and butter, and green beans flavored with bits of real bacon and colorful red onions. She'd eaten all of it greedily, smiling up at him gratefully when he placed another piece of sizzling hot-water corn bread on her plate. Stuffed, she could barely manage to eat but a smidgen of the peach cobbler that was still warm and drizzled with sweet vanilla ice cream.

"Little girl, I've never seen anyone so small put away so much food so quickly. You make me feel like I'm the best cook in the world," he'd said proudly as he watched her eat.

"You are," she said, stopping her fervent chewing long enough to smile up at him. "Your food is the best I've ever eaten."

His smiled waned then, because he knew that the girl probably had little to compare his offerings to, since she'd probably not lived long in a home where someone cooked for her on a regular basis. She was a runaway, and he knew without her telling him that she lived many days not knowing where her next meal would come from. That thought touched him so deeply that he walked over to her and placed his weathered hand on her small head.

Unsure of the man's intent, the girl swallowed quickly and

sat very still when she felt the touch of his warm, dry hand resting on the top of her head.

He began to pray quietly then, "Lord, just this moment *You* spoke to me. Just this moment You told me to get up and come over here and touch this girl, this girl who is *frightened,* this girl who is so *lonely and scared* that she is still not able to even *tell me her name.* I cover this child right now, Lord. In the blood of Jesus, *I ask that You put Your anointing on this child.*

"Lord, keep her safe no matter where she may be, and surround her with Your grace, O Lord . . . I know that one day she will come to You for herself, but until then, Lord, save a special place in Your heart for this child . . . Thank You, Lord; I thank You for Your continuous blessing and mercy in my life. I love You and I praise Your name, O God . . . *Amen.*"

When she opened her eyes and looked up at him, he was wiping tears away from his eyes, and she made up her mind at that moment that it was time for her to go. Sadly she'd packed her bags while he was sleeping and slipped out in the dark of night. Only two blocks from the church, she was picked up by the police. It seemed that the hospital staff had reported her to the police when she ran away weeks ago, and for some odd reason tonight was when the authorities finally caught up with her.

"Okay, girl, you better come with us," said the officers, and they handcuffed her with a plastic tie and put her in the back of the car.

And now she was here at this new place, a locked-in facility—one they told her was especially built for runaways like herself.

The voices of others rang loud in her ears again as the playground sun shone brightly in her face, and the girl sighed and pulled down the frayed cap that she always wore. Tears squeezed from her eyes.

Maybe I should've taken a chance and stayed with him, she

thought. *Maybe everything would've been all right this time.* But she knew that wasn't true, and it seemed that she would never be able to stay anywhere.

Not for long anyway.

39.

Shining Hour

Lynnette looked around the church and batted her eyes appreciatively. "Girl, you didn't tell me all these fine men went to this church. I might have to start coming here . . . Ain't nobody at my church but a bunch of old men." She rolled her neck and, with one more long, approving glance around the sanctuary, added, "God don't care where you praise Him, long as you do!"

"Here we go," said Jayson teasingly. "Tam, I ain't gonna say no names, but some folks just can't stop, can they? I mean, some folks still tryin' to be a player when they supposed to be worshipping the Lord!"

Lynnette responded snappily, "Boy, I don't play like that in God's house!"

"*Please,* don't start, you two," said Tamara with a quick glance at them. Jayson sat on one side of her in the pew this morning, and Lynnette on the other. Frustrated by the constant disparaging comments the two of them made about Sienna, she'd invited them to hear her sing her solo today so they could see another side of the girl. Though it was not the first time that Sienna had sung alone, Tamara's own attendance was spotty, so today would be the first time that she would hear her as well.

Lynnette moved an errant braid away from her face. "Just for you, Tamara, and for the Lord, of course, I'm not gonna let that big-head boy sitting next to you get me upset this morning."

Jayson said, "And because me and God are close, I won't let her bother me, either, *but we do know who got the big head.*" Before Lynnette could respond, he chuckled as he asked Tamara, "So, can little Miss Sienna really sing? Or did she just bad-mouth her way to the front of the choir, too?"

Tamara hit Jayson with her elbow and said, "Stop it, Jay . . . She *can* sing. In fact, from what I've heard, she can sing very, very well . . . You'll see."

Jayson leaned over her then and remarked, "Lynnette, you really do look nice today . . . not like a diva, just like a regular ol' church-going sistah girl."

Lynnette's royal blue knit suit was accented by taupe pumps and a silk printed scarf in shades of royal blue, purple, and magenta that was tied around her neck. Small silver earrings dangled from her ears, and her microbraids were tucked into an elegant French roll. Instead of her usual flashy reds or deep-burgundy nail colorings, she'd used a pale pink color today and left her usual chunky silver at home in favor of a more delicate sterling ring and bracelet.

With a smile Lynnette replied, "Well, thank you, Jay . . . you lookin' good yourself." I've never seen you in a suit before, and I must say, it makes you look almost fly, brotha!"

He straightened out his tie with a dramatic flourish and responded, "Thank you so much, Lynn . . . This is just a little somethin' I threw on, you know." Jayson knew he was cutting a sharp profile, though. His expensive navy blue pin-striped suit was impeccably tailored, and he wore a pair of brown Stacy Adams wingtips to match.

Tamara smiled, happy that the two of them had called a truce and that she would not have to endure their constant bickering this morning.

Shooting her a sidelong smile that showed off his deep dimples, Jayson stated, "Tam, you look good, too, but you always know how to put it together right."

Appreciatively he checked out her bias-cut black and white print georgette skirt topped by a deep-red knit turtleneck sweater twin set. She wore understated sling-back black pumps and carried a matching small black bag. Her ears glittered with the small CZ gold wires that Sienna had bought her for Christmas, and her watch was her only other jewelry today.

Before Tamara could respond to Jayson, Lynnette added wryly, "Yeah, girl, you always look good. You the kinda person who could wear a burlap bag and make it look like it was made by a designer."

Unsure of how to respond to the generous compliments, Tamara replied genuinely, "Thank you . . . I'm glad you like it."

"I agree, you do look very nice today, Tamara," she heard from beside her.

This time Tamara was glad to hear the instantly recognizable husky tone of Isaiah Perry. He'd telephoned her a few times since they chaperoned the Friday Teen Night event, and each time they'd spoken, she'd grown more comfortable talking with him.

"Hello, Isaiah," she replied without even attempting to hide her bright smile when she looked up at him. Happy to see him, for a moment she forgot all about her two coworkers sitting on either side of her.

Not intending to go unnoticed long, Lynnette cleared her throat loudly, and Tamara reddened suddenly, remembering her and Jayson, "Oh, I'm sorry. Isaiah, this is Lynnette Moore and Jayson Johnson. We work together at the Care Agency, and they've come with me today to hear Sienna sing."

Isaiah leaned over and shook both of their hands and said, "It will be a treat for you to hear our Miss Sienna sing. I'm telling you, that girl can blow! Hopefully, you will enjoy Minister Walker's sermon as well, and we will see you here again." Then he turned his attention to Tamara again, "As always, I'm glad to see you here, Tamara . . . I better get going, though; we will be singing in a few. I just wanted to 'holla atcha,' as the kids say," he added before walking away.

Lynnette raised her eyebrows and then gave Tamara a long, searching stare before asking impetuously, "Girrrl, is there something you ain't told us? Brotha man is fine and in church, too? That's a double whammy, almost too good to be true!"

But before she could answer, Jayson commented with a touch of derision in his tone, "C'mon, ladies, let's not pump the brotha up too high. Don't you know that's an old trick? Just 'cause a brotha's in church don't mean nothin'." He patted his chest and said, "The church gotta be in *here,* you know?"

Lynnette rolled her eyes at Jayson and then turned to Tamara and mouthed the word "jealous" before stating adamantly, "Now, where were we? Oh, I know—fine brotha man who just left. Tell me, now, Tam, do you and him 'got a little thang' going on or something, that we don't know about?"

Embarrassed by Lynnette's persistent probing, Tamara answered, "No-o-o, Lynn, there is *nothing* going on! Isaiah is Sienna's teacher, and sometimes when I come here to church we talk and stuff, that's all."

Lynnette batted her large eyes in her dramatic fashion. "Girrrl, I think you might be missing out on something, then. 'Cause that brotha was *not* looking at you like he's just Sienna's teacher; he was lookin' at you like *wasn't nobody else* in this room—and to tell the truth, you was lookin' at him the *exact same way.*"

Tamara said, "No, Lynnette, you are just seeing things," but her wide smile betrayed her true feelings.

Busily talking, neither girl noticed Jayson looking in the direction where Isaiah Perry was standing with the choir. Stroking his goatee, he was studying the man intently, with a scowl on his handsome brown face.

To Tamara's relief, the choir began to sing, interrupting Lynn's persistent questioning.

Tamara recognized right away the John P. Kee song they were singing as one that Sienna played quite often at home, and it sounded especially beautiful today. She sat back in the pew, closed her eyes, and let the harmonious words course through her body. When she opened her eyes again, Lynnette and Jay were standing on their feet and singing with the choir.

Lynnette held her hands high in the air, and her eyes were closed while tears ran slowly down her face. Jayson was rocking from side to side, totally engrossed in the song.

Surprised to see her coworkers so touched by the music, Tamara closed her eyes again. Something about her two friends' obvious emotion made her own eyes swim with tears. Again today Tamara felt that same fluttering inside that had been building each time she attended church, and she was unsure how long she could continue to restrain it. This intense quickening was deep within, and Tamara intuitively sensed that whatever was happening inside her was unexplainable, profound, and very real.

Throughout the Reverend Walker's sermon, Tamara felt as though some long-sleeping part of her was awakening and struggling to be recognized. But though his message was very moving, somehow she managed to hold her feelings within.

The Reverend Walker prayed for a moment, then said,

"Today we are going to do something a bit different. We have been blessed to have a relatively a new member who can sing so beautifully and is so clearly anointed by the Lord with her voice that I wanted her to join me as we call those so inclined to come to Christ this morning." The Reverend Walker turned toward the choir. "Sienna Larson, will you join me, please."

Sienna came down from the choir stand with the microphone in her small hand. Tamara had heard Sienna sing before at home, but she was totally thrown off balance by the beauty of the girl's tone this morning. Without instrumental accompaniment, Sienna began the song in a sweet, high voice that sounded as pure as a bird's. The lyrics described the journey of one struggling through difficulties in life and not always succeeding.

As she continued to sing the beautiful lyrics, the timbre of her voice became more and more resonant until her voice seemed to fill the entire sanctuary. Tamara was listening, transfixed in the moment, and by the time Sienna sang the words that asked how a person can survive alone, Tamara's long pent-up tears began to fall. All she heard was the words of the song then, as it described a better way to live, by asking for help.

She barely heard Lynnette tell her, "Girrl, she *can* sing. My God, listen to that child's voice."

Tamara was dazed, watching Sienna singing through eyes blurred by tears, and suddenly she felt herself taken over by something that she could not stop. She could see Jayson looking at her curiously, but he said nothing, and she could not speak.

Sienna's voice peaked then, reaching a full, high crescendo as she sang about where the help could come from. It could come from God.

As the song ended, Sienna continued to hum the tune in the same sweet voice with which she'd begun the melody, while Minister Walker asked the congregation, "If there's anybody

238

today who would like to invite God into their life, now is the time."

Before the minister had even completed the words, Tamara's feet were moving of their own accord. She wiped away the tears streaming down her face with a tissue that someone thrust at her as she walked down the aisle. In moments, she was standing there at the front of the church, unaware that Denise Jackson was also crying and that Isaiah was mouthing the words silently, "Thank you, Jesus."

Jayson's and Lynnette's eyes were wet watching Tamara standing before the congregation with tears running down her face. The two of them knew that this type of public display was a huge departure from Tamara's normally reserved behavior, and that made the moment even more touching to them.

When the minister looked into Tamara's tear-stained face and asked if she wanted to join Hope Temple and accept Christ as her Lord and Savior, all she could do was nod yes. The Reverend Walker hugged Tamara tightly then, and though the moment was surreal to her, she felt safer and more secure than she ever remembered feeling before. There in front of the entire congregation, she rested her head on his broad shoulder and sobbed happily.

40.

Blindsided

"Tamara, that girl of yours just doesn't like me," said Jayson while opening the car door for her in the parking lot of the Club Rapport, where they'd just arrived for a little dancing.

Tamara had surprised herself by accepting his invitation to come out, but then, she'd enjoyed dancing when they'd come before, and so she decided to try it again tonight. Lynnette was unavailable, leaving the two of them on their own this evening.

"Oh, it's not that she doesn't like you, Jay," replied Tamara while cautiously maneuvering from the car to avoid sliding on an icy patch of sidewalk.

"Watch your step, now, Tam," Jayson said grabbing her elbow to help stabilize her as she stepped down and out of his new Chevy Blazer. Just last week he'd traded in his Malibu and pulled into work later that day in the shiny, black vehicle, with a huge smile on his face.

"Your truck is really nice, Jay," said Tamara.

"I'm diggin' her, too," replied Jayson as he took a long glance at his new four-by-four. "And, unlike your little Sienna girl, my truck is vibin' with me, too."

"Aw, Jayson, c'mon . . . Sienna likes you just fine."

"Well, what is it then, Tam?" he asked. "The girl talks to me like she can't stand me, and I really do try to be polite and nice to her . . . 'specially now since I know that lil' sistah girl can sing like that. Shoot, I want her to remember me in a good way when she signs that first recording contract," he added mischievously.

Tamara snatched her arm from him and gave him a look of teasing derision. "Jay, I'm surprised at you. Why, that's *triflin'*!"

Jayson gave her a look of feigned shock. "Well, listen to *you*. She's rubbing off on you! *Triflin'*, huh, Tam?"

Still laughing, they entered the club, and while the crowd was substantial this Wednesday evening, there were still plenty of open tables for the two of them to choose from.

While trailing Jayson as he searched for a suitable stopping place for them, Tamara recognized the cool soprano saxophone of Marion Meadows filling the air. Along with their growing gospel music collection, she finally was purchasing some jazz CDs for herself as well, and Marion Meadows was one of her favorites.

The mellow vocals *were* a little suggestive, but the musical accompaniment was excellent, and the smooth sounds made her want to dance. Besides this was a jazz club, and many of the songs did not have any lyrics at all, just sweet music, which is what she liked best anyway.

"How about right here?" asked Jayson loudly while pointing to an isolated corner booth.

Skeptically she replied, "Its a little dark, isn't it?"

"No, it's fine to me—close to the dance floor and everything."

A bit reluctantly she agreed, "Well, okay, if you think so."

Jayson helped her out of her coat, whistling loudly once he saw the outfit she was wearing.

Tamara's clingy black knit skirt and sweater set was adorned with a small gold chain belt, which accented her curvy hips. A gray and black silk scarf was tied loosely around her neck, and the long skirt was deeply split in the back, revealing the shapely swell of her calves when she moved.

Jayson stared at her openly, remarking in a low tone, "Girrrl, I ain't never seen you wear nothin' like this before."

Tamara's deep-brown skin flushed red suddenly. She sat down quickly and smoothed her skirt over her legs nervously.

"It was all Sienna's idea," she explained uncomfortably. "She picked it out when we went shopping the other day . . . She seemed to think it was a good choice for me."

His approval was still quite evident as he replied, "Well, for once I agree with little Miss Sienna. That outfit is slammin', girl. It shows *all* your assets." He gave her one long last glance before adding a bit flirtatiously, "Don't you go nowhere, now! I'll be right back; let me get our drinks."

Ignoring his teasing manner, Tamara nodded her head to the music while thinking of how comfortable she felt being here tonight. Reflectively she noted that since she had joined church the other week, she felt more relaxed than usual all the time. With a sudden smile then, Tamara realized she derived a special comfort from knowing that she was part of something larger than herself, and that she had something inside that was special and wonderful.

After she had joined that day, people had crowded around her to congratulate her, but even in the haze of the moment she recognized Isaiah Perry's and Denise Jackson's faces. All her friends seemed happy; Jay and Lynn were smiling, and Sienna . . . well, the teen was overjoyed. The girl hugged her tightly and then said incredulously, "And you joined when I was singing, Tamara . . . when I was singing!"

She smiled back at the girl and said, "Yes, Sienna when *you* were singing . . . I couldn't help myself, because your voice moved me so much. Sienna, you truly have an amazing gift."

The following Sunday, after services Tamara was baptized, and with her eyes closed tightly, she held her breath while the Reverend Walker laid her gently back in the cold water. When he brought her up and Tamara burst sputtering from the water into the warm air, she felt ebullient and refreshed, as though she'd left some unnecessary part of her old self down there in the cold water.

"Whatcha thinkin' 'bout?" asked Jayson as he returned with their drinks.

"No alcohol, right?" she asked before taking a sip.

"Nope, just a virgin drink, like you asked for. You seemed deep in thought, though, Tam. What were you thinking about?"

"Just about the other Sunday, that's all."

"When you joined the church, you mean?"

"Yes. It's all been so strange, Jay. Ever since Sienna moved in with me, so many different things have been happening lately that it's kinda hard to keep up with all of the changes."

"Well, Tam, getting to know the Lord is a good thing. I am far from a perfect person, but even I know that we all need God in our lives . . . There are so many times in my own life when I don't know how I would've made it without my faith in Him. Knowing Him for yourself and having Him in your life makes the difficult days much easier."

"I'm beginning to understand that, Jay."

"The best thang about it all is, even if you didn't really know Him before, He still loved and knew you. It is amazing how many times He carries us when we can't carry ourselves."

Pondering that thought silently, the two of them enjoyed the music and sipped their drinks quietly.

Glancing up at Jay, Tamara was shocked to see that he was looking at her, and the intensity in his eyes made his gaze different from usual tonight. Slightly stunned, she asked, "Jay, why are you looking at me like that?"

Jayson was nursing a double shot of Hennessy, and the warm liquor boosted his courage, enabling him to say to Tamara what he'd been keeping inside for a while. Though he'd always been attracted to her, he had always convinced himself they were meant to be just friends. At least until he saw Isaiah Perry looking at her so intently at church the other week. For some reason, when the possibility of losing her to another became apparent, his feelings for her kept rising to the surface, and now it was too difficult to hold them inside any longer.

Jay's gold bracelet shimmered on his smooth brown wrist as he stirred his drink with one hand before glancing up at her again. "Tamara, what would you say if I told you that I would like this to be a real date?"

Tamara looked at him uncertainly, as if it took a moment or two for the meaning of what he was saying to truly sink in. "A *real* date? . . . you and I?"

Jay's eyes were on his brown drink, scrupulously avoiding her eyes. "Yes, Tam, a real date . . . you and me. For a while now, I've been wanting to tell you how much I like you."

"What do you mean, 'like me,' Jay?"

After another long, slow sip of his drink, he stared directly into her eyes and replied, "Tam, I like you a lot and maybe what I'm feeling is even stronger than just 'like'; you know?" In a rush, words poured from his lips as he moved closer to her, and she smelled the pungent odor of the liquor from the drink on his breath. "It's just that you are so beautiful . . . so naturally beautiful to me, and you're also intelligent and so very sweet. I keep thinkin' you are the type of girl I would like to spend my whole life with."

Tamara tried to disguise her shock. Though Jay was good-looking and lots of fun to be with, she'd never thought of him as more than a friend. Even though he flirted with her now and then, she always thought he was just teasing since she was aware that she was different from the more flamboyant type of girl she usually saw him coupled with.

Stammering uneasily, she replied, "I—I—I don't know what to say, Jay. I've just never thought of you and me in that way."

Jayson turned from her then and, feigning nonchalance, bobbed his head to the music while his face became a mask of unconcern. He shifted gears. "So, do you like this Isaiah Perry guy? Is he your type?"

Thrown completely off balance now, Tamara answered falteringly, "Oh, I don't know, Jay. Recently, it just so happens that we run into each other now and then, and I guess we are kinda like friends, you know?"

His glance was skeptical. "Friends, uh? He wasn't looking at you like you were just a friend at church the other week, Tam. You *can* tell me the truth, you know."

Though uncomfortable with his insistent attitude, Tamara tried to sound lighthearted when she replied, "C'mon, Jay, I *am* telling you the truth. We are nothing more than friends." In a way, though, Tamara knew that she wasn't being totally honest with him, since each time she saw Isaiah Perry or heard his voice on the telephone, her heart danced in her chest and suddenly she felt happier than she had only moments before. But since she didn't know for sure what Isaiah thought of her once she put her own feelings aside they were no more than friends . . . no more.

Jayson set his now empty glass on the table and grabbed her hand. "C'mon, girl, let's dance. That's what we came here for, right?"

"Right!" agreed Tamara, relieved that the awkward moment had passed and glad the uncomfortable conversation was evidently over.

As the mellow melody led them, they whirled, stepped, and danced together to the sounds of Boney James's "Body Language." To her surprise, she hadn't forgotten how to step with the music, and she moved confidently as Jayson twirled her and they glided to soaring horns and tinkling keyboards. Breathless with excitement, she smiled up at him when the song ended, and did not protest when he pulled her close for the next song.

"I like this," he said in a low, hoarse voice.

Thrown off by the unfamiliar huskiness in his tone, she was unsure whether he meant he liked being close to her or liked the song playing now, and Tamara felt her own discomfort start to rise again.

Jayson held her tightly as they swayed to the jazzy, melodious voice of Boz Scaggs filling the room, but when Tamara accidentally caught the reflection of the two of them in the large mirror covering the wall behind them, Jayson's eyes were closed tightly, and he seemed lost in another place.

Unhappily, Tamara realized as she watched him that their earlier conversation was not really over. Right now it looked as if Jayson did have deeper feelings for her than she'd ever imagined. Still, she was hopeful that it was all some sort of misunderstanding, because if it was not, they were on two different wavelengths, and it was possible that their relationship would never be the same.

41.

Caught Unaware

"There's our table over there," said Lynnette, using her sparkly gold-beaded evening bag to point out their seats across the crowded conference room.

Tonight was the annual Foster Parent Dinner and she, Tamara, and several other Care employees were in attendance, representing the agency. Once Tamara spotted the table, she immediately saw Joan Erickson and Jayson sitting there with some of their other coworkers. Despite her hopes, there was a strain in her relations with Jay ever since his revelations during their dancing excursion the other week, and she was doubtful whether the discomfort would be dispelled this evening.

Oh, well, I'm not going to let anything ruin my evening, she thought determinedly. This event only occurred once a year, and it was the one special night when all the state agencies came together to honor foster parents and reward those who had been deemed worthy of acknowledgment. In fact, her mentor and friend Denise Jackson and Denise's husband, Leonard, had been honored with several different awards over the years, in recognition of the couple's continuing commitment to kids without homes.

She glanced at her friend approvingly. "Lynn you really outdid yourself tonight—that outfit is beautiful."

"You mean this old thing?" asked Lynnette, tossing her a teasing smile over her shoulder. Tamara could tell that Lynn was quite aware she was looking good, though. Her full-legged, flowing black silk pants and matching sleeveless buttonhole top were covered by a flowing caftan of brilliantly printed handspun silk, painted in bold African colors of deep gold, burgundy, and brown. Tonight, instead of her usual sterling silver, she wore ornately styled ethnic-design gold earrings that matched her cuff bracelet and wide-woven gold ring.

Her trademark microbraids were lifted high on her head in a bun of sorts, with tendrils of curled hair strategically left free to hang loosely around her face and neck. The hairstyle suited her face perfectly, accenting her natural gifts of high cheekbones and large eyes. Tamara couldn't help but notice how Lynnette moved through the tables with ease, which confirmed her suspicion that Lynn was more confident than usual about her appearance tonight.

At their table Tamara read the small place cards sitting tent-like at each place setting, and was instantly relieved to see that hers and Lynn's had been placed next to each other.

As if reading her mind, Lynnette said snidely out of the side of her mouth, "Girrl, I'm glad they got us by each other, 'cause it's some of these folks I really didn't want to be sittin' by, if you know what I mean. Shoot, I don't even want to be bothered with them at work, let alone after hours."

Joan Erickson offered the two women a tight smile before re-marking, "Now, don't you both look nice? As always, Lynnette, you look just gorgeous, and Tamara, you look very elegant tonight as well."

With her usual sassy aplomb Lynn threw her red-nailed hand out at their boss, smiling widely as she replied, "Joan, girrl, thank you. This old thang is just somethin' I pulled out the back of the closet and threw on. Now, my girl, Tamara, *she's* lookin' good."

Tamara lowered her head to cover her smile at Lynnette's sauciness—only she would have the verve to call Joan "girl" in front of all their coworkers. She was truly one of a kind. Tamara also felt embarrassed—she was always surprised and thrown off guard by compliments about her appearance. Tonight she thought herself underdressed to say the least. Her classically styled deep-violet form-fitting knit dress was topped by a beaded black cardigan sweater and completed with plain black pumps and a matching purse.

"Tamara has quite a figure, and so whatever she wears, she wears very well," said Joan, looking at her with the same tight smile on her face.

"I know that's right," added Jayson. Actually, he had been

uncharacteristically quiet up until then, and Tamara had been hoping that he'd had second thoughts about his revelations the other night. However, his comment made it clear to her that his state of mind had not changed since they were at the club. Troubled by this realization, Tamara tossed a quick glance his way, tightening her lips imperceptibly without saying a word. Sighing, she pulled out the chair next to Lynnette and sat down hoping that, at least, the uncomfortable subject would not come up again tonight.

Thoughts of Jayson soon faded as she and Lynnette chatted. Dinner was served by bored-looking young men and women all attired in white. The food was the usual fare for this type of event: chicken Kiev, rice with vegetables, and green beans. Plenty of fresh bread and rolls with butter were available, and stacked on trays around them were several types of sweet treats for dessert.

Lynnette took a piece of bread, turned, and passed the plate to her, asking, "So, are you still dwellin' in the glow from joining church and accepting the Lord into your life?"

"The glow?" asked Tamara quizzically.

Jayson stuck his head in front of Lynn's, replying, "When you first join church, you get kinda caught up in the emotion of the moment—you know, feeling good and everything."

"Yeah, that's it, the after*glow*," agreed Lynnette. She pulled the warm bread apart and buttered it. "Girrl, the last thang I need is all these carbs . . . Eating this bread is just like applying fat directly to these hips of mine," she laughed.

Jayson continued, "Lynn, don't nobody want to hear about your hips, tonight. Let's just eat, drink, and be merry and all that, okay?" Then he turned his attention to Tamara. "Back to 'the glow' . . . Tam, it's the part after that emotional day that's hard. When you tryin' every day to live life on the good foot, according to the Word of God."

"I know that's right," Lynn agreed again.

Tamara took a roll and chewed the warm bread thoughtfully. They were right about one thing; she *was* riding high. It was so unlike her even to have walked up there and showed her emotions in front of the entire church as she did. Even today she was unsure of what really had happened . . . Maybe she was still in some sort of emotional daze.

"This chicken Kiev is dry," remarked Lynn with her lips turned up. "These events never serve good food, do they? The best thing is always the bread and the sweets, which nobody needs to eat much of, right, girl?" She took a swallow of iced water from the crystal goblet in front of her, "I tell you what, though, girl, that Sienna got a voice on her! Uh! Uh! Uh! That child can *saaang*!"

"She's right," said Jayson. "Your little Miss Sienna *can* blow! What's that girl gonna do with all that talent, Tamara?"

"I don't know," said Tamara. She took a drink of her own water. "I suppose I've never even thought about it like that, and she's never really talked to me about any future in singing, either. Right now she just really seems to enjoy singing in church."

Lynn turned her wide-eyed gaze on Tamara. "Seriously, Tamara, the girl gots mad talent. You might as well get ready for some pressure from folks about her singing future. And y'all need to start talking about it, so that you got a plan."

"Pass the salt and pepper, Lynn," said Jayson. "She's telling you right, Tam. When word gets out about that little girl's powerful voice, she's gonna explode!"

Joan Erickson stopped talking. Evidently, part of their conversation had captured her attention, and she asked, "What's this about talent and exploding?"

The three of them exchanged glances.

"Sienna's got some singing talent," explained Jayson. "Right now she's singing in church."

The woman smiled and commented dryly, "Well, that's probably the only place she can sing right now. She *is* a ward of the state, after all, and she can't do anything without the state's approval."

Flatly Lynnette responded, "We all know that, Joan."

Jayson cleared his throat loudly and wiped his mouth with the napkin.

"Excuse me for a minute," said Lynnette, rolling her eyes meaningfully toward Joan while her lips curved upward derisively. "Don't you need to go to the ladies' room, too?" she asked Tamara pointedly.

Her hint for Tamara to accompany her so that they could vent further on Joan's intrusive remarks missed the mark, though, and the uncomprehending Tamara shook her head no.

As soon as Lynnette exited for the bathroom, Jayson smoothly slid over into her seat by Tamara and, with the napkin in front of his mouth, whispered to her, "She always got to tell us something she think we don't know. We *all* know little Miss Thang—excuse me—*Sienna* is a ward of the state."

Tamara's own voice was low as she replied, "I know. It does get frustrating, Jay, because it's as if she believes we would do something illegal or against the rules to try and promote Sienna into a singing career or something. I don't really understand why she would think that."

"I do," said Jayson. With his eyes locked on Tamara's, he purposefully rubbed the back of his deep-brown hand, demonstrating to her his thought that Joan was again being racist.

"Oh, Jayson, I certainly hope not. Just cause we're black doesn't mean we're stupid."

Quietly, he added then, "I have been stupid, though, Tamara."

She turned to him with a quizzical look on her face. "What do you mean, you've been stupid?"

His stare deepened, and he stroked his goatee while watching her intently. "Stupid to not have told you long before now how I feel about you."

Thankfully, before Tamara could respond, Lynnette returned, tapped him playfully on the shoulder with her purse, and said, "Jay, get out of my seat!" After sliding into her now vacant chair, she added with her usual sauciness, "Now, c'mon, y'all, let's get this party started!" Then, stacking Tamara's plate on her own, she handed both to the young waiter and asked loudly, "It's about time for the show to get on the road, isn't it?"

It was as if those in charge of the event had heard the girl's remarks; no sooner had she finished her comment than the emcee tapped the microphone, saying, "Welcome, all, to the annual Foster Parent Dinner and Award Ceremony."

Tamara was grateful for the reprieve from Jayson's unexpected advances moments before. Clearly Jayson seemed intent on keeping up his uncomfortable pursuit of her, but at least for now she did not have to think about it. Throughout the ceremony her thoughts were unfocused, though, floating and whirling about as she thought about all the changes happening every day in her life. Her newly changing relationship with Jayson was just one more thing to add to the list.

Earlier Lynn had advised her that she might be basking in the afterglow of the highly emotional experience she'd had the other Sunday at church. Quite possibly that was true, since inwardly she felt incredibly light and free, and yet at the same time she felt connected, grounded—as if she were part of something bigger and more important than herself.

"Look at Ms. Joan up there," said Lynn in her ear. "Girrl, Joan might get on my nerves, but she know she can dress, though."

Tamara pulled herself from her musings to look up approvingly at Joan Erickson's deep-emerald, softly tailored one-button pantsuit. The woman wore dyed-to-match strappy high-heeled sandals and had a buttery-yellow raw silk print scarf thrown casually across one shoulder. Her huge diamond sparkled in the spotlight on the stage.

"Why's she up there, anyway?" asked Tamara, fully attentive now. "I didn't realize Joan was presenting anything tonight."

Joan Erickson's voice interrupted her, and as the woman spoke through the microphone, she answered Tamara's question. "I'm up here to introduce someone very, very special tonight. This woman and her husband have probably housed more kids in their home as foster and adoptive parents than anyone in the state of Illinois. Most of us don't want to open our homes to our own relatives, but these wonderful, caring people have fostered over two hundred kids and adopted thirty-five."

She paused several moments for the enthusiastic applause from the audience to subside.

Dramatically the spotlight illuminated the side of the stage, and Denise Jackson appeared in the light. Joan smiled and said, "Mrs. Jackson, please join me, if you will."

Tamara clapped hard, thrilled to see her friend standing there in the spotlight. She thought how typical it was of the woman's humble nature not even to have told her that she was going to receive an award tonight, and yet she was glad to be here to see her accept the honor.

The large woman was regally resplendent tonight in a deep-purple skirt suit with high taupe pumps. A matching large hat sat jauntily on the side of her head as well.

Accepting the microphone from Joan, Mrs. Jackson said, "Thank you, Ms. Erickson. I am honored to be here tonight." She chuckled deep in her throat and said, "Y'all can see I'm glad to be here—I'm dressed in my Sunday best!"

"Wonder where Mr. Jackson is . . . funny he's not up there with her, isn't it?" asked Tamara. Lynnette seemed not to have heard her, since she did not reply, so Tamara turned her attention back to the stage.

The woman continued in her throaty voice, "Only a few weeks ago, Mrs. Erickson came to me and told me that she wanted me to present this special award tonight, and I was so very honored that she asked me to do it. You see, y'all, in this world we live in today, it is rare that we meet a genuinely good person, and the recipient of this award is just that. She's good, sweet, kind, and gentle in spirit. These are traits that aren't often appreciated in this world we live in today, where most folks are out for themselves."

Many in the audience nodded their approval of her statement.

"Anyway, I know that we are all tired, and this is the last presentation of the night, and I'll make it short. As a foster parent I can attest to the difficulty of the task. It is hard taking in any child and especially difficult to take in a teenager. Shoot, y'all know these teenagers are already hormonal, and then with the hardships life has often handed many of these young folks in the system . . . they got other issues as well, believe me!

"The sad truth is that there are never enough foster homes to take in all the young people who need a place to live. And there are some young people that are so hard to place, there is literally no one who will take them in—and even though they may be hard to manage, they are still children who need a home of their own. Care Agency had a young lady like that earlier this year, and when push came to shove, the only person who would accept her into her home was one of their own employees.

"Now, mind you, this young woman is an excellent employee, rarely misses a day, and rates high among foster parents and birth parents for her empathic nature and professional way of delivering services to them. But she accepted this girl into her home . . . and this child is a handful, too, feisty and smart-mouthed, but this young, single working woman has hung in there with her.

"Yes, the two of them still struggle, and I know it is difficult for her sometimes, but the point is, she cared enough to give the girl a chance. The fact is, we don't know where this teen would've gone had Tamara Britton not opened up her home to her."

Tamara's jaw dropped then. She'd began to notice that the story sounded quite similar to her and Sienna's as Denise Jackson delved deeper into her narrative, but she was absolutely shocked to find it was Tamara herself that the woman was speaking of so highly. Questioningly she glanced at Lynn and Jayson, and with one look at the wide smiles they wore, she immediately realized everyone had known about this but her.

"Tamara? Tamara, baby girl, where are you?" asked Denise Jackson while squinting into the packed ballroom.

As if in slow motion, the spotlight turned its brilliant light to where Tamara sat with her friends and coworkers.

Denise Jackson's smile was dazzling then, and she said ebulliently, "Come on up here, Tamara. C'mon, now, baby girl!"

In a daze Tamara rose from her seat and made the long procession to the stage as she prepared to face a crowd again for the second time in just a few weeks.

After hugging her hard, Mrs. Jackson kept her arm around her tightly as she said loudly into the microphone, "For being a consummate professional every day that you perform your job, and for not only opening your home to a difficult young woman, but for being brave enough to open your heart as well, we salute you Tamara Britton, with this special Child Welfare Employee of the Year Award."

Denise Jackson had tears brimming in her eyes as she handed her the award. "Here, baby . . . I love you."

"I love you, too, Mrs. Jackson," the young woman said as her own eyes grew watery and she faced the crowd, saying simply, "Thank you." Later, when she replayed the evening's events in her mind, it wasn't the applauding crowd or even the award itself that stood out most. Instead, it was the three words from Mrs. Jackson that made the night so special. "I love you," she'd said to her.

I love you!

42.

Reminiscing

Where is the house? Tamara asked herself, slowing down her Toyota to a lower speed while straining to see the addresses on the houses as she drove by.

"There's 1128, 1130, 1142—here it is . . . 1148 North Dexter Drive," she read aloud.

Critically she glanced at her reflection in the rearview mirror, ran her fingers through her hair, and then grabbed her briefcase from the passenger seat before closing the car door behind her.

Her confident stride disguised the anxiety she was feeling at that moment. This stop might really be the end of the road. Tamara sighed, and her heart was heavy at the possibility of this being a dead end. If there was no luck here, this would mean no more stones to turn over and nothing left to uncover. She'd been searching so long, it was difficult for her to fathom that one way or another, the search was about to end . . . but if Lillian Lewis could offer her no information about her brother's whereabouts, it really would be over. She would just give up in that case.

Only a few weeks had passed since she'd visited Sissie Bailey for the second time, and Tamara felt an odd déjà vu as she again knocked at the door of a stranger. Looking around, she noted that the older home's exterior was well kept. Even the painted wooden floor of the porch was immaculate, and there was a lovely old-fashioned swing hanging in front of the shiny plate-glass window there.

When she opened the screen to knock again, this time she saw a small doorbell blending inconspicuously into the door-jamb. Pressing it lightly, Tamara immediately heard the corresponding melodic chime of bells inside the home.

The door was opened by a deep-brown-complexioned, tall and regal gray-haired woman wearing a blue cotton flowered shirtdress topped by a matching cardigan sweater. Around her neck was gold cross on a chain, and in her hand she held a pair of steel-blue wire-framed reading glasses.

"Hi," said Tamara as she extended her hand to the woman. "I'm Tamara Bailey; I spoke with you yesterday by telephone about Maurice Lewis the Third—or do you call him Three?"

The woman placed her glasses on her nose and took Tamara's small hand into her own long thin one for a quick moment. Her dark eyes were magnified by the glasses and appeared distorted as she stared at her closely for a moment before she responded in a dry voice, "Hmph, I do not . . . call him that— 'Three,' that is; that's some of that street talk, and Maurice was *not* raised in the streets. He just chose to wallow out there for some reason that I cannot fathom."

If there was one thing that Tamara knew right away, it was

257

that Lillian Lewis was no woman of the streets. The woman's diction was perfect, each word spoken crisply and enunciated precisely in a low, throaty tone.

"Come on in, Ms. Britton."

"Oh, you can call me Tamara," she responded as she followed the woman inside.

"Okay, then, Tamara, and you can call me Miss Lillian," she added, giving the young woman a wry smile of her own.

"Your house is beautiful, Miss Lillian," commented the younger woman as she looked around the room filled with dark antique mahogany furniture. The smell of lavender permeated the air, and she noted that against the far wall sat a butterfly-armed sofa; its pale cream color matched the shades of the brass-base antique lights that sat on the end tables. A huge ornately framed mirror hung above the couch, and other artworks hung on the walls around the room.

Especially eye-catching was the arrangement in the corner of the hallway. There, under a massive painting of a scenic view of Paris, sat an antique table balanced precariously on ornately cut curved wooden legs; and on its shiny top, decoratively placed, were several photos encased in various types of frames.

"May I?" she said, turning to look at the woman as she gestured toward the table.

"Yes, of course," the woman replied as she led her over to the photos.

Tamara gingerly picked up one of the black-and-white photos from the table and gazed at it inquisitively. Pictured was a young couple who looked shyly into the camera from where they sat side-by-side on the step of a house.

"That is our mother and father," said Lillian Lewis proudly. "You know, back then in the 1950s, photos were in black-and-white."

Tamara gently stroked the ornate metal frame with her

thumb while staring raptly at the smiling pair. "It's beautiful. The two of them look like they were very happy."

"They were in love, and they were sitting in front of their very first house. Back then black people—Negroes is what we were called then—did not often get a chance to own a home. They were proud to have been one of the first Negro families to have purchased one in our town."

"What town is that?"

"Glasgow, Kentucky, that's where they both came from . . . old coal-mining town. My granddaddy Maurice Lewis is from there, and then of course Daddy, Maurice Lewis Jr., was born there, too. He met Mother, Maylene Stuart, all the way back when they were in grade school, and then the two of them went to high school together. After they graduated, my daddy went away to the Air Force, and then he came home and got married to Mother."

The woman's eyes began to glaze over as she stared straight ahead, recounting the events of her parents' past. "Daddy tried to work in a factory for a while, but it just didn't suit his personality, and so he decided to go finish his education. Mother worked while Daddy went to college."

"College?" She was shocked to know that Maurice Lewis III's father had gone to college, especially way back then, when that sort of education was almost unheard of for African-Americans.

"Oh, yes. My daddy graduated from college," the woman said proudly. "He even had his master's degree."

"What did he do?"

"First he was a school teacher for fifteen years, and then he was a principal of an elementary school downtown, until he passed. Mother went to school after he got finished, and she became a nurse. Nursed folks at a hospital and then in their homes, till she passed on."

"I can tell you are quite proud of them."

"I was—rather, I am. I am proud of both of them. Mother and Daddy had *honorable* jobs . . . Being a nurse is honorable . . . helping people when they are sick and cannot help themselves. Every person does not have the capability to do that. It takes a special gift."

"I agree."

The woman held her glasses in her hand as she stared into the younger woman's eyes. "But to me, being a teacher is the most important job in the world. I was so proud of my father, in fact, that I went to college and became a teacher myself, and I've been teaching for over twenty-five years now."

Tamara said admiringly, "That's quite an accomplishment. Nowadays kids can be a real handful at times." She thought of her problems with Sienna and added, "In fact, I know now just how difficult they can be from my own personal experience, but I am finding that the rewards many times outweigh the difficulties that are involved."

Lillian Lewis replaced her glasses on her nose and said fervently, "You are exactly right, young lady. The work is often hard, but the rewards are immense. I've found that it is this way with much of life, though. Whenever the work is difficult, the bounty is large when the job is done. So, do you have children?"

Tamara replied, "Yes, I have a child living with me; she's fourteen."

"You look a bit young to have a teenager." Tamara saw her glance at her ringless finger. "No husband?"

"Oh, it's not like that. I work for Child Welfare and I took her in, from the Agency I work for."

"She's an orphan?"

"I guess you could say that. She has no parents, really."

Lillian Lewis gave a definitive nod of her head and said, "Young lady, that's a good thing you're doing, then. Be proud of yourself, there are not many honorable people left in this world."

Tamara sighed; the woman's comments only served to remind her that there was no honor at all about her reasons for taking Sienna in the first place, and she often still had mixed feelings about the whole thing. Sighing, she replaced the photo gently and picked up a small snapshot of a smiling young man. His broad face was deep mahogany brown and handsome, and his broad smile was relaxed.

Before she could even ask, Miss Lillian said, "That's my brother, Maurice. Maurice Lewis the Third, to be exact. We never called him by that street name 'Three' . . . My brother had an honorable name, and he should've carried it with more dignity than he did much of the time."

The thin woman wiped at some imaginary lint on her print cotton dress. She continued without looking at Tamara, "He was about twenty years old in that photo, and he didn't have any children then." With disappointment apparent in her voice, she added, "Now, I think that he has at least two or three kids. I would think that some of them are probably grown by now."

"He *was* handsome," said Tamara as she continued to stare at the picture. She was thinking of Yvette; she could see where the girl got some of her features from—her nose, her eyes, and the shape of her mouth all were Maurice's.

"Let's go into the living room," said the woman.

She looked at the photo once more before setting it gently back down on the table. Following the stately woman into the front room, she took a seat on the couch.

"Let me get you some tea . . . I'll be right back," said Miss Lillian.

Tamara looked around approvingly, taking in all the details of the meticulously decorated room until Lillian Lewis returned with two china teacups balancing precariously on matching china saucers in her hands.

"Thank you, Miss Lillian," she said as she blew on the steaming, fragrant tea to cool it before taking a cautious sip.

Lillian Lewis's deep eyes twinkled as she looked over the top of her glasses, informing her, "I only drink green tea these days. It's good for you. There is something in it—I can't remember exactly what it is, but it helps to fight cancer, they say." The woman looked at her again and emitted a small chuckle before she took a sip herself and added, "We never know who the proverbial 'they' are, now, do we? But I figure, it certainly can't hurt to try it, now, can it?"

"No, it can't," agreed Tamara.

"Now, back to my errant brother, Maurice. What is it exactly that you want to know about him?"

"I'm trying to find out if he's still alive somewhere. I'm looking for the father of an old friend of mine, and I've been led to believe that it might be Mr. Lewis."

The woman set the cup of tea carefully on the doily lying on the shiny mahogany tabletop. "Oh, my, that little brother of mine, Maurice—he was such a heartbreaker . . . how my Daddy *loved* that boy. He broke Daddy's heart, you know? Mother's, too, really. They'd had such high expectations of him."

"They did?" Tamara was very surprised to find that Maurice Lewis had come from a college-educated father and a mother who was a practicing nurse, and that he'd grown up as part of the black nouveau middle class of that day and time. She'd just assumed that he'd had a much tougher young experience that had led him to his unsavory life as a street hustler.

The woman turned down her lips and said, "Oh, yes. Maurice was quite intelligent and well spoken, too. He was a good-looking boy, and he grew up to be a strapping, handsome man."

"I could see that in the picture," said Tamara.

"Those good looks of his are what ruined his life, in a way. Attractiveness is only a blessing if you use it for a good purpose.

262

With Maurice, so many girls chased behind him, they made him feel like he was more important than what he was. He never got a chance, really, to develop himself on the inside." She patted her flat chest. She removed her glasses, wiped her eyes, and continued, "Instead he used his good looks and eloquent speech to become a sweet-talker to women, and a hustler on the streets."

Tamara set her empty cup on the table, careful to place it on a doily as she'd seen the older woman do with her own. "Did he ever marry any of the women?"

"Not that I know of . . . It's like that boy got in them streets and forgot all about his Christian upbringing. He slept with all sorts of women, and when they had babies, he didn't seem to care . . . I never even saw a one of his children. *Not one.*"

Tamara asked in a lowered voice, "Miss Lillian?"

"Yes?"

"Is Maurice still alive?"

Soberly she answered, "Yes. He's alive."

"Where? Do you know where he is?"

Lillian Lewis looked at her out of the corner of her eye. "Certainly I know where he is. He is my brother, and no matter what he was doing wrong, we've always stayed in touch with one another. I do love him, you know."

Tamara sat uneasily on the couch for a moment. Then she asked in a voice that was little more than a whisper, "Miss Lillian, can you please tell me how to get in touch with Maurice?"

The woman shot her an exasperated look. "Well, yes, Tamara, of course I can. After all, that *is* what you came here for, isn't it?"

With a sigh of relief, she replied, "Yes, it is, Miss Lillian. It is exactly what I came here for."

43.

Double Trouble

Shivering as she watched the early sunset on the cold February evening through the window of Jayson's Chevrolet Blazer, Tamara impatiently waited for him to get inside the truck so they could leave. Without even glancing at her watch, she knew that this evening's movie plans with Sienna were ruined.

Her evening plans began to unravel once she received the call from Jayson, informing her they were needed immediately to perform an emergency crisis family intervention. Sara James, one of their clients, had been worried out of her mind when her twelve-year-old son did not come in right after school. Consequently, the mother totally lost it when the boy strolled in hours later, and the resulting argument became so out-of-control that concerned neighbors called the police.

Instead of arresting anyone, though, the police relied on collaborative relationships they'd forged with social agencies within their city, geared toward defusing these types of situations whenever possible and thus keeping the family unit intact. After stabilizing the situation, officers had telephoned the Care Agency and agreed to allow their crisis team to handle the situation. Tamara, Jay, and Alexis Troy, another trained counselor, were the on-call team that evening, immediately dispatched to make sure that the situation was indeed under control.

Entirely engrossed in the situation at hand, Tamara did not

even notice the look of disappointment on Sienna's face as the teen watched her rush out the door after Jayson arrived at her apartment. Alexis Troy was waiting for them at the Jameses' small apartment, and the three of them then sat down to talk with the mother and her son.

Alexis, a middle-aged African-American counselor, was well experienced in these types of situations, and, in less than an hour, she worked her therapeutic magic and diffused what had been a volatile situation. With her sensitive guidance, the concerned mother's screaming, cursing, and yelling eventually dissipated into tears of relief that the boy had come home unharmed.

As Tamara watched Jayson climb into the passenger seat of the truck, she suddenly flashed back to the last home visit they'd made together, and, with more than a touch of worry in her voice, she asked, "Jay, do you think they're going to be okay?"

Jayson closed his door and replied, "Tam, it's gonna be just fine. As always, Alexis really worked through the entire situation well with them. She took the necessary time to help Ms. James understand that her anger was based on her concern for Anthony's safety."

Tamara agreed, "I think Alexis did a good job, too . . . but then, she always does. I guess I just want to be sure that nothing will happen after we leave."

Jayson was silent as he turned the key in the ignition and backed the car out of the lot. He knew that Tamara was once again thinking about their unnerving discovery of the neglected Smith children months ago, and he said gently, "Tam, you gotta let it go. I know what's on your mind, but this situation has nothing to do with that other one. I don't know why it happened, but *please* stop blaming yourself—it was not your fault. You know as well as I that sad situations just happen now and then in child welfare. Thank God that the really bad ones like what we saw are usually few and far between."

She turned from his gaze and looked out of her window before replying thoughtfully, "I know that bad things happen in child welfare, Jay . . . I guess I just always thought it would happen to someone else and not to one of my caseload kids, you know? I promised myself that I would be extra careful from now on, certain I've done everything within my power to prevent anything from happening to a child on my caseload—*everything.*"

"I understand how you feel, Tam—really, I do. It *was* hard looking at those kids like that, and it wasn't any easier watching it played on the news over and over for days afterward—even for me."

They were both silent then, and the quiet in the truck seemed deafening. Jayson's overtures toward her had really shifted the comfortable balance of their relationship. The easy banter they used to share before his unexpected confession was much more difficult now.

Jasyon reached over, turned on the radio, and then, changing his mind, cut it back off after only a moment or two. Clearing his throat, he said huskily, "Tamara, I know you don't want to have this conversation, but I think we need to."

Tamara's stomach sank because even though she did know that they probably needed to talk about what had happened the other week, she really did not want to. Feigning ignorance, she crossed her arms tightly in front of her, still feeling chilled although the truck's heat was blowing warmly through the vent, and asked innocently, "What conversation is that, Jay?"

"Don't play like you don't know, Tamara. Save me that at least, okay? You've always been honest with me; please don't change now. You know what conversation I'm talking about."

She sighed loudly, "Okay, Jay . . . I admit it. I know what you're talking about. But what else is there to say?"

"Tam, there's a lot more I have to say. *I like you* a lot, and I

266

really do want us to spend time getting to know one another better . . . *outside of work.*"

Quiet again, Tamara stared out the window, feeling flustered now and unsure how to respond. Jayson's repeated advances made her feel pressured to a degree, and she did not like that feeling at all.

Persistently Jayson asked, "Tam, please say something."

"Jay, I'm just not sure what you want me to say," Tamara murmured.

Jayson turned the truck into her driveway and parked in the guest spot in front of her town house apartment. "I know what I want you to say, Tamara, and that is that you like me, too, and are interested in getting to know me better, too."

In a small voice, she interjected, "Maybe the timing is just off."

"What do you mean by that?"

"The timing, Jay . . . you know, with Sienna living with me and everything. I don't have much time to date . . . not really."

Jayson twisted his lips and responded, "Hmph, seems like you have time to see Isaiah Perry."

"We are not seeing each other. He's *just a friend,*" she protested.

"C'mon, Tamara, even I can see that guy wants more than friendship from you, and I know that you can see it, too."

"Jay, he is just a friend," she repeated, feeling more flustered each moment the conversation continued. Her trembling had dissipated, giving way to a telltale warmth from the inside out—a sure sign that her anxiety level was rising.

Jayson turned her head gently toward him. "Well, then, Tamara, I want to be a friend, too. I want you to look at me the way that you do him. I mean, I saw how you looked at him when we were all at church the other Sunday."

Tamara looked at him questioningly. "I don't know what you mean, Jay . . . How *was* I looking at him?"

Jayson looked deeply into her eyes and said, "You looked at him like he was the only man in the world, Tamara . . . like you couldn't see anything or anyone else but him."

The young woman shook her head free of his hand, gazing downward as she replied softly, "I guess I didn't realize I was looking at him like that."

"I did, though," said Jayson, and he gently lifted her head again so that she would have to look in his eyes.

Tamara was surprised to see the sadness there, but she just was unable to give him the answer that he wanted to hear. "Jay, I think I should go inside . . . to check on Sienna."

Unexpectedly, he bent over and almost touched his lips to hers, but she pulled her head back just in time to avoid the kiss, turning quickly to look nervously out the window again.

"C'mon, Tamara, look at me," Jayson implored.

"Jay, I've got to go now . . . Thanks for letting me ride with you," she said, and with one deft move, she was out of the truck and on the pavement, walking toward her door.

Tamara quickly turned her key in the lock and opened the door. Only once she was inside did her heart rate began to slow down a bit. The entire situation with Jayson was getting out of hand now, especially since it seemed that his advances were getting more persistent each time the conversation was brought up anew.

She touched her hand to her lips and thought of how he had almost kissed her tonight, and then motionlessly stood by the door until she heard his engine start. Only when the noise from the truck began to recede and finally die out totally did Tamara dare to move.

She abruptly noticed the almost eerie silence in the apartment . . . The lights were strangely dim, and it was uncharacteristically silent. Normally the sounds of music, often too loud, met her at the door, or Sienna was there, chattering and full of energy, ready to tell her about her day. Reassuringly she told herself that most likely a disappointed Sienna had fallen asleep and was somewhere in the house taking a nap now.

"Sienna? Sienna?" she called loudly as she began to walk down the hallway.

Tamara checked in the living room area, but there was no Sienna curled up on the couch or lying on the carpet sound asleep. Unable to discount her rising concern, she flicked on the light with a trembling hand before continuing down the long hallway softly. Sienna's door was open, and a glance inside told her that the girl was not in there.

When Tamara reached the closed door of her own bedroom at the end of the hall, she stood nonplussed, unable to recall closing it when she left in the morning. In fact, she rarely closed her door ever. Even more apprehensive now, gathering her courage, she turned the doorknob and threw the door back. To her extreme surprise, there lying in the middle of her bed was Sienna, intertwined in the arms of a lanky, deep-brown-skinned young man!

The girl jumped up, and her eyes opened wide as she asked, clearly surprised, "Tamara! What are you doing home?"

"I do live here, don't I?" answered Tamara, and her calm tone belied the shock she was feeling inside. This was the last thing that she would have expected from Sienna at this stage. While the girl's classwork still left much to be desired, she had lost a lot of the bad attitude that she'd had initially. She willingly attended church several times a week, and the two of them had been getting along much better. Tamara assumed that Sienna's Christian faith was at the root of much of her change, but this behavior in front of her was certainly not part of that doctrine.

The young man's eyes were on Tamara as he jumped up from

the bed. With one quick, furtive glance at Sienna, he said, "I gotta go . . . See ya, Sienna."

Sitting on the side of the bed, he pulled on his huge sneakers and then bounded down the hallway, stopping only a moment to retrieve his jacket from the living room, and then they both jumped a bit when they heard the door slam hard.

With the boy gone, Tamara turned her attention back to Sienna.

"Well?" she asked, fully expecting an explanation of some sort from the teen.

Instead, Sienna clicked her tongue in the impertinent manner that she'd not used for a long time and rolled her eyes. "Well, what?" she replied, affecting the streetwise, nonchalant look and tone she hadn't used in quite a while. Clicking her tongue even louder, she added flippantly, "Well, I guess you shouldn't have come back so soon, and you might not have seen something you really didn't want to see, huh?"

Tamara's anxiety was giving way to anger now. *"Sienna, stop making that annoying noise with your tongue! And do not use that tone with me!"*

The teen continued to stare her down defiantly. "What you mean, 'tone,' Tamara? I'm just talking like I do normally."

Tamara's voice rose. *"What was he doing here? Or better yet, what were the two of you doing in here?"*

The girl pulled up the sleeve of her blouse and said, "What did it look like we was doing here? We wasn't *doin'* nothin'! Just messin' around."

Suddenly, Tamara felt as if she were on the verge of hysteria. Her pulse was pounding hard in her temples, and her heart was beating a mile a minute. She needed some time alone immediately, and she knew it. "Sienna! Just please, get out of here, right now . . . and pull up your blouse. You're almost exposed."

Sienna slowly pulled her blouse on, and, after making sure to shoot Tamara one parting impertinent look, she jumped to the floor from Tamara's high four-poster bed and walked out of the room, her small body held proudly erect.

Tamara closed her bedroom door hard behind Sienna. She slipped her shoes off, sat on her bed, crossing her feet under her, and held her head in her hands. Tears began to slide from her eyes, and suddenly she felt totally overwhelmed by everything going on in her life.

The very last thing she wanted was for something awful happen to the teen while she was living with her. Suddenly all sorts of what-ifs about Sienna were running through her mind. What if the girl got pregnant? What if somehow she allowed the girl to live out the same situation that she'd come from—to complete the circle of neglect or abuse again? She knew that she could never forgive herself if that were to happen.

Mrs. Jackson's admonishment that Satan was the master of what-ifs was far from Tamara's mind then. Thinking again of the scene she'd just witnessed, she wiped her eyes with the back of her hand, blew her nose, and said aloud, "Sienna . . . what if I've bitten off more than I can chew? What if I'm not the person for you to live with after all?"

44.

Blowup

"Excuse me," said Sienna in a flat voice as she reached over her and opened the cabinet, "I'm just getting the popcorn, if you don't mind—that is, if you don't care if I eat some of *your* food."

Without turning to look at Sienna, Tamara replied in a crisp, even tone, "Of course you can eat, Sienna. Don't be silly."

"Well," responded the girl sarcastically, "I don't know . . . it is *your* house, after all, Tamara, and you want me to do everything the way you want me to do it, right? For all I know, you might not want me to eat."

Tamara held her tongue, surprised that Sienna was even home tonight. Normally she would be at choir rehearsal on Tuesday night, but when Tamara had offered to take her to the church earlier, the teen had replied that she didn't feel well and did not want to go. Tamara had said nothing. In the days since she had caught Sienna wrapped in the arms of that boy in her bedroom, they'd spoken little, and the tension was still thick between the two of them.

In fact, as the days passed, Tamara realized with surprise that Sienna was holding some sort of grudge against her. Clearly, the teen believed *she* had a reason to be angry with her and not vice versa. Tamara was flabbergasted by Sienna's faulty reasoning; after all, the girl had clearly been in the wrong the other night and consequently was totally unjustified in having an attitude of any sort with her!

Inwardly Tamara was working hard to get past the unsavory episode, as her own feelings were still in an uproar about what she'd seen that night. Several times she had set out to talk about the incident anew with Sienna, but each time, a vision of Sienna and the boy lying on the bed together flashed into her mind, and her emotions began to rise so quickly that she backed away from the conversation entirely. The situation seemed to highlight Sienna's disregard of household expectations, and now this subsequent disrespectful attitude was almost too much for Tamara to tolerate. In fact, the entire experience was making her former insecurities about the teen rise to the surface again. Ever since that day, Tamara felt overwhelmed more often than not about the extent of the responsibility she'd taken on.

What made things most difficult was that Tamara was so unused to all these varied emotions bubbling inside at the same time that she was almost afraid of what she might say if her anger rose to the surface right now. Mindful of these complex emotions whirling inside, she replied pleadingly, "Sienna, please just get whatever you want to eat . . . Don't try to pick a fight, okay?"

Ignoring her request for peace, the teen replied loudly, "I'm *not* trying to pick a fight with you, Tamara! If I wanted to fight with you, I would, so don't accuse me of stuff that I'm not even doing!"

"Why are you talking so loudly, then?" asked Tamara quietly.

"Because I can!" answered Sienna, even more loudly.

"What kind of answer is that, Sienna? Please lower your voice," repeated Tamara, but by now she was struggling to keep her own tone even and calm.

"Please lower your voice," said Sienna in a singsongy voice clearly intended to mock.

"Sienna! You stop that, *now*!" Tamara said, her own voice becoming louder.

The teen gave her a defiant glance, "That's all you know, isn't it, Tamara? 'Stop it!' 'Don't!' 'Quit!' That's the problem with you, Tamara Britton; you don't know how to do nothin', do you, Tamara? You just know how to *stop* everything and everybody from anything they want to do!"

Warningly Tamara said once more, *"Be quiet, Sienna!"*

Sienna ignored Tamara, though, speaking fast and furiously now. "You think just 'cause *you* don't have no friends, *ain't nobody* supposed have no friends, and you think just 'cause *you* don't have no man. *ain't nobody* supposed to have no man, either!"

In a quieter voice Tamara said incredulously, "Man? Girl, you don't know anything about a man. That was no man laid up in my bed with you that day. That was a boy, Sienna. That's why he ran out of here so fast as soon as he saw me and knew there was trouble."

"He's more of a man than you've ever had!" the girl retorted.

"You don't know *who* I've had!" said Tamara, even louder now. "In fact, Sienna, you don't know *anything* about me!"

Sienna responded sardonically, "And you know what? I don't care if I don't know nothin' about you, either! You ain't nobody, Tamara Britton . . . In fact, you just *nothin'*, Tamara Britton!"

It was then that Tamara felt a part of herself separate from her body, and though she knew she was going to say some things that she should not, she had no control over what was happening. She could not stop herself from speaking.

Looking Sienna straight in the eye, Tamara said in an icy, crisp voice, "You are ungrateful, Sienna. I am more than you will *ever* be . . . I open my house to you and give you a decent place to live, and clothe and feed you, and you treat me with disrespect all the time."

Surprised at the coolness in Tamara's tone, Sienna uncertainly lowered her own voice a bit, replying, "I didn't ask you to let me stay here, Tamara."

The timbre of Tamara's voice did not change, though, as she continued to stare into the girl's eyes unblinkingly. "I know that you didn't. And you know what? I didn't ask for you to stay with me, either. In fact, the truth is, I didn't *want* you to stay with me in the first place. I just said okay because my boss caught me by surprise when she asked me, and I said yes when I really wanted to say no."

The girl looked stunned for a moment and then, recovering some of her feistiness, admonished, "Well, then, you should've said no, and then I wouldn't have to be here living in your dumb ole' house with you!"

Tamara slammed the kitchen cabinet loudly then and turned to face the girl again. "You are right. I should've said no, because ever since you have been here, Sienna Larson, my entire life has been turned upside down. Before you came, I lived a quiet life, and you know what? I liked it like that, too. Then, all of sudden I feel pressured and let you move into my home, and nothing, *nothing*, has been the same!"

"You should be *glad* your boring life got some excitement in it now!"

"You know what? I *liked* my boring life just like it was, and I didn't need you or anybody else to walk into it and try to change it!"

The teen's sauciness dissipated then. She was obviously thrown off balance by Tamara's unexpected ire. "Tamara, I wasn't *trying* to change your life. I can't help it if you didn't do nothin' in the first place."

But now Tamara's own long-suppressed anger was fully in control, and she continued to speak, her voice crackling with derision. "Oh, you can't help it? You know what, Sienna? That's

275

what I wanted to believe, but I know better. You *can* help it; that helplessness is only a little role you play so that you don't have to take responsibility for your disrespectful behavior. The truth is, you came here only interested in yourself, Sienna Larson. You wanted me to do things that *you* thought were important, and you didn't care what impact your desires had on my life."

Uncertainly Sienna replied, "I didn't ask you to do *nothin'* for me!"

Tamara's voice was louder than she could ever remember it being before. "You ask me to do *everything* for you Sienna! Nothing in my life is good enough for you! You don't like the food I eat! You don't like my work ethic! You don't like the fact that I don't have a boyfriend . . . I guess you'd be happy if there was some crazy man over here who was a child molester or something! Would that make you happy?"

Sienna felt sick now. She wished she had never started this whole thing. She'd never seen Tamara angry like this before, and she didn't know what to do to make her calm again.

Contemptuously, Tamara asked, "Do you want to know something else, Sienna?"

The teen stared at Tamara without answering.

Anger was written on Tamara's face as she replied, "I was *fine* without any of these changes in my life. I was happy just like I was. Nobody but me! No phone calls at my job about someone acting up at school! No one here bringing strange people in and out of my home! No worrying about someone who might get pregnant by a boy 'cause she doesn't listen! I was just fine with no church, no Isaiah Perry . . . *no Sienna Larson!*"

Sienna's eyes brimmed with unshed tears. Tamara, breathing heavily from the heated exchange, turned her back to the girl and busily began to clean the dishes as if to indicate that she was finished speaking and the conversation was over.

Sienna stood there for a moment longer, watching Tamara's

stiff back, and then, with her head down, she walked from the room.

As if finally remembering the girl, Tamara turned toward Sienna again, only to realize the teen had left the kitchen. Feeling shaky and out of sorts, she exhaled several times deeply, fighting to regain her shattered self-control. Never could she recall being this upset with anyone, and never had she ever been quite so angry.

It was as if she were in a fog, speaking from a distant place inside herself. Though she could hear herself speaking, she was shocked by the callousness of the words coming from her own mouth. Now Tamara was replaying the out-of-control scene in her mind, and in her more rational state, she wished she could take her words back—but it was too late for that.

Contritely Tamara whispered a small prayer with a catch in her voice. "Lord, I'm so sorry for what I just said. I was too angry, and it was not my intention to hurt her."

Wiping away a guilty tear, she sighed and turned to finish cleaning the kitchen. Mustering a small amount of optimism, Tamara could only hope that the bass rhythm she heard pulsating from the girl's bedroom was Sienna's way of sending her a signal that everything was going to be just fine between the two of them very soon.

45.

End of the Road

Tamara was trying unsuccessfully to curtail her excitement as she clicked noisily down the long linoleum hallway of the nursing home. She hadn't uncovered any information about Maurice's short stint in the Army, so she'd been surprised when Lillian Lewis told her that her brother was in a veterans' hospital in Sunnyside, California. But Tamara, eager to escape the simmering tension permeating her house, decided on the spur of the moment that it was the perfect time for her to meet Maurice Lewis the III. She quickly had arranged plans for the trip to the West Coast.

Early this morning, Tamara dropped a still oddly silent Sienna at Denise Jackson's home for a long weekend before catching a flight out of Bloomington, Illinois. She was privately hoping that her time away would prove healing for the two of them.

"Can you please tell me where Maurice Lewis's room is?" she asked the red-haired nurse stationed at the reception desk.

The woman gave Tamara a searching stare and then smiled and replied, "Sure . . . Mr. Lewis is in Room two fifty-six. That's almost at the end of the next hallway to your right."

As she quickly walked down his hallway, she was acutely aware of the loudness of her boots in the quiet corridor. Two doors from the end of the hallway she found room 256. Stepping through the door, she immediately recognized Maurice Lewis

III, in all his splendor, calmly lying there in the bed, watching television.

He shot her a look of feigned almost paternal admonishment and then asked with a snort of a laugh, "Was that you making all that noise coming down the hallway?" Then he gave her a thorough, dark-eyed once over before adding, "Naaaw, don't tell me a little ol' thing like you was makin' all that noise. Gal, don't you know when you come up in here to see us sick folks you need to wear some quiet shoes?"

Tamara's face immediately warmed with the man's teasing. "Sorry," she murmured sheepishly. "Let me introduce myself . . . I'm Tamara Britton. L-Lillian Lewis . . . your sister . . . told me about you, and I came out to talk to you," she added falteringly.

Disbelievingly he asked, "Are you from way out in the Midwest, too?"

Tamara nodded.

"And you came all the way out from Illinois to see me?" the man said, with an incredulous look on his face. Obviously suspicious about her motives now, he asked warily, "Girl, exactly what is it that you want from me that you gonna come this far to find?"

Tamara was dumbstruck by his question and stared at him for several moments. Maurice Lewis III looked like the picture of health, joking and laughing in the bed. In fact, he did not look sick at all. His sister had told Tamara that the man's health was failing badly, though, and she knew he suffered from severe hypertension, heart trouble, and diabetes as well as from borderline emphysema from many years of smoking. But according to Miss Lillian, the ailment that had him lying in this hospital bed, often writhing in pain, was his debilitating arthritis.

The one thing that could not be denied was how handsome he still was. Maurice's glowing skin was as mahogany as the furniture in his sister's house, and though his face was creased and lined with the years, the aging of time only served to make his handsome features more striking. Running his fingers through his thick silver-streaked wavy hair, he gazed at her mirthfully with dark eyes framed by thick, long lashes. Yes, Tamara thought as she stared at him silently, Maurice Lewis III was quite a good-looking man, and his playful nature made him even more attractive. Yes, she could understand now why so many ladies found him irresistible.

"Excuse me, Miss Lady, why are you here?" he asked with a suddenly indignant look on his handsome face.

His annoyed look snapped Tamara back into reality, and she replied, "Mr. Lewis, I came all the way out here because what I need to find out from you is quite important. I'm tracking down information for a friend of mine. Her name is Yvette," she added purposefully, hoping he would recollect the girl's name.

The man frowned and said, "Yvette? Sorry, Miss, I don't recall any Yvette."

"How about Jannice, then?" she asked hopefully.

The light of recognition glowed in his eyes this time. He admitted quietly, "Yeah, I remember Jannice. Girl, come over here and sit down . . . Tell me what do you know about Jannice."

Tamara sat by his bed, and to her chagrin as she sank down deeply into the too-soft turquoise vinyl-cushioned chair, it expelled a loud whoosh of air. She giggled inappropriately, a nervous reaction.

The man ignored her out-of-place laughter. Squinting as if trying to see her better, he stared at her more closely now. "What did you say your name was again?"

"Tamara," she answered, now suppressing a curious urge to smile during this serious moment. She knew that the laughter moments earlier, and now this impulse to smile, were just an inappropriate response to her deep anxiety about this long-awaited meeting. "Tamara Britton," she repeated, louder this time, thankful to feel herself calming down as she spoke.

"And exactly who are you to Jannice?"

Having regained her composure, Tamara replied earnestly, "Jannice is the mother of a friend of mine . . . Yvette is her name."

Again his look was skeptical when he asked, "A friend of yours, huh? Miss Lady, I wasn't born yesterday. What kind of friend of yours would make you want to travel all the way out here?"

Tamara forced herself to keep her gaze steady as she replied, "I don't have a lot of friends, Mr. Lewis, and Yvette is someone I met back in grade school and knew for several years after that. She was in state care—'foster care,' so to speak—the entire time, until without warning she was moved to a home in another city, and I've not seen her since."

"Foster care . . . you mean she was an orphan? Well, that stinks!"

"Yes, Mr. Lewis, she was an orphan, though truthfully, that word is not used much these days. I work in child welfare now with young people in the system, and, more importantly, I work with parents to try to stabilize their home environments so that they can keep their children with them, because I agree, Mr. Lewis, that far too often what happens to kids caught up in 'the system' . . . for want of a better word . . . *stinks*!"

He gave her a long, hard look before replying, "What you're doing . . . well, that's commendable of you, young lady."

"Thank you."

Maurice continued to stare at her unblinkingly. "But why would you be looking for me, if you don't even know where this Yvette is right now?"

While Tamara was uncomfortable under the man's probing gaze, her own gaze did not waver from his as she answered confidently, "I'm planning on finding Yvette again, once I get all of the information compiled. I want to surprise her."

Disbelieving again, he commented, "I want to believe you, Miss Lady, but frankly . . . that sounds almost too good to be true. You know, I haven't met too many folks in my lifetime who do something for somebody without getting something out of it themselves."

She held up her chin proudly and directly returned his stare through her almond-shaped eyes. "Mr. Lewis, I am getting something in return . . . peace of mind. It is because of Yvette that I was motivated to go to college and obtain a job in child welfare, and I've done nothing but think of her since she was unceremoniously taken away. I am certain she will remain in my thoughts. I must find out about her past so that if we ever meet again I can share this information with her."

Tamara was quiet, allowing the man some time to soak in all the information she'd given him. After several meditative moments, finally he replied, "Okay, then, Miss Tamara Britton, I do remember Jannice . . . I remember her quite well, in fact. That Jannice was one pretty black gal . . . The girl was built like a brick house, and her eyes turned up on the sides—reminded me of those Japanese girls, you know?"

After breathing an imperceptible sigh of relief that the man had evidently decided to share his memories with her, Tamara listened intently as Maurice reminisced about days long past.

With a knowing look, Maurice added then, "Bad thang about Jannice was that she was more than a little bit on the fast side. We met at a bar I used to hang out at in the city, and that little girl chased me and chased me until she finally got my attention. Fine as she was, though, I didn't jump in the sack with her right away, either . . . though I must admit, I have been known to do that in my time," he added with a mischievous chuckle.

Maurice stroked his chin and shot her a deliberate glance. "Naw, but not with Jannice. We used to talk a lot, and lookin' back at it now, I remember what I mostly liked about her was that she was so dang funny. We would laugh about the dumbest things, and I guess it got so, to tell the truth, I just wanted to be around her 'cause we had so much fun together."

Tamara shook her jacket off and placed it over the back of the square-backed plastic chair. "I think it would be nice to have someone that you had lots of fun with," she replied, and as she spoke, Isaiah Perry's face briefly appeared in her mind.

Languidly Maurice agreed, "Yeah . . . it is nice. Really, everything was all good until we started going to bed together. Should've never done that. First of all, I didn't know that she wasn't no woman; she was just a girl, only a teenager really. We only went to bed together a couple times, and to tell the truth, it wasn't all that much to it, and then she told me that she was pregnant."

"That would be with her first daughter, right?"

"I guess. I did see the baby one time. She said the baby's name was Mauricia. For a long time after that she disappeared from the scene . . . or maybe I did—my memory is a little hazy at that part," he added, smiling wryly. He looked at her and added, "Jannice wasn't the only woman I was seeing, you know? Truth is, I was considered to be a bit of a ladies' man back then, you know?"

"Lillian did tell me that," she replied with a small smile.

The man shot her a semi-sulky sideways glance. "That sister of mine is still tellin' everything, I see." Focusing on the past again, he continued, "Anyway, one night I was in the club having a drink, and one of my boys told me there was someone outside wanted to see me. When I got out there, Jannice jumps out of a car with a baby and said it was mine."

"What did you do?" Tamara asked.

With an ironic snort he replied, "I did what any self-professed playa would do. I denied it." His smile slowly disappeared, and he repeated in a quieter voice, "I denied it . . . I can still see her face that day. She looked at me one time like she hated me and then just got in the car with the baby and left. I never bothered to see who drove her there or anything."

"So then, how did you end up getting back together with her?"

He shook his head. "Believe me, I wish I knew. I heard that Jannice went back downstate, and then after several months I looked up one day and there she was—just like she'd never left. She never said a word about a baby this time, and before I knew it, we just ended up back in the bed again."

"Did you see her after that?"

"Maybe 'bout a year later, and we 'did the do' and parted ways."

"So, she never told you about the other child she had?"

"She had two babies?"

"Yes, Mr. Lewis. Jannice had two kids that she said were yours. Your name is on the birth certificate. They are both girls, and my friend Yvette is one of those girls."

The man looked shocked. "Two? Are you sure?"

"Yes, two."

Again he shook his head disbelievingly while chuckling to himself. "So, two babies with Jannice . . . Where is she, do you know?"

Tamara asked softly, "You mean Jannice?"

"Yes, where is she?"

Solemnly she replied, "Jannice is dead."

His surprise was evident on his face, and he asked, "*Dead?* She's a young girl . . . How can she be dead?"

"Jannice, OD'd five years ago."

Shocked now, Maurice almost shouted, "OD'd! Don't tell me that pretty black girl was a drug addict!"

"Yes, I'm sorry to tell you she was. In fact, Jannice had problems with all sorts of drugs, but her life finally ended with her heroin addiction."

Maurice's look was incredulous then. "Heroin? Whew! That's ugly, 'cause ol' her-on is one drug that don't take no prisoners— it just kills. I had a coupla friends myself that got caught up with it, and that horse held them so tight they never could break free."

"I think that is what happened to Jannice as well," added Tamara. "She couldn't break free—she just couldn't."

He shook his head. "Jannice, dead . . . Man, I'm sorry to hear that!" After a couple of minutes, he asked falteringly, "So, what happened to the children . . . *my* babies? You said something 'bout state care earlier . . ."

Tamara gazed at Maurice Lewis sadly. "That is what happened to the children, Mr. Lewis, state care for all of them. Unfortunately, Jannice's drug addiction made her ill equipped to handle the responsibility of having children. She actually abandoned two of her babies shortly after their birth and neglected the others severely on several occasions, leaving them alone while she searched for drugs . . . The state actually took her last three kids into custody immediately after she had them. Two were addicted to drugs but still were adopted."

His face was sad now. "How many children did she have?"

Tamara replied matter-of-factly, "She had seven, Mr. Lewis. Jannice was the mother of seven girls."

Obviously surprised by her news, he asked, "So, you are saying that I have a couple of daughters out there that I've never met, and they don't have any idea that I'm their daddy?"

"Yes, I would say that's probably the case. You have to understand that unless they have the inclination and the ability to search on their own to find you, there's no way that they could know who or where you are."

"What about your friend—Yvette?"

"She was one of the babies who was abandoned shortly after her birth by Jannice . . . left alone in an apartment and found by neighbors there, who called in the authorities."

"Oh, my God," said Maurice Lewis. "She was left alone to fend for herself when she was just a baby, huh? That poor girl . . . living somewhere on her own without knowing who or where she came from."

Before Tamara could respond, the red-haired nurse turned the corner into the room and, after giving the two of them a quizzical glance, said, "Mr. Lewis, it's time for your medicine." She looked over her shoulder at Tamara and said, "Don't be surprised if he gets a little drowsy—it's the medication."

"Do I have to?" he whined playfully to the nurse with a flash of his teasing smile.

The nurse smiled back and apprised him saucily. "Oh, Mr. Lewis, you've been here long enough that you know the answer to that one. Besides, if you don't take it, you will be quite uncomfortable later—and we don't want that, do we?"

"No, *we* don't, do *we*?" he teased again impishly.

"He's not such a charmer when he's in pain," the nurse commented knowingly to Tamara. "So we try to keep him feeling comfortable."

"Okay, Mr. Lewis, you'll feel a stick now," she said as she jabbed the needle into his arm. "Now, a burn."

"Ouch!" said Maurice Lewis as he made a face toward Tamara. "Even though I'm a grown man, I still hate shots!"

The nurse dabbed the man's arm with alcohol and covered the small puncture with cotton and a Band-Aid before saying perkily, "All done, Mr. Lewis . . . I'm off now. I'll see you tomorrow, okay?"

Maurice gave the nurse a flirty wink. "You have a good night, sweetheart. Don't do anything that I wouldn't do!" he added jokingly.

The woman laughed as she tossed back, "If that's the case, I'd be doing all sorts of things that I don't normally do, huh? 'Cause we both know you're a humdinger, Mr. Lewis!"

The man laughed for a moment and then asked, "Now, where were we?" turning his attention back to Tamara.

Tamara smiled and replied, "We were talking about your daughters, Mr. Lewis."

Maurice began to slur his words a little. "Yeah, that's right . . . It's just hard for me to believe I have two more girls and I didn't even know about them." He laughed ironically. "And now there are three, just like my old nickname . . . *Three*."

"Three?"

"Yes," said Maurice and he covered his mouth as he yawned widely.

"Lillian did say she thought you had two or three kids."

"Actually, I have four," he said as he began to nod a bit. The medication was taking effect very quickly, and he was obviously growing drowsy fast.

"Four?"

"I've been married since I've been out here and I have a son who lives with his mama since we been separated . . . Maurice Lewis the Fourth," he said proudly.

"That's still only three, Mr. Lewis," Tamara replied, wondering if the medication was causing Maurice to lose touch with reality as he became drowsy.

"Naw, Miss Lady, that's three girls I have . . . one boy. My other daughter came from a little 'meet-up' I had when I was visiting Lillian one time and I slid up to the Windy City that weekend. Only one little rendezvous with a petite little blue-eyed blonde—but once was all it took."

Realizing now that Maurice had another daughter she did not know about, Tamara asked, "The mother was white?"

The medicine was taking effect quickly now, and Maurice laughed drowsily, "Yeah, Miss Lady, she was white, not a blonde sistah like you see nowadays."

Curious now, Tamara asked, "Did you ever see the baby?"

"Naw, never did. Just heard about her . . . They said she was a pretty little thing." Maurice laid his head down on the pillow and closed his eyes. He mumbled sleepily, "I 'spect she's probably about fourteen or so now . . . The mama named her Larson after her . . . Sienna is her name . . . Sienna Larson."

46.

Fallout

Glancing around, Tamara was grateful to be traveling home in an almost empty plane, with few people to distract her from her swirling thoughts. Since leaving the Veterans' Administration hospital that morning, her mind had been in an uproar over the information Maurice Lewis III shared with her. Deep in thought, she did not even notice as the plane taxied down the runway and slowly made its ascent into the clouds—her normal fearfulness during takeoff overshadowed by her preoccupation with the shocking news she'd received.

Again Tamara wondered, how could Sienna be Maurice Lewis III's daughter? How could that be? It made no sense. After all, she was looking for Yvette's family, not Sienna's. In fact, Sienna had nothing to do with this—the process of searching for the man had begun well before she even knew Sienna.

Breaking into her thoughts, the dark-haired flight attendant smiled brightly and asked, "Would you like something to drink?"

"Yes, I will have a lemon-lime water, please," she answered, returning the woman's smile.

Tamara had been searching for information about Yvette for a long time now. She'd begun only months after she started working at the Care Agency a little over six years ago. The hunt had been tedious from the start since she had no real information other than Yvette's first, last, and middle name. But ironically, in the end it was those same three names that proved to be enough to put together Yvette's missing family again.

"Here you go, ma'am," said the flight attendant as she placed the drink and a plastic cup filled with crushed ice on the small tray in front of her.

"Thank you," said Tamara. Twisting the top off the bottle of flavored water, she poured the fizzing liquid into the squat cup absentmindedly.

Actually, I can't even take the credit for finding them, she thought. When the antiquated computer system finally had been updated last year and she had entered the three names on it, just like magic the girl's birth information had appeared on the screen. Sipping the water slowly, she thought with a wry smile that it was just like the system to enable you to locate a missing person's information years after the fact.

Tamara had not realized how thirsty she was until the cool carbonated drink slid welcomely down her dry throat. Since leaving the hospital this morning, she'd been in a sort of daze, and she realized with amazement that the water was the first liquid she'd put into her body since then.

Tamara would check the records when she got back into town, but she already knew what she would find out. Sienna Larson was Maurice Lewis III's daughter; she just knew it. "I simply can't get over it," she whispered.

Tamara poured more of the bottled water into the cup and, sipping it again, stared out the small window. Suddenly, the entire moment seemed strangely surreal, and as she gazed into the fluffy white clouds, it seemed as if they were not moving at all, as if the plane were caught somewhere in time and were standing still, even though she knew they were traveling forward at a rapid speed.

Yet, they were moving, and swiftly, just as everything had moved quickly once she typed those three names into the up-to-date computer system. In fact, after that it all had come together at a remarkable speed. But little had turned out the way she thought it would, and nothing had ended in the way that it began. Her first impression of Sissie Bailey was that the woman was simply tough, hard, and unfeeling; however, her eyes misted thinking about the transformation she'd witnessed on her last visit. She saw the woman's hard-lined face soften with the hope that she might have a granddaughter who might come to love her if she met her in the future.

"You just never know, do you?" she asked in a small voice, as if someone were there to answer her question. Like seeing only the jutting tip of an iceberg, Tamara realized she'd been looking solely at what was on the surface in this situation. As time passed, it became clear that the visible point where she'd first focused had given her no indication of all the intricacies and complexities that she would encounter once she looked a little deeper.

Through Sissie Bailey she had met Samyra, her daughter. Again fooled by the superficial, she had misinterpreted the woman's rugged countenance. With a finger Tamara wiped away the wetness from under her eyes as she turned toward the window again. Samyra Bailey's case was so very sad to her. Was it the prison environment that made this vibrant woman's own femaleness seem alien to her now? And even though Tamara knew that Samyra had no right to criminalize another, still she deeply empathized with the woman's anger and pain once she heard the story of her difficult upbringing.

"Is there anything else you would like?" asked the flight attendant, startling her as she was once again deeply enmeshed in her thoughts.

"No, no, I'm just fine, thank you very much," she replied.

Tamara set the empty plastic cup on the tray in front of her, leaned back on the headrest, and closed her eyes. Sleep eluded her, though, and instead in her mind she saw the weathered face of Benzo Taylor, standing outside in the cold of Chicago, selling his wares to the public on the mean streets. Hoarse from years of smoking, he'd told her warningly, "Girl, don't let anyone tell you hustlin's an easy way to make a livin'." With a croak of a laugh, he'd added, "Hustlin' might be easy to get into, but it's a hard way to live, and many a hustler's died tryin' to make a livin'. You remember that, you hear?"

Where did I get the courage even to go there? she wondered as her face warmed again, thinking of the men in the barbershop laughing at her feeble attempts to be strong and in control of the situation, when it was obvious she was not. Then unwittingly she conjured up a vision of a young Maurice Lewis III walking those same cold city streets, warm with youth and anticipation of a night of fun and laughter in his favorite nightclub. She struggled to picture Jannice, whom she had never seen, imagining the woman's face deep brown and beautiful and full of life, visualizing her as she waited excitedly for Maurice to arrive, with no thought or forewarning about the early death that she would encounter.

"It's all so sad, so very sad," she murmured to herself.

Even though much of the family was separated, literally torn apart, it was difficult to blame anyone, because the bad decisions and lack of responsibility that resulted in so much pain and disappointment seemed to be equally distributed among all of them. Tamara supposed that of the group, Maurice Lewis III was the most culpable, though. After all, he was the product of a middle-class home with strong values, and he had a mother and father there to help raise him.

She could smell the lemony-lavender scent of Lillian Lewis's well-ordered, beautiful home. Clearly, had this eloquent woman's handsome brother not decided to leave home for the bright lights of the big city, none of this would have come to pass.

But would that be a good thing? she wondered. If Maurice Lewis III had not met Jannice, there would be no Yvette, and none of her sisters would be living, either. Without Maurice there would be no Sienna.

Without a second thought, she said aloud, "That would be a loss . . . a real loss."

Sienna's bright, small gamine face appeared in her mind, complete with the dancing eyes upturned saucily on the sides. The small pink mouth was almost always stretched into a smile or chattering about something or other, and the teen's diminutive hands were always gesturing or moving about as well. Tamara could not help but smile as she thought of her then—Sienna, a small whirlwind of motion, a compact cyclone packed with energy!

"Oh, Sienna, it is true that sometimes you say the wrong thing at the wrong time!" she whispered. And attitude? Sienna Larson had enough attitude for five or six people, Tamara thought wryly. Though she would never admit it to the girl, the truth was, Tamara rather admired her spunky nature—the teen spoke her mind, and no one would ever steamroll Sienna!

Even if Sienna was totally out of bounds with her attitude and conversation at times, there was no denying that she was always animated and full of life. She simply lit up the room with her presence. No, she could not imagine this world without Sienna Larson. In fact, she really could not imagine her own life without the girl now, and surprisingly, she didn't even want to.

Tamara recalled the inexplicable beauty of Sienna's singing that day when she'd accepted the Lord into her life. Unexpectedly, the girl's voice had drawn her in, and Tamara was no longer aware of where she was, and was unconcerned about everyone else in the room. All she heard that morning was the sweetness in Sienna's tone, and the lovely lyrics of song the girl sang, and it was that sweet purity that had drawn her to God. Yes, one thing was true: Sienna's voice was surely a powerful gift, and the world deserved to hear it.

Sienna Larson and Yvette—*sisters*, she thought again in amazement. *I should have seen the similarities. I suppose I was totally blinded by the difference in the girls' coloring, and the dissimilarity of their demeanors, but then again, I guess it was just not what I was looking for at all. All this time, my interest was in locating Yvette's family, and it never occurred to me that Sienna could be part of that.*

Old thoughts replayed themselves in her head, and Tamara began to have a familiar discussion with herself. It was the system, she thought disdainfully, the screwed-up system that caused all of this, really. What kind of system took children from their homes, causing them to lose their identity in the process? How could these children ever feel whole when they didn't know who they were, where they came from, and who they were even related to?

"What a mess!" she said angrily. Her voice was so loud that the flight attendant, who was without much to do on the almost empty flight, came running over to see if she needed something again.

"I'm sorry for the noise . . . I don't want anything," Tamara said quietly when she saw the woman standing there.

She watched the flight attendant walk away, and once she was gone, Tamara closed her eyes again, and tears squeezed out from under her lashes. This changed a lot, she thought, but then she realized that actually it did not, because in reality everything had already changed well before she knew that Maurice was Sienna's father. Unexpectedly, she had become quite attached to Sienna. Though she'd been uncomfortable at times with the entire process, in retrospect she really was quite pleased with many of the changes that had occurred in her life in the past months since the teen had come to live with her.

While she was lost in her thoughts the time flew by, and now the plane was making its slow descent onto the runway. Tamara sighed, and after a moment she wiped her eyes once more and found her cell phone inside her bag.

"Mrs. Jackson?" Tamara asked once she heard the woman's voice at the end of the line. Absentmindedly she played with one of the small CZ earrings that Sienna had given her for Christmas.

"Yes, this is she. Tamara? Is that you?"

Tamara started to speak rapidly, her adrenaline suddenly running high and her thoughts still awhirl: "Yes, Mrs. Jackson, it's me. I am on my way home now. Instead of staying the extra day, I took an earlier flight out. Something happened while I was there. Something quite unexpected happened. I can't tell you all the details right now, but I will say that I've inadvertently found Sienna's father."

There was long, almost eerie silence at the end of the line.

Suddenly concerned, Tamara asked falteringly, "M-Mrs. J-Jackson, are you still there?"

Mrs. Jackson sighed loudly before answering in a voice that seemed vague and distant, "I'm here, baby girl . . . I've got something to tell you, though. I didn't want to call you while you were out there, but I am glad that you are on the way home. Sienna is gone, Tamara. She ran away last night, and we haven't heard one word from her."

In disbelief, Tamara asked, "Sienna? Gone?"

Sighing again, Mrs. Jackson replied, "Yes, baby girl, she's gone. Don't you worry, though. These kids do this sometimes, and they usually come right on back in a day or two."

Tamara's heart sank, and fear clenched her chest as she remembered the ugly words she'd yelled at the girl so unfeelingly during the big argument they'd had days ago.

"Tamara? Don't you worry now . . . just come on home."

"Okay," she replied. Unable to say more, Tamara hung up the telephone and held it in her lap. Tears began to overflow from her eyes and run slowly down her face, and she no longer tried to hide them.

Tamara knew she was hurting the girl when she said the callous words the other day, and yet she'd never apologized. And the worst part of it was that she really hadn't meant most of what she'd said. She'd just figured that she would have time to make it all right, and now it seemed that she did not.

Barely able to contain herself, Tamara sobbed, "Oh, Sienna, not now . . . Why did you have to leave now? I'm sorry. I'm so, so sorry."

47.

Finally Free

The girl had carefully chosen her clothes that morning. Once dressed, she'd stood in front of the mirror, rehearsing her speech time and time again for the judge, trying to make sure she would be totally prepared for this morning. Yet now that she was here in the courtroom, all the well-practiced words seemed to have slipped from her mind, and all she could do was nervously smooth her plain black pants down over her legs.

"Don't worry," said Marsha comfortingly as she gazed into the girl's worried face. The African-American woman was her court-appointed advocate, and she'd stood, staunchly supportive, by her side each time the girl had to go before the judge. "Everything is going to be all right. In fact, I really think today you are finally going to get your wish."

"I hope so," the girl replied, but she was too afraid to believe it might happen. This was her third trip in front of this judge in the past two years. Each previous time she'd been hopeful, only to leave the courtroom disappointed and vowing to try again as soon as she could.

Much to her surprise, Safe Haven Home had proved to be a decent place to live. In fact, she'd only run away one time during the couple of years that she'd lived there. After Judge Rosenberger told her that she'd never become emancipated if she didn't stay put, the girl had done so.

Nothing bad happened to her there. Her friend James Jordan made sure of that. Although she'd not trusted him at all on that first day she'd met him, the stocky, light-complexioned boy had designated himself her protector, and he'd kept her safe for the entire time she was there. If she got to leave today, she would miss him as much as she could miss anybody. He was really the first and only friend she'd really ever had.

"She just called you," said Marsha softly as she put her arm around her shoulders and gave her a gentle push.

The girl rose and walked nervously up to the podium, where she stood in front of the judge.

Judge Rosenberger smiled at her and said, "Well, young lady,

I see we meet again. I must say, I admire your determination. Emancipation must be something you really want for yourself."

"Yes, ma'am," she answered without looking up at the Judge.

The woman put her reading glasses on her face and began to peruse the file in front of her. "Let's see . . . this is good; you have completed some schooling now. You've gotten your GED now, and you are enrolled in some college classes for the fall."

"Yes, ma'am," she answered again, in a low voice.

"This is good, too . . . It says here that you have also been working. It seems that you have a job after school, and these letters of recommendation from your employer speak highly of you."

The girl kept her eyes down and said nothing.

Judge Rosenberger removed her glasses and said in an almost stern tone, "Young lady, look up at me. If you are going to face the world on your own, you must learn to look it in the eye and face it squarely right now!"

Slowly the girl raised her head, bringing her dark eyes up to meet the judge's blue ones.

The judge closed the folder in front of her, looked Yvette deeply in the eye, and in a quiet, even tone said, "Young lady, I think that it is clear that you have the intellect, the drive, and most importantly, the spirit required to live as an emancipated minor. There is no reason to stop this process—you are within months of your seventeenth birthday, and Marsha has agreed to be your state-appointed guardian till then."

The girl looked at the woman disbelievingly. *Can it be?* she thought. *Can it be that I'm really going to get what I want this time?* Uncertainty was written on her face when she turned to give Marsha a furtive glance, but after one look at the woman's wide smile, her heart leapt happily.

"Take these papers to the young lady," the judge said to the bailiff standing by her desk.

The man took the papers from the judge, walked over to the podium where the girl stood, and laid the legal-size documents in front of her.

By then, though, the girl's emotions were overflowing, and so were her eyes. Unable to see very well, she struggled to read the words on the paper as she wiped away the tears that would not stop falling.

Touched by the girl's obvious joy, the judge said in a quiet voice, "I will tell you the thrust of what it says.

"As of today, February 14, 1988, the court finds Tanisha Yvette Bailey to be an emancipated minor."

The girl gazed happily at the judge through her tears.

"Ms. Bailey, what that means is that you may live wherever you like, with or without whomever you like, and it's all legal."

"I'm free," said the girl as she grinned at Marsha and began to cry in earnest. Half-sobbing, half-laughing, she repeated the words as if she could not believe it. "I'm finally, finally free."

48.

Meltdown

Tamara walked slowly into Hope Temple, feeling heavy, weighed down with guilt and worry about the still-missing Sienna. The teen had been gone now for three whole days, and Tamara's optimism that she would return was fading. Instead of working these past two days, she'd walked up and down the city streets throughout the day and driven through those same streets late into the night, searching for Sienna. Sabrina and Terry helped her by calling all her friends from school, but it was spring break and there were no sightings of her by anyone from school.

Isaiah Perry called each night and repeatedly offered his assistance in helping her look for Sienna. Tamara felt far too ashamed to accept his help, though, knowing that it was her cruel and hurtful words that made the girl leave in the first place. In fact, Tamara's guilt was so deep that the friendship that was blossoming between her and Isaiah seemed lost, and the small inroads he'd made with her were closed again, leaving her as standoffish and reticent as when they'd first met.

Her distant stance perplexed him, and each time that his efforts failed to draw her out of her shell, he would say resignedly, "Know that you and Sienna are in my prayers, Tamara."

Each time, Tamara could hear the sadness and confusion in his voice, yet she was wallowing too deeply in her own misery about her part in the girl's disappearance to explain. So she simply would thank him for his call and hang up the telephone quietly, feeling more alone and sadder than before.

Even once she'd joined Hope Temple, a part of her had remained convinced that she attended services mainly to satisfy Sienna. But strangely, since the day that Mrs. Jackson told her the teen was missing, she'd begun to long for the comfort she remembered feeling inside the church's walls.

As if being drawn by an unseen force, Tamara's feet moved steadily toward the pew that she and Sienna had shared the first time they came to church together. As she made her way there, someone tapped her shoulder and said, "Don't you worry, Sister Britton, Sienna's gonna be all right. We're all praying here . . . We love her, too, you know." Tamara nodded dumbly, twisting her lips up in a semblance of a smile at the face that she couldn't seem to recognize right then.

Once seated in the pew, she took out her Bible and began to turn the pages absentmindedly while struggling to gather her thoughts together.

"Sienna?"

Tamara glanced up into the worried face of Isaiah Perry. "How are you?" he asked, and concern was evident on his handsome face.

"I'm fine," she replied quietly.

"Are you sure?" he asked in a gentle voice.

"Yes," she replied, but he could see that Tamara's usual generous smile was spare, and her eyes dim and lacking their normal glow.

"Tamara . . . ?"

She looked up at him again.

"Anytime you need me . . . anytime, okay?"

Tamara heard his words but was not able to respond, feeling oddly displaced at that moment, as though her body were wrapped in cotton, making everything seem softly distorted and unreal. With effort she forced herself to nod her head quickly and then turned her gaze down toward the Bible again, until she sensed intuitively that he was no longer standing there.

Tentatively Tamara raised her head. Looking around, she seemed to see people looking her way curiously, and she imagined they knew about the wicked words she'd uttered and about the guilt she bore for Sienna's disappearance. As she touched the small earrings that Sienna had given her, Tamara thought how all along everyone gave her more credit than she deserved regarding the teen. In her heart Tamara knew that she had not let Sienna move into her home because she cared, or even because she was such a warm and giving person; the truth was that she'd opened her home to Sienna because she was a wimp.

When Joan Erickson had cornered her that day in her office and asked her to take the girl in, Tamara had been too much of a wimp to say no. Each time someone had paid tribute to her about Sienna, she'd felt like an impostor, because she was. If she'd had any backbone, she would not even have accepted the award so generously presented to her by Denise Jackson from the Foster Parents Association that night. Yes, she knew the truth, which was that Tamara Britton knew nothing about love or caring or concern, because her motives had been self-serving all along.

Sister Walker took the microphone then. The finely boned brown-skinned wife of the pastor said in an ebullient voice, "Welcome, everyone, this morning! Let's just give some praise to the Lord, because He woke us up this morning and He started us on our way and the Lord is blessing us right now!"

Tamara was not feeling blessed at all, but obediently she looked up into the woman's smiling face.

The woman continued, "Many times in our lives we find ourselves in situations that are unfair. Life is sometimes difficult, and we find ourselves without anyone to talk to about what we are going through. But know that you are never alone! God loves you, and He is always there with you!"

"Amen," said several members of the congregation.

"The times when life is tough are those important times of growth for us, when God is getting us ready for something greater He has in store for us one day. Our hardships today will certainly be our testimony tomorrow, and these difficulties will serve to make us more confident in our faith once we realize that He's been with us all the time. Truly, truly, truly, I say to all of you today, just like it says in the Word of God, Romans eight, verse twenty-eight, 'Be encouraged, church, persevere through your hardships, because all things work together for the good for those who love God and are called according to his purpose.'"

The musicians began to play, and as the choir sang the introduction, the woman began to hum along, and then she sang,

"When difficulty finds its way into our life,
We struggle to find a reason,
But, remember, our Lord always has a plan,
And these hardships will only last but a season.
Everything is for the good,
Yes, everything is for the good!
All things work together for the good,
For those who love the Lord . . ."

Tamara stood unconsciously rocking from side to side, while listening to the words that seemed to permeate her entire body. *All things work for the good for those who love the Lord,* she thought to herself.

When the selection was finished, the words of the song continued to run through her mind while she sat there fighting her anxieties. Inwardly she was in a state of flux, and it took all she had to keep herself seated and remain outwardly calm.

Still lost in thought, she put her offering into the tray when it passed by, and then stood as the choir began to sing its main selection, a popular song about praising God through the good and bad that life brings. She'd bought this CD by Shekinah Glory Ministry because it was one of the first songs she'd heard Sienna sing and because it was a favorite of the girl's and the congregation's. Today as they sang, some of them held their hands up to Jesus, and she wondered just how they could praise Him even in the midst of their difficulties. Tamara watched them, wanting desperately to understand how going through bad times could make a person better, and moreover, desiring to understand how to love and trust God regardless of what she was going through.

In the days since Sienna left, Tamara had come to realize that the teen had been a catalyst for change in her life. Just like a lightning rod, Sienna had pulled all sorts of new energy from Tamara. Not only that, Sienna also touched her in a way that Tamara had never known before, and now that she was gone Tamara missed her terribly. Her home and her life, which had seemed so complete before Sienna came, seemed empty and barren without her.

The greatest irony was that Tamara's anger about her own discomfort had made Sienna run away, and yet now she understood that the uneasiness she had been experiencing was simply part of the necessary adjustment to change; and without change, life would be stagnant, lacking growth and substance.

"Church, let us rise for the prayer."

Tamara stood, and lowered her head, and closed her eyes.

"Lord, we praise Your name today . . . and just like my precious wife, Sister Walker, said earlier, we thank You, Lord, for all of the hardships that we have faced and will face in our lives, for we know all is in Your plan. Lord, we ask that You help create in us a clean heart—a heart that is free of deception and open and transparent for the world to see. We know that You know us fully and that You have already forgiven us for any sin we may have committed, and that You love us just as we are. Oh, what a blessing it is, God, to be loved just as we are."

Tamara whispered, "A clean heart, God, that's what I want."

"Lord, we thank You for Your love, and each day we ask that You show us how to love others just as You do us: unconditionally, fully, and without reservation. Amen. You may be seated, church."

She sat back down and then turned her swollen eyes upward the minister.

"Church, for the past few months we have been talking about learning to walk in love, and over the past few weeks we have learned that this is no easy stroll. But, if we are striving to be like Jesus, we must learn to love others like He loved us."

The minister looked out into the congregation and said,

"You know it's easy to love folks that are close to us. When we look at our children, they look like us and they often talk like us; they remind us of ourselves, and if we are good parents, we find it easy to give them love. But oh, church, it's not so easy to love folks that aren't in our family—is it?

"Turn in your Bible to Romans eleven. I'm gonna show you somethin' here that will just blow your mind when you think about it. You see, salvation was not really for us in the beginning; salvation was for the people of Israel, and they rejected it. Read Paul's words with me beginning at verse fifteen: 'For if their rejection is the reconciliation of the world, what will their acceptance be but life from the dead!'

"See, it was then, when the people of Israel rejected the salvation that God turned their rejection into good, when He offered to the world the salvation that had only been for them:

"'If the part of the dough offered as the first fruits is holy, then the whole batch is holy; and if the root is holy, then the branches are also holy . . .'

"Now, listen here, church, keep in mind, the root is God, ' . . . and the branches are made holy by the root.'"

The minister told them, "Now, stay with me, church; let's move on down to verse seventeen:

"'But if some branches were broken off, and you, a wild olive shoot, were grafted in their place to share the rich root of the olive tree, do not boast of the branches. If you do boast, remember that it is not you that supports the root, but the root that supports you.'"

He stopped there for a minute. "Church, this verse is a warning for us. It reminds us to stay humble, lest we get bigheaded, as we can do sometimes, thinking that everything stems from something great we have inside ourselves. We are here because of God, because He loved us enough to graft us onto the tree and feed us His Word. God does not treat us like stepchildren because we got in the game late, either; He treats us like His own, because He made us His own."

Tamara looked up, thinking how amazing it was that God's love was so consistent, strong, and unconditional.

The minister removed his glasses in his customary manner. "Now, church, we have seen that we have been made a part of salvation through God's love for us, and now let's read how we as Christians should claim that salvation for ourselves." He replaced his eyeglasses and said, "Turn your Bibles to Philippians three, verse twelve.

"You know, at the time Paul wrote this, church, he was in prison. In fact, this book is comprised of letters he wrote to the people of Philippi while he was there. So he wrote about difficult times from personal experience. In other words, Saint Paul could relate to what he was talking about here, 'cause Paul was livin' it, too! Brothers and sisters, Paul was talkin' the talk *while* he was walkin' the walk!"

"Amen," said several members of the congregation, amid a smattering of laughter.

"Y'all understand that, huh? Y'all must know something about that, then," added the pastor with a chuckle.

Tamara could not laugh with the others, though. Her mood was too somber, and she solemnly waited to hear the remainder of the sermon, still feeling fluttery and off balance inside.

"Okay, church. Read with me . . . chapter three, verse twelve: 'Not that I have already obtained this or have already reached the goal, but I press on to make it my own, because Christ Jesus has made me his own.'

"Remember, now, church, we are His now; He's grafted us onto the tree of salvation, and we are connected to Him. He's our root, our sustenance."

The minister continued, "Church, don't stop reading now. C'mon . . .

" 'Beloved, I do not consider that I have made it my own, but this one thing I do; forgetting what lies behind and straining forward to what lies ahead, I press toward the goal for the prize of the heavenly call of God in Christ Jesus.' "

Tamara closed her Bible then, and so did the minister. The words she'd just read with him were in the forefront of her mind now.

"We have hard times, church; yes, we do, but know that God works them altogether for the good, sisters and brothers. We can't let life's difficulties and hardships make us bitter or too frightened to love, because it is through love that we best reflect the Holy Spirit within us."

He looked into the congregation, and his voice choked with emotion. "My brothers and sisters, I know it's hard sometimes, during those difficult times when life has been tough and it seems that no one understands or cares what you've been through or what you are going through, but *be assured* that God has His hand on you. Believe me, even if you have been through the most severe of difficulties, you *can* trust enough to love again. You must remember to *forget* those things that lie behind, and *press forward* toward the high calling of Jesus Christ."

It was as he said those words that Tamara felt something within begin to break apart. Her mind would not be still, and she couldn't stop its movement; it was filled with swirling images of the girl and thoughts of Yvette, Isaiah Perry, Denise Jackson, and all the people she'd met in the past few months. Although she could hear his words clearly, she could only stare straight ahead unseeingly as the minister continued to speak.

"Press forward, church . . . *press forward*. It's all about love. It's all about learning to love like God loves us."

He leaned on the podium, glasses in hand again. "Before I stop today, church, I want to share this prose with you. This year I found some Christmas cards. They weren't expensive cards or

306

made by a special person; in fact, my wife and I picked these up at Wal-Mart. But they were the most beautiful cards because of what they said. I have one with me today, and I'm going to read it to you to close the sermon."

He put his eyeglasses on and began to read. "It says, 'God . . . *the greatest person* . . . so loved . . . *the greatest degree* . . . the world . . . *the greatest company* . . . that He gave . . . *the greatest act* . . . His only begotten Son . . . *the greatest gift* . . . that whosoever . . . *the greatest opportunity* . . . believeth . . . *the greatest simplicity* . . . in Him . . . *the greatest attraction* . . . should not perish . . . *the greatest promise* . . . but . . . .*the greatest difference* . . . have . . . *the greatest certainty* . . . everlasting life . . . *the greatest possession.*'"

Tamara began to cry then. Slow tears coursed down her smooth brown face, and each time she wiped them away, more came just as quickly. She'd cried so much in the past few days that truly she thought there were no tears left to cry, but she did cry now, and the tears flowed unceasingly.

It seemed that Minister Walker was looking right at her then, and he said, "God makes no mistakes, my church . . . There is a plan for your life, and nothing, *nothing*, is an accident. Never be afraid to walk in love, just as Jesus walked in love for us . . . Know that no matter where we come from or where we've been, there is exceedingly abundant room in God's heart to love us, and we always have room in our hearts, too, church! Plenty good room to love!"

Then the minister began his altar call. "If anybody would like to come today and accept God into their life, come now . . . come now."

Tamara was crying in earnest, lost in her own emotions, and totally unaware of what was going on around her other than the sound of the preacher's voice.

In his low, gravelly voice, Minister Walker began to slowly sing the old Negro spiritual he'd sung at Bible study weeks ago:

"There's plenty good room,
plenty good room in ma Father's Kingdom,
plenty good room, plenty good room
—just choose your seat and sit down."

Tamara's sobs became louder, and she lost all control. It was as if a dam had burst inside her, and she was unable to hold back the emotions she'd suppressed for so very long.

"I can't take it anymore," she cried as she sobbed loudly and sat down hard in the pew. "Oh, God, I just can't take it anymore. Help me, God, please help me," and through her tears she continued to say those words over and over until Denise Jackson ran down from the choir stand to help her out of the sanctuary.

49.

Finding Faith

Isaiah Perry almost had to carry a weakened Tamara from the church before putting her into Denise Jackson's car. While unsure of why Tamara was so upset, they both knew that in her state of mind she was obviously in no position to drive herself home.

Isaiah Perry's husky voice was heavy with concern when he asked Denise, "Do you want me to come with you?"

Denise looked at the young man. "No, I think it will be better if I take her alone, Isaiah. Now, you try not to worry, baby, and I promise I will call you as soon as I get her calmed down a bit."

"Please don't forget, Mrs. Jackson," he said. "Good-bye, Tamara," he added, glancing over at her, but the young woman showed no sign of having heard him and instead just continued to wipe away the silent tears still flowing down her cheeks as she stared out the window.

Once in the apartment, Denise Jackson gently led Tamara into her bedroom, opened her drawers, and picked out some comfortable clothes. Tamara had finally stopped crying and now stared straight ahead, as if she were in a daze of sorts, clearly still very upset and suffering through some sort of severe inner turmoil.

Denise Jackson pulled back the coral comforter on the bed and plumped the pillows. "Baby girl, I'm gonna make us some tea. Now, you get comfortable and then just get right up in the bed until I get back," she added as she patted the pillow.

When she returned a few minutes later with two cups of steaming Red Zinger herbal tea, Tamara was sitting upright in the bed. Her legs were crossed in front of her, and she continued to stare ahead blankly.

"Baby girl?"

Tamara's eyes were swollen so tightly closed that when she turned to look at Denise, they were like mere slits in her round face.

"Oh, baby girl . . . ," said the older woman sadly as she set down the cups of tea.

"I'm okay," Tamara said hoarsely, but her sad expression clearly did not match the words coming from her mouth.

"Baby, is there something else going on? I know that you are upset about little Sienna leaving and all, but it seems like more.

What did you mean, you 'can't take it anymore'? What did you mean when you kept saying that, Tamara?"

Tamara did not reply but instead slowly stretched out first one leg and then the other and got down from the bed. Almost mechanically she walked over to the closet and opened the metal door. Standing on her toes, she pulled out an old, green duffel bag from the corner of the back top shelf. Without looking at Denise Jackson, she wiped the dust off the top of the bag almost lovingly before she opened it and reached inside. In a moment she'd retrieved a worn black Bible, and with it in hand she walked back over to the bed and sat down.

Denise Jackson looked at the girl curiously but, for once, kept quiet. She could sense that whatever this was that seemed to be eating at the girl's insides, it would have to be handled by her in her own time and in her own way.

Tamara pulled her legs up under her again and said in a voice that was so quiet, it was little more than a whisper. "You know, I had a friend who knew a minister that preached at a church called Hope Temple—just like the church we go to now. It was a long, long time ago, but it's still pretty ironic, huh?"

Denise gazed at Tamara straightforwardly and answered, "It's not ironic at all. Remember, our God is not one of irony, Tamara! Your friend might have gone to the first Hope Temple founded by Reverend Davis, God rest his soul. He was Minister Walker's stepfather—took care of him just like he was his own, though."

"Reverend Davis?" she said in a surprised voice.

"Yes, baby, Reverend Davis. He was a good, kindly man."

She closed her eyes, then opened them again and said quietly, "Yes, he was good and kindly . . . He took care of my friend, too."

"Your friend?"

Tamara said, "Yes, my friend . . . For a long time now I've

been trying to help this friend of mine. She's someone I knew a long, long time ago. This friend's struggle was the reason that I became involved in Child Welfare—because I knew what she'd gone through and I wanted to make a difference, you know?" Slow tears had began to course down the girl's face again as she clutched the worn Bible close to her.

Curious, the woman asked, "So where is your friend now?"

Tamara continued speaking just as if she had not heard the woman's question. "This past year so very much as happened. And finally, after so many months and years of searching, I was able to find them."

"Them?"

"Yvette's parents—*my friend* Yvette's parents. I've met her grandmother and her aunt and found out that her mother is dead," she said as she choked back a sob. "Her mother, Jannice Bailey, died of a drug overdose . . . all alone." She wiped her newly flowing tears with the back of her hand almost angrily. "Then, I met her daddy . . . I met her daddy," she repeated.

Uncomprehending, Denise Jackson asked again, "So, do you know where your friend is now?"

Tamara slowly brought the Bible down from her chest into her lap and opened it to the first page. She read the words that were written on the inner sleeve aloud. "'God loves you. Never forget that.'

"Yes, Mrs. Jackson," said Tamara, and tears were streaming down her face again. "I know where she is."

Denise Jackson was concerned that Tamara once again seemed so distraught. "Baby girl, I just have to say this to you. I don't know what is going on, why you are so upset, but I want you to think about Minister Walker's words today. Tamara, everything works together for the good, baby girl—*everything*."

Between her hiccuping sobs, Tamara said morosely, "B-b-but, Mrs. J-Jackson, I've made such a mess of everything.

S-Sienna was trying to be kind to me in all the ways she knew how; she l-l-liked me and I wouldn't accept it. I expected t-too much of her, and I said things to her that I thought I meant, b-but now I know I did not."

Denise Jackson pursed her lips and said, "Shhh! Just hush now, baby girl. You are a sweet and loving person, and you are being way too hard on yourself. Truth be told, you should've given Sienna a good talkin'-to a long time before you did."

Tamara glanced up at the woman and said in a rush, "I'm not a good person; I'm not; I'm not. Everyone thinks I took Sienna in because I'm so good. The truth is, I took her in because I was afraid to tell my boss that I would not."

Denise Jackson sat on the bed by her and rubbed her back gently. "Oh, Tamara, baby, no. That is just a deception of the enemy. *God* put it into your heart to open your home to little Sienna, and even if you were afraid and you did it anyway, that makes it so much more of a wonderful thing for you to have done. You were submitting to His will *without even knowing it.*"

For the first time that day, hope appeared in the girl's eyes when she looked at her. "God was with me then?"

"Baby, God has been with you all the time. Even during those times you thought you were alone, you were not, because He was right there watching you and loving you all the time."

"But, Mrs. Jackson, it was so hard sometimes . . . and I felt so alone."

"Baby, all of us have difficult times, and I don't know what you've been through, but I know that all of it was a preparation for this moment, this time, this day, and the plan that God has just for you. Baby girl, you didn't feel Him with you, because you didn't stop and listen to His quiet voice inside. But He was there; He was there."

Tamara wiped her swollen eyes and said quietly, "All things work together for the good . . . *all things.*"

"Yes, baby," said Denise Jackson. "All things work together for the good. God doesn't make mistakes, and you and your life were no accident. He was preparing you then *for this moment, now.* Be assured that you've had a profound effect on that girl, and I know that she will be back."

"Oh, Mrs. Jackson, do you really think so?"

With certainty Denise Jackson replied, "I think so. Sienna's probably just somewhere with a friend, and when she gets tired and misses you enough, she'll be back. Sienna loves you, Tamara, so she has to come back . . . Love will bring her back."

"She loves me?"

"Yes, baby girl, Sienna loves you. You are the most stable person she's had in her life, and she admires you and she loves you deeply, and what's more, Tamara . . . you love her, too."

Tamara inhaled deeply and then sighed as she opened the book and read the words again: "God loves you. Never forget that."

Denise Jackson looked at her curiously and asked, "Is that your friend's Bible? Is that why it seems to mean so much to you?"

"Yes, it is my friend Yvette's Bible. It was given to her by Reverend Davis, a long time ago. He was so very kind to her when no one else was."

"You and she must be very close. She seems to have shared a lot with you."

Tamara turned and opened the nightstand drawer then. She moved aside a worn copy of a paperback book, *Hind's Feet on High Places,* by Hannah Hurnard. Then from inside a large brown envelope she pulled out a piece of paper and handed it to Denise Jackson.

The older woman put on her glasses and began to read silently. "Why, this says something about a Tanisha Yvette Bailey being an emancipated minor . . . Is this your friend?"

"My name is Tamara Britton, with no middle initial." The younger woman gave Denise Jackson a small smile and said, "I couldn't think of one for 'Y' . . . Tanisha became Tamara, and Bailey became Britton."

Not fully understanding, Denise Jackson looked down at the paper again and then gazed up at Tamara.

Tamara continued in a low, emotionless voice, "I lived as a runaway most of my life when I was young. I was abandoned by my parents, victimized within the system, and then finally, finally set free. I was ashamed of who I was and what type of life I'd come from . . . and so I made up a whole new identity."

"Oh, baby girl," the woman said compassionately, at last comprehending fully the gist of what Tamara was telling her.

Tamara shook her head sadly and then continued to speak, "It was no good, though, Mrs. Jackson, because I still could not run away from the memories of what happened to me. Now I know that my mother died of a drug overdose, my grandmother lives in the projects with my nephew, my aunt is in prison, and my father is alive, and I've met them all. The funny thing was that I'd told the lie so long, it was almost as if Yvette was a separate person, and so when I saw my relatives, I still did not even claim them as my own."

Denise Jackson was quiet as she took in all this new information. Suddenly the woman sat up alertly, and her expression was quizzical. "But, baby girl, I thought you said that the man you found in California was Sienna's daddy."

"He is," said Tamara as she watched the woman carefully.

The woman's eyes widened, "But, you were looking for *your* daddy . . . Oh, Lord, so what that means . . ."

"What that means is that Sienna Larson and I are half sisters," said Tamara as she turned her swollen eyes from the woman and stared unseeingly toward the bedroom door.

Denise Jackson shook her head and said with an astonished

look on her face, "Imagine that! The two of y'all sisters and never knowin' it . . . Ain't that something? My, my, my . . . sho' ain't no doubt that the Lord *does* work in mysterious ways!"

"He sure does, Mrs. Jackson." Tamara added quietly, "For the longest, I've been searching for my family, and months ago my own sister, Sienna, showed up on my doorstep, and she'd been with me all this time."

The older woman chuckled, "It's just a human trait, Tamara; sometimes we just cain't see what's right in front of us, for lookin'! But, don't you worry baby girl, He's gonna work this all out—just you wait and see."

Tears filled the younger woman's eyes again. "Do you think so, Mrs. Jackson? Do you really think God will bring Sienna home?"

"I know He will," said Denise Jackson firmly. "I know He will."

50.

Finger-Poppin' Time

"How you feeling today, girl?" asked Lynnette. To Tamara's surprise, her friend had stood by her resolutely during the past week. Not only had Lynnette come into the office to work each day, she also had called her several times each evening, making it her business to help keep Tamara's spirits up anyway she could.

Time was passing, though. It was already Friday, and Tamara still had not heard one word from Sienna. "I'm okay," she replied. "I was really praying that we would hear something this week, though . . . School is back in session, and I was hoping hard that she would appear there."

"Don't you worry, Tam . . . She's gonna show up," said Lynnette reassuringly, but she looked worriedly at Jayson, who was standing behind Tamara.

Tamara continued, "Last night Isaiah came over, and we searched all through the west side of town, but we didn't see her anywhere. He's been asking people at school, but so far he's had no luck, either."

"Tam . . . I know that after all you've been through, you, more than any of us, know that God's got her in his sight. She's gonna be all right," said Jayson. "Besides, she has to come back. You know that child's not finished terrorizing you yet!" he added with a smile.

Tamara smiled as she twisted one of the small earrings that she'd worn every day since the girl had been gone. "It's amazing, Jay-Jay; I really do believe she's okay, because I truly believe God *is* watching her, and I know that He loves her."

Jayson looked serious, and after quickly glancing toward Lynnette, he asked, "Tamara, tell me if you mind me asking . . . I know that you said that you were a runaway, but how *did* you manage to live like that so long?"

"Jayson! That's not really any of our business!" said Lynnette as she shot him a warning look. "Tamara, you know that you *do not* have to answer that nosy boy's question."

Tamara smiled at the two of them. "It's okay. I can understand why you have questions. I know for you it probably seems hard to understand. Actually, looking back at it all now, it's difficult for me to figure out how I survived. I really don't know how I did it . . . I suppose it's like Mrs. Jackson said—God was with me all the time."

"He had to be," said Lynnette. "Girl, you were a mere child during some of those times you were off living on your own. Anything could've happened to you. It had to be the Lord that kept you through all of that. All I can say is that He must have some real special plans for you!"

Jayson asked, "But, Tam, weren't you scared?"

"Yes, I was very frightened at first, but because of the bad stuff that happened to me in foster placements, I became more frightened of being in the homes. Living in any home became scarier than living in the streets."

Jayson shook his head and stroked his goatee. "And to think I was believin' that you was weak and everything; but, little girl, you got me beat! You are one strong cookie to have made it through all that you have!"

Lynnette threw back her microbraids, which were hanging loose and free today, and said, "I agree with that." She smoothed down her off-white lightweight wool and then pulled the sleeves of the matching lamb's-wool turtleneck sweater. "Baby, it's whenever we think we are weak that somehow God gives us just what we need to be tougher than we ever thought we could be."

"It's funny that most of the time, I don't feel very strong at all . . . but I guess I am, aren't I?" Tamara said with a half smile. "And even when I'm not, I've learned now that God does care for me and He's always with me. It's so strange that the very man who fed me and treated me with kindness back then was the stepfather of the minister in the church I now attend."

"Girl, that's not strange; that's just God." Lynnette widened her large eyes and pursed her lips. "It's like the Word says: 'God won't give us more than we can handle' and 'He'll always give us a way out when things get really tough.' Minister Davis was your way out back then Tamara. God put him in your life at *ex-actly* the moment you needed him most. It just goes to show, the Lord *always* knows what He's doing. Shoot, the Word says He knows how many hairs we have on our head."

"And the Lord gotta be the man to know that about you, Lynn, since yo' hair count changes by the week, every time you get a new weave," said Jayson with a smirk.

Lynnette rolled her eyes and then threw him a derisive glare. "Well, at least I got some hair to count—more than I can say about you!"

Tamara giggled, happy for their verbal sparring this time, since it gave her an excuse to laugh for a moment.

"Sounds like we're having fun over here!" said Joan Erickson.

The three of them became quiet as they exchanged quick looks, perturbed that the woman had again slipped up on them quietly when they seemed to be playing instead of working.

Joan turned her attention to Tamara, though, and said in a voice that seemed full of genuine concern, "I've heard about everything you've been through, Tamara. This type of news just travels, so don't feel bad. Please, know how much I admire you for having the willpower not just to live through such a harrowing early life, but to also actually have overcome it all with such style and grace. Know that your experience makes you invaluable to the youth we serve and their families, and I don't think that we could have a better person working for us here at the Care for Kids Agency."

Tamara was dumbstruck by the woman's unexpected kind words. For so many years she'd been ashamed of her past and had separated herself from it so carefully that she'd almost begun to believe that all the bad things she'd experienced so many years ago had happened to another person.

She had only been fooling herself, though, and she knew it when Sienna ran away and it all came crashing down upon her.

Since then she'd received only support, concern, and comfort, rather than the retribution and judgment that she'd imagined people would respond with once they learned the truth about her. Even though Sienna was still missing, Tamara was thankful the truth was out, because she felt lighter and freer than she ever had in the past.

Then, to Tamara's complete surprise, Joan Erickson reached over and hugged her around the neck hard. She could smell the expensive Chanel no. 5 cologne in the woman's hair as she said in her ear, "If I can help you in any way, please let me know. *Please.*"

Tamara felt herself soften under the woman's kind words and said, "Thank you, Joan. Thank you."

"See, I told you she does have a heart after all," said Jayson when she walked away.

"Boy, shut up! You ain't told us nothin'! You the main one always talkin' 'bout the woman," said Lynnette.

"Now, don't start again, okay?" said Tamara, but when she looked up to smile at Jayson, he was looking over her head at something or someone behind her.

"Tamara, somebody is here to see you, girl," said Lynnette. "It's that fine man from your church—you know the one I mean."

Tamara spun around to see Isaiah Perry standing in front of her.

Instantly concerned, she began to question him. "Isaiah! Nothing bad has happened, has it? You haven't heard any bad news about Sienna, have you?"

Isaiah shook his head and smiled widely, and then suddenly from behind him, Sienna's small face popped out around the corner of a neighboring cubicle.

"Ain't nothin' happened to me!" The girl postured and

319

saucily clicked her tongue loudly. "*Shooot,* I can take care of my-self . . . Ain't *nobody* gonna mess with me!"

Jayson twisted his lips and replied in a low voice, "I can be-lieve that, little Miss Thang!"

Tamara's face lit up when she saw the girl, and she jumped out of her chair happily. "Sienna! Where have you been? I've been worried sick!"

Sienna gave her a pouting look before saying in a hurt tone, "*You* the one said you was tired of me and everything."

Tamara looked into the girl's eyes and said, "Yes, I did, Sienna, and I can't tell you how sorry I am for saying that. I was angry, and I said things I should not have. I did not mean it . . . I did not mean it at all."

"You didn't?" The girl's stare was skeptical for a moment, and her voice lightened. "Really, Tamara? You didn't mean it?"

"I didn't. Come here, Sienna," said Tamara as she moved closer to the girl.

Tentatively the girl walked over to her, and as soon as she was close enough, Tamara grabbed her by the arms, pulled her close, and hugged her hard. When she looked at Isaiah, her eyes were wet with tears, and so were his. "I've missed you so much, and I've got *so* much to tell you."

"Okay, okay, enough of this mushy stuff," the teen replied, quickly wiping her eyes with the back of her hand. "And don't think I'm cryin', either, 'cause I ain't no punk like that . . . I just got somethin' in my eye," she added hastily.

From behind her Tamara heard Joan Erickson say, "Tamara, why don't you take the rest of the day off? Lynnette and Jayson can cover for you; and you and Sienna can enjoy a long week-end."

Tamara looked at her two coworkers—her two *friends*—and Lynnette grabbed her coat and said, "Don't worry, we got it cov-ered, Tam. Enjoy."

"If you like, I can drive you two ladies home," said Isaiah. "It will give you time to talk."

Tamara gave him a grateful smile and said quietly, "Thank you, Isaiah."

Sienna took over the conversation then as she began chattering mercurially, jumping from subject to subject while making it clear to everyone that she'd lost none of her spunkiness while she was away. "Mr. Perry, we probably gonna have to stop at the store. Shoot, I know Tamara ain't got nothin' good to eat since I ain't been in the house, now, do you, Tamara? And, Tamara, can we get some movies or somethin'? You know, a sista gots to have somethin' to do on a long weekend."

Suddenly the girl stopped talking and looked around, as if she'd just noticed that all the attention was on her. Clicking her tongue in her now all-too-familiar fashion, she cut her eyes toward Tamara and asked sassily, *"Why everybody lookin' at me?"* She rolled her neck dramatically and added, "Y'all act like y'all ain't never seen a *person* befo'!"

Tamara couldn't help but laugh loudly before chiding the girl gently, "Sienna, hush! Let's go."

"She-e-e's ba-a-ack!" said Jayson with a huge smile. He looked bemused and shook his head from side to side, noticing how Sienna now held Tamara's deep-brown hand firmly in her own pale freckled one. He whispered to Lynnette, "I just would've never guessed it—*sisters,* you know?"

Isaiah heard his comment and, with a smiling glance over his shoulder, replied, "It wasn't for us to know, Brother Jayson, but God knew, and He *always* works all things out for the good!"

"I'll give you two snaps up on that one, brotha man, 'cause I'm wit'cha when you right!" said Lynnette with a tilt of her head and a saucy double pop of her red-manicured fingers. And wearing a huge smile on her face, she watched the three of them walk away.